HEDGE FUND
WIVES

By Tatiana Boncompagni

HEDGE FUND WIVES
GILDING LILY

HEDGE FUND
WIVES

Tatiana Boncompagni

AVON

An Imprint of HarperCollins*Publishers*

This is a work of fiction. Names, characters, places, and incidents are products of the author's imagination or are used fictitiously and are not to be construed as real. Any resemblance to actual events, locales, organizations, or persons, living or dead, is entirely coincidental.

HarperCollins books may be purchased for educational, business, or sales promotional use. For information please write: Special Markets Department, Harper-Collins Publishers, 10 East 53rd Street, New York, NY 10022.

FIRST AVON PAPERBACK EDITION PUBLISHED 2009.

Interior text designed by Rhea Braunstein

Library of Congress Cataloging-in-Publication Data
Boncompagni, Tatiana.
    Hedge fund wives / Tatiana Boncompagni.—1st ed.
        p. cm.
    ISBN 978-0-06-176526-1
    1. Rich people—Fiction.   2. Wall Street (New York, N.Y.)—Fiction.   3. Chick lit.   I. Title.
    PS3602.O6564H4   2009
    813'.6—dc22
                                                              2009002481

09   10   11   JTC/RRD   10   9   8   7   6   5   4   3   2   1

For Max

Acknowledgments

Above all others, I must thank my amazing editor, Lucia Macro, who not only helped conceive this book, but provided unflagging enthusiasm and helpful guidance during its writing.

I am greatly indebted to the incredible team at Avon Books and HarperCollins who have worked on *Hedge Fund Wives* in one way or another, especially Esi Sogah, Aurora Hughes, Pamela Spengler-Jaffee, and Kyran Cassidy, as well as my mountain-moving publisher, Liate Stehlik.

My literary agent, Joe Veltre, gets an enormous gold star for nudging me in the right direction when the book was in its early stages and for championing my interests throughout the publishing process. I would also like to express my unending gratitude to Alan Fisch, Joseph Drayton, and Lisa Katz of Kaye Scholer LLP, for wise counsel and tenacious representation.

Art Rolnick of the Federal Reserve Bank of Minneapolis, Mark Quinn, Greg Reposa, and others provided invaluable background information and ideas. To Tina Craig, Kim Harrington, Gigi Howard, Auna Jornayvaz, Sarahbeth Purcell, Karen Quinn, Margery Tanjeloff, and Beth Waltemath Lewicki, thank you for cheering

me on and lending an ear (and sometimes a tissue) when necessary.

Last, I am fortunate to have the support of my family—in particular, Camilla, Freddie, and Bunker. My children, Enrico and
Valentina, and husband, Maximilian, give meaning to everything
I do. Thank you for your patience and love, and for all the well-
timed hugs and kisses.

1

Baptism by Champagne Fountain

When I first opened the invitation to Caroline Reinhardt's baby shower, I thought I'd received it by mistake. I barely knew anyone in the city besides my husband John, who six months earlier had been recruited from his desk at the Chicago Mercantile Exchange to trade energy derivatives for a New York-based commodities-focused hedge fund. They made an offer we couldn't refuse, and in the short span of a week, we were packing our boxes for Manhattan and toasting the Windy City goodbye with vodka gimlets in the bar at the top of the John Hancock Tower.

Now, half a year later, it was early December, and I was surrounded by hedge fund wives. With the sun shining bright against a clear sky, the air refreshingly cool on the necks of the fur-and-diamond-clad shower guests as they streamed past a pair of gargantuan front doors—doors that had reputedly once graced a fourteenth-century Venetian palace—and into the lavishly decorated home of Dahlia Kemp, wife of billionaire hedge fund manager Thomas Kemp, the day held nothing but the promise of pleasure. Once inside and relieved of their furs, the women would fill their flutes at a free-flowing Perrier-Jouët champagne fountain and nibble on passed hors d'oeuvres of beluga caviar and jamón ibérico, all the while studying (furtively, of course) the Kemp's impressive art collection and gossiping in excited half-whispers about the expense to which Dahlia must have gone for the event.

Certainly a three-course gourmet meal accompanied by rare vintage wines, a five-tiered Sylvia Weinstock cake and goody bags stuffed with diamond earrings and four-figure day spa gift certificates had to amount to an important sum, even for the wife of a man who had cleared "three point two" (billion) the previous year. Even the invitations, which had been hand-delivered by a white-gloved courier and sent with a small gift, an Hermès silk scarf, to underscore the party's theme (Rue du Faubourg) and dress code (French chic), were absurdly costly. No, no detail had been skimped on or forgotten for Caroline's shower, and years later all of the guests would remember the party as the last of its kind.

Although no one spoke of it, the economy had begun to sour and every day brought fresh tales of falling fortunes. Most of the women assumed that their vast monetary reserves would protect them from having to alter any aspect of their enviable lives, but of course they were wrong. Wealth is relative by nature, and if one day you have a hundred million dollars and the next you have only fifty, the things that were once within reach—the private jet, the home in Aspen, or even five-tiered Sylvia Weinstock cakes—are suddenly out of it. Under such circumstances, it's not long before a marriage built around material possessions and predicated upon the shared responsibility of their care and maintenance, begins to crumble.

But on the day of Caroline's shower, at least, the wealth flowed as freely as the champagne, and I was more than happy to partake in the merriment. Not because of the gourmet morsels and vintage bubbly—I'm more of a cheese plate and glass of white kind of girl—but because I was desperate to make some friends. I'd done little to no socializing since we'd moved, partly because shortly after arriving in New York I'd fallen pregnant—I later miscarried—and partly because I was, to be completely honest, deeply afraid of the other wives. They all seemed so . . . well . . . perfect; and fitting in with them felt like such a daunting task. Ergo, when the invitation to Caroline's shower arrived, I had originally assumed there had been a mix-up at the calligraphers. I was just about to post the response card back with a little note alerting the host to the error, when John returned home from the office and assured me that the invitation really had been intended for me. Apparently one of his new colleagues at Zenith Capital had a wife who was expecting their first child and wanted to invite me to her shower.

On the day of the party, I had my hair blown out at the hair salon on the corner, and after getting caught with a stylist who was convinced they could pump more volume into my unrepentantly limp locks, ended up arriving a bit late to the Kemp's four-story Upper East Side townhouse on a tree-lined block off of Fifth Avenue. I was only ten minutes late, but already the first gush of guests had trickled out of the entry foyer and into the first-floor living room, allowing me to make a mostly unnoticed entrance, which turned out to be a stroke of luck. When I spotted the rack of designer furs in the front hall, I realized that my bright pink puffer would have stuck out, literally, like a sore thumb among all that sable and mink; and I crossed my fingers that no one but the maid, whose sole job it was to keep an eye on the coat rack, would connect me with my pink marshmallow parka. Chicago's anything-goes-as-long-as-it-keeps-you-from-getting-frostbitten approach to outerwear clearly didn't apply in New York City. This was a chinchilla-or-bust kind of town, and I made a mental note to go shopping for a new winter coat as soon as possible.

Taking a deep breath I made my way through the mirror-walled marble foyer into the Louis-XIV-antiques-decorated living room,

and surveyed its contents: a couch and several arm chairs upholstered in lustrous dove-gray silk; marble-topped side tables and a
coffee table made of mercury glass; a huge ivory oriental rug and
a pair of gargantuan Lalique vases filled with fresh-cut pale pink-
and-white flowers. A large Dutch pastoral painting hung on the
far wall just above the couch, and a slew of Impressionist paintings from Renoir, Degas, Monet, Cézanne, and Pissarro covered
nearly every available inch on the others. I counted about twenty-
five female guests milling about, each wearing at least eight carats
of diamonds and shoes that cost as much as my first car.

I took another deep breath, fluffed my hair a bit, and decided
to introduce myself to Caroline. Only problem: nearly everyone
was pregnant. And not just a little pregnant—at least half of the
women there were sporting basketball-sized bellies, making it
next to impossible to know who I was supposed to be congratu-
lating. Luckily, I didn't have to take more than three steps toward
a tray of mini croques monsieurs and Gruyère gougères before a
striking blonde greeted me with a double air kiss.

"Marcy, I'm Caroline," she said. "Thanks for coming."

Caroline Reinhardt had pin-straight blond hair that hung in
an impossibly thick curtain down her back, dark blue eyes, and
rubbery lips. She was wearing a wool pencil skirt and sleeveless
ivory silk blouse that showed off her toned arms, perky, full breasts,
and flat stomach. In other words, there was no way this woman
was pregnant. It took me a second, but when it finally dawned on
me that she was having the baby via surrogate I managed to eke
out a passably hearty congratulations.

"Thanks so much for inviting me," I said, given that the usual
"you're glowing!" and "how do you feel?" were obviously not ap-
plicable.

"Of course we had to include you. There was no question," she
smiled, revealing a row of perfectly white teeth. Veneers, no doubt,
and from the look of them, the best and most expensive kind

($50,000 easily). "How are you finding the move?" she asked, crossing her long arms right below her perfect breasts.

"Decorating our new place has kept me pretty busy, but to be honest I've been really lonely. It's no fun shopping alone for armchairs," I said.

"Don't tell me you're not working with an interior designer?" she balked.

I shook my head, helping myself to one of the Gruyère puffs. Cheese was my one big weakness in life, a mild obsession that would forever necessitate the wearing of body-fat encasing (or restructuring, as I liked to call it) undergarments.

"Not to worry. I'll call Jasper on Monday and ask him to see you straightaway. He's finishing up our place on Bank Street. He's marvelous and does so many of the girls' homes here," she said.

"Did he do this place?"

"Oh Lord no. He's much more, shall we say, décor forward? But Thomas Kemp is such a stick-in-the-mud traditionalist," she said, conspiratorially. "Anyway, there's a chance Jasper's in Chicago doing a taping with Oprah but I know I'm going to see him next Tuesday. Should I tell him to give you a ring?"

"Oh no, don't do that," I said, wondering exactly how much Jasper Pell, an interior designer who makes regular pit stops on *The Oprah Winfrey Show,* charged for a telephone, forget in-person, consultation. "I'm doing it on my own. Well, really John and I are doing it, but—"

"Ohh, *you're* an interior designer. No one told me," she said, suddenly excited. "Will you come over and tell me what you think of the nursery? I can't decide if we should go with the faded sea foam or dusty wisteria color palette. Which one do you think is more progressive yet soothing?"

I told her she'd gotten the wrong idea, that I wasn't an interior designer and was useless when it came to such dilemmas.

"Oh," she sighed, her lips furling with disappointment. Then

she started scanning the room in search of someone else to introduce me to, and I knew I'd blown it—my one big shot to make a
good impression, and hopefully, a friend. John wasn't kidding
when he said that if in the real world you get one chance to get in
someone's good graces, when it comes to the superrich, it's thirty
seconds.

"Have you met the party host, Dahlia Kemp, yet?" Caroline
asked distractedly.

We walked over to the couch where two women, both thin and
blonde and dressed in pastel tweed skirts, silk blouses, and gold
necklaces, were bent over their BlackBerries, tapping out emails.
I couldn't be sure, but I thought I recognized the one on the right
from a copy of *Vogue* that I'd thumbed through at the hair salon
that morning.

The one on the left spoke first. "So tell me Caroline how are
you staffing up for the baby's arrival?"

"We're thinking a cook, baby nurse, and a nanny should do it."

Three people for one little baby?

"We did the same when Carolina and Alexander were born,"
Dahlia sniffed. "It's so important to have a back-up nanny in case
of emergencies. Of course now that our children are six and eight,
we've had to staff up with specialists: language and culture tu-
tors, tennis, golf, and swimming instructors, and so on. But you
don't have to worry about that just yet. And whoever handles
your domestics headhunting can help vet your candidates."

Caroline said she would have to remember to ask for more
details at a later date, and then put her hand lightly on my shoulder before introducing me. "Dahlia Kemp, Ainsley Partridge, this
is Marcy Emerson. Her husband John works with Fred at Zenith,"
she said, taking a small step away from me, almost as if I were
being presented at court. For a moment I had the distinct yet surreal impression I was meant to curtsey.

"Lovely to meet you," I said, offering my hand across the mercury glass coffee table. I waited for Dahlia to grasp it but she didn't. Instead, she daintily fingered one of the multiple Van Cleef & Arpels clover Alhambra necklaces strung around her neck and looked away while Caroline hissed in my ear, "She doesn't shake."

What, like the pope? Confused and embarrassed, I withdrew my outstretched hand and stuffed it in the little front pocket on my dress, and as I fumbled with the pocket, it occurred to me that maybe I *had* been meant to curtsey before.

"You have a beautiful home," I said finally.

Dahlia looked around the room as if she'd never really noticed how nice it was and parted her thin lips, hesitating for a second before gesturing to the portrait hanging above a large marble-topped armoire. "I'm not sure about the Cézanne over there. Thomas just bought it at Christie's. What do you think, Ainsley?" she asked, turning to the blonde seated next to her.

"I like it." Ainsley shrugged and looked back down at her BlackBerry.

"Well, anyway," Dahlia sighed, rolling her wide-set, almond-shaped eyes at Caroline, who snorted quietly into her hand in response. "I suppose we could always put it in the Greenwich house when that's finished."

"How's that going?" Caroline asked.

"Meier is gouging us. Twenty million for the glass porte-cochere alone. The bastard refuses to get bids from other contractors. Thomas is considering firing him, but I've talked him out of it, thank God. Could you imagine the scandal?" Dahlia said.

Caroline shook her head. "Would be a nightmare. But tell me, I've been meaning to ask. Preston Bailey or David Monn?"

"Bailey was busy today so Monn planned the event. Personally, I think they're both talented but Monn does better florals," Dahlia replied before sliding open the golden pyramid covering the face of her wristwatch to check the time. "I think we should start lunch," she said, motioning to one of her many housekeepers to begin ushering the guests into the dining room.

I did my best to make my way gracefully over—the women, I noticed, didn't so much walk as they did waft—to the dining room, where four round tables, each set with ten place cards, had been draped in baby blue linens and set with white china and silver. I found my place card, sat down in my seat, and for an agonizing three minutes (I apparently hadn't wafted slowly enough) I waited alone at the table, reading and rereading the lunch menu:

Fava bean and mint salad

Kobe beef filet mignon with blanched white asparagus
and chanterelle toasts

Or

Grilled wild salmon in black currant sauce,
sautéed mushrooms and a wild-rice timbale

Herb-scented sorbet trio and Chocolate-and-espresso cake

I was just about to get up from the empty lunch table and excuse myself to the ladies room when a petite woman with straight, shoulder-length light brown hair, luminescent olive skin, and sharply defined facial features plopped herself into the seat next to mine. She was breathing hard, as if she had just run a couple miles in her Roger Vivier pumps.

"I don't think we've met," she said once she'd caught her breath.

"Marcy Emerson. I'm new. My husband and I just moved here from Chicago."

"Jillian Lovern Tischman, but everyone calls me Jill," she said, extending her hand.

I sighed with relief and shook her hand. "So this is not a totally *verboten* form of human contact after all?"

"Oh, did you met Dahlia already?" she replied, placing her Hermès Medora clutch on the table.

I nodded and took another big sip of my champagne.

"Pace yourself," she warned, eyebrows raised, as the tables filled up around us. "These things have a way of dragging on forever."

"Sounds like you go to a lot of baby showers."

"I've done the math, and by my calculations I'll go to one hundred and fifty of them before everyone's done spawning."

"How do you get to one hundred and fifty?" I asked.

"Fifty women, give or take. Three babies each because three's the new two, four's the new three, and, well, you get the point."

I told Jill that John and I hoped to start a family, but didn't delve much deeper into my recent reproductive history. "My dream is to have a house full of kids, but in general I try to avoid, becoming a cliché," I said.

"Well, good luck. Because try as you might, you're probably destined to end up in one of the seven categories of hedge fund wives."

"You make this place sound like Dante's *Inferno.*"

Jill thought for a second. "You know, it's actually an apt comparison," she said before lifting her glass and taking a long swallow from her own flute.

So much for pacing oneself.

2

The Accidental, the Westminster, the Stephanie Seymour, the Former Secretary, the Socialite, the Workaholic, and the Breeder

I was curious to hear more from Jill, but before I could get any more out of her, Dahlia stood up to give a speech about Caroline and we all had to be quiet. I didn't have a chance to chat privately again with Jill until we were all shunted upstairs to eat cake in the second-floor sitting room, which itself resembled a petit four with its mint and cream décor and huge Venetian glass chandelier suspended from the center of the ceiling. I asked the woman cutting wedges of cake for a large piece and sat down next to Jill to watch Caroline tackle her mountain of presents—including the cashmere baby blanket I'd brought.

"If there are seven kinds of hedge fund wife, which one are you?" I asked Jill, digging into my chocolate-espresso-cream confection.

"Oh, I'm an *Accidental*," she demurred. "When I met my hus-. band I thought he'd end up in politics like the rest of his family.

Glenn moved from being an equity analyst tracking tech stocks for Merrill to a fund called Conquer Capital when we were engaged, and unlike most of the other hedge fund brides, I actively opposed his transition into this world."

"But why?"

"Because I knew it would mean that I'd spend the rest of my life at parties like these, listening to someone prattle on about their latest trip to a five-star, obscenely expensive resort where they lunched at the table next to Diane von Fürstenberg and Barry Diller's and sunned in beach chairs next to Ben Affleck and Jennifer Garner." She rolled her dark eyes and slouched in her chair.

"So how do I spot other *Accidentals*? They sound like my people."

"We're usually the last to arrive and the first to go. We're also the least likely to host a social gathering or send out holiday cards."

I was enthralled as Jill broke down all the different types of hedge fund wives, or HFWs, as she sometimes referred to them. According to her the *Westminster* (as in pedigreed and pure bred) has a recognizable and respectable last name (which she's kept, non-hyphenated), belongs to all the right clubs (Junior League, Harvard, and Doubles) and is more likely to subscribe to Emily Post than to the *New York Post*. While the *Westminster* always looks groomed, she isn't gauche about it (no false eyelashes except for black tie functions, no breast implants, etc.) and strives above all to appear elegant and natural. She may have a job but it isn't all-consuming, and thanks to her years of co-chairing this and that, she's constructed a first-rate social network. If you need a letter for the co-op board of the building you are hoping to buy into, the *Westminster*'s your gal. Applying for membership in, say, Piping Rock, the most exclusive golf and beach club on Long Island's North Shore, she's the first call you make. Ditto for nursery school applications, benefit committee aspirations, etc., etc. But as like-able as the *Westminster* is, "her perfectionism can rub some the wrong way," Jill sniffed.

Later, I would learn that Jillian Lovern Tischman, in addition to being a mother of two, was a contributing editor for *House & Home*, a monthly glossy magazine that mainly featured the city, country, and vacation homes of socialites and B-list celebrities. She was also on the boards of numerous noteworthy charities and cultural institutions around town, and thus far more *Westminster* than *Accidental*.

Named for the famous supermodel who, by settling down with Peter Brant, a massively wealthy investor, art dealer, and racehorse breeder, inspired droves of models to secure their own hedge fund honey pots, the *Stephanie Seymour* is so used to get-ting away with being nasty and rude—even their husbands let them treat them like dirt—that they've actually forgotten how to be gracious. They also tend to only want to talk about shopping, their last session with the physical trainer (whom you get the sneaking suspicion they might be having an affair with), or their last trip to the dermatologist's office (ditto). They have kids, but you never hear about them unless they're referencing a plastic surgery procedure, as in, "I had the breast lift six months after I gave birth to fill-in-the-blank Junior." *Stephanie Seymour* wives take the whole yummy mummy thing to another level, make that universe.

Without a doubt, Caroline Reinhardt was a prime example.

The third kind of HFW, the *Former Secretary,* is self-explanatory. Their husbands were too lazy or busy (or both) to go look for a wife, so they simply married the first girl who did a decent enough job organizing their lives at the office. They also never talk back and give surprisingly good blow jobs. *Former Secretaries* are often the snobbiest of all HFWs because they feel so insecure about their lowly backgrounds, and tend to be the most protective of their territory (i.e., husbands) because they have the most to lose. Unlike the *Stephanie Seymours*, they don't have good looks to fall back on, and since they aren't terribly charming, they also don't have many friends who would side with them in a big city divorce battle. After hearing this description, it shocked me when Jill said that none other than Dahlia Kemp was this category's reigning queen.

"That's the point, you're not supposed to be able to spot them. Their whole *raison d'être* is to blend in with the other HFWs," Jill said.

The fourth category of wife, the *Socialite,* cares about one thing and one thing only: social status. She's as vain as the *Stephanie Seymour,* as connected as the *Westminster,* as cutthroat as the *Former Secretary,* but has a past as cloudy as the East River. Even the ones that come from upper-middle-class backgrounds, like Ainsley Partridge, have skeletons bursting out of their closets, which, it should be noted, are stuffed with borrowed dresses they just "happened" to forget to return. The *Socialite,* Jill said, was a shameless cheapskate and never paid for anything—not her clothes, her hair, her makeup, her transportation, her gym membership, or her meals. The list goes on and on. In fact, if there is one way to tell a *Socialite* from the rest of the HFWs it's that she will stick you with the bill for lunch while the other four won't even let you see it.

The *Workaholic,* on the other hand, will inform you that you'll be splitting the bill even before the waiter takes your drink order—and even though both of you know she'll be expensing it, along with the black town car hovering outside the restaurant's front door and the holiday gift—a crate of halfway decent California cabernet—she'll be sending you in December. Like her husband, the *Workaholic* is married firstly to her high-powered, although not-quite-so-lucrative job as a magazine publisher/interior decorator/real-estate broker/corporate lawyer. She has no children and has talked herself into believing that she'll be able to easily reproduce up until the age of fifty. But before you start feeling too sorry for the *Workaholic*, remember that she has a closet full of perfectly tailored Akris suits and Manolo Blahnik heels, takes pleasure in tearing her workplace underlings to shreds, and has a seven-figure bank account in the Cayman Islands that even her husband doesn't know exists. "What's his is mine and what's mine is mine," is her motto. Welcome to the hedge fund wives' version of women's lib.

Of course, the *Workaholic*'s exact opposite, the *Breeder*, is hardly a poster child for the feminist movement either. Of all the hedge fund wives, the *Breeder* is the easiest to identify. She's often sporting a big, pregnant belly and either carrying a new tot in a shearling-lined Louis Vuitton baby carrier or pushing one in a Bugaboo stroller. And in case you happen to catch her without one of her three, four, or five children, she wears their bauble-equivalents—little enamel and gold shoes—on a chain around her neck.

By the time Jill had finished schooling me on the seven types of hedge fund wives, the cake plates had been cleared and Caroline had opened all of her gifts (I'd never seen so much Tiffany silver in my life). Jill walked me down to the entry foyer, where we were both given our gift bags and stood waiting for our coats when Ainsley sidled up to Jill to ask her if she was coming to her annual holiday party. "I can't come. Glenn's parents are expecting us in Oyster Bay that weekend," she said.

"Oh really, that's too bad," Ainsley pouted.

"Why don't you invite Marcy and her husband John?" Jill suggested.

Ainsley protested, stammering through a half-cooked explanation that it was really just a small get-together and her husband Peter was already complaining about the number of people she'd invited. Jill pointed out that since she wasn't coming, it wasn't like John and I would be adding to the final number of guests. I felt stupid standing there as the girls argued about me, but I'd also visited the champagne fountain enough times over the course of the afternoon to dull my sense of shame and self-pity.

"I suppose two more isn't a big deal," Ainsley finally growled at Jill, tossing a handful of her long, pale blond hair behind her back. She turned to face me. "The party is in two weeks, Jill can fill you in on the rest," she said. Then she grabbed her fur from a patiently waiting maid and stomped outside.

"Now you get to see Ainsley's apartment and meet some of the other wives who weren't here today," Jill said. She was quite pleased with herself, having exercised her considerable social power for seemingly good use.

"I know. I can't wait, I just wish that you were going to be there."

"You'll be fine," she said before wafting outdoors into the brilliant sunshine, "as long as you don't wear that coat."

3

Missing Spanx and Other Morning-after Anxieties

Two weeks later, on the morning *after* the Partridge's annual Christmas party, I woke up with a lethal case of cottonmouth, throbbing head, and little memory of what had happened after half-past one the night before. Plus I couldn't shake the feeling that I'd done something really life-altering embarrassing, like maybe-I-need-to-move-to-Dubai-now embarrassing. Then the phone rang, punctuating the merciful silence of my darkened, cool bedroom with a sound so shrill, so loud, it made my brain feel like it was imploding on itself, and I lunged for the bedside table to snap it up, if only to prevent it from ringing again.

"Hello?" I croaked.

"Good morning." It was John, my husband, who was predictably at work even though it was a Sunday, and according to the clock on my bedside table, not even nine o'clock.

"Oh, I get it—you're being ironic," I said.

I quickly calculated: The man had had at most four hours' sleep the previous night. How and for God's sake *why* he had made it into work when his appearance wasn't required was beyond me.

Was he in a bad mood because he felt just as hung over as I did or because of something else? Something involving me and the bottle of tequila with which I had spent the better portion of last night familiarizing myself?

"How are you feeling?" John asked humorlessly.

"About as bad as I sound, maybe worse," I said. "What happened last night anyway? I don't remember anything after we ordered that second bottle of Patron."

"So you don't remember the incident?" he asked.

"Incident? What incident?" I didn't like the sound of that word. It sounded like something that required the involvement of the police and lawyers, documents and affidavits, judges and juries. This couldn't be good.

"There was an altercation at the bar," John continued.

"With who?"

"With whom," he corrected me.

My husband, the grammar nut. I blamed his pedantry on his mother, a former middle school English teacher turned real estate broker, with whom (*thank you, John*) I had what I called a "civil" relationship. Let's just say that after almost seven years of marriage I'd learned to put up with the things I couldn't change.

"Okay . . . whom?" I asked again.

"A girl. She meant to throw her drink at Ainsley, but Ainsley ducked and it hit you instead."

"It did?" I couldn't believe that I didn't remember having a drink thrown in my face. The only other time I'd blacked out was during my sophomore year of college, when I drank one (okay, six) too many beers while tailgating a Northwestern football game. "So then what happened?" I asked.

"You threw your drink right back at her."

"I did?"

"Then she said something and you shoved her and then she socked you in the face."

Feeling the tender spot around my eye, I uttered, "Are you serious?"

"Yeah. I would have tried to protect you, but it happened too fast."

"Do you know why I shoved her? I mean it's not exactly like me to engage in bar brawls."

I heard John shuffling some papers, the sound of a drawer opening, and I knew there was something he wasn't telling me. He always went into organizational mode when he was holding something back. It was his tell.

"Spill," I said.

"The girl who hit you . . ." He paused, weighing his options.

"Yes?"

"She told you to put your girdle back on."

"Spanx. Girdles are for grandmothers. There's a difference."

"I'm just repeating what the girl said. Can we not get lost in semantics, please?"

"Alright, why were my Spanx off?"

"You tell me. You're the one who took them off."

"Did I take them off . . . in public, in front of other people?"

"Yes," he said.

Oh fuck.

"You took off your stockings, too," he added, unbidden.

Doublefuck.

"But I wasn't wearing any underwear!" The dress I'd worn was a little (okay, a lot) on the short side. Everyone in that club must have gotten an eyeful of my Britney Spears. For a moment everything went dark, and I had to move a pillow under my head.

"Everyone must think I'm a lunatic. Why didn't you stop me?"

"Marcy," he sighed. "Of course I tried to stop you. But you wouldn't listen."

"Did I slur?" It was a masochistic question, but I needed to know everything.

"There was slurring, drooling, stumbling, spilling, nudity, and fighting. Shall I continue or was that enough?"

"John, help me out. I'm mortified!"

"Well then that makes two of us," he said, and I realized that as stupid as I felt, John must have felt ten times more embarrassed. After all, I didn't ever have to face these people again if I didn't want to, but John had no choice; he worked with them every day.

I cleared my throat. "I'm sorry, honey. I know what a big deal it was to you that I make a good impression," I said.

"Actually you sort of did," he grumbled. "Peter thought you were hilarious and Ainsley felt so bad after that girl decked you. They want us to all have dinner after New Year's. Go figure."

I'd rather let John control the TV remote for the next five years than have to go to dinner with the socialite and her husband.

I groaned dramatically.

"Marcy, we aren't in Chicago anymore. New York works differently. Deals aren't made in conference rooms, but over cocktails and dinner tables. Zenith rewards rainmakers, the guys who are good at reeling in potential new investors. If I could do that, I could be pulling in much bigger bucks."

"But, John, we have plenty of money."

"My portfolio has outperformed all the partners' expectations, and I've been rewarded for that, but I'm never going to move up the ladder if I don't start bringing in new capital. And to bring in new money, we need to be out there meeting the people who have it."

"You want to rub shoulders with rich people. I don't understand how this requires my involvement."

"I'd like for you to get us invited to more parties like the Partridge's. Last night I met a Venezuelan banking scion and an Ecuadorian flower exporter. They want to set up a dinner and talk about Zenith's investment returns. And why? Because they saw us with the Partridges and figure we're connected. Marcy, despite, or maybe because of the crap you pulled last night, people here love you. You had tons of friends in Chicago. I know that if you set your mind to it you could get us invited to the right parties and fundraisers."

"John, you know I'm not big on schmooze fests. Can't you just go out without me?" I gulped down the glass of water on his bedside table since mine was already empty. My headache was getting worse by the second.

"It looks bad for a guy to be at parties on his own. People will think I'm trolling for chicks."

I spit my water back into the glass. "Say what?"

"My point is that I want you with me. All you have to do is be your normal, charming, and hopefully not inebriated self, and I'll do all the real work. We might have to throw a few dinner parties when our apartment is ready, but otherwise your actual input is minimal."

"I don't know, John. I thought we agreed that we were going to focus on getting pregnant again. What I want is a baby, for us to be on diaper-duty, not schmooze-control every night of the week. That's not at all how I pictured our lives here."

"So you're telling me that you have no interest in making friends and having fun? Because basically that's what I'm asking you to do. And I don't think it's a good idea for you to get pregnant again before you have a chance to form a social network. God forbid if anything happens next time, you'll at least have some friends to lean upon for support."

"I'd rather lean on barbed wire than any of the wives I've met." I snorted.

He sighed with exasperation.

"John, one woman wouldn't shake my hand, another snubbed me because I don't have an interior decorator, and just last night someone sneered at me because she didn't like my dress."

"They can't all be that bad."

"There are two nice ones," I confessed.

"I know you miss Chicago, but it's time you start trying a little harder to settle in."

"Umm, need I remind you of what happens when I attempt to settle in? I get blind drunk and moon people."

"How about you try skipping the tequila next time?"

"Sober socializing? No, thanks. My couch is way too comfy," I joked.

"You owe me after last night," he said, in a tone that suggested I not attempt to breathe any more levity into the conversation.

In the spirit of moving forward, I decided to make a concession. Also because I felt really guilty about having made such a total idiot of myself in, of all places, the Rose Bar in the Gramercy Park Hotel. It was *the* hot spot in New York; on any given night it was filled to capacity with the city's most influential editors, wealthiest power brokers, and hottest model-actress-socialite-whatevers (the new ubiquitous hyphenate). If it were up to me I'd never set foot in there again, but if I ever wanted to get the baby I'd dreamed of having, it sounded like I had to.

"Okay, John, but once I have a so-called social network, then can we try again for a baby?"

"Whatever you want, Marcy."

"Then I guess we have a deal," I said.

"That's my girl."

"I mean, what's the worst that could happen?"

Oh, if only I'd known.

4

The Worst Hedge Fund Wife on the Planet

Heaving myself out of bed, I guzzled down the rest of my glass of water and threw on an old T-shirt and a pair of John's boxers. Sunlight poured through a gap in our curtains, illuminating a wedge of vanilla carpet where my outfit from the previous night lay in a sad little heap. I picked it up and tossed it in the little hamper we used to collect our dry cleaning, then retrieved my shoes, a pair of leg-lengthening, bank-breaking black pumps, and my quilted black satin clutch, both from Chanel, both carelessly scattered around the room. I shelved them in their appropriate tissue-lined boxes while at the same time eyeing the floor for my stockings and Spanx.

Oh right, I'd left those at the club.

Along with my self-respect.

Nice.

I needed coffee, lots of it. Without it, I knew I would be unable to function for the entire day, not that I had anything in particular to do, but still. I slipped on my fleece slippers and padded over to the kitchen, where I sloshed some milk in a saucepan, ground some coffee beans and dumped the entire grinder's worth of grounds into the liner. Once it was brewed, I poured a couple cups of the coffee into the saucepan with the warmed milk and then emptied the whole mixture into the red-and-white snowflake mug I'd used since high school. If there was one thing I had down to a science, it was making coffee just the way I liked it.

Taking my first gulp of the hot, dark liquid, I peered inside the refrigerator, where I found the signs of a drunken, middle-of-the-night food binge—the pumpkin pie I had made two days earlier was almost entirely eaten and one of my earrings was nestled in between a half-eaten round of Camembert and a carton of orange juice that had been full when we had left for the Partridges' but was now mostly gone. Feeling even more disgusted with myself, I closed the door of the fridge and looked down at my stomach. It was bloated and distended.

Gross.

My head pounded behind my left eye socket, and without thinking I reached up to apply pressure on it, causing a thunderbolt of pain to rip through my head as soon as my fingers made contact. I stooped down to check my reflection in the mirrored backsplash, only to have my fears confirmed: I had the beginnings of a black eye. A real, Oscar-de-la-Hoya-worthy shiner. It was gonna be ugly.

Gulping down another mouthful of coffee, I started trying to piece together the previous night's timeline. There had been three glasses of champagne, which I had downed in rapid succession. Not advisable, obviously, but I always drink quickly when I'm nervous, and that night, surrounded by John's hyperwealthy colleagues and their expensively maintained wives, I certainly had cause to be. You see, it was pretty clear that most of the other wives at the Partridge's party grew up with nannies and private school kilts hemmed just so, while I had carried a house key around my neck on a dingy white shoelace and braved the Minnesota winters in multigenerational hand-me-downs. Even last night, wearing a new designer dress and multiple coats of a new mascara the woman behind the cosmetics counter swore was what all the movie stars use, I still felt like a prairie girl among princesses.

However, for John, I put on a brave face. He seemed to be reveling in our transition into a higher tax bracket and new city as much as I was floundering in it. Since being recruited by Zenith from his desk at the Merc, John had been completely obsessed with his work. His job as a specialist in trading energy derivatives required him to, for example, predict, hopefully correctly, how much the price of a barrel of oil was going to rise over the next quarter and why. It was all tremendously complicated, time-consuming, and stressful, but it turned out that John was really good at it, and in the span of less than a year, he'd managed to make the fund an obscene amount of money, which had in turn made us wealthier than we'd ever dared to dream.

For anyone without an intimate understanding of what hedge funds do, in a nutshell they invest other people's money. We're talking super-wealthy individuals who have the five to twenty million dollars you need to play ball with these funds just lying around, gathering dust, twiddling its little green thumbs. If everything goes right, the investors get back whatever profit (or return) is made, minus twenty percent and two percent of the total investment that the fund keeps as compensation. (A few managers take a full fifty percent of the profits, but they're more the exception than the rule.)

For a long stretch of time everything did go right—the rich got richer and a bunch of guys in the right place at the right time minted huge fortunes virtually overnight. And then the economy tanked, and the party was suddenly over.

John and I were a total anomaly. While we were upgrading our furniture and researching luxury vacations, the rest of Wall Street was taking it on the chin. The banks had all underestimated their exposure to the subprime mortgage industry melt-down and had been forced to write off billions of dollars. As they started reining in on the amount of loans they were making to small and large businesses, deal flow slowed and with fewer deals in the pipeline, profits dipped. Soon thereafter pink slips started to fly. The Federal Reserve intervened to save the banks from going under, but at the expense of the dollar, which sank even lower in value. To make matters worse, the boost U.S. exports received as a result of the weak dollar was far smaller than previously anticipated or hoped for, and the president's pro-ethanol policy was making the cost of all food higher as Midwestern farmers ditched less profitable crops in order to grow corn. To top it all off the Saudis were once again raising the price of crude, mainly because of the weakening dollar. The long run of American prosperity was coming to an end.

But not for us. Ours was just starting.

Although we were lucky, I didn't feel like it. Moving to New York had been difficult for me. Okay, gut wrenching. Shortly after our relocation, I had gotten pregnant. A dream, since we'd spent a year trying before it finally happened. You could say that I was—and am—totally obsessed with babies. I love the way they smell, the sounds they make when they eat, their tiny little hands making angry little fists when they cry. It hadn't mattered to me that I vomited five times a day and could only stomach Saltines and cheese sandwiches for the duration of the whole first trimester. I'd watch those Gerber baby commercials on television and just melt with happiness. I was going to be a mom.

Everything was going great until I hit the twenty-week mark and started bleeding. First it was just some spotting, but when the flow got heavier, my doctor put me on monitored bed rest in the hospital and they shot me full of drugs that were supposed to help. But it was too late. I miscarried. It wasn't meant to be, the doctor said. We'd try again, John said. A lot of people said a lot of things, but nothing could allay the pain. My world was black. I couldn't stop crying. For weeks, all I did was cry. Cry and eat cheese—Burrata, fresh off the plane from Tuscany, weeping with moisture, and Stilton from England, massive slabs of the salty, piquant stuff. John brought me only the best, unpasteurized, illegal cheese. I could eat it now: I wasn't pregnant anymore. There was no danger of ingesting a piece of Listeria-laden fromage and losing the baby.

I had sat on our new couch, my misery wrapped around me like a blanket, and thought of my baby. I wondered what he would have looked like, whether he would have inherited John's blondish hair or my dark locks, John's lean, athletic build, or my softer, shorter one. Would he have been popular? Bookish? Funny? Preferred pancakes to waffles, bacon to sausages? I'd never know. All I could do was imagine. Imagine and then weep. I told John that I wanted us to move back to Chicago. New York held only unhappiness for me. I missed our old lives and I missed our friends.

"We'll make more," he assured me.

Now in the kitchen, I considered the empty seat at the breakfast table and silently cursed John for making me go to the Partridges'. I had wanted to stay home and watch an episode of *Lost*, but he wouldn't hear of it. "I promise, once you have a glass of wine and start talking to people, you'll be glad you're there," he'd argued, and when I still refused to budge from our big comfy couch, he pulled out the heavy artillery: "My bosses will be there. It won't look good if you're not with me."

I harrumphed, unimpressed.

"We haven't been out in months. Don't I deserve a night out with my wife every once in a while?"

Thus reminded that I, baby or no baby, still had some wifely responsibilities to perform, I pried myself off the couch and let him prod me into our bedroom in the direction of our walk-in closet, where I squirmed into my trusty Spanx, a pair of stockings, and that stupid dress. And although I had resigned myself to spending the night quietly sipping champagne in a corner, hoping that no one noticed what a big, friendless loser I was, I actually ended up having a good time.

The highlight of the evening had been—no, not the tequila— but meeting Gigi Ambrose, the well-known caterer, cookbook author, and frequent *Today Show* guest. With masses of auburn hair, Jessica Rabbit curves, and enough Southern sass for a whole cotillion's worth of debutantes, she was the kind of woman you want to hate, but can't. She was too charming, and on top of that, her recipes had always served me well in the kitchen. Even so it had taken me half an hour to work up the nerve to walk up to her and introduce myself.

"I love the kumquat glazed chicken skewers," I'd said in reference to one of the hors d'oeuvres being passed around on silver trays that evening. There had also been caviar-topped quail eggs, blue cheese and candied fig tartlets, not to mention grilled polenta squares and seared tuna bites. But the chicken skewers had been my favorite, and as a conversation opener I had asked Gigi if she'd included the recipe for them in her next book, a home entertaining guide she'd already started promoting on her *Today Show* segments.

"Oh, I'm not catering tonight," Gigi had drawled in response. Her voice was deep and warm, and she smelled of vanilla and rosewood. "Ainsley went with another company, which is more than fine by me. I'm here with my husband."

"I am, too," I said just as a woman in a chinchilla coat clomped through the doorway on five-inch platform heels. She had raven hair, large, probably surgically enhanced breasts, and a thin gold phone pressed to her ear. She was barking something in Russian into it. Later I would learn from Gigi that the fembot's name was Irina and she called herself a matchmaker, but most believed her to be a madam. Irina set up pretty Russian girls, many just off the plane, with rich old men who wanted hot young things to take to dinner—and then home to bed. Eliot Spitzer was rumored to have been one of her better customers.

"Darling, hello. I haven't seen you in a while. It's so nice to see you," Irina purred, leaning down—she stood six feet two in her heels—to give Gigi a double air kiss salutation.

"Have you met Marcy Emerson?" Gigi asked, putting her arm around my waist and giving it a reassuring squeeze.

Irina shifted her eyes, a pair of icy blue slits rimmed in heavy black liner, to me.

She was intimidating all right, and I had fumbled for my words, finally sputtering something like *"its cold out there, isn't it?"* thinking that I'd be safe talking about the weather.

But I'd thought wrong.

"In Russia we have a saying," Irina said, her voice as frosty as her glare. "There is no such thing as bad weather, just bad clothes." She had made a show of looking me up and down before stomping off into the living room.

"Umm, is it my imagination or did she just sneer at me?" I asked Gigi.

"Not your imagination."

"Well, then, what a friendly lady. I'm so glad I came."

Gigi laughed. "You couldn't get out of tonight, either, could you?"

"Is it that obvious?" I replied, and for the next ten minutes Gigi and I swapped our bullet-point biographies. She was originally from North Carolina, recently married her husband, one Jeremy Cohen, an ex-Goldman Sachs banker who'd originally made his money trading junk bonds (à la Michael Milken, minus the jail time). His particular knack was distressed investment, which meant that he bought and sold stock in troubled corporations. He'd started his first vulture fund, in the late nineties following the International Monetary Fund crisis in Asia. After making a killing flipping undervalued companies in South Korea, Jeremy launched another fund and amassed yet another fortune buying securities in a string of utility companies across Texas. Immediately after Gigi married Jeremy, she got pregnant with a girl, now six months old and named Chloe, and moved into Jeremy's gargantuan, feng shui-ed apartment in a newly refurbished luxury condo/hotel on Central Park South. I told her that I'd grown up in a suburb of Minneapolis, went to college in Chicago, where I worked post graduation at an investment bank, most recently as a relationship officer for the bank's wealthy clients, and met John, whom I had been married to for five years.

Gigi and I finished our glasses of champagne and agreed it was time to join the others in the living room; our husbands were probably wondering if we'd left without them. Gigi suggested we take the long way back, through the Partridges' dining room, where we gawked at a china hutch full of plates etched with two fancifully entwined *P*'s and an *A*.

"Monogrammed tablewear," Gigi whispered, rolling her eyes. I giggled and she leaned in close to my ear to dispense a torrent of insider information, the importance of which I would realize only later, once it was too late.

"I actually shouldn't be making fun of poor Ainsley. Jeremy told me earlier tonight that Peter's closing his fund. He started it three years ago and it never reached critical mass."

I nodded. Critical mass in private-equity-speak referred to the amount of capital he had been able to raise. It was a common death knell for hundreds of start-up funds.

"Plus he cleared all his trades through Bear Stearns," Gigi continued.

In the aftermath of the subprime lending debacle, Bear Stearns, once one of the most venerable banks on Wall Street, was forced to sell itself to JP Morgan for less than it was worth. Much of its well-paid staff, including several of Peter's friends, had been laid off, leaving Peter to scramble to forge relationships with new brokers.

"And to top it all off, Peter was personally heavily invested in Bear stock. He'd worked there for ten years before he left to do his own thing. When Bear sold to JP Morgan for a pittance, the Partridges lost just about everything they had. Lord knows why they're throwing this party. They really can't afford it."

"I can't imagine what it's like to lose so much so quickly."

"Hey, this is New York. Fortunes are made and lost every day, especially in a market as volatile as this one."

This, I knew to be true. John and I, for example, had profited from fluctuations in the energy markets. We were overnight success stories, but we were the exception. Far more had lost their shirts. No one could have anticipated that Greenwich, Connecticut, aka hedgefundlandia, would become rife with home foreclosures.

"Hey, let's have lunch next week, my treat. Do you like Nello?" Gigi asked, mentioning the name of a popular Italian restaurant on Madison Avenue.

"I've never been, but John has and he tells me it's good."

"It is. The pasta is incredible. Tuesday at noon work for you?"

"Absolutely," I'd said, and for the first time since the miscarriage, I actually had something to look forward to.

Gigi handed me her card in case I had to cancel—which I promised her I wouldn't, my agenda being completely empty and all—and we walked back toward the living room, where the party was just starting to pick up steam. The music had gotten louder and drinks stiffer. At around eleven, Gigi bade us all goodbye—she'd promised her babysitter it wouldn't be a late night—but before she left she introduced me to Peter Partridge, who immediately plunked a pair of felt antlers on my head and asked me to pose with Ainsley in front of their fifteen-foot Christmas tree.

Clad in a strapless chartreuse mini, her hair tumbling in her trademark flaxen waves over a pair of lightly tanned shoulders, Ainsley was every inch the Woman About Town. She had the kind of haughty aura that is particular to people accustomed to being at the center of attention anywhere they went. Ainsley's parents were upper middle class, but socially ambitious enough to know that by sending their daughter to Exeter in Massachusetts for boarding school and then to Rollins in Florida for college, they would be giving her an opportunity to join the ranks of high society. They were right: Ainsley met Peter at a charity benefit while she was working as a summer intern for *House & Home,* however it wasn't until she bumped into Peter two summers later at Piping Rock that the pair began to date. They were married a year and a half later (a picture appeared in *Town & Country* magazine), and Ainsley gave up her job working in *Vogue*'s fabled fashion closet to dedicate herself to charitable works full time, or so she told the *New York Times Vows* columnist at the time.

For several subsequent years, Ainsley and Peter were considered New York's golden couple. She had beauty and charm, he, pedigree and (it was assumed) tons of old money—still the best kind. They were photographed at parties, written about in all the newspapers, celebrated everywhere. I would be lying if I said that it wasn't thrilling to be momentarily allowed into their inner circle, even if Ainsley had kept calling me by the wrong name. (Where she got Tricia from Marcy, I'll never know.)

I had been sitting on the couch for a while, pretending to listen to John and one of his colleagues discuss the latest round of firings at an investment bank downtown, when Peter suggested that we all do a round of shots, which, when they arrived, turned out to be closer in size to tumblers, filled close to the brim with tequila. Everyone threw theirs back in one, and I, not wanting to stand out in the crowd, followed suit. It was a bad move. The quails' eggs and tiny tartlets might have been delicious, but they hadn't provided much in the way of stomach lining. I was immediately drunk.

I found John in the hallway between the kitchen and dining room, talking to Ainsley. Tugging lightly on his shirt, I tried to get his attention.

He didn't notice, so I tugged harder. "Honey, I'm going to get my coat," I said.

"Really?" he asked, looking at his watch.

I nodded and swayed, and John moved to steady me. But Ainsley moved faster. Clasping a skinny, sinewy arm around my waist, she pouted prettily and said in a surprisingly husky voice that I simply could not go, that she was just getting to know me. (*Err, Tricia?*)

"C'mon, Marce, let's stay a little longer," John seconded.

I agreed—*stupid me*—and whiled away some time thumbing through a stack of coffee table books (most of which featured Ainsley in some way or another) in front of the fake fireplace in the Partridges' living room. Three-quarters of an hour later, I was no longer tipsy but tired and truly ready to go home. But when I went to find John, I stumbled into Peter, who somehow talked me into accepting a glass of Montrachet from him in the kitchen. He'd just opened the bottle, the last in a case he'd won at a charity auction and said it would be a shame not to drink it. Okay, okay, I relented. And, yes, I could have declined Peter's offer and left the party, slipping out into the foyer and through the front door without anyone noticing, but the thing is that I really felt like it would have been rude to turn down the guy. He'd just lost his business and the majority of his savings. The least I could do was share a bottle of Montrachet with him.

From then on my recollection of events starts to get blurry. I do remember that all of us piled into a couple of cabs and headed downtown to the Gramercy Park Hotel, where there was a velvet rope that Peter and Ainsley had no trouble transcending, and inside the music was great, the vibe electric. Bottles of champagne, tequila, fresh orange juice, pomegranate juice, and soda crowded every square inch of our table. Once we were all settled, Peter handed me another drink, a tequila mixed with the pomegranate juice, and I honestly don't remember anything of what happened after finishing it—no idea how or why I'd disrobed in front of a room full of the city's most sophisticated, well-connected movers and shakers, or started a fight with a girl whose face and name I cannot, for the life of me, remember even to this day.

5

Becoming a Rules Girl

"Honey, all of us hedge fund wives have to put up with the same Goddamn quid pro quo," said Gigi Ambrose.

Gigi and I were having lunch at Nello, home of the fifty-dollar plate of pasta. No joke. The smoked salmon ravioli actually costs fifty-five dollars. But despite the exorbitant prices—or maybe because of them—and the fact that Christmas was a mere three days away, the place was packed, buzzing with the kind of excitement such extravagance tends to generate. You feel the same thing walking into Bergdorf's shoe salon, but there it's overpriced platform heels that get everyone salivating, while at Nello, it's the overpriced veal chops.

"What quid pro quo?" I asked, craning my head forward with interest.

"Your husband may make tons of money, but you never get to see him."

I laughed. "Too true."

I took a bite of my penne rigate, which I must admit tasted like heaven—the hot and sweet sausages somehow managed to be both delicate and hearty—and surveyed the room. There was a maitre d' hovering by the bar, nervously keeping an eye on all the tables. Waiters in black vests and white aprons tied at the waist were zipping around, taking orders, delivering plates of aromatic delicacies—artichokes drizzled in white truffle oil, pan roasted veal chops with sautéed wild mushrooms, and Chilean sea bass cooked in a lobster, saffron velouté. On one side of me a pair of older women with shopping bags at their feet pushed forty-two dollar tuna tartares around their plate; on the other side, a foursome of men, all devouring the veal and wearing wedding bands, openly ogled the lithesome young girls seated at the table next to theirs.

"Rule Number Two," Gigi continued, snapping me back to attention with a flick of her hand, the same hand that happened to be sporting nine carats of flawless, colorless diamonds (Grade: F, Color: D, for those in the know). I was learning that one diamond wasn't good enough for a Hedge Fund Bride; nothing less than three would do. Take Gigi's engagement ring for example. There was the center stone, an emerald cut stunner that was, to my untrained eye, at least five carats, and then two triangle-shaped stones, each about two carats, flanking it. In Chicago, my three-carat engagement ring was considered flashy; here, it was barely worth flashing.

She had made it her mission that day to school me in the art of hedge fund wifehood and I, having been the ignorant newcomer I was, was most grateful for the lesson.

"Never ask him about work. If he wants to talk about it, he will. And make sure you keep people who want stock tips, or in John's case, predictions about fluctuations in the price of crude far away from him at social functions. There's nothing that grates on Jeremy more than someone who wants free market advice."

"Is that Rule Number Three?" I asked, trying to keep up.

"No, three is to never talk about your own problems, especially any that might be work related, if you do happen to have a job."

I opened my mouth to comment, but Gigi pressed on. "Rule Four," she said. "Keep the baby talk to a minimum. Children should never be a disturbance, especially at night."

With that, Gigi bent her head in concentration over her fettuccine al funghi, and I couldn't tell if she was a) focusing on the flavors, trying to discern the ingredients; b) trying not to get any of the rich mushroom and cream sauce on her ruffled silk blouse, which I assumed was made by a famous designer, and therefore wildly expensive; or c) thinking about the last thing she said, the thing about keeping children off the conversational menu.

It occurred to me that I hadn't observed Rule Four over the previous six months. In fact, I had vagrantly violated rules one *through* four. I was a fantastically shitty hedge fund wife. I didn't fit the mold at all, but for that matter, neither did Gigi. She seemed too outspoken and vivacious, and she had her own thriving career. Plus she clearly loved talking about her daughter Chloe. She had spoken of nothing else during the first half of our lunch.

As Gigi expertly twirled her pasta around the tines of her fork, using the bowl of a spoon to anchor the pasta, I took the opportunity to continue studying her face. She had wide-set eyes, a straight nose, and full lips, but in the sunlight I could see that she was wearing a thick layer of foundation and that there were wrinkles creeping out from around her eyes and lips. She looked older and less sprightly than she did on television or on the cover of her book jackets, but she was still arrestingly beautiful.

When we were finished with our entrees, Gigi ordered a bowl of gelato for us to share and spooning the creamy, cold ice cream into my mouth, I was reminded of my childhood in Minnesota. Whenever my sister and I did well on our report cards, my father would take us for ice cream at Byerly's, an upscale grocery store in the suburb where we lived. This happened pretty infrequently since Annalise rarely studied—she was too busy with boys and cheerleading practice—so more often than not my father would take just me. We usually went on Friday nights when Annalise had a game to cheer, so she wouldn't feel bad about her academic shortcomings, or at least that's what my father said. Now, in hindsight, I think Dad was more concerned about making *me* feel better. After all, I was the one stuck at home on a Friday night when most kids were out with their friends, partying and whatnot.

Gigi wanted to know about my sister, so I told her that she had been the popular one and I the smart one. "A family of two daughters usually gets one of each," I said, adding that Annalise wasn't exactly prettier than I was, but she had a better figure—larger breasts, longer legs—and had been the recipient of braces (whereas my parents, in their infinite wisdom, had decided I could go without) that had given her the killer smile that would eventually grace our local Dayton's department store newspaper advertisements for its annual three-day back-to-school sale. Annalise, considered a minor celebrity in our high school thanks to those ads, was named Homecoming Queen her senior year. She had a string of boyfriends, tons of friends.

I didn't.

I imagined this was why she couldn't believe that I had married "well" and she hadn't. She was stuck in a shabby two-bedroom house with a husband who spent too much time watching sports (hockey, football, you name it . . .) on television and drinking beer (from a can, "not even a bottle" she once complained bitterly to my mother, who then told me, even though I had on several occasions made it clear to her that I no desire to know the inner-workings of my sister's marriage). It was down to Annalise to raise their two rambunctious boys—Jack, five, and Trevor, three—and fix things up around the house. My beauty-queen sister had to empty the gutters, mow the lawn, rake the leaves, shovel the snow, and on top of that clean the house and cook breakfast, lunch, and dinner on a grocery budget so small that they sometimes had to have hot dogs for dinner—five nights in a row. She couldn't help but compare her life to mine and wonder where she'd gone wrong. It's like I had disturbed the correct order of things, and she resented me to no end for it.

I explained this all to Gigi, who told me that she had a sister who was married, too, who was always jealous of her big city life until the day that Gigi started dating a Greek shipping magnate. In the beginning he was romantic and sweet and incredibly generous—he took her to nice restaurants and on lavish trips, and bought her expensive shoes. He also liked to rub her feet.

A little too much.

'After a few weeks of dating, Gigi started noticing that her Greek magnate was getting a little too much pleasure out of touching her feet, and liked doing it at inappropriate times, like when he was driving them home from dinner or to his beach house in Bridgehampton. "He'd get hard just from touching the soft skin on the underside of my arch," she said. "That was his favorite part."

Still, he was kind to her and seemed serious about their relationship—"he told me that he couldn't wait to introduce me to his parents"—so she put up with his sexual quirk. But then, he got mean. A few months into their courtship he started criticizing her. "If *one* of my nails was chipped, he'd tell me that I looked like a mess." One day she told him that if he cared so much about her nails, then maybe he should pay for her manicures. His response was to call her a gold digger and cut their meal short. Around the same time he became controlling about what shoes she wore. Sometimes, Gigi said, she had to change them four or five times before they went out.

She told me a story about one of their last weeks together, when they planned on meeting some friends for brunch at Felix, a restaurant and bar in SoHo. It was a cold Sunday in February and there was ice and snow on the ground. Gigi chose a pair of flat boots to wear with her jeans and sweater, but her Greek boy-friend pointed out that she'd already worn the boots once that week. "So I changed into my other boots that happen to have a lot of buckles, and he freaked out. He said they would be too hard for him to get them off. He threw a tantrum," she said.

The next day, she dumped him, and being a short man with a massive Napoleonic complex, he didn't handle his dismissal well. For six months following their break up, he harassed her with vulgar, cruel phone messages and emails, and told all of their friends that *he* had dumped *her* because he figured out she was only interested in him for his money. "All rich men end up saying that. Even Jeremy has and John, if he hasn't already, probably will."

Gigi suddenly looked stricken and covered her mouth with her hands. "What am I doing? I've broken the most important rule of all. Rule Number Five: Never talk bad about your husband."

I assured her that I was not going to tell anyone. "Who would I tell? I have no friends in New York." I reached across the table to squeeze her hand reassuringly.

"No, sugar, you've got me now," she said.

The waiter cleared the bowl of gelato and took our coffee orders. One espresso dopio for Gigi, who explained that she needed the caffeine because she had been up all night with the baby and had to go to a meeting at her publisher's after lunch. I ordered a cappuccino, extra foam, and told her that she didn't have to justify her coffee order to me. "I drink way more than I should, and I don't have kids or a job to legitimize my caffeine addiction," I said.

Gigi asked if John and I planned on starting a family soon, and, given the confessional turn of our lunch, I told her about my miscarriage. I didn't say much about what happened in the hospital, because nobody wants to hear the gruesome details, but I did talk about the grief that followed and how I was trying to pick up the pieces of my life. She was careful not to ask too many questions and to dab the tears from her eyes before they had a chance to ruin her makeup.

Then, because our lunch was coming to an end and I didn't want to leave her on a sad note, I told Gigi that I knew John and I were fortunate, that there was a lot in our lives that was a lot better than before. Better and bigger and brighter.

"Our apartment has floor-to-ceiling windows in the living and dining rooms and we're updating all our furniture to eco-conscious midcentury modern. It's all clean lines, natural wood finishes, dye-free textiles, that sort of look. It's what John likes."

"And you?'

"Me? I don't know the first thing about interior décor. Nothing matched in my house growing up. What do I know about bamboo flooring and hemp silk?"

"Everyone likes splurging on something. What is it for you? Shoes, handbags? Mesotherapy?"

"Meso-what?"

"Nevermind. Better you not know."

"I guess I do like eating well. It's nice to be able to order whatever I want when we go to restaurants. No more 'Just the house salad for me, thanks.'"

She laughed. "Poverty is the best diet in the land."

"But really, there's so little off limits, it blows my mind," I continued. "We bought brand new cars for our fathers. This summer John wants to rent a nice house in Southampton and last weekend he ordered a couple of custom made suits and a ton of shirts from a store on Fifty-Seventh Street."

"Turnbull & Asser." Gigi nodded knowingly and crossed her long alabaster arms over her ample chest as she leaned back in her chair.

"Yes! And his shoes cost fifteen hundred dollars."

"John Lobb."

"John says you have to have these things. People notice."

"It's true."

"Who knew men were such label whores?"

"They can be worse than women." Gigi nodded.

"I mean, bespoke cashmere? Have you ever heard of anything more pretentious in your life?"

We both snorted.

"John is a little confounded by my thriftiness, but I just don't see the point in blowing a thousand dollars on a purse that will be declared 'out' on the pages of *Harper's Bazaar* in three months. And besides, I feel like a bad feminist spending his money. When we lived in Chicago I had a job and if I wanted something, I'd use my own money."

"So get a job here."

"I know. I should. I've been meaning to start making some calls. But I can't seem to motivate. Our couch is just too comfortable."

"Well, if you're looking for some part-time work while you look for something permanent, I could use your help with a few catering events I have coming up. You could help me with advance prep, or with room décor if you don't like kitchen work."

"Oh no, I love baking. I'll do whatever you need."

"Can you work the events too? I have one coming up the first week after New Year's. My friend is a contributing editor for *House & Home* and she's hosting a party celebrating next month's designer of the year issue. She's a hedge fund wife, but one of the good ones. You'll love Jill."

"Jill Lovern Tischman?"

"You know her?" Gigi asked.

I nodded and told her all about Caroline's baby shower—the goody bags, the cakes, the mountain of presents Caroline received.

"I heard that the surrogate wasn't invited," she said.

I had assumed that whoever was carrying Caroline's baby lived in Idaho or something and Caroline would be going there to retrieve her baby once it was born, but apparently the Reinhardts were putting the woman up in their West Village townhouse and had plans to keep her on as the child's wet nurse once the baby was born. The day of Caroline's shower she'd stayed home, but as Caroline had later boasted, she'd remembered to send the woman a piece of the Sylvia Weinstock cake home with her driver. *As if it was so darn thoughtful of her to save her a slice of cake, and then not even personally deliver it.*

I tossed my napkin on the table, and Gigi checked her watch, a white oversized one with a diamond bezel.

"So can you help me for Jill's event? The other wives will probably think it's weird that you're doing it, but I'll tell them I begged you to pitch in," she said, standing up. "Do you think your husband will mind you spending an evening out with me?"

I raised my eyebrow at her. "Are you kidding? John's never home before ten, most nights it's eleven."

"Oh right. I forgot. You're a hedge fund wife."

"Don't remind me," I snorted.

Together we exited the restaurant, bundled up in our heavy coats, ready to face the inclement weather outside. It had begun to sleet, and the freezing pellets of rain struck down on us as soon as we set foot on the sidewalk.

As I bundled my coat against the precipitation, I received a text on my BlackBerry.

John: Fred and Caroline Reinhardt have invited us to Aspen for New Year's. Please find appropriate housewarming gift. (Budget: $3,000-$5,000) We'll discuss wardrobe needs tonight. Love, me.

6

Parties Galore

It took me half a dozen tries to get the right hostess gift for the Reinhardts. My first instinct was to buy a case of wine, since it was guaranteed not to go to waste, but John said my suggestion lacked "originality" and "panache," and that all the other "dolts" in his office had already shipped crates of Château Margaux to the Reinhardt's sprawling Aspen chalet weeks ago. So it was back to the drawing board and Madison Avenue for me, and after having several more of my ideas shot down because they were also too "pedestrian" or "obvious" we went over budget and settled on half a kilo of Royal Sevruga caviar ($6,000) and three black lacquer globe *presentoirs* (at $350 a pop).

Our invitation was for only three days, but we took twice as many bags. John had gone a little crazy with the ski gear and had bought two entirely new outfits for himself, another ski outfit for me, including a little fox fur hat that looked like something Ivana Trump would have worn in her 1980s heyday, as well as top-of-the-line skis, boots, and poles for the two of us. I ski, but I would hardly consider myself an enthusiast, so the cash outlay on all the paraphernalia that I knew I would be using at most once a year seemed completely ridiculous. But then again, so was spending six thousand dollars on half a kilo of fish eggs, so I kept my mouth shut. It was John's money, after all.

As soon as we touched down in Aspen John received a text message from Fred saying that his chauffeur would be waiting outside of baggage claim to help us with our things and drive us to their home (in one of the three black Hummers they kept on hand for guests and staff to use). The Reinhardts' home was located just north of town, on Red Mountain, which was apparently where the best properties were found. A Saudi prince owned the most impressive estate—its main house boasted fifteen bedrooms, a racquet ball court, and indoor swimming pool, and sat on ninety acres of closely guarded land—but there were others with values estimated at fifty million dollars and beyond. And bear in mind that these were homes that were used at most two to three times a year by the actual owners, and the rest of the year were tended to by armies of caretakers and staff who were under strict orders to keep everything ready in case the owners decided to make an impromptu stopover.

The Reinhardts' mansion, or chalet, as Caroline liked to call it, was every bit as spectacular as I would have guessed it would be. The main house comprised of eight bedrooms, most of which had their own adjoining bathrooms, plus a screening room, full-size exercise room and Pilates studio, indoor pool and separate steam and sauna rooms for men and women. The great room, overlooking the city of Aspen, featured vaulted ceilings, a huge chandelier made of wood and real deer antlers, giant widows, hardwood floors, stone accent walls, and a double fireplace connecting the dining room and bar area. The room was also stuffed with exotic furniture—think zebra wood commodes and Biedermeier armoires and vitrines—and accessorized with fox fur and mink blankets, pewter lamps, and a huge ostrich-skin-covered ottoman that doubled as a coffee table. Our bedroom was similarly decorated with antique hunting prints, a stack of fur-trimmed cashmere blankets, and a real Tiffany lamp perched atop the demi-lune console.

By the time John and I were unpacked, and ready, and had transferred our hostess's gift to the appropriate staff member (later that same housekeeper would hand me a handwritten thank you note from Caroline acknowledging her reception of the gift) we were instructed by the butler that the Reinhardts had headed over to the après ski at 39 Degrees, the luxe lounge at the Sky Hotel, a swank ninety-room mountain lodge, and wished for us to join them if we were so inclined.

One of the drivers—there were three on staff—whisked us up to the hotel and bar in question, and I swear, walking into that room, I had never seen so much mink in my life. Every single woman was blanketed in some form of animal pelt, and two of the toppers were gold furs made using a process pioneered by Fendi to meld real twenty-four-carat gold with fur via vacuum technology. Plus the jewelry! Diamonds glinting from every earlobe, wrist, and finger. I adjusted my J. Mendel hat (apparently still in fashion given the number of women wearing similar models) and grabbed John's hand as we threaded through the crowd toward the Reinhardts' table at the back of the lounge.

Caroline was sipping a glass of champagne, dressed in a matching white puffer jacket, pants, and ski goggles all marked with the Chanel logo, when she spotted us walking toward her. She hopped to her feet, past a man who I had to assume was their bodyguard from the grim expression on his face, black-on-black uniform, and foreboding presence, and came over to greet John and then me.

"Kisses, love," she said, bussing John on both cheeks before turning to me. "Did you find everything all right? Is the room okay?" she asked.

"Yes, absolutely," I said. "Thank you so much for having us."

John walked toward the table, where Caroline's husband Fred, a large man in both stature and girth, with a potato-shaped nose and pink skin that suggested German ancestry, slapped him on the back and poured him a glass of champagne.

Caroline assessed my hat. "That's a nice one," she said, before turning on the heel of her boot and returning to the table.

I decided to take her stilted compliment as progress, and made my way over to the table. Dahlia nodded a frosty hello to me before flicking her attention back to Caroline, and there were a couple other women I didn't know but knew of seated around the table. One of the women, Magdalena, was married to Herb Zimmer, the head of ZAC Capital, an equity-market focused hedge fund. She had dark olive skin, large breasts, flashing dark eyes, and masses of chestnut-colored hair, and as I would later learn (in one of Caroline's saunas, from another houseguest) was often the subject of mean-spirited gossip.

It came with the territory since Herb was one of the wealthiest and most successful of all the hedge fund kings; his net worth was close to seven billion according to *Forbes* magazine's annual survey. He'd grown up on Long Island, the son of a prominent local businessman and librarian, went to Harvard business school and eventually, after a stint in arbitrage, started his own fund. His first marriage ended in divorce after twenty years—the wife was said to have grown tired of his eccentricities—and Herb suddenly found himself alone and desirous of female companionship but not interested or willing to go through the usual dating rigmarole. So instead he asked his psychologist to help him make a list of all the attributes he wanted in a new wife—from physical traits to professional background and weekend hobbies—and he forwarded this list of "requirements" to his closest friends. Hundreds of women sent in pictures and biographies and Herb, again with the help of his psychologist, narrowed the applicant pool down to ten candidates. Over the course of the next six months he took each of the women out on a date (always to the same restaurant, the Four Seasons in New York) and asked them each to complete a Myers-Briggs test to determine their personality type. With each round of dates he came closer to finding his candidate and eventually, after only four rounds, settled on Magdalena.

They married in a simple ceremony with Mayor Bloomberg presiding, and Magdalena, an interior designer from Argentina, quickly settled into Herb's life as, it was often joked, "the forty-third staff member." (At the time of their wedding, ZAC Capital had forty-two employees.) Magdalena couldn't care less that everyone gossiped about her behind her back. Say what they liked, Herb was king of the hedgehogs, she was queen, and no one could take that scepter away from her.

I took a seat on the far end, as far away from Magdalena, Dahlia, and Caroline as I could manage, and ordered a Coca-Cola from one of the waiters perpetually hovering around the table. The altitude was making me a bit nauseous, and I was feeling overwhelmed by the buzz of chatter and competitive energy in the room. Not two seconds after I took my first grateful sip of pop (we Minnesotans call Coke and Sprite and most other carbonated, sugary beverages "pop") Jill Lovern Tischman floated into the room, looking cozy and warm in a chocolate mink cape that she held closed with her delicate hand. A massive sea-green opal sparkled from one of her fingers.

Fur and baubles aside, I couldn't have been more excited (and relieved) to see her. She spotted me in the crowd and came right over, enveloping me in a big Gardena-scented hug, and made me feel instantly at ease. Across from me, Fred Reinhardt made room for Jill on the banquette and she instantly began peppering me with questions: Had I ever been there before; did I snowboard; and had I gotten a room at the Sky Hotel? I barely had a chance to tell her where John and I were staying—she and Glenn had their own "little" chalet on Red Mountain and were there with her children

and two nannies, plus some friends with their own brood in tow—
before Irina Khashovopova descended on the table and took the
seat next to mine.

Dressed in a chinchilla vest and hat, gray leopard print jeans,
and fur-lined boots, Irina scooped up the champagne bottle and
poured a glass out for herself and Jill before sitting back down
and sighing dramatically. She whipped out her phone, punched
out a telephone number with a finger that was adorned with a
pink tourmaline-encrusted frog, barked into the mouthpiece in
Russian for thirty seconds before snapping it closed and slipping
it into her vest pocket. After draining her glass of champagne and
ordering five more bottles for the table, she announced gravely, "I
just come from the boutique in Little Nell. They will not honor my
discount."

"What discount?" Jill inquired, running a hand through her
light brown hair.

"I told lady, Bergdorf give me twenty percent off J. Mendel but
she no listen. I try to buy a hat. Just a fucking hat. Do you know
how much I spend on J. Mendel fur? Hundreds of thousands, and
they will not give me a twenty percent discount on a fucking hat?
I told lady I never shop J. Mendel again. From now on, I get all my
fur from Fendi."

"But how can it be J. Mendel's fault if the Little Nell won't give
you a discount? They're just a retailer," I said.

Irina sneered at me. "You obviously don't know who I am.
Karl Lagerfeld put me front row at his Chanel show last season.
Denise Rich won't throw a party on her yacht unless I am there.
Angelina Jolie sends me Christmas cards, so who the fuck are
you to question my right to ask for a discount?"

"Irina, I get that you're mad, but that's no excuse to take it out
on Marcy," Jill said.

Jill's comment only served to fluff Irina's feathers more. Grit-
ting her bright white teeth, she said, "Is the principle of the matter.

I spend so much money. I'm good customer. And they want to argue with me over a measly three hundred fucking dollars. *Nyet.*"

Jill wisely decided that she wasn't going to engage Irina any further and we let the matter drop. As the hour wore on, I removed my hat and set it on the seat next to mine. The lounge was heating up and one of the bodyguards, this one belonged to the Kemps, kept bumping me on the head as he reached over me to hand Dahlia her phone and then take her coat and ear muffs away from her.

As the hour wore on, the group jostled around—I noticed several of the guys, including John, heading to the bathroom with suspicious frequency—and I ultimately found myself seated next to Caroline, who was by then well into her cups. She slurred as she addressed me, and reiterated how glad she was that we had made it, that her husband really, really loved John, and that she wanted us to go out to lunch in the city when we got back. I was pleased that she was being nice to me—I'd thought I'd blown it when I couldn't tell her what color I thought she should paint the walls of her nursery—but also highly skeptical of her true motivations. I was smart enough to know that Fred could have put her up to hosting us and getting to know me, in order to find out more information about John. We were playing in the big leagues now, literally rubbing elbows with some of the wealthiest people in America, and I had to be on my guard.

I sipped my Coke and asked Caroline what she had in store for all of us. The Reinhardts were hosting a 100-person dinner in a heated tent on the great lawn of their home on New Year's Eve. This was the third year they were throwing the party, and John said that in years past they had blown everyone away with private performances from Jay-Z one year and Mariah Carey another. This year it was rumored that they had lined up Rihanna, but Caroline wouldn't confirm that for me. She, however, did divulge that she and Fred had flown in the acclaimed Belgian artist and

photographer Jean-Luc Moerman to paint temporary tattoos on
guests and a number of ex-Cirque de Soleil contortionists to perform during the intermission. Before she stood up she placed her
hand on mine and gave it a good squeeze. "Oh you have no idea
what it takes to put this party together. Even working with an
event specialist, it all ends up resting on my shoulders," she said,
and for the first time I could see that the stress was, indeed, getting to her.

"Caroline, honestly, I'm in awe," I said. "I wouldn't know
where to begin."

She seemed to appreciate my accolades greatly. "I've made up
my mind. I'm putting you and John at the table with Al Gore and
Leonardo DiCaprio. John would like that, right?"

Forget John. I was so excited I thought I might pee in my pants,
but I smiled and said that yes, indeed, John would be thrilled
since he was very passionate about environmental preservation.

"Oh, good," Caroline hiccupped, "because Fred just sent the
jet this morning to pick up Leo and his girlfriend."

The Reinhardts' New Year's party was, according to local gossip,
not quite as fabulous as the previous year's. But you could have
fooled me. Everywhere I turned there were famous faces and
bold-faced names, trays of champagne flutes, and six-foot floral
arrangements. I felt, as usual, underdressed in my simple jewel-
toned column, especially when I saw Jill in a partially see-through
dress that was made of silk and tulle, with a front panel of close-
cropped gray mink. Her shoes, open-toed sandals, were constructed entirely of peacock feathers. Caroline, meanwhile opted
for an asymmetrical fire-engine-red gown with a crystal-encrusted
bodice and short hemline, while Dahlia chose a discreet ecru satin
party frock and matching fox-trimmed bolero, that was pinned
with a large diamond and pearl orchid brooch.

After a sumptuous five-course dinner with our new friends Al and Tipper Gore (Leo was a no-show) and a performance by Maroon Five (the Rihanna rumors were wrong), I went to the ladies' room to powder my nose and get away from Al, who, to be honest, didn't know when to stop talking. On my way out my heel caught on a duct-taped ridge covering one of the power cords leading toward the stage, and I knocked into Dahlia, who nearly had a heart attack when I instinctively grabbed her forearm to steady myself.

"I'm so sorry," I said. "I tripped. I know you don't liked to be touched."

"You should watch where you are going, Marcy," she said flatly. "And I mean that in more ways than one. Clumsy is not cute, and neither is playing the naïve little wife. I've seen a dozen women like you come and go, and as sure as I know my children's names, I know that you will not last long. Your kind never does. Either your husband will not bear out to be the whiz kid that all the other men seem to think he is, or he will dump you for someone else. And whichever one of these comes to pass, believe me, Marcy, no one here will care."

"And a joyous and prosperous New Year to you, too, Dahlia," I said.

She regarded me contemptuously before continuing on her path through the throng of well-dressed guests.

I was stunned, but not hurt. Dahlia lived in a bubble; she was totally lacking in social grace, not to mention delusional and completely removed from reality, and I wondered what it would take for her to come back to her senses and realize that she was no better than me, or the dozens of assistants and shop girls, nannies and waitresses she probably verbally assaulted every day.

It was close to midnight, and Justin Timberlake, along with Caroline and Fred, took to the stage to lead the crowd through a countdown to the next year. John found me in the swarm of bodies near the shockingly true-to-life ice sculpture of Caroline's naked body and pulled me to him and kissed me warmly on the mouth as the gold and silver confetti fell from the ceiling and onto the crowd.

"I love you, Marcy," he whispered in my ear. "This is going to be our year. Look around at all these people. By this time next year, we'll be just as rich as them. You watch and see," he said, lifting his glass to me.

I took a long swallow of the champagne and smiled, but inside I was wondering if my husband truly meant to sound like a greedy asshole or if it was just the cocaine talking. By then I was almost sure that he was using. All the trips to the bathroom, dilated pupils and dry mouth, not to mention the sniffing that he kept on blaming on the frigid temperatures and high altitude? Give me a break. As if I wasn't supposed to put two and two together. It incensed me that John wouldn't volunteer that he was snorting lines, and I didn't know what made me more upset, that he was trying to keep it a secret from me, or that he was using a drug that up until recently he considered something only trust-fund-addled playboys blew their money on. I tried to confront him about it a few times, but we were so rarely alone—there was always another houseguest or staff member around—that I decided to leave it until we returned to New York.

As the festivities continued late into the night, I tried to remind myself that I was lucky to have a husband with big and clear goals, even if it would have been nice, that is to say I would have respected him more, if he had been motivated by something other than the deepening of his own already deep pockets. I thought of the heavy, secondhand autobiography of Lee Iacocca my father toted around with him to some of the football games that Annalise cheered in high school. My father was a liberal Democrat, like most of the people in our middle-class Midwestern neighborhood, but he looked up to Iacocca because he had resuscitated Chrysler and had saved and created jobs in the process. This, according to my father, was capitalism at its best. Iacocca deserved every bit of his success

John did not.

In fact, most of the people around us did not. They made money for the pure sport of it, and didn't manufacture a product or create jobs. Sure, there were the dozens upon dozens of people they employed to take care of their offspring and belongings, and I supposed that in this regard their good fortune had trickled down to the nannies and busboys, cleaning ladies and garage mechanics, but was that enough to buoy an economy forever? I did not think so, but most of the people making merry in the crowd did. And they partied despite the darkening economic clouds, despite the millions of foreclosure signs popping up across the country like little red flags. A storm was coming, but no one wanted to see it, least of all, of course, the wives.

7

Setting the Table

Jillian Lovern Tischman lived in Gramercy Park, a neighborhood named for the private park to which only the residents of the buildings abutting the manicured green square were given access. Her apartment was actually two apartments that had been combined into one a few years prior to my visit. It was on the same square as the Gramercy Park Hotel, aka the scene of my latest humiliation, which I could just make out if I hung my head out of Jill's kitchen window and squinted through the trees of the park. It was in this position that Gigi found me when she swept into the room in a cloud of her vanilla and rosewood perfume.

"Girl, you better get your head out of that window. I can't afford to lose one more person tonight," she clucked. "The bartender's not returning my calls and one of my servers called to say she's come down with the flu, which knowing this one means she's been asked out on a date. Probably by some jerk who's gonna take her to a fancy restaurant, have his way with her, and never call her again. I keep telling her not to put out on the first date, but Lord have mercy does she ever listen to me?"

"We've been wasting our breath," said Gigi's chef, Bear, an

older German man who was large and huggable enough to make his name seem appropriate rather than silly. He was vigorously stirring a chocolate sauce over a double broiler and paused mid-stir to add, "I'm starting to think she is the kind that never will learn."

Gigi sighed, and turned to look at me. I was wearing a black Ralph Lauren cashmere turtleneck sweater and skirt, and the pearl necklace John had bought me a few months ago for my thirty-fifth birthday. "Thank you so much for doing this," she said as she walked over to the butcher's block-topped kitchen island and pushed aside four stacks of industrial-sized, plastic-wrapped baking sheets to make room for her plastic binder. Flipping through the notebook, she found the page she was looking for and started explaining to me the timeline of the evening, starting with prep work, followed by the cocktail hour, and finally dinner service. Around ten we would clear the tables and rinse the dishes before restacking them into their plastic crates. Then they would be sent to a facility to be scrubbed clean inside industrial-sized dishwashers.

"*House & Home* cut their budget down by a third," Gigi said as I perused the menu over her shoulder. "And half of my purveyors have jacked up their prices by twenty percent, so between the budget cut and price increase, we're producing this event on a shoestring. Of course everything still has to look pretty. These design people couldn't care less about how the food tastes, as long as it looks good."

"Seems like a metaphor for my life," I said before I could stop myself.

Gigi set down her notebook and peered at me over her reading glasses. "Is there something you want to talk about?"

"I'll elaborate when we don't have thirty people due for dinner in less than two hours," I said in an effort to deflect any more questions.

I wasn't ready to talk about it yet, but John and I had gotten into an argument in bed on Saturday night when I finally had a chance to tell him about my plan to help Gigi with her catering business while I started looking for a full-time job. John's objections were two-fold: First, he didn't want me to work as a catering waitress, which he deemed ridiculously below me; and second, he didn't want me to go back to work—period. He said that people would get the wrong impression if I was seen slaving away for Gigi and asked if I wanted them to treat me even more dismissively than before.

"Do you even realize that your job will entail scraping other people's half-masticated meals off dirty plates?" he asked, his face turning a frustrated shade of crimson. He set down his copies of *Alpha* and *Trader Monthly* magazine, which could be best described as the hedge funder's *Vogue* and *Harper's Bazaar* for all the obsessive reading it inspired.

"John, I'm doing this," I said. "You're the one who said I should make friends."

"Let's be clear on one thing—Gigi will be your employer, not your friend, if you do this."

"Can't she be both? Geez, John, according to you everyone's either a master or a slave. This isn't ancient Egypt. What are you, Hegel?"

"Actually, Marcy, it's less far off than you think. But I tell you what I'm going to do. I'm going to let you learn that for yourself. Maybe then you'll understand what I'm trying to accomplish for us, instead of fighting me at every turn." He picked up his magazine and began reading again.

"Well, I'm so glad you approve," I said acerbically.

John glared at me before flopping over on his side and opening the drawer of his side table. He pulled out his bottle of Ambien, popped a pill in his mouth and swallowed it with a swig from his bottle of Evian.

Shortly after we moved to New York, John started having trouble sleeping. I encouraged him to stop reading his finance magazines in bed and offered to make him chamomile tea or hot milk, but he insisted on going to the doctor to get a prescription.

"All the traders take the stuff on a nightly basis," he claimed, and so, he, too, started relying upon the drug to get to sleep. I didn't think it was a good long-term solution, but I also knew that he was under a lot of stress at work and, like me, was still getting acclimated to our new life. I was also relieved that the cocaine binge (which we never discussed) had ended in Aspen, and hoped that once John settled in to his job and had become used to its demands and pressures, he would be able to quit the Ambien as easily as he had seemingly quit the cocaine.

Washing down the pill, he lay back down and shifted over on his side (away from me), sending his magazines in a flurry to the floor. He didn't bother to pick them up but announced without turning around to face me, "Just don't expect me to dry your tears when Gigi scolds you for serving from the wrong side or showing up with a stain on your collar. *Then* we'll see how you define your relationship."

I said nothing, but in my head, I thought: *Man, my husband's becoming an asshole.*

Gigi was nervously chewing on her bottom lip, reading through her notes, and jotting a few words down here and there in the margins when the doorbell rang. Jill's nanny, a diminutive Filipina woman with a tidy appearance, ran to get the door and two pretty young women appeared in the kitchen's doorway.

"Where are the aprons?" asked one. She had dark brown hair and bore a heavy resemblance to Katie Holmes, pre-Tom Cruise and her Scientology-condoned makeover.

Gigi closed her notebook and plucked four starched white aprons, still in their dry cleaning bags, off of a coat rack in the corner of the kitchen. "Here you go, Maggie," she said, unwrapping an apron and handing it to the dark-haired girl, before doing the same for each of us. "I need you two to start assembling the canapés. You're on the mini BLT towers," she said, nodding to Maggie. "Can you manage the vichyssoise with truffle-foam shot glasses, Gemma?" Gigi asked the other girl, this one with sea glass-colored eyes, freckled skin, and shoulder-length strawberry blond hair.

"Yeah, no worries," she said. Her voice was soft, and she had a lovely British accent.

"And, Marcy, I'd like you to help the girls and then set the tables. The china is already out in the living room in crates, and you should find the tablecloths and silver there as well. The flower arrangements are lined up in the foyer—I'm sure you saw them coming in. Once you're done with that, would you put out the place cards? Here's the layout," she said, handing me the evening's seating chart. "Each one should be tucked into the silver clam shells you'll find in a box with the salt and pepper shakers."

I slipped the crisp white apron over my head, tying its waistband in a bow at my back, the way Gigi had styled hers, and got to work assisting Maggie and Gemma with their prep work. Maggie said she was working every day that week with A Moveable Feast and had taken on extra hours with another catering outlet. Her boyfriend, a mortgage broker, had been sacked from his job and wasn't able to cover his share of the rent. They were both scrambling to find a cheaper place but in the meantime Maggie was working at all hours and had missed several casting calls because of it.

Gemma, meanwhile, was possibly going to have to withdraw from NYU because her father, an office-supplies salesman, had promised to pay for her tuition but the credit crunch had also taken a toll in the U.K. and he hadn't made enough in sales commission to be able to afford Gemma's school fees. Even Bear was having money problems. He'd lost a bundle on the stock market after he'd followed a bad tip given to him by a drunken dinner guest. To make matters worse, he commuted to work from up-state New York and the spike in gas prices was biting into his monthly income. He and his wife had been forced to tap into their IRA accounts to make ends meet. Their plan to move to Florida and retire in five years had been scrapped entirely.

Their stories made me feel guilty. It didn't seem fair that so many people were struggling to keep their dreams alive—you couldn't watch the news or open a paper without being con-fronted with a dozen similar tales—and I, one of the very few, very lucky ones whose lives hadn't been negatively impacted by the economic downturn, didn't feel particularly lucky.

After the girls had moved on to assembling other hors d'oeuvres, I made my way across the foyer into Jill's living and dining rooms. I nearly gasped as I entered the living room, which bore the hallmarks of what was known as mod-baroque design: lots of color and bold geometric patterns, and plenty of eclectic, ornate furniture and decorative *objets*. For example, in Jill's din-ing room a carved wooden sideboard, painted in high-gloss paint, was topped with a collection of large Murano vases and set against a wall covered in lime-green jacquard wallpaper. A chandelier constructed out of champagne flutes, hugged the ceiling, and the walls were covered with abstract oil paintings, one of which had to be a Willem de Kooning, an artist whose work I'd seen at the Museum of the Art Institute of Chicago. In the adjacent living room, there was a sky-blue area rug, a '50s era dark purple velvet couch, and a pair of antique armchairs covered in real zebra hair; sculptures constructed of neon lights stood in the corners and a set of sexually charged out-of-focus black and white photographs hung on the walls. I'd never seen anything like it.

Unable to help myself, I tiptoed down the hall toward the

Tischmans' private quarters. Passing a small office, which featured indigo blue walls, a writing table encrusted in seashells spray painted Ferrari red, red-and-white-striped Roman shades, and an inky leather chair made out of ebonized oak, I reached Jill and her husband Glenn's bedroom. It was painted in gray and hung with chartreuse graphic-printed silk curtains that coordinated with the upholstered headboard and a bench stationed at the foot of the bed. A large Dorothy Draper yellow screen painted with Grecian urns was tucked behind a gray suede fainting couch. Above the bed hung a partially nude portrait of a young Japanese girl, her schoolgirl socks still on and legs spread wide. Pressing forward down the hall to the last room, I found an incredibly messy guest bedroom—there were ties and men's shirts scattered on a Chevron striped rug, half-empty water bottles crowding the surface of a puce Lucite bedside table, magazines and newspapers piled high on a mother-of-pearl tray on the floor next to the bed. Across the hall were the doors to the children's rooms, behind one of which I could hear a cacophony of yelps, cries, and screams.

I glanced at my watch and realized that I'd spent enough time ogling Jill's apartment and needed to get started on setting the tables before Gigi discovered my delinquency and had a nervous breakdown. But just as I was about to high-speed tip toe back down the hall to the dining room, I heard a loud crash and the door to one of the children's rooms banged open, revealing a little girl dressed in a navy jumper dress and gray cable-knot cardigan, her light brown hair clipped back by two plaid barrettes, her plump cheeks flaming red and streaked with tears. "I don't love you anymore," she yelled behind her shoulder, before running smack into my thighs.

She reeled backward, and I braced her shoulders to keep her from falling. Once she regained her balance, she shook me off and raced back into her room. Her nanny appeared from inside the bathroom and regarded the fragments of what looked to be fine porcelain scattered all over the hardwood floor. "Ava," she said, shaking her head. "What did you do now?"

And with that, the girl burst into a fresh wail and threw herself on her pink shag rug. "But Mommy said she would have tea with me before my bath and Mommy doesn't like drinking out of plastic!" she cried.

I ventured into the room, which was decorated in various shades of pink, with butterfly-themed wallpaper, silk balloon shades, and a fuchsia crystal chandelier. A child-sized table was set with an elegant fine china gold and ivory tea service, minus the teapot. As the nanny began picking up the pieces, I carefully approached Ava and knelt down next to her writhing, kicking body.

"Can I have some tea please, Ava? You've set such a nice table. And I'm so very thirsty."

With a snivel, she raised her head and studied my face through her long, wet lashes. "Who are you?" she asked.

She had her mother's olive skin tone and fine features. I told her my name and that I was there to help with her mother's party. "But I'm suddenly very thirsty," I said, clutching my throat and swallowing hard. "Would you please, please share some tea with me?"

She nodded solemnly and rested her hand on mine. "You poor dear," she whispered. A post-tantrum hiccup escaped from her small mouth as she guided me to her table, where she instructed me to sit and stay until she returned with another teapot. After searching frantically through her toy box, a gorgeous little chest painted with butterflies and flowers, she finally found a teapot made of pink plastic, and poured me a cup. For the next few minutes, we sat like that—Ava pouring and I drinking and remarking on the delicious flavor and subtle aromas of her make-believe tea, as the little girl fussed with the imaginary pots of sugar and cream—until the nanny emerged from Ava's en suite bathroom and clapped her hands together, calling an end to my diversion and her play.

"Bath time," the nanny announced. "Say goodbye to your guest."

Ava set her tea cup down carefully and circled around the table. "Thank you so much for coming," she said before bestowing me with a dramatic air kiss. "Let's do this again soon."

Regretfully I left her to her bath and returned to the dining room and my chores. I quickly laid down the white linen tablecloths and set the tables with the floral arrangements (long glass troughs tightly packed with raspberry-colored English garden roses) glasses (stemless red and white wine goblets) and plates (hand-painted with flowers and made of fine bone china) and began working on the place cards. I recognized quite a few of the names—Caroline's was on the list, as was Dahlia's and Ainsley and Peter Partridge's. Jill, the evening's hostess, was seated next to Jasper Pell, whom *House & Home* was honoring that night as their "designer of the year" and who happened to be the very same decorator Caroline had suggested I hire at her baby shower.

The memory of Caroline's quick dismissal of me at her shower made me suddenly realize that John was right about one thing: I wasn't about to score any points with the other hedge fund wives by working as a server for A Moveable Feast. Cringing in anticipation of facing Caroline and Dahlia wearing an apron and carrying a tray of quivering canapés, I knew that it was too late to back out—I wouldn't dare leave Gigi in the lurch, especially since she was already short-staffed for the night—and as much as I wasn't looking forward to facing the other women's sneering faces, I was genuinely happy to be working again.

Back in Chicago, before we moved to New York, I worked in private client services for Bloomington Mutual, a Midwest-based, multinational bank with brokerage, commercial, and investment arms. I'd started there fresh out of Northwestern University as a research analyst, and had always felt grateful for my job. Out of the fifty-two students who applied for the job from my college, I never thought that I'd be the one to land it. My grades we good, but so were those of the other applicants, and they'd all held prestigious internships at banks and law firms and showed up at the Bloomington Mutual informational meeting looking like they *already* had the job. I remember walking in and seeing them all there assembled in the career center's main receiving room, their neat leather folders and Mont Blanc pens poised for note taking, the girls in fresh-pressed navy wool suits that didn't look like they'd once belonged to their mother (like mine had).

But to my great surprise the Bloomington Mutual managing director in charge of recruitment had been impressed with my work history. "There's nothing like a nine-to-five to teach a kid *real* responsibility. These unpaid internships are a bunch of malarkey," she had grumbled during our one-on-one interview the following day. I got the impression that she'd worked her way through college and high school like I had and perhaps even recognized a younger version of herself in me. Or maybe she just liked the cut of my mother's DKNY. Who knows? What matters is that she picked me and after briefly returning home to Minnesota to reorganize my belongings and earn some cash to pad out my near-empty bank account, I moved into a small apartment near Wrigley Field with a couple of my girlfriends from school and started working at the bank.

I was good at my job. I didn't mind pulling all-nighters in preparation for a big pitch or meeting, and loved trying to make sense of the endless charts and graphs that we were forced to produce. My strengths, according to the progress reports I received, were in proofreading documents and writing deal memos, rather than in the more analytical aspects of my job. To be honest,

I was happy to leave the number crunching, and economic modeling to the other analysts, and they were happy to turn to me for help synthesizing complex deals into readable reports.

Little by little I started making a name for myself at BlooMu, which is how we referred to the bank in-house. As I mentioned earlier, my bosses liked me. I think it was because I was respectful and always on time, and didn't bring my ego into the office every day like a lot of my contemporaries. No task was too menial, no deadline impossible. When my two-year research-analyst program ended, I was asked to stay on as an associate, received a nice bump in pay, and a lot more responsibility. My managing director, a forty-something man who resembled a geekier Richard Gere, took a liking to me, and brought me on overseas trips—I saw London, Seoul, Hong Kong, and Berlin—all on one deal, a merger between two liquor conglomerates. I made polite and witty (if I do say so myself) conversation at client dinners and cocktail parties, took copious notes at meetings, and never, ever took advantage of my corporate card. Five years and many deals later, when my MD was promoted and a vice presidency spot opened up, the word at BlooMu was that I was a shoo-in for the job.

But around this time things had started getting serious with John. We had met at a mutual friend's housewarming and he asked me to lunch. I didn't hear from him for a while, but then one night he called and asked me if I wanted to come over for a drink. It was a booty call of course, but, hey, I was lonely. My brutal work schedule didn't exactly leave much time for socializing and I had no better prospects beating down my door, begging me for a date.

The same was true for John and after about twenty-or-so of these late night calls, he invited me to go to Wisconsin with him for the weekend for a friend's wedding. We had a nice time, and so when the next wedding cropped up, he asked me again, this time introducing me as his girlfriend. A bunch of his friends got married that year—I think I went to six nuptials in all—but it was the one in Minneapolis that I remember best. The bride came from Swedish stock, and in the old tradition of the Vikings, you had to drink a shot of aquavit every time someone got up to speak. Needless to say, John and I were both completely drunk by the time the herring appetizers had been cleared, and over a plate of meatballs smothered with lingonberry sauce, he told me that he loved me.

I nearly choked on my Wasa bread when he said it. I'd only ever thought of our relationship as a warming drawer—nice and toasty, but not exactly fiery—and he'd never once given me the impression that he thought I could be The One. But then it occurred to me that John wasn't the passionate type, and I'd been misreading his signals all along. He asked me to move into his apartment, and then a year later he asked me to marry him. That's when we started talking about our future together, where we wanted to live, how many kids we wanted, the mistakes our parents had made that we didn't want to repeat. That sort of thing. John was easy on a lot of fronts, but he felt passionately about one thing: Once we had children, he wanted me to stay home and take care of them.

His mother Penny, short for Penelope, had been first a school teacher—she taught sixth-grade English at a private school in Bloomfield Hills, Michigan, the posh suburb of Detroit where John grew up (and attended public school). She later became a real estate broker, and according to John, once she left teaching for real estate she became a real shrew. Penny was habitually rude to John's father, who was a life insurance salesman and often brought home less income than she did, and was always too tired or too busy to make dinner (or breakfast and lunch, for that matter) or throw birthday parties for John and his younger brother Jake. She wore nothing but pastel twinsets and slacks, and had her nails done every Friday afternoon no matter what. John tells a heart-wrenching story about breaking his arm in Little League and having to wait on a plastic chair, his injured arm cradled in a makeshift sling while his mother's fingers and toes were painted silver-flecked mauve.

Penny once confided in me that she'd gotten pregnant with John by accident and then, a couple years after he had been born, figured she'd have another baby so that John wouldn't always be pulling on the bottom of her cardigans ("stretching them out"). "He needed a playmate," she had said, smoothing a lock of dyed blond hair behind her ear.

John still resented her.

"There's no way I'm going to be like Penny," I told him over and over during our engagement, when it still seemed useful to discuss hypothetical middle grounds, like, what if the bank gave me a four-day workweek, or what if I could work from home. Eventually we figured out that there was no telling what the future would hold for us, but I knew for sure, that I, unlike Patty, *wanted* children. I wanted nothing more than to spend the rest of my middle-age years baking chocolate chip cookies, reading bedtime stories, and cheering at soccer games. I wanted nothing more than to become a mother. I liked working in finance but I didn't want it to be my whole life.

Still, as much as I wanted to start a family with John, I was afraid of being dependent on him for financial security. I enjoyed the independence of having my own source of income, the feeling of empowerment that came with knowing that I could take care of our family if need be. What if the dynamics of our relationship changed for the worse? And what if John ever left me?

After much consideration, I eventually agreed to quit my job when I got pregnant with our first child. As afraid as I was of losing my independence, I was more fearful of losing John. He made me feel so safe. With him, I never felt alone, and the awful memories of my childhood didn't seem to affect me as much. My parents had fought constantly and sometimes violently, and I knew that with John I'd be able to give our children the sense of security my sister and I had lacked growing up. And really, that's what mattered most to me: creating a peaceful home environment. No lying, no yelling, and no hitting.

Caving into John, however, meant that even if I got the promotion to vice president at the BlooMu, I would eventually have to quit. But I never got to make that decision for myself, thanks to Michelle, a blonde from Evanston, Illinois. Pretty and well put together, Michelle had enough ambition and charisma to make up for what she lacked in intelligence and diligence. I sometimes had to cover for her at work, but she ingratiated herself with me by teaching me a battery of useful tricks, like how to use hair powder when I didn't have time to shower or that tying a scarf through the belt loops of my suit pants could add a little flair to my outfit. My big mistake was confiding in Michelle that I wanted the vice presidency but was planning on leaving the bank as soon as I got pregnant. The next day she marched straight past me into our MD's office and told him what I'd said. Before the end of the week, Michelle was announced as the bank's newest vice president.

Michelle did her best to drive me out of the bank, and I did my best not to hurl her little plastic deal trophies at her face every time she called me into her office. But it wasn't for another year when I was passed over *again* for a promotion (for reasons I still don't understand) that I started thinking about requesting a transfer to another department.

The only thing open at the time was a job in private client services. Whenever anyone on the investment banking side went there, we joked that they were being "put out to pasture," or that they weren't "hungry," meaning they'd lost their drive and couldn't hack it in the big leagues. Some of the other bankers referred to it as "early retirement." But I was desperate and determined, and spent the next three weeks begging everyone who would listen to me why I should be allowed to become relationship officer for the bank's high net worth clients. Thankfully I'd built up enough goodwill at the bank to win the job on probation.

If the bosses at BlooMu had banked on me growing bored with client relations, they must have been surprised at how quickly I took to it. Even I hadn't expected to find my new post as stimulating as my last, but it was. Whoever said figuring out how to weight a client's portfolio in stocks, bonds, and alternative assets was less challenging than, say, charting the expected increase in economies of scale following a corporate merger was dead wrong. Plus in private wealth management I went to a lot of charity balls and fancy dinners and learned all about gourmet food, fine wine, flowers, décor, and etiquette—basically all the things that the daughter of a Post-it Note salesman (my dad worked as a B-to-B account manager for 3M) wouldn't have been exposed to otherwise. I went on golf weekends in Palm Beach, wine tours in Napa Valley, and to the Art Institute of Chicago's big gala when Bloomington Mutual was one of the fundraiser's main sponsors. Michelle got the big job, but I got the better one—one that, lo and behold, had prepared me better than I could have ever imagined for my new life in New York. It would be many months before I had this epiphany, but when it finally came, it would be worth the wait.

"I'm home, sorry I'm late," Jill called out as she flung open the front door to her apartment and raced through the foyer, past the dining and living rooms on her way toward the bedrooms. I heard her purse and the black garment bag she'd been carrying over her shoulder fall to the floor of the hallway, and the sound of her heels being kicked off and hitting the wall.

"Goddamn it, Rami," she swore. "I warned you about Ava and my good porcelain. One of these days she is going to break something. I see one of the cups from my Minton set, which was a limited edition release using *real* gold. It's practically *priceless!*"

I didn't want to be within earshot when Jill discovered that not only had her three-year-old daughter been playing with her best tea set, but that she'd also broken the most important piece, the teapot. I found Gigi in the kitchen, working side-by-side with Chef Bear, sprinkling a handful of finely chopped Italian leaf parsley on a tray of porcini and robiola tartlettes. After I informed her that I was finished setting the tables and up for another task, she sent me back out into the living room to set up the glasses behind the bar. I was just fanning out a set of raspberry linen cocktail napkins when the bartender finally wandered into Jill's apartment.

He was young, no older than twenty-one or twenty-two, with dark wavy hair, blue eyes, and a sly grin. He had that preppy, clean-cut appearance and the sort of swagger inherent in boys who had grown up wearing varsity letters on their high school jackets and feeling up girls in the backseats of their cars. But this guy also had a compelling measure of vulnerability, like Chris O'Donnell in his *Scent of a Woman* heyday.

I had to remind myself not to drool.

"Hey," he smiled, revealing a gorgeous set of dimples that I found myself fantasizing about licking chocolate out of in a dark bedroom—or linen closet.

"I'm Blake," he said, snapping me back to the real world.

I stammered something about telling Gigi he had arrived and walked back to the kitchen. I didn't trust myself around a guy that cute. Not that I was in danger of doing anything inappropriate with him—I was no cougar—but my palms had gotten sweaty just looking at him. And sweaty hands and crystal stemware don't exactly mix. Last thing I needed was for Jill to start yelling at me for breaking some of her no doubt *priceless* stemwear.

I found Gigi in the kitchen and told her Blake had arrived, at which point she sighed heavily with relief and announced that everything was set for the party. "Let's go check up on Jill," she suggested.

In Jill's boudoir, a mirror-lined powder room, I took a seat on a tufted stool and took in the gilt-framed mirrors layered over the wall mirror, hand towels embroidered with gold fleur de lis and a bronze faucet cast to resemble a cascade of lemon leaves. I watched as Jill opened double doors to another room that was as big as Ava's. The walls were lined with shelves for shoes and handbags (I counted five Birkins and two Kellys) and there were racks and racks of clothes. She plucked a silk navy dress from a lineup of cocktail frocks and slipped it on over her head. The front of the dress featured a prim cascade of ruffles, but the back was almost entirely cut out, revealing Jill's surprisingly toned back. It was elegant but a little subversive, too, and it fit Jill's body like a glove.

"Wow," I gasped, when she emerged from her closet and twirled around for us.

"It just came in this morning. The boutique had to messenger it over to my office. Could you take off the tag?" she asked, turning around and motioning to the back of her neck.

While removing it, I couldn't help but notice the price—it cost nearly ten thousand dollars. My wedding dress, the most expensive garment I'd ever purchased (and I purchased it for myself) had cost exactly two-tenths of that.

"Wow," I said again, sucking my breath in hard. Subversive elegance sure didn't come cheap.

"I know, pretty pricey, huh? But I had to have it. Besides, I put it on Glenn's card and considering that we're not speaking at the moment, I don't think I'm in any danger of getting a lecture."

"What, you didn't tell me this? How long has this been going on?" Gigi asked.

Jill sat down at her vanity and slicked a coat of deep red lipstick over her lips. "God," she paused, her dark, wispy brows furrowing in thought. She pressed a pale pink nail against her forehead. "I don't know, maybe a month or so? I mean, it's not like we never talk to each other. But beyond swapping schedules there's not a whole lot of conversation happening."

"But what about over dinner? Don't the kids notice?" I asked.

"What dinner? Glenn gets home at ten most days, after the kids are asleep. He's your typical five-minute father. He says hi to them in the morning, asks them what they're going to do that day and then it's 'see you later, be good for mommy' and he's out the door."

"Even on weekends?" I asked.

"Even on weekends. Either Glenn's working in the home office with the door locked and his noise canceling headphones on or he's at the office. You know, when I first met Glenn he had this dog, a golden retriever named Jimmy, and he was so good to it. Took it to the dog run, bought him birthday presents and washed him in the bathtub all the time. I figured this was a guy who was going to make a great father, not like my dad, who was gone all the time. And that's one of the reasons I fell in love with Glenn, because I thought he would be there for our kids, that he would be *different*, that I wouldn't have to do every fucking little thing on my own like my mom did. When I had Justin five years ago I couldn't believe that Glenn didn't want to be more involved. He didn't want to change diapers, or give him baths, or feed him carrots. Honestly, I felt like I'd been hoodwinked. If I wanted to marry someone who wasn't there for our kids, I would have chosen someone *far* richer. You know, I had plenty of options back then."

"Oh puh-leez, wealth isn't everything!" Gigi said. "You think Jeremy's even touched one of Chloe's diapers? Uh-uh."

"I don't mean to point out the obvious, Gigi, but Jeremy's older. He has a grown daughter already. It's not like you expected him to be a hands-on dad, did you?"

"Yeah, you're right about that. Jeremy warned me plenty that he wasn't interested in having more kids, wasn't gonna wake up at night to feed the kid and all that. I think he said something like, 'been there, done that,' but, and I don't mean to point out the obvious, Jill," she winked, to show that she meant to be funny, not snide, "but I'm no spring chicken, either. So I promised Jeremy he wouldn't have to lift a finger for the baby—I would do all the work myself—but if he wasn't going to give me a child, I was going to a sperm bank."

"And he agreed to that?" Jill asked.

Gigi shrugged. "Look, I know it wasn't the most normal arrangement in the world, but I was thirty-eight. Time was a-ticking."

"Well, this proves my point. Jeremy never led you to believe he would be an involved father. Everyone told me not to freak out, that most dads don't really get interested in kids until they're a bit older. But now Justin's five and they have common interests. Glenn likes baseball, Justin loves baseball. Glenn loves cars, Justin loves cars. But has he ever taken him to a Yankees game or the Auto Show? No. With Glenn, it's all excuses, all the time. And if the kids happen to misbehave on the rare occasion he makes it home in time to have dinner with us, it's my fault if they won't stay in their chairs or won't eat their steak. Of course it's my fault! Because it can't be his if he's never around!" Jill hissed, the color rising up her neck to her face.

"What about going to see someone, like a therapist or couple's counselor?" I suggested.

"Talking about our problems isn't going to change anything. The only thing that's going to make a difference is if Glenn stops taking me for granted."

Gigi and I listened to Jill as she enumerated the many ways in which she felt her husband had failed her. Not only did he lack an acceptable degree of interest in their children, but he was, like so many men in the hedge fund game, entirely focused on making money—not that he was even that good at it. "It would be different if he was pulling in even a hundred or fifty mill a year, but he's not," she sniffed.

"But why? How would more money change your feelings about his parenting skills?" I asked.

"Because it would just *justify* it," she said matter-of-factly. "Gigi understands what I'm talking about."

Gigi stood up and looked at her watch. "The guests will be here any second," she said.

Jill continued, undiverted. "I loathe going on vacation with him alone because he never wants to do anything but read his books and papers and sit in the hotel room. Before breakfast, he doesn't talk, period, because he can't be civil until he gets his coffee. But even at lunch and dinner, we barely exchange words. And if he does open his mouth, it's usually to criticize me. He thinks I'm frivolous and silly, but we all can't be financial wizards and political geniuses."

But the worst part was that they were no longer having sex, Jill said. As much as he had disappointed her, and as tense as their limited interactions with each other were, come nightfall, Jill still wanted him to touch her. She was a woman with a healthy sex drive, she complained, and she shouldn't be expected to live the life of a nun just because her husband felt stressed out at work. On numerous occasions Glenn had refused her advances in bed at night. Five times she had crawled on top of him naked, only to be shoved off as Glenn rolled onto his side, muttering something about being tired. So Jill had thrown him out of their bed.

"If he's not going to make love to me, then what's the point?" she said, fastening a gold and diamond cuff around her wrist.

8

Nip Slips, Gilded Cookies, and Screen Sex (In other words, dinner at Jill's)

As the doorman buzzed from downstairs to announce the arrival of the dinner's first guests, Jill stepped into a pair of red-soled cobalt crocodile pumps. "I can trust you guys not to share any of this with anybody, right?" she asked.

Gigi and I both nodded and vowed never to breathe a word of what she had just told us. Then we all returned to the living room, where Jill made a beeline for the bar and Gigi handed me the first of many trays I would hold that evening.

I wish I could say that my heart wasn't thudding in my chest or that my hands weren't trembling so hard that I nearly dropped my tray of cayenne-dusted cheese straws, but, alas, they were. The first guest to arrive was a tall, handsome black man, whom I instantly recognized as Jasper Pell, the evening's honored guest and favored designer of hedge fund wives everywhere. He was accompanied by an equally handsome blond man whom I over-heard him introducing as his partner. Several other couples arrived in quick succession. The men were all dressed in dark suits, with or without ties, and the women in designer cocktail dresses, tasteful makeup, and statement accessories.

As Blake poured out endless glasses of wine for the women, and vodka drinks for the men, I circulated with BLT towers, careful to hold the tray aloft with my right arm, napkins at the ready with my left. Most of the women were light eaters, save a couple larger-sized ladies dressed in dark dinner suits and major jewels, who consumed the morsels of food with gusto, but the men were the easiest sell of all. They didn't even care what they were eating; they just picked each hors d'oeuvre up, not even breaking eye contact with the man or men they were speaking with (the men and women having immediately segregated themselves into opposing clusters) and plopped it into their mouths.

Caroline arrived on her husband's arm dressed in a chic black bandage dress and leopard-print platform slingbacks that showcased her thin frame and long legs. She wouldn't have even recognized me had I not made a point to say hello to her.

"But, Marcy, what are you doing holding that tray?"

I explained to her that Gigi had drafted me to work for her, and I was going to be helping her out with events like these from time to time. "But couldn't you just loan her one of your staff members?" she asked, incredulous.

"The point is that I wanted to work. I need the activity," I responded, which served to confound Caroline even more, and she flitted off to greet and congratulate Jasper on his *House & Home* cover story.

Aside from Caroline, only one guest made any sort of conversation with me other than to give me a drink order (never mind the bar was never more than ten steps away) or hand me a linen napkin balled around a half-chewed piece of food. He stood alone, near the bar, and seemed a little nervous, like he was out of his comfort zone. I wondered if he was waiting for his wife or girlfriend—she being the one who actually belonged in this milieu—and was making small talk with me to fill his time before she arrived. But since he was a good eater and would gamely try at least one of everything I had to offer, I was happy to return to him and keep him company.

"Spicy pork empanada with cilantro crème fraîche dipping sauce?" I asked, presenting him with a silver tray.

"Do you really have to ask?" he said, plucking one up. He held it at eye level—his were brown, with little green specs—before putting it in his mouth. I watched him chew, and couldn't help but laugh as he rolled his eyes with pleasure. "What's in that one?" he asked after he'd swallowed.

I told him I would ask the chef if he really wanted a precise list of ingredients. "Tonight's my first night working for this catering company and I'm not terribly familiar with the menu yet," I admitted.

"First time, huh?" He smiled, breaking into what I thought was an incredibly cute, if slightly lopsided grin. Judging from the cut of his navy suit, and the discreetly expensive watch on his wrist, not to mention the fact that he was at Jill's dinner at all, I knew he must be successful. Plus he was pretty good-looking, if you like athletic, dark-haired men. (And who doesn't?)

But given that I was married and had already done enough karmic damage by fantasizing about the college-age bartender, I quickly excused myself and headed back to the kitchen, where I found Gigi, who was busy discussing something with Bear, and who, after taking one look at the expression on my face, ordered me to sit down at the table.

"The last thing I need is for you to faint in front of everyone," she said, bringing me a sixteen-ounce bottle of water. "And don't even think about getting up until that whole bottle's gone," she added before returning to the stove and the half a dozen duck breasts she had left searing over high flames.

I tilted my head back and began chugging the water, but just as I finished the bottle, I heard my BlackBerry bleating in my purse, signaling the arrival of a text, and went into the pantry to check who it was from. I scrolled over to the instant messaging application and read.

> John: Finished work early. Think I could stop by?

What? He'd given me nothing but grief about working this event and now he wanted to show up, uninvited? No way. I punched out a reply and hit send.

> Marcy: You know I can't invite you. It's a seated dinner.

I was standing in the dark, waiting for John's reply, when Jill walked in. "The bitters are in here," she giggled, then stopped up short when she saw me. "Oh," she gasped, nearly tripping, and Blake stepped in to steady her, snaking his hands around her tiny waist. I looked down at my BlackBerry, which was buzzing in my hand.

> John: So set out another plate.

I looked up at Jill, who was scanning the shelves for her bottle of Angostura bitters. "Someone wanted a Manhattan," she said, rolling her eyes. "Can you believe it?"

Blake snickered behind her.

I grabbed the yellow-capped bottle from off the shelf and handed it to Jill. "I'm so embarrassed to ask you this," I stammered, "but is there any chance we could set another place for my husband? I can't believe it but John actually wants to come."

"Of course he can come, just check with Gigi about the seating," she said, handing the bottle to Blake with a little sigh. "Here you go," she said, sashaying out of the pantry and kitchen, back toward the party. Blake followed her out as I typed out my last text to John.

> Marcy: Please hurry. Dinner starts in twenty.

To my surprise Gigi was thrilled to hear that John was coming for dinner. Apparently Ainsley had arrived without her husband Peter and if John hadn't shown up they would have had to scramble to remove the empty place. Whipping out her seating chart, Gigi got to work checking the name cards in the dining room against the list of guests that had already arrived, and I embarked on another tour of the living room, which was now full of guests, with a tray of morsels, this one bamboo skewered curry-spice langoustine. I noticed that Jill was having her white wine topped up once again by Blake, while her husband Glenn—I could recognize him from the framed family photos I'd seen in Jill's boudoir—was listening to Caroline's husband Fred crow about his latest art acquisition, a Damien Hirst formaldehyde-preserved animal that was going in his Greenwich estate.

"We got it for a steal at eight mil. Stevie Cohen paid twelve for his. Caroline arranged the whole thing; she's more than tits on legs, that one!" he whispered in Glenn's ear, slapping him on the back.

Hearing Fred's off-color remark about his wife, I swerved away from the men even though I wanted to get a better look at Glenn, who appeared, at least from a distance to be cocky and handsome (olive skin, floppy brown hair, tennis player's build). Threading through the crowd I caught tiny snippets of conversation, making my already queasy stomach churn like it was making butter for the Minnesota State Fair.

"I finally got an appointment at that new gyno spa. The waiting list is nine months long," whispered one woman dressed in what looked to be a splatter-painted potato sack.

"Christ, I got my chartreuse Birkin faster than that," responded her friend.

One langoustine down, nine more to go.

"If my brother was on the Fed's board of govenors I might have cleared three bill last year, too," said a man with an unfortunate overbite.

"The bastard just laid down thirty-one-point-three for his place in Southampton," replied his pointy chinned companion.

Three langoustines each, only three left now . . .

"I heard the porte-cochere alone is costing them twenty mil," gasped another woman.

"Yeah, but Meier hates working with them. So they can kiss the front cover of *Architectural Digest* buh-bye," sniggered her friend, a pale, petite woman with boyishly short hair and a flat chest.

No takers.

I walked toward another pair of men who looked like they could still be in business school. The shorter one wore rimless glasses and a striped oxford shirt only partially tucked into his rumpled chinos, and the other had on a Harvard baseball cap, a white oxford shirt, and jeans.

"Man, I'm so bummed. My Aston Martin's in the shop again," said the one in the glasses.

"All I can say is that I feel your pain, dude."

There was a tiny flutter of noise at the door and both of the men turned to look at Thomas and Dahlia Kemp, who was dressed in an ivory taffeta shift with a matching fur-trimmed cashmere cardigan and stacks of white-gold and diamond bangles at her wrists. Dahlia, unlike Caroline, noticed me as soon as I approached her with one of the two remaining skewered crustaceans on my tray.

"Isn't it funny how one always ends up returning to their roots," she said, her thin lips quivering and nostrils flaring as she sailed past me toward Caroline and Magdalena Zimmer.

On my way back to the kitchen I saw Thomas Kemp tapping out a text on his BlackBerry, totally oblivious to the fact that he was less than a hand's distance away from Ainsley, who was quietly sipping a glass of champagne, the long, square-shaped nail of her pinkie finger jutting out like an eagle's talon. Once again her blond Princess Bride hair looked to be professionally arranged and her makeup expertly applied, while her deep-cut dark green velvet dress showed a surprising and, if you ask me, inappropriate amount of cleavage. Not to overstate the obvious but Ainsley did not look like a woman having money troubles. Nonetheless I'd already overheard several of the other party guests whispering about the closure of her husband's hedge fund and rumors that the Partridges had quietly placed their apartment on the market.

At nine o'clock Jill announced that dinner service was starting, and all the guests made their way to the tables to locate their name cards and commence the duck salads with pomegranate dressing that Maggie and Gemma had already placed on the tables. I was in the kitchen, running for another bottle of St-Estèphe, when John came in, and by the time I had come back out I found him already at his table, shaking hands with Fred over one of the raspberry rose centerpieces. He was seated next to Ainsley, who was facing away from him toward her other dining companion, the man in the navy suit with the lopsided grin. I watched as she tipped her head back to laugh at something he had said, her breasts very nearly spilling out of her dress.

The man, to his credit, turned immediately red and looked away. Seeing my stunned expression, he shrugged his eyebrows and chuckled softly, and I made a mental note to ask Gigi or Jill about him as soon as either of them had a free second. I was dying to know which of the other women was his date.

Making my way around the table, I refreshed everyone's glass of wine, except Thomas Kemp's, who had neither touched his salad nor his wine and whose smooth face was still bent over his BlackBerry, and finally arrived at John's seat just as he was finishing telling a story to Ainsley. Her breasts had thankfully resettled back inside the bodice of her dress, but still threatened to break free at any moment.

"Hey there," I said, leaning in to give John a peck on the mouth, which ended up landing on his ear when he turned back toward the table.

He lifted his wine glass for me to fill it.

"Thanks, Marcy," he said distractedly.

"Oh, it's you! From the Christmas party!" Ainsley exclaimed, lifting her wine glass for me to fill. "John didn't mention you were here tonight."

"I was just getting to that," he said. "Marcy's helping out Gigi. She's so bored to tears she's willing to do anything just to get out of the house."

"Really? I could spend all day in bed," Ainsley said, giggling.

"My wife apparently loves scrubbing dishes. Don't you, Marcy? Now if I could only get her to keep her closet door closed."

What the hell?

Mr. Navy Suit excused himself to go to the bathroom and I returned to the kitchen to get another bottle of wine and simmer down. Inside I was fuming at John for snubbing me and then making fun of my work. When we had discussed the matter privately, he hadn't minced words about not wanting me to work for A Moveable Feast, but making it apparent to others that he was ashamed of me was an entirely different story. He didn't have to come to the dinner if what I was doing bothered him so much.

Returning to the tables I fought the urge to empty the bottle of wine in my hand on John's head and reminded myself that John's issues were his, not mine.

The next hour and a half passed in a blur. I shuttled cocktail orders back and forth from the table to the bar, showed guests to the bathroom, and made the rounds with bread rolls that no one wanted and bottles of wine that everyone did (with the sole exception of Thomas Kemp). Jill gave a little speech about Jasper Pell and then Jasper announced his new line of gilded furniture, which drew some polite applause from the dinner guests. I doled out little bundles of chive-wrapped haricots verts and spooned white truffle gravy over pink slices of panko-crumb-crusted sirloin steak. I also brought out specially prepared plates of steamed grouper for Dahlia (as a sufferer of celiac disease, she followed a gluten-free diet) and vegetable and tempeh lasagna for Jasper (he was a strict vegan who hadn't consumed any animal food products since 1995).

I was just starting to clear the entrée plates when I noticed the strangest, most outlandish thing I have ever witnessed at a dinner table. Thomas Kemp's mother, a rather large woman who was dressed in a navy silk caftan and massive jeweled brooch, bent down to retrieve her silver box clutch from underneath her chair (which, because of her girth, was no easy feat). Opening her handbag she procured a small golden spatula and began methodologically scraping the gravy off of her plate with it until the entire plate was licked clean. Everyone seated at her table noticed, but pretended they didn't. No one was going to make fun of the woman when one stock tip from her son could turn them into multimillionaires overnight. As the wealthiest person at the table, Thomas Kemp could have defecated in his seat and no one would have murmured a word. That was the power of money: It gave you carte-blanche to be as eccentric or vile as you—or any of your family members—chose to be.

Half an hour later I was scraping plates myself. For dessert chef Bear had prepared individual Black Forest cakes made with alternating layers of chocolate meringue and chocolate cherry mousse, which tasted divine (Bear gave me a generous portion of a cake in the kitchen) but was a nightmare to clean off the dinner china. And since the kitchen sink was already clogged up with the grease from the seared Muscovy duck breasts, Gigi asked me to go ask Jill for permission to use the sink in the laundry room.

I went to look for Jill in the dining room, but all of the guests had abandoned their tables and were either milling about in the living room or had slipped outside into the apartment building's stairwell to smoke cigarettes. I searched for Jill in both places and when I couldn't find her concluded that she must be in one of her children's rooms, putting them back in bed. Tiptoeing back down the hall, I waited outside Ava's door for a couple of minutes until I heard a set of voices inside Jill's bedroom.

I didn't even have to press my ear up against the door to hear Glenn's angry voice.

"I understand your needs plenty. I get a credit card statement telling me all about them every month. Thirty thousand on your AmEx. Another ten on your MasterCard? One month, and you whip through forty thousand dollars on nothing—clothes, shoes, jewelry. How does that even happen?"

"I shop because it makes me happy," she said stridently. "Truth be told, it's the *only* thing that makes me happy anymore."

"Wonder how the kids would feel if they heard that. Nice mothering, Jill."

"How dare you bring up my parenting skills? At least the kids could pick me out in a police lineup."

"Don't you realize that the reason I never see my kids is because *I* have to work to keep *you* in the style to which you have become accustomed." His voice had turned stingingly virulent.

Jill laughed. "That's insane."

"Aren't you always complaining about how hard it is to juggle your work and motherhood? Well how about coming straight home after one of your boozy magazine lunches instead of stopping in a store to buy yet another fucking overpriced dress. That rag you're wearing makes you look like a cheap slut."

"Oh, that's rich. So now I'm a cheap slut?"

"I take that back, Jill. You're not cheap. You're a motherfucking expensive slut," Glenn said.

"And you're an ungrateful, parsimonious asshole," she yelled back. "Don't think I don't realize what your job entails. Or that I haven't heard about your trips to the strip clubs."

"Yeah? Well at least those girls pretend to care about my happiness," he said before slamming the door to the bathroom shut.

I returned to the kitchen, where Gigi enlisted me to help Maggie, who was supposed to go stand by the door and hand out goody bags to the guests as they left. Each bag included a copy of the *House & Home* issue featuring Jasper Pell as well as a set of Porthault hand-printed cocktail napkins, and a couch-shaped sugar cookie that had been decorated with twenty-four-carat gold and ivory icing. When I was done assisting Maggie with the bags, I helped Gemma restack the wine glasses in the catering crates. Midway through this process I heard my Black-Berry beeping in my purse in the pantry again.

There was a message from John, who told me he'd left the party and asked when would I be coming home. I replied that I didn't know, maybe in an hour, around 11:30 p.m. I knew that he was probably worried about me waking him when I came back home—he could be such a prima donna about getting enough sleep—and suggested that I sleep on the couch so I would be sure my arrival wouldn't disturb him.

A second later, I received his response.

John: Good idea.

9

Gynomania

I thought that John would be in a horrible mood the day after Jill's *House & Home* dinner party, but he was just the opposite. Humming softly to himself, he brewed a pot of coffee (usually my job), toasted a couple slices of multigrain bread, and fried up a trio of eggs (ditto). The smell of the bread grilling underneath the oven's broiler woke me up from my makeshift bed on the couch and I ambled into the kitchen readying myself for an argument which never came.

"So last night was fun, huh?" he said, reaching for a plate above my head.

I could smell his designer deodorant—he'd recently upgraded from Speed Stick to Carolina Herrera for men—and my antifrizz hair serum.

"Did you use some of my hair stuff?" I asked.

"Yeah, so?"

I gave him the look that my sister used to give me when I insisted on wearing ankle socks with my penny loafers.

Scraping a generous wedge of butter on his toast, he flipped his eggs on to the plate and sat down at the kitchen table. "Anyway," he said, taking a sip of his coffee, "the food was great, wine was great, people were great. I had a blast."

"I'm so glad," I said, trying not to sound too acetic.

"Couldn't have been that much fun for you, though."

"Why do you assume that?"

He stuffed a piece of toast in his mouth and shrugged.

"I really wish you wouldn't act like you're embarrassed by me. There's no shame in working in catering."

"Well, as long as you're happy, Marcy. I thought you wouldn't feel comfortable being, you know, *servile* to the other wives but clearly it doesn't bother you."

"Not in the slightest," I retorted.

This was a lie of course, but I wasn't about to admit that I'd felt incredibly awkward serving Dahlia, Caroline, and Ainsley their dinner. I consoled myself with the fact that not all nights would be as bad as last night. Before I left Jill's apartment Gigi had gone over her January and February schedules with me and the majority of events she had coming around the bend—a private dinner with mainly music industry execs, an engagement party for the mayor's daughter, and so on—did not include any of the other hedge fund wives we knew. Gigi's book launch was at the end of January, and Caroline, Dahlia, and everyone else would be invited to it, but she insisted I attend the party as a guest.

"Okay then," John said before shoveled a heaping forkful of hot, runny eggs into his mouth. He turned his attention to one of his energy industry newsletters.

While toasting a couple slices for myself, I pulled out the raspberry jam, sloshed some milk in a saucepan for my coffee and sat down at the table. It was strange that John was willing to give up so easily on the subject of me working for A Moveable Feast; he usually fought these sorts of things to the death if I didn't comply with his wishes immediately. But maybe he was learning to be more flexible, open-minded. After all, New York was a more progressive town than Chicago.

I retrieved my toast and sat back down at the table. "Doctor Delgado's office called to confirm our appointment. It's at twelve-thirty," I said, reminding him of my check up with the gynecologist.

I had made the appointment more than a month ago and I had to wait another few weeks to get the coveted lunch-hour time slot, but it was important to me that John was there to hear what the doctor had to say. I was banking on Dr. Delgado encouraging us to start trying to conceive again. Maybe he could convince John that we had no reason to think the next pregnancy was going to end in miscarriage, and that, in fact, there was no time like the present to get moving on our baby plans.

"You won't miss much work since its lunch time," I said, offering to pick up a sandwich for him in case we had to spend some time in the waiting room.

John grumbled something about lunch hours not really existing in his line of work, which I chose to ignore, and tossed his half-read newsletter in the trash. I would fish it out later, like I did most mornings, and read it while I ate my breakfast. The energy sector fascinated me; I loved how world political events, economic developments, and weather all played into determining the price of a barrel of oil or kilowatt of energy.

"See you later," I said, following him to the front door. John retrieved his new black cashmere wool coat from the front hall closet and stepped into his bespoke wingtips, also a recent purchase. "I emailed the address to your assistant, so she should have it. But if you need me to send it again or are running late, text me."

"Sure," John said, kissing me lightly on the cheek. And then he was out the door.

A few hours later I was sitting in Dr. Delgado's office, which occupied half of a two-story townhouse on a quiet Upper East Side block in the Sixties. The décor was meant to be soothing—all muted beiges and grays—with one large fish tank in the upstairs waiting room, and some nicely framed sepia-toned prints of beautiful, big-eyed children on the first level. There was an array of celebrity and women's magazines, including the latest copy of *House & Home*, as well as a bookshelf lined with copies of a reproductive health book he had co-authored with an alternative medicine guru from London (available for purchase), and a flat screen television tuned in to Fox News. The big story of the day was that the Federal Reserve was coming to the rescue of yet another bank that had gotten in trouble buying up mortgage-backed equities. I tried to zone out and think happy thoughts, but as the minutes ticked by, I became more agitated. *Where was John?*

By the time Dr. Delgado's nurse called my name and escorted me to a small, all white room, I was already in meltdown mode. The nurse stared at me for a moment before leaving the room. She returned with a Valium and a small cup of water. I refused the pill and promised her that I just needed to take some deep breaths.

Shaking her head, she motioned toward the iPod docked into its player. "How about some music? Something soothing, like Enya," she suggested, and scrolled down toward the album she was looking for.

"I'm waiting for my husband," I explained and asked her if someone could bring him to the room if he arrived while I was in with the doctor. She patted my hand maternally.

"Sure thing," she said. "But most of the men don't ever come."

Needless to say, John never arrived. I texted him a dozen times, each time sounding more panicky and angry, and received nothing back. Then I started worrying if he had been in an accident on his way over and even called his office, but the only information his assistant had was that he had gone out. It was so unlike John to completely flake on something as important as this, I was sure something had gone terribly awry. As Dr. Delgado greeted me and asked me how I had been feeling, as he instructed me to put my legs up in the metal stirrups, as he squirted lubricant on a vaginal ultrasound wand and inserted it between my legs, even as he showed me on a the little screen that my uterus, cervix, and ovaries all looked to be in working order, I thought of nothing besides John's absence, feeling simultaneously scared and angry. "From what I see here, you can get pregnant again as soon as you like, Marcy," said Dr. Delgado, shaking my hand before he vanished out of the darkened room, oblivious to my anxious state.

Three excruciating hours later, John finally called me on my cell phone and gave me a lame excuse for his disappearing act—something about a conference call running over, followed by an impromptu lunch with a guy up from Washington, D.C., who had an inside track on U.S. drilling prospects in Alaska. I told him that I would never forgive him for leaving me there like that, and that the very least he could have done was send me a text or call me to let me know I shouldn't be expecting him. Then I'm pretty sure I called him a few choice names, including "selfish asshole" and "total prick" before hanging up the phone and making myself one very tall vodka cranberry.

It was when I had finished that and had taken a long, fitful nap on my living room couch that my BlackBerry finally came back to life. I propped myself up on my elbows and picked up my phone, which was vibrating against the top of our new, sustainable wood coffee table. There was another apology text from John and an email from Jill inviting me to a long, boozy lunch at Michael's, a see-and-be-seen lunch spot in Midtown, the following afternoon.

I fixed myself a plate of cheese (a salty aged Gouda, creamy St. André and tangy, herb-dusted chèvre) and crackers, and then, after debating a couple of minutes, decided to go ahead and open one of John's prized bottles of Château Mouton Rothschild. Sitting down in front of the television, I flipped through the channels, bypassing a marathon of *The Real Housewives of New York* in favor of *Denise Richards: It's Complicated.* I'd just finished watching my first episode and second glass of wine when John came home looking nervous and guilty. In one hand he carried a very large bouquet of yellow roses (my favorite) and in his other, a little bag from Bulgari.

"Marcy, I'm so sorry," he said, his eyes welling with tears. "I messed up."

I'll admit that my first instinct was to leap over the coffee table and rip that bag out of his hand to see what was inside it, but I also knew that I couldn't let John think that he could buy his way out of trouble. Not this time.

I took a sip of wine and carefully placed my glass back on the table. (John, I was sure, was itching to remind me to use a coaster, but he knew better than to mention it.) "You really disappointed me today," I said slowly, trying not to sound overly emotional. "You've made it pretty clear that you prioritize your work ahead of me in the past, but to not even take two seconds to let me know that you weren't going to come to my appointment, well, John, it leaves me wondering where we can go from here."

"I know, Marcy."

"It feels like ever since we moved to New York all I've been doing is apologizing to you for getting drunk, or for wanting to work a stupid job, or for losing the baby. You make me feel like a child. And I'm not."

"I know you're not," he interjected.

"And then, today, leaving me wondering if you've been killed in a car accident, not responding to my texts until *three hours later*? It's beyond disrespectful."

"I didn't realize my BlackBerry was off," he said, taking a few steps toward me. He removed a coaster from the drawer inside our coffee table and placed my wineglass on it. Even in the dim light, I could see his nostrils flaring and cheeks rouging.

"Don't lie, whatever you do."

John turned away from me to lay his suit jacket over the back of one of the Frank Gehry corrugated cardboard (i.e, eco-friendly) Wiggle Chairs. "I knew I'd screwed up by the time your first text arrived and then I was scared to deal with your anger afterward," he said, turning around. "I guess it's still hard for me to think about getting pregnant again . . . after everything that happened."

"But, John, we've discussed this. You know I want a baby. And now that I've made friends I have a social network should anything go wrong, which Doctor Delgado assured me today we had no reason to believe it would. And on top of that, I'm thirty-five. If you want a baby with me, we have to start trying as soon as possible. My fertility is only going to go downhill from here."

John nodded, sat down beside me, and handed me the bag from Bulgari. "This is for you, Marcy, for putting up with me recently. Work is stressful, I have so much weighing on me, but I know that's no excuse for acting like such a jerk. Can you forgive me?" he asked.

I could have sworn I smelled liquor on his breath, but his face was twisted and ashen, the picture of remorse. I had to get over myself and forgive him. The whole point of my visit to Dr. Delgado was to convince John that it was time for us to move forward and start working on having a baby again, and there was no way I was going to get pregnant if we weren't at the very least sleeping in the same bed. Jill and Glenn already had their two children; it was all fine and well for them to be sleeping separately and indulging in their spats. For me, however, time was of the essence.

"I forgive you," I said.

He shook the golden bag in my hands. "Open it already."

I put my hand inside and pulled out a small flat leather box, which I immediately opened, revealing an incredibly beautiful, undoubtedly costly pair of Art Deco-style diamond earrings. They were the sort of baubles a movie star might wear down a Hollywood red-carpet and certainly finer than anything I've ever owned.

"Oh, John," I gasped. "Really? We can afford this?"

"Put them on," he cajoled, and in another second I was at the mirror in the guest bathroom, sliding them on to my ears.

John came up behind me and lifted my hair to get a better look. "Is all forgiven?" he asked, kissing my neck and sending the good kind of shivers down my spine.

"It will be if you have sex with me right now," I murmured, turning to him.

And we did.

The following afternoon I met Jill and Gigi for lunch at Michaels, a restaurant and power-lunch spot in Midtown. I dressed again in my black cashmere sweater and jeans, my new trench coat (not quite a mink, but a big step up from my pink puffer), and stiletto boots (which *did* cost more than my first car, even if I subtracted the amount of money I'd made working the *House & Home* dinner). I'd bought the boots that morning on Madison Avenue and hadn't quite gotten the hang of walking in such high shoes. Gripping the railing, I tottered past the hostess stand down the short, green-carpeted staircase to the restaurant. Gigi was already at our table at the front of the room (prime placement) and witnessed my sorry-looking entrance.

"Didn't your mama teach you how to walk in heels?" she demanded, taking a sip from her cappuccino. "Sheesh."

I might have been offended if I didn't know Gigi as well as I was beginning to so I laughed and reached for my napkin before responding, "As a matter of fact, she did, but her heels were about two inches high and these are five, so give me a chance to catch up, all right?"

She leaned over the side of the table to get a better look at my shoes. "Nice," she said. "At least you'll look good when you're falling on your face."

The waitress brought me a menu and took my drink order—a Coca-Cola since I was still feeling a little queasy from all the wine and vodka I'd drunk the day before—and as I studied the menu I couldn't help but overhear the movie publicist seated next to us squawking into her cell phone about the budget for a premiere she was planning.

"I don't care if they're defaulting on their creditors and can't pay their production assistants. Find me some money to promote this flick or I'm going to cancel the whole fucking screening . . ."

I asked Gigi if she'd gotten any feedback on Jill's party.

"Not much. Jill wasn't pleased that Ainsley messed with the seating. That girl is so totally shameless," she said.

"Wait, Ainsley changed who she was sitting next to?"

Gigi nodded and asked me if I remembered the guy sitting next to her.

"John?" I asked. Why would she want to sit next to him?

"No, the other guy. The one in the navy suit? Supergorgeous and superrich?"

Yeah I remembered him.

"I think so," I said, trying to sound casual and noninterested, the way a happily married woman should sound when discussing other men.

"His name is Warren Robbins and he just, and I mean *just*, started socializing again. He lost his wife to breast cancer about a year and a half ago. All the money in the world, the best doctors and best care and he still couldn't save her. She left him with a little boy to raise all on his own."

"What a horrible story. That poor man."

"Jill was shocked when he agreed to come to her dinner and we all figured that he was finally ready to start meeting other women. But then Ainsley had to go putting herself next to him and probably succeeded in scaring him back to that big old house of his in Greenwich for another couple years."

I told Gigi about Ainsley's near nipple exposure.

"You know she's never going to land a guy like that. Warren can see she's only interested because he's got money."

"But she's married!" I said, taking a sip from my Coke.

"Who's married?" asked Jill as she sat down at the table, once again breathing hard from running. "Sorry I'm late, you guys," she added. "My trainer made me do some extra sets."

The waitress approached our table again to take Jill's drink order and tell us about the daily specials. Gigi and Jill both ordered "the usual" (I'd later learn that it was a good idea to cultivate a "usual" dish at places like Michael's because then you could show off to your friends that you were a frequent patron and hence one of the city's movers and shakers), which was a thirty-six dollar Cobb salad for Jill and a thirty-three dollar roast chicken for Gigi. I settled on the thirty-five dollar burger (with extra Gruyère).

"So, did you have a good workout?" I asked.

Jill cracked a coy smile. "You could say that."

"If you're fucking your trainer I'm gonna bop you on the head right now," said Gigi.

Jill laughed and shook her head.

"Don't pay any attention to her. She's being belligerent today," I whispered to Jill, loud enough so Gigi could hear.

Gigi flicked me with some of her water. "I was up with Chloe all last night. She's teething. I'm tired. I need sleep."

"What you need is for Jeremy to pitch in," Jill and I both said in tandem.

"Anyway," Gigi said, crossing her arms over her chest. "You

were telling us about your trainer at the gym. You belong to Equinox, right?"

"I do, but that's not where I was. I was at this new spa that specializes in making you tight . . . down there."

"The gyno spa? Don't they have a nine-month wait list?" Gigi asked.

"Not for friends of Irina's," winked Jill. "She's got some pull there. I think maybe she's an investor."

"Irina the maybe madam?" I asked.

Jill nodded and proceeded to bestow Gigi and me with all the details of her "workout," how the doctor who runs the spa measured the strength of her vaginal muscles by making her contract them while her fingers were inside her ("gloved, of course"), and the electrostimulating instrument that her personal trainer used to help her increase her "tone."

"I bought these," she said, lifting a couple of packages from her monogrammed Goyard tote. "They're for using at home."

I took the one that was marked vagina weights and turned it over in my hands. Inside the plastic coating there was one white rounded plastic cone with a blue string on the end and five silver and white weights in increasing size and heft. The weights looked a lot like the eco-friendly, spiral-shaped compact fluorescent bulbs with which we had replaced all of our regular incandescent light bulbs, and I knew from that moment on I was never going to be able to look at a light bulb the same way.

"Forgive me if this is a stupid question, but why on earth's sake are you doing this?" I asked.

"I want to be better in bed," shrugged Jill as she returned the vagina weights to her bag. "The Russians have been doing this for years. That's why men love fucking them—they've got vaginas as powerful as vise grips. My trainer says that by the time she's done with me, I'll be able to shoot maraschino cherries out of my pussy."

"I don't know what's more shocking, that you just said the word *pussy* or that you, a Princeton grad, mom of two, aspire to shoot cocktail fruit out of it," said Gigi, grabbing the other package out of Jill's bag. "Let me see this."

I leaned over to study the other package. It was made of white plastic and shaped like a penis, with a slit down the center and a handle bar at the end. There was a small knob on the handlebar.

"Can I please have my Kegelmaster back?" Jill asked.

"It says here that you're supposed to work to fatigue. Up to six sets of thirty reps each, three times a week. What are you, training for the Vagina Olympics?"

"Give it back, please," Jill asked again.

"First you have to tell me how this works. It looks like a kitchen utensil," Gigi snorted, waving the wand in her hand. "Like a handheld pasta maker."

I laughed so hard I had Coke up my nose. All of Michael's was watching us, agog.

"You both can laugh all you want. But you," she hissed, pointing to me, "haven't had a baby and you," she pointed to Gigi, "had a friggin C-section. Neither of you have any idea what vaginal births do to your vagina. I had a second-degree tear with Ava. My stitches took six weeks to heal."

Our waitress brought our appetizers and Jill's glass of red wine. Gigi took a bite of her roast chicken and said quietly, "For the record I didn't *choose* to have a C-section. Chloe was breech."

"I know," Jill acknowledged. "And I'm sorry. I shouldn't have said that. I don't know what's gotten into me lately. My assistant just quit and told my boss it was because I was a crazy bitch and now I have to go in for sensitivity training. It's such a nightmare. I think maybe I need to up my Xanax or go on vacation or something. Are either of you interested in making a quick trip down to Miami? I could do a write-up about that new hotel in South Beach for the magazine and expense the whole thing."

I bit into my burger. It was hot and juicy and incredibly delicious. "How are things with Glenn?" I asked, remembering the argument I'd heard them having in Jill's bedroom.

"No better," she responded glumly.

"No sex? Then what's the point of lifting vagina weights?" Gigi asked.

"The point is that when I do finally have sex again, I'm going to be really good at it," Jill answered.

"I hope Glenn's ready to have his mind blown," I said.

"And speaking of mind blowing, can you guys believe that Ainsley switched her seat so she could sit next to Warren? She's clearly looking to trade up. Wearing that dress, coming out without poor Peter—"

"And then flirting her ass off with him," Gigi interjected.

"Even though he clearly wasn't interested," I added.

Jill leaned in and whispered over the table. "Let's just hope he stays that way . . . I swear I just saw her in the waiting room at the vagina spa and you know what that means."

"Lock up your husbands, girls," Gigi said, slicing into her chicken.

10

And the Socks Come Off

In early February, Gigi's third home entertaining guide, *Wow Their Socks Off,* hit bookstore shelves nationwide. Dubbed as a how-to for the ambitious hostess, *Wow Their Socks Off* featured such lines as, "Why serve regular deviled eggs when you can delight your guests with deviled *quail* eggs topped with truffle caviar foam?" and included recipes for acai-glazed salmon with hen-of-the-woods-mushroom ragout and goat milk dulce de leche with brown sugar bacon. At the last minute Gigi's publisher, worried about the depressed economy, encouraged Gigi to add a couple chapters catering to the budget-conscious reader, but even with the additions the preponderant content of the book remained ultragourmand, and as such was totally out-of-step with the current zeitgeist.

Gigi and I were in her all-white kitchen—white Carrara marble floors and countertops, white wooden cabinetry and appliances, white farmhouse basins, and so on—preparing some hors d'oeuvres for her book-party launch later that evening. In the background we were listening to, but not watching, the flat panel television that was switched on to CNN. The news was bad all around: falling home prices across the country; rising unemployment and crime rates; and more credit crunch woes for investment banks and insurance companies that had bet too heavily on mortgage-backed securities.

"I'm screwed," she said. She held in her hand a piece of perfectly seared filet mignon.

"You're not screwed," I said, as I rolled my thirty-fifth sage-scented veal meatball between my hands. Only one hundred and fifteen more to go.

"Oh yes I am. The food critics are eating me for breakfast. They're saying that I've grown out of touch with Middle America because I'm married to a billionaire and that my dishes are off-putting and pretentious. And to top it all off, my publicist told me this morning that *The Today Show is* thinking about pulling my segment. With *Cooking A Moveable Feast* and *Memorable Feasts,* my other two books, all three of the morning shows were all duking it out to get me on first." She laid the slice of beef on top of a piece of house-made rosemary crostini, topping it with a dollop of caramelized onion and a sprinkle of finely chopped flat-leaf parsley.

Disappearing into the living room, Gigi returned with a stack of computer printouts. "My reviews," she said, handing the papers to me. I read one that accused Gigi of being not only out of step with the economic climate, but also insensitive to the rising cost of food and gourmet food in particular, another from an animal rights advocacy group condemning Gigi's use of veal and goose liver (foie gras) and calling for a boycott of her books, as well as one from an environmental watchdog group outraged by Gigi's inclusion of Chilean sea bass and Atlantic salmon, both of which were nearly endangered due to several consecutive years of overfishing. One essay, printed on a newspaper's op-ed page, even criticized Gigi as oblivious to those with gluten intolerance.

I held it up to her. "This is a joke, right?"

"Those nut jobs. I swear the next book I write, if I ever get to write another book, is going to be titled, *In Praise of Gluten*."

I returned my attention to the stack, reading through a couple of online items that had gleefully pointed out that Gigi had failed to make it clear that certain garnishes (like the gold leaf on the dark chocolate ganache opera cake) were optional or provide more affordable substitutions for costly ingredients (one radish canapé called for Dutch butter and Himalayan sea salt). Both sited her recent marriage to an enormously successful hedge fund manager as a possible reason for the "glaring absence of economically sensitive alternatives." Even the *New York Times* had turned uncharacteristically snarky. The last paragraph of their review was particularly eviscerating:

> Petrossian caviar and dry aged porterhouse steaks? Who does Ms. Ambrose think her readers are? Other hedge fund wives? Well, this may or may not come as a surprise to the author, but those people don't cook their own food and they certainly don't buy home entertaining guides. They have *people* for that, and we're pretty sure that, after reading this book, Ms. Ambrose does, too.

I did my best to raise Gigi's spirits and stop her from assuming that everyone cared what the reviewers and critics had to say, but the truth was that her nerves were legitimate. She'd received a very large advance from her publisher on the basis that her next book would sell as well as her first two, and if this one was a failure and her publishing house took a big hit because of it, her future as an author was as good as dead. And since everything had been built around the books—the regular appearances on the morning shows, the catering business and endorsement deals (Gigi was an ambassador for a line of high-end cured meats)—she stood to lose everything she'd spent years of her life building.

"I think I made a big mistake with doing this project at all. I wasn't really into the concept when my editor presented me with it, but the money was so good and I needed to pay for my dad's hospital bills."

Gigi had confided in me that she was currently struggling to pay for her father's medical care. She'd grown up with a decent amount of money (by North Carolina standards) but while she was in college her father lost a big chunk of their savings on a risky investment scheme and her mother was diagnosed with breast cancer. Her mother's care drained the last of their savings, and Gigi had to wait tables to pay for the last two years of her tuition at the University of North Carolina. But her mother survived and had been in remission with no signs of the cancer returning, and Gigi picked up her love of food while working in a gourmet restaurant in Chapel Hill. Everything was going well for the Ambrose family, until Gigi's father had a stroke, leaving him mentally incapacitated to the point that he required constant surveillance—he had developed a tendency to strip naked and walk out onto the street—from someone physically strong enough to pick him up and take him back inside the family home. But help cost money.

Gigi sent checks, but her long-term goal was to move her parents to an assisted living facility in Miami. Jeremy had an apartment in South Beach and liked to spend a considerable amount of time there in the winter so he could be closer to Lauren, his daughter from his first marriage whom Gigi described as "tragically spoiled." Lauren went to Rollins, a Florida college that was popular with privileged Southern spawn who couldn't buy their way into the Ivy League, and dutifully visited her dad on weekends—mainly so she could hit Intermix with his credit card. She also often flew up to New York (First Class tickets for a nineteen-year-old!) and was in town that week to go to Gigi's cookbook party, however, Gigi suspected Lauren had ulterior motives.

"Lauren can't stand me and, believe me, the feeling is mutual. If I had my parents in Miami, I could go for the day to see them when she comes over. That way Jeremy would get to spend all the time he wants with his daughter and I'd get to see my parents more often," Gigi had said. "Everybody would be happy."

"Sounds like a great plan to me," I said.

But there were problems. Gigi didn't have enough cash in her bank account to cover the down payment on her parent's new place. She'd already sent them so much for her father's hospital bills, and a few years ago she had to pay for the plumbing to be updated in her parents' house. She'd asked her siblings to pitch in but they'd scoffed. "You're the one married to a billionaire. Ask Jeremy,'" they said.

Jeremy, however, was in no mood to be charitable. His hedge funds were having a bad year. Although his investors weren't yet defecting, his portfolio was in the tank. "He doesn't like to talk about it, but I know when he's nervous about work. He gets stingy, stops leaving big tips at restaurants and grumbles about little things, like the bill from the gardener in Southhampton or the cost of valet parking the Bentley in Miami," she explained.

For Jeremy wealth was a state of mind. There would always be some other mogul or hedge fund manager who had more money than he did, who ranked higher on the Forbes 400, or simply made him feel poor in comparison. Jeremy was jet rich but he aspired to join the ranks of the yacht rich, and because he was going to end the year even less wealthy than the year before (and thus that much farther away from buying his own megayacht) he was feeling, according to Gigi, completely impoverished. "The man has his own jet, four homes, and untold millions invested in stocks, bonds, and other assets, but he believes he can't afford to put a roof over my parents' heads. It's like he's got bank-account dysmorphia," she said.

Unfortunately, given the abysmal reviews for her cookbook, it didn't look like Gigi would be able to afford the down payment on her parents' new home on her own. She sighed and looked at the ceiling. "I should have followed my instinct and done something on gourmet Southern cooking, but my editor said that Paula Deen and Katie Lee Joel already had that niche covered. Why didn't I stick to my guns?" she moaned.

"We all cave in too easily sometimes," I said. "How were you to know that the economy was going to tank? That's what this is all about, you know. Everyone's looking for a whipping boy—or girl—for what's happening and you're an easy target since you're married to Jeremy. You're a victim of circumstance."

Gigi gave me a grateful look and suggested we get back to work. By three o'clock we had finished all the prep work in her kitchen and moved to her living room, which was filled with minimalist furniture (low, white modular couches, white goat-hair rugs and boxy glass and a white-painted steel coffee table) and featured Ming and Qing dynasty Chinese porcelain vases, a stunning collection of jade-green celadon ornaments and plenty of lacquerware. Jeremy had eschewed the ubiquitous black and gold Coromandel screen and Tang dynasty horse (which any Eastern scholar knows is a funeral ornament and as such carries bad chi) in favor of Three Kingdoms jade figurines, a series of brightly colored Japanese Hiroshige woodblock prints, and a dozen bonsai trees and ikebana flower arrangements. The look, if I had to describe it in three words, was High End Zen.

As Gigi and I settled into our white custom-ordered Tom Dixon wingback chairs, Gigi's nanny, a plus-sized Jamaican woman in an all-white uniform (to go with the all-white décor, I imagined), brought in Chloe, who was dressed in white cotton pajamas and contentedly clutching a bottle of formula. Gigi clapped with happiness at the sight of her child and took her in her outstretched arms. I got up to leave—I knew how much Gigi prized her time alone with her little girl, especially since Jeremy had put an end to their family dinners, calling Chloe a "tremendous distraction" and an "unnecessary source of stress."

Admiring the little girl's juicy cheeks and halo of auburn curls from afar, I told Gigi that I didn't want to intrude on her time with her daughter and would see her later at her book party.

"No, stay. I asked Betty to bring her out after her nap because I wanted you two to meet."

"Oh, in that case," I said, and walked over and crouched down to Chloe's level to introduce myself, making some funny faces in hopes of entertaining her. She was still drowsy with sleep and mostly preoccupied with sucking down her bottle of formula, but she looked at me through her half-opened eyes and reached her plump little fist toward my nose.

"Why don't you hold her?" Gigi said, handing her to me.

In my arms Chloe felt heavy and moist, like a ball of rising dough. As she drank her bottle she gazed up at me, her eyes smiling expectantly, and I made some silly animal noises until they and I had lost our novelty value and she began to wail for her mother.

Gigi showed me Chloe's nursery, which was decorated in pale lavender, with stenciled birds flying in a flock across one wall and lots of mod nursery furniture lined up against another, and we spent a good deal of time there, cooing over Chloe, before Chef Bear arrived with the catering van to transfer our food to the Reinhardt's kitchen. Then I watched Gigi gave Chloe a bath, and we dressed her in fresh cotton pajamas—these were white but adorned with pink whip-stitches at the neck, arm, and feet holes—before we all returned to the kitchen so Chloe could have her next bottle, sitting at the round white-lacquered table. I watched Chloe gulp down her formula once again, while Gigi held her nose and tried to stomach a glass jar full of green juice.

"What is that sludge you're drinking?" I asked.

"Kale, parsley, celery, apple, and ginger," she said, pulling a face. "Today's my last day of the juice fast and boy-oh-boy I can't wait for that big glass of wine tonight. They say you're not supposed to have alcohol for three days following the fast for maximum health benefits, but I only did this so I can look good in the pictures. And since I'm not going to be doing much TV as it turns out, it won't matter if I put all the weight back on tomorrow."

"See, I told you there was a silver lining to all that bad press," I joked.

"If I'm not mistaken, I'm not the only one who's dropped a little weight in the past couple weeks." She took another sip of her green juice and eyed me over her glasses.

It was true that I'd been watching my cheese intake, and together with the extra physical activity I got by working for A Moveable Feast, I had been able to shed a few pounds. It wasn't much, but besides dropping some weight, I also felt more energetic and happy now that I was getting out of the house with adequate regularity. Not that John had noticed.

Gigi checked her watch and said she had to take a quick shower before her hair dresser, makeup artist, and stylist arrived to get her coiffed, made up, and dressed for the party—a process that would take a couple of hours from start to finish. Then Jeremy's driver was picking her up in Jeremy's Maybach to take her to Caroline and Fred Reinhardt's SoHo loft, where the party—cocktails and passed hors d'oeurves for seventy-five of Gigi's closest friends and select members of the press—was to take place.

Originally Gigi's publisher had planned a massive party for three hundred in the ballroom of the newly renovated Plaza Hotel. Then some of the bookstores started scaling back on their orders and a couple of the women's monthlies unexpectedly axed their features on *Wow Their Socks Off*, so her publisher pulled the budget for the event entirely.

"It was the Reinhardts' or here," Gigi explained, "and it looks bad if you have to throw your own book party. Plus, let's face it, I have a better chance of getting my party covered by *New York* magazine if they hold it. Their apartment is a riot!"

"Couldn't be more out there than Jill's," I said.

"Just you wait," Gigi laughed, swallowing the last of her green juice.

I hoisted myself up from the table and blew a kiss to Chloe. "Well see you there," I said.

John was supposed to accompany me to Gigi's book launch that evening. His assistant called me after I left Gigi's apartment to tell me that she had arranged for me to be picked up via car service at 5:45 p.m. Then, she explained, I would swing by Zenith Capital's Park Avenue office to pick up John, and together we would head downtown to the Reinhardts' front door. Factoring traffic, our estimated time of arrival was 6:30 p.m., exactly thirty minutes after Gigi's book party had begun. If it had been up to me we would have gotten there five minutes *before* the party had commenced, so I could make sure that Gigi was feeling peppy and confident (and ply her with a shot of tequila if need be), but when I finally convinced his assistant to put John on the line so I could argue with him over our departure and arrival itinerary (you'd think we were flying overseas for all the coordination that seemed to be required) John absolutely insisted that we arrive late.

"This way," he explained over the phone, "we can make an entrance."

The condescension in his voice was just too irksome. "As opposed to skulking in through the window?" I asked.

He didn't find my sarcasm amusing. But he had once, before we'd moved to New York, and I was having trouble breaking the habit. I mean, for a long time witty barbs were my trademark, and our exchange of them—our spirited repartee, I'd called it—had been one of the things he liked best about us. I wanted to point this out to John and ask him where all his humor had gone, but after rolling a hundred and twenty-five veal meatballs and icing another hundred sock-shaped cookies, I was too tired to argue.

Besides, tonight, I had bigger things on my mind.

Starting with my appearance. I'd been doing some shopping. In addition to those stiletto boots (the ones that caused me to stumble like a drunken toddler in front of Harvey Weinstein) I went back to the Ralph Lauren store. I ended up purchasing a pleated beige silk jersey dress and a pair of open-toed high-heeled shoes (now that I was getting the knack for them, I loved how tall and powerful they made me feel), which I was planning wearing that evening. To be honest, I was beginning to understand Jill's obsession with clothes and shopping. The saleswomen treated you the way you wished your husband still did: They noticed if you had your hair trimmed or if your skin looked more dewy and youthful; they complimented your taste and your body and they called you at home, during the day, directly and not through an assistant.

But I wasn't about to resign myself to a life where the only people who kissed my ass were people making money off of it. My husband would not ignore me forever! Before Gigi's party I spent a little longer than usual on my makeup and hair, pulling it back into a neat little chignon, and clipped my new earrings, the diamond ones John had given me, to my ears. I looked, I thought, very much like a proper hedge fund wife, and hoped that John would be pleased.

And that he would have sex with me that night.

Since the night he'd missed my appointment at Dr. Delgado's office and begged for my forgiveness we hadn't made love once. That was almost a month ago and I'd gotten my period. I knew, from peeing on one of those ovulation test sticks and also the careful charts I'd been keeping since shortly after the miscarriage, that I was ripe for conception. My heart beat a little faster in my chest knowing that if I could get John to have sex with me tonight there was a very good chance I'd get pregnant. *A baby,* I thought, *a I heartbeat, a growing little body.* Then I forced myself to take a deep breath and remember my mission for the evening—to be so charming, sophisticated, and beautiful that John would want to leave the party early just to make love to me.

I can do this, I told myself. *He loves me.*

Except, when I went downstairs and got in the car and swung by John's office. I waited there for fifteen minutes before he sent me a text. He was stuck in a speed-reading seminar (which was part of Zenith's larger campaign to teach traders to learn how to read faster, retain and gather more information, and delegate more efficiently) and would meet me at the party. That's when I started to doubt very much if he still loved me at all.

It was clear to me he was slowly drowning—in his greed, in his stress, something—and I was losing him. With each day that passed, he grew more distant, more impatient, more *distracted.* The only hope I had of getting his attention once again was getting pregnant again.

Before the miscarriage John had taken such good care of me. When the morning sickness set in he brought me toasted poppy seed bagels with cream cheese and hamburgers and French fries from the neighborhood deli. Once when I complained of being cold while we were watching television he ordered me a cashmere blanket online and paid extra for it to be overnighted so I would have it as soon as possible. He came to my doctor's visits, read my pregnancy books, and massaged my feet—all unbidden.

A baby was my only hope, in so many ways.

11

I Say Oblivious, You Say Ubiquitous

After giving my name to a young woman with a clipboard in the building's downstairs reception area, I rode the elevator up to the Reinhardts' loft. The doors opened directly into their sitting room, which was cavernous in size and scale. If the décor of Jill's apartment was a little nutty, the Reinhardts' was downright nuts (and rated NC-17). Contemporary art's biggest names were all present and accounted for, from Chuck Close photorealist portraits to the Jean-Luc Moerman psychedelic landscapes, but there was also a series of black and white photographs of Caroline simulating (I hope) sex with a muscled model and a realistic, life-size topless bust of her hung on a wall near the dining room table. (I wondered if they would transfer it to another locale once their children were old enough to be embarrassed by it.)

As I made my way through the guests and publicists swarming near the front entrance, I took in the entirety of the Reinhardts' art collection. It was clear that they had a soft spot for pop and neopop art, as there were plenty of works from Lichtenstein, Warhol, Hockney, and Hirst. Atop a hot pink Lucite coffee table sat a Jeff Koons balloon dog, and four Teletubbie-like alien heads were suspended from the ceiling above a chartreuse crocodile couch (yes, you read right), but the most startling piece was the Takashi Murakami fiberglass mushroom that stood rooted in the center of the room casting an even deeper sense of the surreal over the party.

Boy, I needed a drink.

Hiding behind a crush of foodies, who were busy criticizing the hors d'oeuvres and one-upping each other with references to antiquated cooking techniques (what was "sous vide" anyway?), I found the bar. Blake was tending again, a silly, callow grin plastered on his face as he handed a drink to a stick-thin young woman (nineteen years old, if a day) with lips painted the same pink as her too-short bandage dress.

"Vodka cranberry," I mouthed to him over the din of the gossiping foodies at my back, and he nodded, making my drink order first even though there were two other couples waiting to be served. I would have felt guilty for jumping the line but there aren't too many perks to working as a catering waitress, and I wasn't about to forfeit taking full advantage of this one.

Drink in hand, I pushed through the mob of editors, writers, and bloggers to find Gigi, and considered what I was going to say to her. Congratulations didn't seem right, but neither did a concerned "how are you holding up?" Perhaps I could say something like "Great party!" since it was certainly shaping up to be one. Gigi had been fretting that nobody would turn up, because of the horrible review in the *Times* and other bad press, but surveying the room, I estimated that there were already close to seventy people there, including plenty of familiar faces.

I spotted Irina, dressed in an animal print minidress, barking into her cell phone (of course), her icy eyes surveying a crowd of pasty-faced men, who were in turn ogling the naked bust of Caroline. Dahlia stood cowering near the Murakami, probably trying to avoid making any form of contact with the reams of plebs inching ever closer to the golden hem of her cocktail frock. Ainsley, meanwhile, sat in the center of a mod, egg-shaped chair that had been entirely covered in fluttery fabric squares resembling petals. Sipping at a glass of champagne, she peered across the room at Caroline and her new baby boy, whose picture was being taken by the trio of photographers covering the event for various media outlets. Ainsley tried not to let her agitation show on her face, but as she was not the best of actresses, her annoyance was about as obvious as her cleavage, which was once again hoisted toward her clavicle.

To be honest, I didn't know Ainsley well at that point, but she intrigued me and I couldn't help but gobble up every photo of her or piece of gossip about her I happened to stumble across while reading the morning papers. For a long time I wondered what everyone found so special about her, why she, out of all the other socialites and women about town swanning from charity benefit to charity benefit, had captured the interest of the public at large. She wasn't breathtakingly attractive, nor did she have any discernable talent. But then one day, it dawned on me: Whereas most of the hedge fund wives actively discouraged press, Ainsley courted it—and skillfully so. She had calculatingly and flagrantly flouted the rules of high society and private equity by giving the general public a peak inside a world they had never had access to before. She had come to emblemize the superrich in most people's minds, so much so that if you said hedge fund wife to your mailman or the girl behind the cash register at the Food Emporium, it would be Ainsley's face that he or she would picture.

No doubt, she had succeeded in getting the one thing she wanted most—fame. But as the tides of public opinion turned against the rich, so too was it turning on Ainsley. Unemployment was at a seven-year high and the price of milk, beef, and flour had all increased exponentially. No one cared about what the spoiled wife of a blue blood fund manager was doing or saying or wearing. In fact, if anything, they were actively angered by the existence of people like Ainsley and wanted nothing more than to see her downfall. The latest buzz had Ainsley's accessories line yanked from the shelves of stores across the country and a previously green-lighted lifestyle show placed on indefinite hiatus by one of the larger cable networks. The Guggenheim Museum had bumped her as the co-chair of their annual fundraiser; fashion companies weren't asking her to host their cozy little luncheons (because most had done away with them altogether); and at cocktail parties and movie screenings, photographers no longer clamored to take her picture. Just like Gigi, the clouds of economic uncertainty were raining all over Ainsley's parade, but unlike Gigi, who was a mother, author, and business woman, there really was nothing more to Ainsley than her social status. It was the house of cards upon which all was built. And now that Peter's fund had gone belly-up, she would have nothing if it disappeared. Absolutely nothing.

Ainsley turned to look in my direction and caught me gazing at her. I expected her to give me one of her fake, open-mouthed smiles or even ignore me, but she shot up and pranced over to me, throwing one of her Pilates-toned arms around my shoulders. "Hiiii," she squealed. "I'm so glad you're here!"

To say that I was surprised by her warmth (regardless of its authenticity) would be an understatement. Knock-me-over-with-a-feather-flabbergasted is more like it. Not long ago Ainsley had to be bullied into letting me and John come to her Christmas party. Now she was greeting me like we were old friends. Had things really gotten so bad for her that she was now turning to *me* for friendship? It certainly was possible. And although I saw straight through Ainsley's glimmering eyes and charming banter,

John was nowhere to be found and Gigi was still out of my line of sight, which meant that I could either talk to Ainsley or lie low under the Murakami mushroom next to Dahlia. I chose Ainsley.

"Nice to see you, too," I responded. "You look wonderful tonight."

It's true, she did. Her flaxen waves were as glossy as ever, her skin glowing.

"Thanks," she said. "Love your dress."

Once the pleasantries were dispensed with, Ainsley could then get down to business: "Can you believe the fuss everyone's making over Caroline's new surro-baby?" she whispered in my ear. "I mean, it's not like she gave birth to the thing herself."

She did make a good (if ridiculously shallow) point, but I couldn't be sure if she was setting a trap for me. I shrugged noncommittally.

"Oh wow," she said, zeroing in on my diamond earrings. She fingered them with her silk wrapped talons. "L-O-V-E these. Bulgari's new collection, right?"

"How did you know?"

"Oh, it's my favorite jewelry store. Van Cleef is just too oblivious, you know?"

I had to think for a second. "You mean, ubiquitous?"

"Oh God," she giggled, covering her mouth with her hand. "I am so dumb."

Which, of course, was meant to prompt me to say, "Oh no, it's easy to confuse the two," when in fact, it wasn't. Ainsley was too old to be flubbing words like *ubiquitous*, but since everyone let her get away with it, she had no impetus for change. It occurred to me that Ainsley had probably never had a reckoning of any kind in her life and that she probably didn't even realize that one was biting her on the ass, right then and there as we spoke.

You could say she was quite *oblivious*.

Either that, or she was playing the part perfectly.

I needed another drink.

But before I had a chance to suggest we hit the bar for refills, a photographer asked us to pose together for a picture. I noticed Ainsley bristle almost imperceptibly, her spine straightening and chin dipping slightly toward her chest with umbrage, when the photographer made a motion with his free hand for us to move closer together, but she caught herself and gave me yet another one of her toothy grins. She was too smart to kick me, the woman she'd been clutching like a life preserver not even a minute earlier, to the curb over one lousy photo op. For some reason, I was no longer inconsequential to her. Why I wasn't, I hadn't yet figured out, and when I finally did, it would already be too late.

After the picture was taken, Ainsley read my mind and nodded in the direction of the bar. We walked over together, through the foodies, who stood rooted like mushrooms to their places, and she ordered me another vodka cranberry and champagne for herself. As we stood there waiting in line—Blake had been relieved by another server I hadn't met before—she proposed we have dinner sometime. "A double date" was how she put it. Whipping her BlackBerry out of one of her Ainsley Partridge purses (you could tell by the interlocking *A* and *P*), she threw out a few dates in the following two weeks that would work for both her and Peter. I had little choice but to agree to the following Wednesday evening.

Breezing past us, clearly in a rush to get somewhere, Jill smiled and wiggled her fingers, sending an armful of Hermès enamel cuffs tinkling down her arm. "See you ladies later," Jill called.

But Ainsley wasn't about to let her old friend go by with such a meager salutation. She grabbed Jill by the arm.

I could see Jill's aggravation in her eyes as she gave Ainsley a kiss on the cheek. "Can you believe the art? Talk about protomodernism at its best."

"Oh, so *that's* what they call this?" I joked. Of course, no one laughed except me.

Jill glanced down at the blinking red light on the upper right hand corner of her BlackBerry. "I'm sorry, ladies, but I need to—"

Ainsley cut her off. "So, we were just arranging a dinner. Next Wednesday. Can you and Glenn make it?"

"Um, I don't think so. Glenn has to prepare his reports on Wednesday nights. Those are *always* late night for him. Why don't you guys work out some dates and email them to me?" Her mouth was pursed hard in an expression of annoyance.

"Hmm, I'm just wondering where should we do it?" Ainsley asked. She looked at me.

"We could have it at our place," I offered. *And why not? It would be fun to host a dinner party.* I could roast a chicken and mash some sweet potatoes and make my grandmother's secret recipe for cheesecake for dessert. It wouldn't take too much effort to do that, and John would be thrilled at the prospect of having both the Patridges and the Tischmans in our home.

After Jill departed, promising us both she'd call us, Ainsley said she needed to find the bathroom, leaving me suddenly on my own.

I walked through the crowd of guests in search of either Gigi or John, hitting a logjam of bodies near Caroline, who was sitting on the chartreuse crocodile skin couch, cradling her two-week-old baby boy in her arms. The baby was dressed in soft white cotton and wrapped in a white cashmere blanket. He was an incredibly tiny bundle, with red, bumpy skin, and blue-gray eyes that fluttered open every once in a while, usually when the flash of a camera popped in his face.

I was standing at the foot of the daybed, behind Caroline, when Dahlia sat down next to her. I turned my back so that they wouldn't notice me standing there—not because I was trying to eavesdrop—and did my best to melt into the swarm of bodies.

"I can't hear you," I couldn't help but overhear Caroline say. "You have to talk louder."

"Thomas," Dahlia repeated. "He's decided to direct the lion's share of our charitable contributions to the Prosper Fund."

"Oh? I've never heard of it."

"It's a charitable group that helps unemployed men and women from low-income neighborhoods find jobs. Thomas is worried about rising crime rates in the city and thinks this group is the answer. I told him if he was so worried about crime, he should give the money to the NYPD."

"But you're still giving to MoMA?" Caroline asked, distraught. "I told them Thomas was a lock for ten."

As in ten million.

"We are, of course we are. Thomas never goes back on a promise. You know that. But we'll be making our donation anonymously. Thomas hates publicity, and especially considering the economic outlook . . ."

"But didn't I just read a huge article in *Forbes* about him?"

"Oh, that." Dahlia frowned. "I just don't see why he has to bring up his past all the time. Every article, it's the same story. Dad abandoned him at six. To make ends meet, mother stocked shelves at Bergdorf's. It's as if he's *proud* he grew up poor."

Poor Thomas, I thought as I walked away from them with a lump in my throat. I could relate to his need to talk about his lean upbringing—my parents seemed to always be struggling to make the mortgage payments on our home, and my sister and I learned pretty quick never to answer the phone during dinner hours because that's when the credit card collection agencies called. My whole childhood, all I ever wanted was a sense of security, to know for certain that someone wasn't going to show up on our doorstep and force us to move out of our home, or take my mom's car, or take my dad to prison for not paying the bills. That feeling never leaves you, no matter how many diamonds you have hanging off your earlobes.

The thing that most people don't know is that hedge funds are chock-a-block with coddled offspring of the very wealthy; it is as nepotistic and clubby an industry as there ever was, and because of that you'd think that Thomas Kemp would have a massive chip on his shoulder. After all, he hadn't attended the right boarding schools and colleges, rode his bike in the right neighborhoods, or swam in the right pools. Didn't it seem reasonable that he'd *want* to flaunt his billions, his incredible success, in front of the silver-spoon set he'd probably had to contend with as he clambered his way up on the Forbes 400 rankings? But now, he had resolutely refused to buy the trendy art or give to the trendy charities or let Richard Meier build him a porte cochere for twenty million dollars when it really cost a fraction of the price to construct. Thomas Kemp was a smart man, smart enough to know that people were gossiping about him, calling him parsimonious and cheap, and that his wife was growing to resent him a little more each day that he refused to buy into all the bullshit everyone was trying to sell them. They were like fruit flies, these art consultants and real estate brokers, decorators and architects, wardrobe stylists and hairdressers. And Dahlia, she couldn't get enough of them.

"Marcy," I heard John call from behind me. "There you are."

I was relieved to see him. He looked handsome in his gray suit, especially compared to all the jowl-faced food critics and overweight finance guys milling about. "You made it," I said, smiling broadly and waiting for him to say something about how I looked, or at the very least, about the Bulgari earrings.

"So," he said, meeting my gaze for a mere instant before he began searching the room for something or someone in particular.

"I'm wearing the new earrings," I said, shaking my head a little for effect.

He took my drink from my hand and took a sip. "Nice," he said. "They look great."

"You've barely looked at me," I whined, knowing, even as the words were falling from my mouth, the same mouth I'd painstakingly painted with a lip pencil, lipstick, and lip gloss (three *fucking* products, just for my lips), that I was blowing it. *Shut up Marcy, for fuck's sake. Needy is not sexy. Be the kind of wife he wants—aloof, confident, sophisticated, and worldly.*

John looked at his twelve hundred dollar shoes.

"Anyway, should we go find Gigi?" I asked.

"Yes," he said, exhaling sharply. "I've been wanting to meet Jeremy. Is he here tonight?"

"Supposed to be," I responded, but John didn't hear me. He was already making a beeline for Gigi and the famous (or infamous, depending on who you asked) Jeremy Cohen.

Let me start by saying that I had seen Jeremy on CNBC's *Squawk Box* on numerous occasions and had also seen pictures of him at various parties around town, usually in the *New York Times* or in *New York* magazine's Intelligencer section. On television he came across as sharp and quick-witted if somewhat cocksure, which to me is never an admirable quality but to the hedge fund community is deeply essential. The party pictures told a similar story. In them he looked smug and self-satisfied, stocky and short-legged in his wool, velvet, or linen Nehru jackets (depending on the season and occasion). I had been dreading the day that I would meet him because, first of all, Gigi hadn't painted the best picture of him (despite her rule that one should never talk badly about one's husband) and secondly because based on what she had said about him I didn't think he would like me.

I was right.

"Sugar," Gigi yelped, enveloping me in a big hug. "I am so glad you're here."

"Congratulations on your book," John said, giving her a cheek-to-cheek air kiss. "It looks fantastic. Am sure it's going to be a hit. A bestseller!"

John couldn't have been more off the mark, but Gigi had the good grace to not draw attention to his ignorance. "Thank you," she demurred. "Now, I'm sure Marcy hasn't told you, she's so modest, but she almost single-handedly ran one of my events last week. I got held up and couldn't get on-site to set all the preparty wheels in motion but she knew exactly what to do and was cool as a cucumber. I hope you haven't minded me monopolizing her all these nights."

"Oh, no, not too much. Of course I miss her, but all that matters to me is that she's happy."

It was the kindest thing that he had said about me (or to me) in a long time and I took it as proof that John still cared about the health of our marriage. Most everything else about his recent behavior seemed to prove otherwise, but I chose to believe that he really did still love me.

"Well aren't you just a big lump of sugar," Gigi remarked, surreptitiously mouthing the words "that was sweet" when John was reaching behind us to grab two glasses of champagne off of a waiter's tray.

Handing one glass to Gigi, John kept the second for himself. I still had my cocktail and Jeremy had a scotch on the rocks in his hand. As I would later learn, Jeremy was well known for drinking only single malt Scotch and only the best: Glenfiddich 40 Year Old. In fact, he went so far as to bring his *own* bottle to parties where he thought the host might not have a stash of the $2,500 liquor.

While Gigi and John were chatting about food, I decided to

try and make small talk with Jeremy. It made me happy to see John making an effort to get to know my new best friend, and I thought that I should do the same for Gigi.

"So, I met your daughter today," I said, and was about to add how cute she was and how I could now see the similarities between them—Chloe had his pink, Clara Bow lips and the cleft in his chin—but then he made a sort of grunting sound and cut me off.

"Which one? Lauren or Chloe?" he asked.

"Chloe."

"Oh," Jeremy said, now totally disinterested.

"But I saw Lauren here tonight and she's beautiful, too. How old is she?" I asked.

"Nineteen."

"So she's in college now then?"

He took a long sip of his scotch and jangled the two ice cubes in his glass. "Yes and no," he answered, finally making eye contact with me.

I figured that I had him, that I was on to something he might like to talk about. If I could get him to open up to me about his personal life, there was a chance he would come to like me. Perhaps it was silly, but having the imprimatur of my new best friend's husband was important to me.

"Can I ask you what that means, yes and no?" I inquired.

"No you may not," he responded stridently before moving his focus over my shoulder to the crowd behind me. "Hey, is that Mario Garaviccio?"

I turned around to see the celebrated restaurateur and star of the Ovation Channel's cooking competition series. He was heavy set, wore a bandana around his balding head, and a sprig of rosemary in his jacket lapel. Grabbing two deviled quail eggs off of Gemma's tray with one quick swipe of his hand, he stuffed them both in his mouth at the same time.

"Excuse me," Jeremy murmured, pushing past me, his shoulder knocking into mine and causing me to spill my entire drink down the front of my dress. My brand-new silk knit jersey, *beige* dress was covered in cranberry juice. And this being a swanky, foodie party, the bartender had used real, one hundred percent cranberry juice, i.e., not Ocean Spray but the kind that stains.

Holy eff eff eff!!!

I wanted to cry.

"Jesus, Marcy. What happened?" John asked. His tone wasn't the nicest. *What happened to Mr. All-That-Matters-Is-That-She's-Happy?*

If it hadn't been for Gigi, who quickly came to my defense, I might have lost it. "Jeremy bumped into her; it was an accident. Please send me the dry cleaning bill, and if they can't get the stain out, I'll replace the dress," she said.

"Oh no, I couldn't let you buy me a new dress," I said, dabbing my front with my napkin.

Out of the corner of my eye I saw John glance over to Jeremy and Mario, who were clapping each other's backs and laughing uproariously. John moved his weight from foot to foot—he was irritated that he had missed his chance to make nice with the great Jeremy Cohen.

"I'm just going to go say hello. I never had a chance," John said predictably. He walked away to join Jeremy and Mario, not waiting for my blessing.

"Let's get you cleaned up," Gigi said, grabbing my hand.

"Oh no, you can't leave your own party," I insisted.

"Are you kidding me? Of course I can. And anyway, I think the photographers are more interested in taking pictures of Caroline than of me."

I could tell she was grateful for the excuse to excuse herself from the festivities, so I let her lead me into the Reinhardts' private quarters. It was as we turned the corner of a hall wallpapered in Warhols that we bumped into Blake. "What are you doing away from the bar?" Gigi demanded.

"Just heading back now," he panted. His upper lip was slicked with sweat.

"Are you okay?" I asked.

"Yeah," he said, jogging off.

Gigi and I looked at each other and shook our heads.

12

Eco-disaster

"I still think we should reupholster it in silk hemp," John said, planting his hands on his hips determinately.

He was referring to the couch, our suede, so-comfy-I-could-live-there sofa, my favorite piece in the whole apartment. "Don't even think about touching it," I warned.

"But, Marcy, suede is not eco-friendly. The tanneries dump toxins into the rivers."

"Okay, maybe you're right about that. But this leather has already done whatever damage it's going to do. Can't we just keep it until it falls apart and then replace it with the silk hemp? Or maybe by then, they'll have figured out how to produce an environmentally conscious suede?"

He grumbled and muttered something about cohesive design and lifestyle identity, whatever that meant, and went to check on the bottles of biodynamic wine and organic vodka he had chilling in the refrigerator. "Why aren't the chickens in the oven yet?" he yelled from inside the kitchen.

"They don't need to go in for another half hour," I yelled back.

It was an hour before our dinner party was set to begin and John and I were doing some last minute preparations. Well, *I* was preparing while John was obsessing, moving around knick-knacks, fretting about wrinkles in the curtains (at least *they* were silk hemp), and tinkering with his iPod mix for the cocktail hour. It had been like this for the last three weeks, ever since John found out that we were having Ainsley and Peter and Jill and Glenn over for dinner.

The looming deadline of houseguests had pushed him into decorating overdrive. He went on a weekend-long buying spree of eco-friendly home furnishings—from recycled cashmere throw pillows to a new credenza made of kirei grass (a woodlike material fabricated from Sorghum plants). We hired our doorman to paint our apartment in low VOC paints in creamy avocado and oatmeal hues, switched our towels and bedding to 100 percent organic cotton and replaced our old Oriental rugs with sisal and vegetable-dyed wool ones. John also managed to convince (i.e., bribe) our contractor to install our new icestone (concrete and recycled glass) kitchen and bathroom countertops and bamboo flooring a week earlier than previously scheduled. Not a day went by that I wasn't running around town, scouting out everything from a new LED task lamp for John's office to end tables made from salvaged acacia wood. Everything had to be perfect in time for the party, and everything had to be "green," as in environmentally friendly.

I couldn't quite understand how all this consumption was good for the planet. It killed me to spend $15,000 on a commode and $1,500 on a pair of recycled silver candlesticks when I knew how far that money could go in Maggie's or Gemma's hands, for example. When I expressed this sentiment to John, he told me that I was missing the point.

"I don't get it," I said, crossing my arms. "I feel like we're being hypocritical. Buying all this stuff and tossing out all our old stuff? You know where all our old stuff is going, right? To the landfills."

"Actually, I bet a lot of it is being looted by freegans. They're like human bottom feeders, the snails that sit at the bottom of fish tanks and eat up all the other fishes' shit."

"John, that's disgusting," I said, wrinkling my nose.

He shrugged and started to walk out of the room, toward our bedroom, no doubt to gaze at the walls again and wonder aloud if we should have gone with the Sage paint instead of the Sprout.

"You haven't answered my question," I said, rooting myself in front of him.

"Remind me again what it was," he said calmly.

"How exactly buying a fifteen thousand dollar armoire benefits the environment?"

"Because when we buy furniture, like the armoire made of sustainably harvested walnut and low-VOC lacquer, we promote eco industry. We're creating the demand for these products," John said, a self-satisfied grin spreading across his clean-shaven and unnervingly handsome face. "And besides all that, this is our point of differentiation."

Say what?

"The Kemps are into Impressionist paintings. The Reinhardts collect pop art and furniture, Cohen does Chinese antiques, and the Tischmans do contemporary. Eco-conscious is our niche," he explained, rubbing his hands together. "Our identity."

"Except it's not my identity," I said, but he didn't hear me. He'd already placed his iPod ear buds back in his ears and was scrolling through his dinner party mix again, probably debating whether New Order still fit into our music "identity." I couldn't wait to find out—or for our guests to arrive. Five more minutes of alone time with John and I'd be tempted to smother him with one of our organic-dry-cleaned-recycled-cashmere throw pillows.

Thankfully the buzzer from downstairs rang, announcing the arrival of Maggie, whom I'd hired to help me serve dinner and clean up afterward. Since Gigi wasn't coming to dinner—she had gone off for a book signing in her hometown in North Carolina—I was glad to have someone's help in the kitchen.

Maggie helped me finish plating some of the hors d'oeuvres, and afterward I probed her for an update on how her boyfriend's job search was going. She said she was worried he had resigned himself to remaining unemployed for the foreseeable future, and to make matters worse, his boredom and depression had led him to start drinking in the early afternoon. Most nights he passed out on their couch after polishing off a couple of six packs of beer or whatever he could find in the liquor cabinet. Maggie was thinking about breaking up with him.

After dispensing some solicited advice—I thought she should give him a few weeks to turn things around and then break up with him—I left her in the kitchen and finished setting the dinner table in the dining room. I lit the soy candles and laid down the cork placemats, stone runner, bamboo cutlery, recycled glass plates and water and wine glasses, and slipped the organic hemstitch linen napkins into their raffia lotus blossom napkin rings. I'd found an organic florist online and had ordered a half-dozen potted phalaenopsis orchids, a couple boxwood topiaries, and a large arrangement of dark purple and ivory Vermeer calla lilies for the table in the entryway. Then we went into the kitchen to put the free-range chickens in the oven, dumped a bottle of Belgian beer into the cast-iron pot and set out the raw milk cheeses and artisanal flat breads and crackers on the slate serving platter to warm. My cheesecake, made with organic cream cheese, was in the fridge, already on the ceramic, hand-blown cake plate, and the locally grown sweet potatoes had been whipped with caramelized shallots and butter. All Maggie had to do was dress the raw fennel and microgreens in the hand-hewed maple salad bowl, and finish steaming the farmer's market haricots verts and sautéing the Brussels sprouts in garlic and onion.

I poured myself a glass of the wine and ran to my bedroom, where I threw on my latest purchase, a stretch wool garnet-colored cocktail dress with some strategic darting around the bust and waist, and debated adding my diamond earrings before deciding it would look like I was trying too hard. The doorbell rang just as I was slipping into my new vegan Stella McCartney heels—my one concession to John's new *eco-identity*.

Maggie answered the door, as John had instructed her to not five minutes earlier, and I joined John in the living room just as Glenn came through the arched doorway. He was wearing a green striped shirt, green tie, and navy suit and seemed both surprised and annoyed at being the first guest to arrive—it was already ten past eight and we'd requested that everyone arrive at seven-thirty. Glenn asked if we'd heard from Jill. "She's usually late, but not this late," he added, checking his watch, one of those square models with two smaller dials embedded in the main face.

"I'm sure she'll be here soon," I assured him, and the bell rang again, heralding the arrival of Ainsley and Peter.

"Hey, Glenn, Jill running late again?" Ainsley asked teasingly. Her long hair was arranged in a messy, low ponytail and her eye makeup was smudged for a smoky, high-fashion effect. Dressed in a soft pink silk slip with one of those oversized gray cashmere sweaters over her shoulders, she looked as if she had just rolled out of bed or, conversely, was about to roll into one. Accepting a glass of wine from John, she took a seat on the couch, and seemed immediately comfortable in her surroundings, which I tried not to let bother me. I had put so much effort into our first dinner, I was damn well going to enjoy it.

"This place is so cool," she said breathlessly. "Can I have a tour?"

"Sure," John said, taking a glass of wine off of the bamboo tray Maggie was holding out for Glenn and me and disappearing down the hall with Ainsley.

Peter joined the two of us on the couch and I instructed Maggie to leave the cheese and wine trays on the coffee table.

"So, man, I heard about your fund," said Glenn. "It's a brutal time."

"Yeah," Peter responded, slicing off a large wedge of aged goat cheese and depositing it on a cracker. He was dressed in jeans, a pink shirt, and navy blazer that he quickly unbuttoned to reveal a large belly I couldn't remember him having at his Christmas party, just three months earlier.

Peter finished chewing his cheese and as he made up another generous bite, he added, "At least now we've unloaded the apartment. That mortgage was like an albatross around my neck, and the maintenance was killing me."

"I know what you mean. So what's your next step? You looking for something, because I can keep my ear out." It was a generous offer but I couldn't quite tell if it was sincere, and given what I knew of Glenn from Jill and had heard him yelling at her behind closed doors, I had to assume that it wasn't.

Glenn and Peter talked like that for a while, about the markets, how various funds they both had friends at were performing, and revisited the high cost of living in the city—"it's getting worse every day, a hot dog's three bucks now!" exclaimed Peter, his voice rising high with indignation—before I had to excuse myself to go check on dinner. By the time I had returned, Ainsley and John had reappeared and Jill had finally arrived. The men were gathered at the couch, attacking the cheese, hacking it with the sharp edges of their crackers, while the women hovered by the credenza, near the soy candles and potted orchids.

I went over to greet Jill, who was wearing a little lace-edged camisole top, dark jeans, and grommet-studded boots, looking not a day over twenty-five.

"Sorry I'm late," she said, "Ava wouldn't go to bed until I read her *Pinkalicious* another time."

Ainsley wrinkled her nose. "Can't the nanny read to her?"

Choosing to ignore Ainsley's question, Jill turned to me and said, "This place is fantastic. Its eco but also luxurious. I could imagine *House & Home* doing a shoot here if that interested you and John at all."

"Did you hear that honey?" I called across the room.

John had rolled his right shirt sleeve back to show off his new watch, a Vacheron Constantin with a cushion-shaped face and alligator strap. It had cost thirty thousand dollars, which to me was a jaw-dropping sum for a wristwatch, but to John was a totally responsible, if not meager outlay of capital. He'd wanted to go for the palladium version, which cost double his titanium edition, and I'd barely managed to talk him out of it.

I began to tell him that Jill wanted to shoot our apartment—I knew how pleased that would make him—but Ainsley interrupted me, jumping to her feet and joining the rest of the men on the couch, before I could.

"Is that a Vacheron Constantin?" she asked, leaning over for a closer look. She smiled up at him, holding his wrist lightly between her fingers.

Was it just me, or was she flirting with my husband?

In my own freaking home?

With her husband standing right there?

Clapping my hands together, I shooed all the men off the couch. "Okay everyone, dinner's served," I announced briskly.

In the dining room, Glenn sat next to Jill and Peter took a seat next to Ainsley, while John and I anchored either end of the rectangular table. We started on the salad course and as John circled the table pouring out the wine, the topic of children came up. I mentioned that we were hoping to get pregnant soon, and although John didn't say anything, I could tell he wasn't happy with the direction of the discussion. He tried twice, both times unsuccessfully, to redirect everyone's attention to the compact fluorescent light bulbs hanging above our heads.

"Kids are so great. You guys should definitely go for it," Glenn said, spearing a chunk of raw fennel. "But keep in mind that they're a lot of work, and you end up fighting about them all the time."

"You can say that again," Jill interjected.

"And if you want to raise them in the city, they cost an arm and a leg. We're trying to get our eldest into Pruitt, where tuition *starts* at thirty thousand dollars a year, and it's as if Justin's applying to college—the test scores, the essays, the letters of recommendation. Man, such a rigmarole; we've had to hire a counselor to make sure everything gets done on time, Then, on top of all that, you have to know someone on the board *and* pledge a donation. It's got to be done verbally, though; you can't just send in a check because that would be considered bribery. As if any of us would ever dream of doing that," he said mockingly.

"Don't listen to my husband," Jill said, rolling her eyes. "It's really not as bad as he makes it sound. It's true that you do have to be proactive to ensure that your child's application stands out, but mostly the schools care that the kids are well adjusted and happy and show an interest in learning, which ours do."

From the tone of their voices and the way they avoided making eye contact with each other, I deduced that the two of them had not yet patched things up.

"Well, I am *so* not ready to have children," Ainsley said. "And now that I'm the major breadwinner in the family," she said, casting a sidelong glance at Peter, "there's even less reason to do it. I mean it would be one thing if I was like Gigi Ambrose and had a husband like Jeremy Cohen and could afford to have a nanny full time and jet off for book signings and what not whenever I wanted. But that's just not the reality of our situation, is it, sweetie?"

Peter visibly shrank about two inches as she spoke. He reached across the table for the sweet potatoes and helped himself to a large dollop. "These are great, Marcy," he said as he brought another forkful to his mouth.

"My husband has a bottomless stomach," Ainsley said, sitting back from the table and crossing her arms. A look of disgust spread across her face.

Peter patted his belly. "It's getting bigger all right. Ever since I quit working. I think it's from the lack of activity."

"Umm, or maybe it's because every third second you're gnawing on a Krispy Kreme? You eat them all the time," she said before opening her mouth wide and flailing her hands toward her face as if she was stuffing it with food.

I cringed with embarrassment for Peter as he dug his fork into the potatoes again. "Once upon a time Ainsley, we ate Krispy Kremes *together*. You liked them, too," he said softly.

"Well, things change, Peter," she said coldly, before reaching for her wine glass.

From there the dinner went quickly south. Ainsley continued drinking and casting disgusted looks as Peter helped himself to a large piece of my cheesecake. Neither Glenn nor Jill made any effort to diffuse the tension, and each took exactly one bite of the cake and made some polite comments about how good the dinner was and how nice it had been of us to have them over before speed walking out of our apartment as fast as humanly possible. On her way out Jill said she'd call me as soon as she'd spoken with the editor in chief of *House & Home* about our apartment, but asked that in the meantime I take some digital photos and email them to her. Then the elevator arrived and they both slipped between the bronze doors. She wiggled her fingers goodbye at me as they closed.

Back in our apartment, John, Peter, and Ainsley had moved the party to the living room. I could tell Peter wanted to go home because he kept looking at his watch and yawning, but Ainsley was in no rush. At a quarter to eleven, she asked me if we had any dessert wines, and I went into the kitchen to retrieve the organic icewine that was chilling in the refrigerator. Once in the kitchen, I asked Maggie to bring out the wine and glasses but to leave the tray of artisanal chocolate truffles behind. "No one wanted them, so why don't you take them home," I told her, but the truth was that I was afraid that Peter and Ainsley would get into another argument if Peter dared to eat one. And there was no telling what I would do if I had to watch her berate and humiliate him one more time. I'd kept my mouth shut all through dinner because I figured that what goes on between them is a private matter and my meddling would probably only make it worse, but my tolerance for her behavior was wearing thin.

Any idiot could see that Peter's low self-esteem was contributing to his overeating, and as unintelligent as Ainsley was—or pretended to be, according to some—there was no way that she was so obtuse that she didn't notice the effect her callous comments were having on her husband. Maybe he could stand to lose a few pounds for his own health, but pointing out his gluttony in public was just plain heartless.

She had shown that she had a tremendous capacity for cruelty that night, and as I hovered between the kitchen and living room, not wanting to return to the tensely electro-charged atmosphere of the latter, but also not willing to cede the floor to a woman who had the gall to flirt with my husband on my own, supposedly sacred turf, I made up my mind that Ainsley was a dangerous person to know. Like Michelle, my turncoat of a friend who stole the BlooMu vice presidency right out from under my nose, Ainsley would stop at nothing to get what she wanted or what she truly believed she deserved. Feelings of entitlement make people do horrible things, or, rather, they allow them to do horrible things without feeling the slightest inkling of guilt. These people wake up the morning after shattering someone's livelihood, family, and psyche, and wonder nothing more but how long it will take for room service to deliver the coffee.

And I was about to learn this first hand.

13

Surprise, Surprise

At the end of April, John announced that Zenith was sending him to Miami for a conference on South American oil and gas investment opportunities. He'd mentioned it to me at some point, probably over coffee in the morning since that was practically the only time we saw each other, and I said it was fine. Actually, I think I said something like, "nice work if you can get it," and left it at that. But when his secretary emailed me the dates of the trip in mid-May and I noted them down in my daily planner, I noticed that the days he would be gone also happened to coincide with the point in my menstrual cycle when I was most fertile. I hadn't gotten pregnant the month before, and if we missed having sex that week it would be a whole other month before we could try again, which was an unbearable thought for me.

I called John at the office and told him about my discovery of the business trip, ovulation overlap. His response was to sigh with exasperation and then inform me that Zenith had already booked him into the conference and there was no way he could cancel the trip.

"So why don't I come with you?" I asked.

"I'll be at the conference all day and have business dinners every night. It's not like I'll be able to hang out with you by the pool."

"As long as you make love to me once a day, I don't care what you do for the other twenty-three hours and thirty minutes."

"Thirty minutes, huh?" he laughed.

"I'm including foreplay," I said, sure that I'd won him over. "So should I book my tickets or do you want me to email your secretary and ask her to do it?"

"Hold up, Marcy. I didn't say I thought you should come."

"But why not?"

"Because I know you, you'll get lonely if you have to spend the whole day without anything to do."

"No I won't. I could really use a vacation, a little time in the sun. I can read by the hotel pool, go on walks on the beach, do some shopping."

"You'll be eating every meal alone."

"That's okay."

"No it's not. I'm not okay with it. It wouldn't feel right abandoning you every morning. What we should do is take a real vacation together to someplace warm. Let's go to Mexico, just for the weekend. Fred Reinhardt just got back from this birthday party in Las Ventanas and said it was amazing."

I gave up. It was clear that John didn't want me to come along with him on this trip for whatever reason. And a trip to Mexico did sound appealing. Besides, he was right in that I wasn't good at spending an entire day whiling away the hours in a sun chair by myself. On our last trip to a five-star resort in Aruba, John had signed us up for an excursion to a nearby island reef for snorkeling and scuba. I've never been much of an enthusiast for underwater diving—I feel a little claustrophobic under all that water, like I could have a panic attack at any second—and convinced John to go on without me. I stayed behind, with plans to read my novel, a wonderful beach book I'd been saving for weeks, and hit the resort's gym to sweat out some of the alcohol I'd been imbib-ing nonstop since we'd arrived, but ended up spending the day locked up in our hotel room eating the cheese (and not even good cheese at that) out of the minibar. By the time John returned from his day trip, I was miserable and furious with myself—not exactly the kind of person you'd like to be moored in paradise with. No wonder he didn't want me to come to Miami.

Still, I was disappointed. Everything had been going so well between us. We were both busy—I worked at least a couple nights a week for A Moveable Feast and John often had to work late or go to dinner with a fund client, potential client, or energy industry powerbroker—but on the rare nights when we were to-gether, things were great. John seemed happy and more energetic, and was once again acting affectionately toward me. He kissed me on the neck every morning before he left for work, sent me flowers for no reason, and squeezed my waist when he brushed his teeth behind me at the bathroom sink at night. He was finally satisfied with the state of our apartment and said so often, and, to my enormous relief, he no longer seemed to care about whether or not the other married couples at his hedge fund liked us, or rather, me.

Because *everyone* liked John.

And as they should: He was Zenith's new golden boy.

For all his previous bluster about needing a wife who could help him land rich clients for the firm, John was doing a pretty spectacular job on his own, without one drop of my assistance. Sure, I'd gotten him into Jill's dinner and Gigi's book party, but he'd found his own way into dozens of other similar events. And each dinner or cocktail party seemed to spawn a meeting with a rich European magnate, Russian oligarch, or trust fund-addled playboy. But not only was John landing new capital from untapped overseas sources, his portfolio was flying high, with double-digit returns well within grasp. He said that it was like he couldn't make a bad call, like he had been sprinkled in magic dust, and if things kept going this way, we'd be able to buy a massive house in the Hamptons or Greenwich, if we wanted. He was even talking about breaking off from Zenith and going it alone. The only down side to John's success was that he was under a considerable amount of stress, enough to affect his libido.

I tried—believe me, I tried—to make John want me. Every night I prepared for bed carefully, taking a shower and shaving my legs, then adding the tiniest dab of John's favorite perfume behind my ear before changing into a soft cotton nightgown (that could be easily removed or pushed aside). I tried initiating sex in the evening and in the morning, but John was never interested. He either was too tired or had to get to the office, or, as he told me one day, had too much on his mind. "I'm sorry, Marcy," he said, propping himself up on his elbows. It was half-past five in the morning and still dark outside, but I could see his face well enough to read the remorse on his face. "This has nothing to do with you. It's work. The stakes are so high and I'm afraid I'm going to blow it." I told him that he was brilliant and no matter what happened I loved him. Then I decided to stop bothering him until I knew I was ovulating again. The last thing he needed was a wife who was badgering him for sex all the time.

The morning that John left for Miami I called Gigi. John's secretary had emailed his itinerary—a practice John had put in effect during my pregnancy so that I'd be able to reach him in an emergency—and according to his schedule John's return flight was booked for Monday morning, which meant that I wouldn't see him until Monday evening because he would go directly from the airport to the office. I knew that if I didn't line up a lunch or drinks with one of my friends for over the weekend, I'd probably end up padding around our place, watching more bad news about the economy on CNBC (unemployment was up to 7 percent, 95,000 jobs had been cut in the previous month), and feeling worried about the world in general. I left a message on Gigi's voicemail asking her to call me back when she had a second.

She rang back a couple minutes later and explained that she'd been on the phone with Jeremy. Gigi never took calls while they were talking; she'd once told me that Jeremy hated it if she ever dared to click over to the other line, since according to him his time was too valuable to spend it on the phone holding for her. I snorted and pointed out that if there was anyone he should be willing to spend time on hold for, it should be her, but Gigi stuck up for him and said that, *anyway*, it was so hard to get him on the phone that by the time she did, she usually needed to talk to him more than whoever else was trying to get a hold of her.

"You sounded sad in your voicemail," Gigi said as soon as we connected. "Is everything all right?"

"Yes and no," I replied, telling her about how John wanted us to go away together for a romantic weekend but was missing my peak fertility days.

"Where is he, again?"

"Miami," I replied.

"Well, that's a no-brainer. Let's go!"

"Gigi, John doesn't want me there. I wish he did, but he doesn't."

"You know what my mama used to tell me? You can wish in one hand and shit in the other and see which one fills up faster. Now if you ask me he didn't want you there because he didn't want you to be stuck in a hotel room eating a wheel of Brie and watching soap operas while you waited for him to get back to the hotel. Can't blame a man for not wanting to be pounced on and expected to perform the moment he walks through the door to his hotel room," she chuckled.

"First of all, I'm not even capable of pouncing," I said defensively. "And second, I've been watching my cheese intake."

"My point is that now that you're going down with me, on Jeremy's plane, he has no reason to worry."

"For real?"

"Yes. We're going. And we'll be there in time so you can meet John for an after-dinner drink in his hotel."

"I should bring a dress," I said, thinking aloud.

"And sexy heels," Gigi added. "What hotel is he staying in?"

I had to go over to my computer to look up the itinerary again. It included all John's flight and hotel booking information, plus all the seminars and dinners he was expected to attend. I learned early on in my career to treat my assistants, and John's, like gold. Our secretaries received flowers and day spa vouchers on their birthdays, chocolates and cashmere sweaters on holidays. In return my assistant made sure I was in the loop about office gossip and anything else she thought I needed to know, and John's secretary, Elizabeth, kept me up to date on his travel schedules and whereabouts when I needed to reach him.

"He's staying at the Mandarin Oriental," I told Gigi. "Looks like Zenith booked him a suite."

"Ooh, that's a great hotel. They have a sexy little martini bar, an infinity pool, and these great cabana beds."

I logged online and took a look at the hotel's Web site for myself. "Of course, wouldn't you know it: The rooms have bamboo flooring. That's so John."

"You should wait till we get down there to tell him. Make it a surprise."

I agreed. John wasn't the most spontaneous guy and he might try and stop me from coming down. If I were already there, he'd have no choice but to meet with me. We'd have a drink in the bar—John loved a good martini—relax, and perhaps a dip in the

free-standing marble bathtub the hotel's Web site listed under the
suite's amenities before moving over to the bed.

I was so excited I could barely stand it. "Gigi, you are the best
friend a girl could ask for."

"Oh don't be silly, sugar," she purred. "Jeremy was planning
on going down to check in on Lauren, and now I have a reason to
tag along, too. Can you meet me here at two o'clock and we'll head
to Teterboro together?"

Jeremy Cohen owned a Gulfstream V, a private jet that could
comfortably transport up to sixteen people, fly nonstop from
New York to Tokyo if need be, and cost forty million dollars
straight off the lot, plus another one million a year in operational
and maintenance fees. Up until quite recently it had been *the* top
private plane and the mode of transport of choice for the American
superrich. Gigi said Jeremy bought one because Larry Ellison,
the co-founder of Apple computers and Jeremy's idol, had one.
(Larry Ellison also had one of the world's biggest yachts, but I
knew not to bring that up in Jeremy's presence.)

Gigi, Chloe, Betty, and I made it to Teterboro at six o'clock,
about thirty minutes before Jeremy did, so we waited in the lounge
until he arrived. When he finally make an entrance, he barely
said hello to me and boarded the plane ahead of us. There was
hardly any time to check out the cabin before wheel's up, but I
saw at the front of the plane, just behind the cockpit, two cushy
beige leather armchairs, each with its own lacquered maple fold-
out desk. Behind the chairs was a sliding glass door, followed by
a long sofa upholstered in a Chinese brocade, and a square table
surrounded by four smaller leather chairs on swivel stands. Another couple freestanding chairs faced a large flat-panel television
screen on a back wall, behind which stood a good-sized bathroom and a small kitchenette stocked with champagne, fresh
juices, fruit and vegetable plates, and even some nice-looking

cheese (but no crackers, since Jeremy avoided noncomplex carbo-hydrates).

After we took off, I helped myself to a glass of fresh-squeezed orange juice and a little plate of snacks and settled into my seat. Gigi set Chloe down for a nap in the portable crib Betty had as-sembled for her and joined me at the table, while Jeremy closed the glass divider between the back of the plane where we were and the front, where he was, and whipped out his laptop.

"I was going to thank him for letting me hitch a ride," I said, frowning in Jeremy's direction.

"You can do that later, after the Asian markets open," she said.

"And when's that?"

Gigi looked at her watch. "In about an hour or so. Tokyo opens at seven East Coast time, and Jeremy usually clocks out at about eight. Then he'll come back here and open the champagne and relax a little with us before heading to the way back of the plane to watch one of his documentaries. Right now he's working through a series on the planet Mars. Bores me to tears, so I just usually flip through my contraband," she said, opening her croco-dile carry-on to reveal a stack of celebrity magazines.

"Goody," I said, clapping my hands together and rubbing them. "Champagne, trash magazines, and my pick of six leather seats? I think I can get used to this."

"Okay, Orphan Annie, you can give it a rest," Gigi teased.

At eight o'clock on the dot Jeremy logged off his laptop, re-moved his iPhone ear bud, and opened the glass divider. He said a polite hello, took off his Nehru jacket, rolled up his shirtsleeves (revealing an expensive-looking watch), and poured us all glasses of Crystal. Then he sat down at the table, just as Gigi had said he would, and asked her how her day had gone.

She filled him in on her publisher's decision to cancel a few more stops on her book tour, and her television agent's grim suggestion that she "lie low" for the foreseeable future, as well as our plan to surprise John in Miami. He seemed disinterested in Gigi's problems and offered her little in the way of helpful advice and encouragement, seemingly bored by our banter.

I couldn't help but wonder what Gigi saw in him besides his material wealth and the creature comforts it allowed her, but I pushed the thought out of my mind because it felt disloyal to Gigi—how could I pretend to understand their relationship—and hypocritical, given John's recent treatment of me.

I thanked Jeremy for the ride down and marveled at how *nice* the plane was, which was, in hindsight, the wrong thing to say to a nothing's-ever-good-enough man like Jeremy.

"Well, it's not a BBJ3," he said with a sheepish grin, referring to a larger, more expensive plane than his G5. "But it suits our needs just fine." Then he asked Gigi if she had cued up the correct DVD, and when she nodded her indication that yes, she had indeed placed the third episode of the Mars series in the player and all he had to do was press the play button, he wished me good luck with my mission and meandered to the back of the plane, where he covered his ears with yet another set of headphones and watched his documentary until we had arrived in Miami.

Gigi and Jeremy dropped me off at the modern, brightly lit Mandarin Oriental Hotel with instructions to call if I had any problems getting in touch with John. They had an extra room and could send one of their housekeepers to pick me up at any time. I told them not to worry, that I was sure everything would go swimmingly and would call tomorrow so I could meet Gigi, Chloe, and Betty for lunch at the Casa Casuarina on Ocean Drive in South Beach. Gigi said I couldn't miss going to see Gianni Versace's former home, an over-the-top rococo mansion, which had been converted into a private, invitation-only club for wealthy Miamians, and then we'd drive south to the Shops at Bal Harbour, an upscale mall, for a little shopping. There was an Agent Provocateur boutique there, and I figured that some racy lingerie, perhaps a sheer baby doll or lacy merriwidow, would help put John in the mood after spending the day listening to lectures and networking with other energy traders and analysts.

Standing outside the entrance to the hotel, I took a deep breath of the warm, salty ocean air and walked into the lobby. It had soaring ceilings, easily four or five stories tall, and the floor-to-ceiling windows looked out on the Biscayne Bay and farther afield the Miami skyline. The interior was decorated with lots of curved Art Deco-style armchairs, sofas upholstered in warm colors, and glass coffee tables, and imparted an immediate sense of calm and luxury. It was also virtually empty. Nationwide the tourism sector had been in the doldrums for several months, but you didn't see this as starkly in New York as you did in a city like Miami, which relied more on leisure, rather than business travelers.

At the hotel's front desk a very pretty woman dressed in a freshly pressed Mao-collared jacket asked me if I had a reservation or needed to book a room for the evening. She looked down at her sleek, flat panel screen and positioned her manicured hands over her computer keyboard.

"Umm, the thing is that my husband is staying here," I said, swallowing hard. Jeremy had warned me that they may not give me the key to John's room even if I could prove I was his wife, and I was nervous that the front desk would blow my surprise arrival.

The woman behind the desk looked back up at me, her expression the perfect mixture of pleasant and expectant that must be taught in tourism schools. "His name?" she asked finally.

"John. Emerson. He's here for the oil conference."

The woman typed quickly and squinted at the screen. "Oh yes, he is here. He's with us until Monday. And he has one of the

Brickell suites, which are quite nice," she said, looking back up at me with that same pleasant expression.

"Ooh," I said. "I can't wait."

As she tapped some more keys, I unearthed the print-out of John's itinerary out of my purse. "I have the hotel booking confirmation right here," I said, handing it to her.

"Ah, wonderful," she said, taking the paper. She looked at the computer screen and then frowned. "Is he expecting you? The only problem is that I don't see a note in the computer. Although it does say that he has requested two key cards."

"I can show you my driver's license," I offered. "Or a credit card with my name on it."

She placed a beige phone on the counter, dialed a number, and handed me the receiver. "If you could just ask your husband to let us give you a key that would make things easier."

It rang and rang, but there was no answer. Then I tried his cell. No answer.

"He might be sleeping already? I know he had a long day. If you just tell me the room number, I can go up there and knock on the door."

The woman studied me for a second clearly debating whether she should follow protocol, which was probably along the lines of not releasing room numbers or keys without the express consent of the guest, or trusting her instincts and giving me the darn room number. To my surprise she looked back down at her screen, jabbed a few more keys and produced a little envelope on the counter. Inside I found a key card and the room number.

"Enjoy your stay, Mrs. Emerson," she said warmly.

Feeling giddy with excitement, I rode the elevator up to the seventeenth floor and found John's room at the end of the hall. After slipping in the key card, I pushed the door open and walked into the suite, careful not to make too much noise in case he was already sleeping. As I tiptoed through the living room I noticed that the door to the balcony was open, letting in a delicious breeze of warm night air, and that the hotel had left a complimentary plate of chocolates and a bottle of champagne on the glass coffee table. I'd help myself to that once I'd showered, but first I wanted to put down my bag and hang up my clothes before I was too tired. Sliding open the rice paper screen door separating the living room and the bedroom, I realized that the woman at the reception desk must have given me the wrong key.

There was a naked woman in the bed.

But then I realized that I knew the woman, or rather, I knew her *hair*, an unmistakable tumble of flaxen waves. It was Ainsley, and John's hands were grasping her tiny waist as she gyrated herself against him.

"I'm gonna come," she moaned. "Come with me."

I opened my mouth to speak but nothing came out. My throat had closed, and my legs felt like they were encased in cinderblocks. I couldn't talk, couldn't move. I could only watch.

Thirty seconds of agony later, I managed to speak. "John," I gasped, my voice barely above a whisper. "Stop," I said louder.

But he didn't hear me. He was too busy having an orgasm.

"Oh fuck, I'm coming," he said.

"Come inside me," Ainsley said, grinding harder, faster. And I couldn't help but notice the smooth firmness of her backside.

In a crescendo of yelps and moans, she and John came—*at the same time.*

John and I had never managed that.

And then he said it:

"I love you, baby."

And I wanted to die.

14

Of Course

Standing there, watching as my husband professed his love to a woman twice as glamorous, sophisticated, and well-connected as I was, my only thought was *of course*: Of course they were having an affair; of course John would choose Ainsley over me; and of course Ainsley would want to steal my husband. We were rich now! No, scratch that. John was rich and I was going to be the one he traded in for *her*, his trophy. His blonde, thin, socially well-connected trophy. She was all that I wasn't, John's ideal wife. Everything clicked into place. The whole nightmarish, tawdry scenario unfurled in my mind, leading to this horrible moment and this horrible hotel room and the realization that I had practically handed John to her on a silver platter exploded in my brain like a marshmallow in a microwave.

How could I have not seen this coming?

"John." The voice was not mine, it was Ainsley's. She had sensed me or seen me, or both. My husband was lying underneath her, his penis growing limp inside the wet cavern between her legs as he sucked on her right nipple. She pushed off him, grasping at the white bed sheets and wrapping her naked, cellulite-free body in them.

Why suddenly so shy? I thought angrily. I wanted to rip every single strand of hair off her head. My anger was as red as her nails, redder.

He grabbed at her playfully. "You're not getting away so easily. I just started fucking you."

"John. It's Marcy," she said.

"What, is my phone ringing again?"

She jerked her head backward, toward me, but didn't look back. That would mean that she would have to face me, and what she had done. "She's here," she whispered, as if I couldn't hear her, as if I wasn't standing mere feet away from her naked, deceitful little ass. John turned his head around slowly. He was on his knees and as he twisted I could see his torso in profile, and that he was, although not fully erect, still very much aroused.

The man who had claimed to be too stressed out, too preoccupied with his work to make love to his wife, now had enough stamina to fuck Ainsley Partridge twice in a row, without rest. It had been *years* since we'd done that. I hated her, him, myself.

John cursed and scrambled toward the bench at the foot of his bed for his boxers as Ainsley slipped into the bathroom and shut the door.

"What are you doing here?" he asked.

I wanted to tell him that he wasn't in a position to start asking questions, but I was having trouble breathing, making speaking a very distant priority. Every inhalation felt sharp and short, like the breath you take right after someone's punched you in the stomach or you've fallen off a bike and hit the ground at several miles per hour. I kept expecting the sensation to go away, but it didn't. I held my hand to my chest and pressed against it, willing my breath to regulate itself and my heart to slow down.

"How could you?" I finally sputtered.

"Marcy, I didn't want to hurt you. And I certainly didn't want you to find out about us this way."

"Us, us? You and me, we're the *us*."

"Let me get dressed and we can—" he started to say, but I didn't want to hear another word or look at his face for another second. I wanted to gouge out his eyes and rip off his lips. There was nothing that John could say at that moment that wouldn't make what I had witnessed that much more awful.

So I fled.

I picked up my overnight bag and ran out of the hotel room, down the hall and into the elevator. Then I took a cab to Miami International. I knew I could have called Gigi and spent the night at her house, but that would mean that I would have to tell her what happened and that would somehow make it more real. If I could keep it a secret for just a bit longer then I could pretend I hadn't lost John to Ainsley and that my life wasn't over.

Waiting overnight in the airport, I held in my tears. I did not want to cry in public, not because it would be hugely embarrassing (although it would have been), but because I could not do it properly with other people watching, and the Miami airport was surprisingly busy at three a.m. I stopped at a vending machine and bought a Coke and a bag of pretzels and found a comfortable enough chair in a waiting area near my plane's gate. Then I fished out my novel and tried to read it, or tried to look like I was reading it, while I was really replaying the events of the previous hours in my head, over and over. My mind was stuck on a sickening loop: Ainsley's perfect body straddling my husband, John's semi-erection, his face, pained and pitying, still flushed from the vigor of their sex. My memory allowed me to freeze each excruciating frame and bisect the whole sordid scene so that I could see not only the events but my own twisted face as it clenched and contorted in response to the acts I was witnessing. I could see my reaction as clearly as I had seen the sweat dripping between Ainsley's perky breasts or the pleasure on John's face before he realized that I was there. I willed myself to stop, but I couldn't.

And yet somehow I made it through the night and boarded the plane. I sat alone, and drank one sip of the watery, impotent coffee before falling asleep. I awoke again in New York, with the stewardess shaking my shoulder lightly. "Miss, we've arrived," she said, more annoyed than concerned. I wiped a small amount of drool from the side of my face and was halfway down the aisle before remembering that my overnight bag (still stuffed with the sexy dress and heels that would forever go unused) remained in the bin above my seat.

Still dazed, I took a taxi back to my apartment and turned on my phone. There were messages from Gigi, who wanted to know if we were still on for lunch at Casa Casuarina, and from John, who begged me to call him back, urgently. I'd even received a call from his secretary, reiterating John's desire that I call him as soon as possible. I decided to go home, shower and call Gigi. Hopefully she would know what I should do, because I certainly didn't.

"Get a lawyer," Gigi said once I'd finished telling her what had happened.

"It's over, isn't it?" I sniffled. In the shower I had finally allowed myself to cry, and I'd started sobbing again once I heard Gigi's voice.

"Well, no, it doesn't have to be if you both don't want it to be. Maybe John said that he loved Ainsley in the heat of the moment. Maybe he didn't mean it. But I still think it would be smart for you to meet with a lawyer so you can start protecting your assets in case he does want a divorce."

Gigi gave me the name of a lawyer who had helped a friend of hers, and I promised to call him right away. Right after I hung up, I received another call from John and decided to answer it. Maybe he didn't really want to leave me for Ainsley, and although it would be incredibly hard to trust him again, I was willing to try. We had built a life together and I had sacrificed my career for him. What other choice did I have but to try and save our marriage? Plus, I was thirty-five; my fertility had entered a period of "rapid deterioration." (I'm quoting Dr. Navarro verbatim.) If John and I got divorced now it might be *years* before I got married again, and then wouldn't my chances of getting pregnant be close to zero?

"You're all right," John said, exhaling with relief.

"I'm alive, John, but not all right."

"I know, and I'm sorry," he paused. "Marcy, I'm so, so sorry. You have to believe me."

"When are you coming back?" I asked. I didn't want to have this conversation over the phone.

"Monday," he said.

"Monday," I repeated. Monday meant that he was staying for the remainder of the conference instead of racing back home to me. Monday meant that *she* might—no, probably—was staying with him until then and that they were probably still having sex. Monday also meant that he really did love her and was leaving me.

"She's there with you still," I stated.

"She is."

"It wasn't a question," I snapped.

"Marcy," John said, his voice soft and irritatingly piteous.

"Did you fuck her again after I left?" After I said the words, a sharp cry involuntarily escaped from my mouth, and I had to drop the phone to cover my mouth to keep myself from wailing. I vowed to myself then and there that John would not hear me crying for him. He would tell Ainsley, and she would pretend for his benefit to be very sorry for me even though deep down she couldn't care less about my feelings. She would act contrite because she was smart enough to know that that was what John expected and wanted from her.

Oblivious, my friggin cellulite-covered ass. If anyone had been oblivious around here, it was me.

"We should meet. When I'm back in New York on Monday. Can I take you to lunch?" he asked.

"I don't want to meet you for lunch," I said angrily.

"We have to talk."

"Fine. Come home. Tomorrow."

"Okay, then. Tomorrow. I'll see you at the apartment at eight."

On Sunday, I spent the day cleaning the apartment even though I didn't need to—we had a housecleaner come in three times a week to ensure that I didn't. But I couldn't sit still and it felt good to scrub and reorganize. I went through my drawers and tossed a lot of things out, mostly old sweaters and jeans that I hadn't worn in a while. I threw old food out of the fridge, condiments and leftovers, a carton of orange juice. I itched to take my kitchen shears to John's beloved suits and ties and his four-figure shoes, but I didn't. It would only serve to liberate him from his guilty conscience. John was still a Midwesterner at heart. He needed to think of himself as good and ethical. If I were to shred up his beloved collection of Turnbull & Asser custom shirts, he would then be able to say that I was a crazy bitch and that his straying wasn't his fault, but mine.

So instead of destroying his belongings, I packed some of them up for him in a suitcase and garment bag. I was careful to make sure nothing would get wrinkled, stuck socks in his shoes, rolled his ties into neat balls and folded in some extra boxers in case he would only be able to send out his laundry once a week. I snuck in extra toothbrushes and toothpaste, new razors and shaving cream—everything he would need to get by. And as I did this, I decided that I would let him go and be with Ainsley for now. Eventually he would see her for what she really was and come back to me.

* * *

John arrived at a quarter past eight. He used his key, which irked me, and called my name as soon as he passed through the door. I met him in the living room and offered him a drink by shaking my half-drunk glass of organic vodka and cranberry juice in my hand. He shook his head at my offer and took a seat on the couch.

"I packed your bags," I said. "They're in the—"

"Foyer. I saw them," he said. "Thanks."

"So, you're leaving me?"

"Why don't you sit down?"

"Because I want to stand. Now, just tell me, John. Tell me that you want a divorce."

And then he told me what I already knew in one way or another, that he and Ainsley had what he conveniently dubbed a "chemical attraction." He had found himself inexplicably drawn to her, he said, and had initially fought his urge to "be" with her, but in the end the pull between them was too strong. He told me that he had been unhappy in our marriage for a long time, even before my miscarriage or our move to New York, but that those two events had served to deepen the cavern between us. The pressure I had put on him to get pregnant again had exacerbated his feelings of being "stuck" in our marriage, but even so he planned to stay with me. Until Ainsley came along, that is. She was unhappy in her marriage, too. They had this in common, and they talked about it. And then, before either of them knew what was happening, they were falling in love.

He wanted to talk in generalities, but I needed specifics. "When did you two first have sex?" I demanded.

"How does that make any difference now?" he responded testily.

He fidgeted with his watch and I wondered if he had made plans to meet Ainsley somewhere for dinner. Then it occurred to me that Ainsley still might be living with Peter.

"Does Peter know?"

"Yes," he said, sitting up taller in his seat. "She's telling him now." He could not conceal his pride, and I could see clearly how he considered Ainsley as a prize, a prize that he had *won*.

"She's telling Peter now? So you two coordinated this?" I seethed. It took every ounce of strength in my body not to hurl my drink at his face.

"We're in love. We're going to get married."

He said this firmly and was sure to look me in the eye, so that I would see his resolve and know how serious he was. He probably thought that it was the right thing to do to be direct and clear about his intentions, so that I would not hold out any hope for reconciliation. Like a considerate executioner at the guillotine, he'd sharpened his blade in hope of making it quick for me.

"For someone so smart, you sure are easy to manipulate," I said. "Do you really think Ainsley would give you the time of day if you weren't suddenly making tons of money? She's not interested in you. She doesn't love you. She loves your money. And she'll leave you, just like she's leaving Peter, the second you lose yours."

"I'm not going to lose mine," John said.

"For your sake, I sure hope you don't," I responded.

"And for yours. I plan to take care of you, Marcy. Why don't you move back to Chicago? I know you miss living there. I'll buy you an apartment, something like we used to have. You were happy there."

"Was, as in past tense."

"And a car, something sensible of course, and I'll give you a monthly allowance, enough to pay for food and utilities, etcetera, until you find a job," he added.

"Was this Ainsley's idea?" I asked. Call me crazy, but finding out that another woman had stolen my husband from right under my nose had made me a touch paranoid.

"No," he said firmly. "This is my attempt to make things right."

"It's too late for that," I said, crossing my arms.

He got up from the couch and walked toward the foyer. I followed him.

"Marcy, I'm really sorry about all of this. But I believe we can both be happier with other people. Will you take my offer?"

He leaned in to give me a hug. I wanted to shove him off and ask him how he dared to touch me again, that while his new gold digger of a fiancée could be bought off with money, there was no way he could buy my forgiveness. Not in a million years or with a million dollars—no, make that a hundred million dollars. But then I took a deep breath and reminded myself to be smart about this. John and I were getting a divorce. He'd made it clear that he wanted one, and even in the off-off chance that he miraculously came to his senses and realized what a manipulative, cold-hearted bitch Ainsley was, I knew I couldn't take him back. Not after this, not after he hurt me so deeply.

I would let him go and give him the divorce he wanted, but not without *compensation.* I had forfeited the Bloomington Mutual vice presidency for him, uprooted myself and moved to New York for him, decorated the apartment and searched high and low for furniture, flooring, and fixtures made of sustainable materials for him. I had established a household budget, hired staff, organized vacations, and cooked and cleaned for him. For seven years I had put his needs before mine. There was no way that wasn't worth *way* more than the cost of a run-down one-bedroom apartment in Chicago, "sensible" new car, and temporary monthly allowance.

I'd bet my lactose tolerance on that.

But I kept all these thoughts to myself and allowed him to hug me.

"Thank you so much, John. It's truly a generous offer, but I'll have to think it over," I said.

"Of course," he said, before picking up his bags and walking out the door.

15

Drinks Anyone?

The second John left I drained my drink. If I was going to get through the following weeks, I needed a little help, if you know what I mean. I wasn't about to start popping pills when alcohol was cheaper, didn't require the involvement of my doctor, and had the added benefit of being highly refreshing. I fixed myself another cocktail and dialed Gigi, who was at dinner with Jeremy, but picked up anyway. I filled her in on what John had said and she applauded my cool head during what could have become a much more heated conversation. Then she gave me *again* the number for the tough-as-nails lawyer, whom she praised as a "real bastard, the best kind." I thanked her profusely (at that point I was halfway through my second drink and feeling more than a bit buzzed) and clicked off.

Then I got well and truly drunk and watched a marathon of *Denise Richards: Its Complicated* that I'd taped with my DVR. I'd always liked her, but now that we had so much in common—she was divorced, I was getting one—I loved her even more. If she could survive her nasty, highly publicized divorce with her humor and dignity (somewhat) intact, surely I could survive mine. I mean, it's not like either John or I was famous, and we both were pretty reasonable people.

Yes, I would get through this, I thought.

And then I passed out.

The following morning, after drinking a few cups of coffee and downing enough Tylenol to kill a small dog, the first call I made was to Henry Sullivan, the lawyer whose name and number Gigi had given me. His secretary answered and grilled me on the purpose of my call, then informed me that Mr. Sullivan was extremely busy and could not meet with any prospective new clients for several weeks. I asked her what it would take to get a meeting with him sooner than that and she said something along the lines of "Mr. Sullivan exclusively handles cases involving high net worth individuals," and I had no other choice but to tell her that my soon-to-be ex husband worked for Zenith Capital and was a very successful hedge fund trader. Without skipping a beat and with a beguiling lack of chagrin, she told me that she could pencil me in for a meeting on Thursday afternoon.

My next call was to Gigi, who told me she was already back in New York and wanted to meet me for lunch. She had called Jill, and they had already made reservations at Serafina, a child-friendly (Gigi was bringing Chloe) pizza and pasta café on the Upper East Side. I didn't really want to go—my plan had been to take a shower and riffle through John's papers and financial documents in the office—but Gigi wouldn't hear of it. It was dangerous to keep my feelings bottled up inside me; I should let my friends help me through this, she insisted. After hanging up the phone, I took a fast shower, threw on some clothes, and flew out the door.

My destination was Bergdorf Goodman, temple of luxury, mecca for hedge fund wives everywhere. There, I worked fast and with purpose, starting with shoes. One pair of black platform pumps, one pair of nude peep toes, one pair of strappy golden sandals, and one pair of chartreuse suede slingbacks and I was done. I found a few dresses in ivory, plum, and black, and two suits in navy and black. (Fashion designers, taking a cue from the stock market, had lowered hemlines and returned to solid bets like well-tailored skirt suits and sheath dresses.) On another floor I added two silk blouses and a couple pairs of jeans to my haul, before heading back down to the first floor, where I selected three pairs of sunglasses, a quilted navy purse with a gold chain, a structured black shoulder bag, a printed silk envelope, and a glossy alligator skin clutch, plus one very, very expensive gold necklace. With only an hour and a half before I was due at Serafina for lunch, I popped in for a quick visit to the John Barrett salon on the ninth floor, where I had my eyebrows professionally tweezed and my hair deep conditioned and cut into a sleek, shoulder-grazing bob.

I couldn't wait until John received my AmEx bill.

Even though it was in the middle of lunchtime, the restaurant's sunny, glass-enclosed back room was close to empty, and there were several busboys and waiters in black pants and white shirts leaning against the brick wall, biding their time. By the time I arrived an uncharacteristic fifteen minutes late (unpardonable, I know), Gigi and Jill were already situated at a square table with little Chloe propped up in a wooden high chair, gnawing on a piece of bread. When they saw me carrying all my bags, with my new sleek hair and big black sunglasses, their jaws immediately dropped and their worried expressions quickly shifted to ones of shock.

"I see someone's not wasting any time getting even," Jill said, embracing me warmly. "I didn't figure you for the type to go on a shopping binge."

"More like rampage," Gigi quipped.

A busboy moved aside one of five empty tables in our periphery to accommodate all my purchases.

"This is just the beginning," I responded coolly. I sat down, slid my sunglasses off my face, and placed them on the table next to my water glass.

Gigi gasped. "Oh sugar, I can tell you've been crying. Your eyes are all puffy."

"Thus, the sunglasses," I said, waving my new pair in the air. "I bought two more pairs, just to be certain I'd have a pair to coordinate with all my clothes."

They both eyed me skeptically.

"What?" I said. "My husband is leaving me for a size two, bottle-blonde harlot. You tell me how I'm supposed to act."

"She's not a real blonde?" Jill asked.

I shook my head. "And that comes from someone who's seen her pussy in action."

"Okay, let's not get distracted," Gigi said, pursing her lips. I knew she wouldn't like me cussing, but I felt entitled to my coarseness.

The waiter came for our orders and I asked for a salad with seared tuna, the same as Jill, and Gigi ordered pasta. While we waited for our food, I recounted everything that had happened from the second I set foot in the Mandarin Oriental to John's visit the previous night, when he explained his side of the story and conveyed his wish for me to "find a man who really and truly loved me."

At that, Jill guffawed and flicked a handful of light brown hair behind her shoulder. "What a prick," she said as her BlackBerry began buzzing from inside her cavernous black patent-leather purse, which, having just seen it on a shelf at Bergdorf's, I knew cost a few thousand dollars. She dug her arm into the bag to fish out her phone, checking the screen to see whom it was before tossing it back in with the seemingly endless contents of her purse. "Work," she explained. "My assistant."

Gigi and Jill wanted to know if I was okay, and kept asking how I was feeling, but I didn't want to talk about my emotions. There would be plenty of time to discuss how betrayed, angry and hurt I felt later on, once I felt like I was walking on solid ground again. In the meantime, however, delving into my feelings was not an option. What I was willing to discuss was my own stupidity.

"I've spent the last seven years not using the brain that God gave me. I figured that if I was with him, I'd be taken care of, so why should I bust my ass at work, you know? He didn't want me to, and it's not like being a banker fed my soul."

"But John did?" Gigi asked.

"No but he did make me feel so *secure*, and I'm not just talking about money. With him I never felt alone, or like some big friendless geek. He gave me license to feel okay about myself, like, hey, if he loves me I must not be so bad."

"Oh, Marcy, how could you think that about yourself?" Gigi said.

I shrugged. "In hindsight, I know how stupid it sounds, but when John and I met I didn't think very highly of myself, or at least of my ability to make a man fall in love with me, and I was so afraid of losing him that I never stood up to him or fought for what was important to me. I gave up my career, let him call the shots about our vacations, where we lived, who we hung out with. And look where that got me? All along I thought I was being the perfect wife, but in reality, I was becoming this spineless creature that even I couldn't respect. No wonder John left me."

"You're being too hard on yourself," Jill said softly.

"No. No, I'm not. But I'm done with the self-sacrificing. You know, at the time, when John and I were getting serious and I had two very clear paths in my life—him or my career—I thought, I

were divorcing?" I asked. "I can't even fathom having to face John without some sort of intermediary present."

"She went out every single night of the week, and she stayed out as late as she could. I remember her being the last to leave a lot of the catered affairs I was doing that year. And sometimes if the party ended early she'd help us clean up. It was like she had nowhere to go."

"Why didn't she get a boyfriend?" Jill asked. "Then she could have slept over at his place from time to time."

I knew the answer as clearly as I knew my own heart. "You can't just shack up with another man after being hurt so badly. Her self-esteem, I'm sure, was in the gutter, and she probably never wanted to fall in love again. I for one am done with men. They're all selfish assholes that only care about two things: their pleasure and their ego."

Gigi patted my hand and told me that I would fall in love again. Although she had never been married before Jeremy her heart had been broken more times than she wanted to remember by men for whom she'd deeply cared. Most of her relationships hadn't lasted more than six months, and she was almost always the one who got left, not the other way around. Jill said it was because Gigi had chosen "difficult" men who were worth a lot of money and at the top of their profession—she had dated quite a few publishers, authors, and editors, as well as a healthy handful of traders and bankers—and were therefore used to having women fawn all over them.

She agreed, but insisted that it hadn't been her selection of suitors, but rather how she treated them.

"I was too nice!" Gigi cried out, her heavy metal fork hitting the side of her pasta bowl with a clang. "These powerful guys like the thrill of the hunt. If they don't have to compete for you—"

"You're not a prize worth winning," interjected Jill.

"Top prize. Ainsley was John's," I whispered.

Gigi nodded soberly. "I hate to say it, but it's true. Jeremy only asked me to marry him because I played hard to get. I would be really nice and sweet to him when we were together, but then I wouldn't call him back for a few days. I played him like all the men who had played me before. And guess what? It worked. Even now, every once in a while I give him the impression that I don't really *need* him. They need to know that you're not afraid to leave."

"It's too late for me," I said glumly, pushing away my plate.

"No, it's too late for John," said Jill. "Ainsley's got him in her grasp and she's going to suck the life out of him until there's nothing left, just like she did to Peter, and then John's going to come running back to you with his tail between his legs."

"Literally," said Gigi.

"But first, we have to get you through this divorce," Jill said, leaning forward. "Do you have a good lawyer?"

"I've not only got a great lawyer, but I've got all of John's financial statements. In my purse I have records of John's retirement accounts, stock investments, and private loans he's made to his family and friends over the years, the deed to our apartment, papers for his health and life insurance. I have his birth certificate, social security card, and passport. I have everything. I just wish I'd thought to tape his confession of his affair," I said. .

"Oh, I think it's illegal to tape someone when they don't know it," Jill said, finding her BlackBerry, which was once again buzzing in her purse.

"Work again?" I asked.

Jill looked down, her face more pale and drawn than normal. "I have something to tell you guys," she said, pausing to make sure we were both listening carefully. "I kissed Blake and now he won't leave me alone."

"Nineteen-year-old Blake? The bartender?" I exclaimed.

"Quiet," Gigi and Jill snapped at me in unison.

"When did this happen?"

"Weeks and weeks ago. At one of your events, actually."

"Jill, Jill, Jill," Gigi tsked, shaking her head.

"What? A woman my age is at the peak of her sex drive. What am I supposed to do when my husband refuses to sleep with me?"

"You only *kissed* Blake?" I asked.

It didn't seem likely that Jill would just kiss him—I mean, we were grown women, not teenagers hooking up in their parents' basement—and it was also absurd that Blake would be hounding her for "weeks and weeks" if they'd only locked lips. Her story, if you asked me, sounded quite suspicious and I was pretty sure that Jill wasn't telling us the whole truth.

"Yes, we only kissed!" Jill yelped, pushing back a lock of glossy light brown hair. "But I may have given him the impression that we were going to have a relationship." She bit her lower lip and looked down at her half-eaten plate of seared tuna.

"He'll get over it, but you have to make it clear that nothing *more* is going to happen between you two. Look, the guy is nineteen, all he thinks about is sex. If he realizes that he's never going to get it from you, he'll start investing his energy in someone else, someone he hopefully won't have met while he's supposedly working at one of my events."

"And maybe someone closer to his own age," I added.

"Hey, I'm not some geriatric, okay?" Jill whined.

"Once he gets some from someone else, he'll forget he even met you. And pretty soon he won't even be able to remember your name."

"I hope you're right," Jill said. "If not, I could lose everything."

Two hours had passed and we all needed to get back to our work. Jill had to get back to *House & Home* to check on a layout she was supervising, and Gigi had to visit a new bread supplier (who hadn't yet raised prices twenty percent like most of the other bakeries around town). As for me, there was a photocopier at Kinko's with my name on it.

Thanks to my purchases from Bergdorf's, I showed up at Henry Sullivan's Park Avenue office looking like a million bucks, and ready to ask for ten times that amount. The morning of my meeting I put together my outfit with extreme care, selecting the sleeveless ivory silk blouse with ruffled front, navy slim skirt, nude heels, and quilted navy purse. Around my neck I had clasped the heavy gold link necklace from Faraone Manella and in my ears a pair of one-carat diamond studs that John had given me on one of our anniversaries, before we'd moved to New York. I had all of John's financial and personal documents organized in a folder and was ready to get down to business.

As it turned out, so was Henry Sullivan. His waiting room, which was decorated with horse prints and hunter green carpet, antique wood occasional tables, and banker's lamps was bustling with activity. It was more than evident that business was booming for Henry Sullivan. He certainly seemed to be in a good enough mood when I entered his office. While I took a seat in a plush velvet-covered wing back chair, he asked his secretary to bring us some coffee and water and then inquired why "on God's green earth" I wanted to end my marriage.

"Who said I wanted to end it? My husband is the one who wants a divorce. He's found a woman that he likes better than me and wants to marry her," I said.

"And you know this for a fact?"

"Yes, he told me. He's offered to buy me a one-bedroom apartment in Chicago—that's where we moved here from about a year and a half ago—and a car. And he says he'll give me money until I get a job."

Henry laughed loudly, tipping his oversized head backward

so he was looking at the coffered ceiling. "So let me get this straight?" he said. He ran a thick hand through his wavy red hair and smiled broadly. "The guy sleeps with another woman, leaves you, and thinks he can buy you off with a shitty apartment, a car, and a little spending money? Oh man, this one is going to be fun," he added, rubbing his hands together.

What can I say? I liked him immediately.

Henry asked me a lot of questions, like how long John and I had been married (seven years) and whether I had signed any pre- or post-nup agreements (I hadn't) as well as if any of the assets were in my name (the apartment was in both of our names, as was our savings account). We discussed health insurance and life insurance benefits, personal financial accounts and credit card debts and use. I gave him all the documents I had photocopied and he seemed pleased with my forethought. He wrote down everything I said on a legal pad and then, when I was done telling him about John's affair with Ainsley, he informed me that New York was a no-fault, equitable distribution state, which meant that all property would be distributed equitably between the couple and it didn't matter who was at fault for breaking up the union.

"But what's equitable?" I asked.

He laughed again. "What the court decides, or a mediator, if you decide to go that route."

Henry elaborated a bit on his answer, explaining that equitable distribution was different than common law, which a few other states followed, in that property and assets that were earned, gifted or inherited were also up for division. This was an important distinction because it meant that what John brought to the table before we were actually married was also up for grabs. Since neither John nor I had started off rich, that wouldn't be too big of an issue but Henry said that I was an ideal client because I could prove that I had sacrificed my career to support my husband's and that my husband had become phenomenally successful with me at his side. Other factors that the court would consider would be whether or not we had children, our ages, and both real and potential future earnings. Most men wanted to broker deals that limited their spouse's claim on future income, but we would certainly argue for spousal support that increased commensurate with John's earnings.

"Before we start talking about what you need to be able to walk away happy, financially speaking, I want to lay down two laws. Your husband already broke one of them, and that was telling you what he was going to do, i.e., that he wanted to remarry and was leaving you for good. Divorce is like war, and in any war, information is king. We're going to want to keep him in the dark and throw a lot of disinformation at him. Are you prepared to do that?"

"Absolutely," I said.

"Do you hate your husband?"

I hesitated. I was angry at John and no longer in love with him, but hate? "I don't know," I said.

"You don't have to, but I strongly encourage it. It's easier to go through a divorce when you can view the opposing side as your enemy."

He slid a book across the table at me: *The Art of War.*

"Read it," he said. "Before our next meeting."

I nodded dutifully and tucked the book in my purse.

"This week I'm going to draw up the petition for divorce and will send it to you for review. Once you sign off on it, we'll have it delivered to your spouse. There's a chance he's already contacted a lawyer and will file for divorce first. If that happens, don't worry. Just call my office and we'll send a messenger to pick up the papers."

Henry instructed me to alert my bank of my impending divorce and have them freeze John's and my joint checking, banking, and equity accounts, if John hadn't done so already himself. I was also to freeze our joint credit cards, which made me more than a little nervous, especially since Henry said I should tender my resignation to A Moveable Feast immediately. Whatever money I made would be reported to the court and could negatively impact the alimony for which I was eligible. This obviously left me in quite a pickle.

"What am I supposed to live on in the meantime?" I asked, knowing that I didn't have any personal savings outside of our joint account to rely on. I could always sell the Bulgari earrings John had just given me, but I was sure I would get only a fraction of what they were worth. (There was a glut of second-hand jewelry on the market as half of Park Avenue was trying to liquidate theirs.) And then there was the maintenance and mortgage on our apartment; there was no way I could pay for that, even if I could continue earning a paycheck as a catering waitress.

"Don't be silly. John will cover those expenses," Henry assured me. "It would be against his own self-interest to default on either and be fined or lose the apartment."

Still, there was the matter of being able to meet my personal needs, however small, before the divorce was settled, and Henry's solution was that before freezing the bank accounts I take out a small amount of money, enough to get by for a couple of months but not so much as to anger my spouse (and put him on "attack mode") or offend the court. Remembering my recent purchases at Bergdorf Goodman, I got a little nervous and asked Henry if he thought I should return some of the unused clothes and shoes, but according to my lawyer a $25,000 shopping spree after you'd discovered your husband cheating on you didn't qualify as an egregious misappropriation of funds. I could tell by the look on his face that Henry thought he was delivering me good news, but hearing this just made me angrier. I had been a good wife. I had been responsible with our money! All this time I could have been shopping for jewels and couture, and John had never appreciated my prudence—or me.

Still, I didn't think John was the kind of guy who would leave a woman destitute and was convinced that I would only be inconveniencing myself by freezing our bank accounts. He still wanted to think of himself as a do-gooder. And besides that, wasn't he far too busy being Zenith's rockstar trader by day and Ainsley's love slave by night to concern himself with moving our assets offshore?

"Don't be so sure, Marcy. Divorce brings out the worst in people from my experience. Which is why when I go into one, I only go in with a warrior at my side. To the outside world, I want you to continue looking and acting like a hedge fund wife. Dress well and act reserved and gracious. But on the inside I want you to transform yourself into a soldier ready for battle. The only way to walk away from these things the victor, is if you're willing to go the distance. That's my second rule, you must be willing to go for the jugular."

It was just the pep talk I needed.

"Oh let there be no mistake about it. I am out for blood. He may have made me cry, but I am going to make him bleed," I said, my voice steely with determination.

16

Asset Stripper

I spent the following four months waiting for the divorce proceedings to move forward and following Henry's instructions to the letter. I didn't work, talk with anyone about the particulars of my divorce (besides Gigi, my one and only confidante), and I did my best to keep it together and present a brave and elegant face to the world. I had taken thirty thousand dollars out of our joint savings account—which barely put a dent in it, in case you're wondering—and knowing that I had to make it last for an indefinite period of time, I lived really simply compared to what I'd gotten used to as Mrs. Marcy Emerson. No more two hundred dollar dinners, three hundred dollar trips to the hair salon and day spa, no more shopping expeditions down Park and Madison Avenues snapping up decorative items for our apartment.

I thought I wouldn't miss all the trappings of life as a hedge fund wife, but the truth is that I did. Not having to worry about money was *nice*. So was being able to waltz into any store and buy anything you want. Even if I never abused my spending power (pre-divorce) just *knowing* that I could shop to my heart's content gave me a certain confidence that the saleswomen and doormen and everyone else trained to decipher the haves from the have nots could pick up on. In other words, because I was rich, most of the people I encountered every day treated me with respect. And now that I wasn't, they didn't.

And it sucked.

I missed having money, which made me disappointed in myself. I had somewhere along the way convinced myself that I could take it or leave it, and that it wasn't the measure of who I was as a person. When my parents and sister marveled at my good fortune, I'd always laugh it off and say something like "I still take my coffee the same way." This was my indirect way of insisting that no, our wealth had not changed me, not one bit. And to that same end I resisted adopting the mannerisms and appearance of a rich woman.

My humility had become a point of pride, so much so that I'd nearly built my entire (new) identity on the fact that we were wealthy but you wouldn't know it by looking at me. Oh, how self-righteous I had been about remaining "down-to-earth" despite the meteoric rise of our finances—and how hypocritical: Now I knew that it was easy to act like you don't care about money when you have loads of it.

But beyond feeling surprisingly depressed about my limited budget, I also missed working for Gigi. Doing prep work side by side with Maggie and Gemma all those nights, we had plenty of time to swap life stories and had become more than just co-workers, but real friends. When Maggie's boyfriend moved out, we comforted her and when Gemma had to withdraw from college because her father couldn't pay the tuition, I secretly vowed to loan her the money once I received my divorce settlement. There were a lot of other servers and chefs who worked for A Moveable Feast, but Gigi knew we three enjoyed one another's company and made sure we were always teamed together. After the divorce went through, I wasn't sure that I would go back to working for A

Moveable Feast, but I sure hoped that wherever I landed, I'd find the same spirit of camaraderie.

It was the middle of July when I heard from John. He called one morning and at first I didn't know who it was. After more than eight weeks without any form of direct communication with him, I'd forgotten how deep and serious his voice was, and it was strange to hear it again. He was on his way to work and the sounds of traffic and street sounds—horns honking, jackhammering—as well as a spotty connection made it next to impossible for me to hear him. I told him to call me later, once he was on a landline, but he was insistent on talking to me then and there. I knew why: Once he got to the office time was money, and apparently I wasn't worth either of his anymore. The old Marcy would have sat on the phone and put up with the static buzzing in my ear. I would have expended my mental energy trying to decipher the meaning of his broken sentences, but the new me was not as tolerant. I hung up the phone and didn't answer it again for another forty-five minutes, when I was sure he'd gotten to his office and was already on the clock.

"Hello," I answered.

It was John's secretary. "Mrs. Emerson I have Mr. Emerson on the phone for you," she said, her voice two octaves higher than usual.

"Elizabeth, how are you?" I asked, knowing full well that John was most likely sitting at his desk in the next room, waiting for me to be put through.

"I am, umm, well. I'm okay," she stuttered nervously. "And you?"

"I've been better, but given the circumstances I could be much worse. Thanks for asking," I said.

"I'm putting you through to Mr. Emerson, Mrs. Emerson."

"Elizabeth, you know me. Call me Marcy."

She patched me through and John came on the line.

"Marcy," he said.

Henry had said I should take it as a good sign if John tried to reach out to me. He either wanted to settle, or he knew that he was losing and wanted to try and trick me into revealing some of my playbook. (As if I would let that happen!) Henry instructed me to talk to John if he called, but I wasn't to tell him anything about my current life (whether I was working or interviewing for jobs, or if I was dating anyone new, for example) or agree to anything without consulting him first.

"Are you there?" John asked.

"Yes," I responded coolly. "I'm just waiting for you to tell me why it is that you are calling me."

"This divorce stuff is getting crazy. It's time we settle and move on with our lives."

"If you want to settle, you can communicate that through our lawyers."

"I'm obviously trying to simplify matters and speed things up by calling you directly," he said, testily. "All the lawyers want to do is drag this out so they can keep racking up billable hours. And the more we spend on the divorce, the less money there is for us to divide up."

"Divide, huh? Fifty-fifty?"

He grumbled. "I have a very generous proposition for you."

"I know what I'm entitled to so why don't you let me decide what's generous?" I said.

"Jesus, Marcy. What's gotten into you?"

"Umm, let me think," I said sarcastically.

"How about I drop by tonight? To the apartment, and lay it all out for you?"

I wasn't sure if I was ready to see John again, but he sounded desperate, and I was confident that I had the upper hand. "Be here by seven," I said. "And don't be late."

When I called Henry to tell him that John was coming over, he advised me to have John put his settlement terms in writing and that I should not sign or verbally consent to anything. "Let the jackass throw you some bones," he said. "At least we'll know what he's comfortable giving up. If it's a decent sum, we'll push for more, and if it's paltry then we'll know that we're in for a long court battle," he said.

I spent the day cleaning the apartment (I had fired the various housekeepers we employed weeks ago). After mopping the floors and vacuuming the carpets, I scrubbed the kitchen countertops, bathroom sinks and toilets, and wiped the windows and other glass surfaces with the eco-conscious cleaners that John had asked me to buy in bulk when we were still together. Then I took a long bath, applied a facial mask and deep conditioned my hair, shaved my legs and armpits, dyed the hairs on my upper lip, plucked my eyebrows and filed and painted my nails before blowing out my hair, putting on my makeup and slipping into my plum-colored dress, nude pumps, and pearls. By seven o'clock, I was ready for combat.

The doorman buzzed me to tell me that John was on his way up, and I opened the door in anticipation of his arrival. Even though he had been making the mortgage and maintenance payments on the apartment, I still didn't want him using his keys to enter the apartment. This was my turf now.

He walked out of the elevator with his key poised, just as I suspected he would, and a determined look on his face. I knew John well enough to know that he had been going over in his head what he wanted to say to me, as if he was preparing for a meeting with an energy company CEO. When he saw me, and realized that I had read his face—and mind—his cheeks flushed and facial features rearranged to convey his aggravation at being caught unaware.

"Good evening," he said once he had regained his composure. He quickly gave my body the once over, allowing his eyes to linger for a moment at my waist.

"I've lost weight," I said.

"I noticed. You look good."

He was lying. I looked like hell. Skinnier, made-up and dressed-up, but hell all the same.

"Come in," I said, pushing the door open with my back so he had to walk by me.

He hesitated for a second, annoyed by the obvious power game I was playing, before striding into the foyer and walking straight through to the living room, where I had put out one of his prized bottles of French Grand Cru. I knew it would make him nervous to see it there and would lead him to wonder if I had been slowly making my way through his extensive collection of expensive wines. (I had.)

"The Mouton Rothschild!" he exclaimed.

"Would you like a glass?" I asked, pouring one.

He swallowed hard and took a seat on the couch. "Yes," he said through gritted teeth.

I handed him the glass along with one of our recycled linen cocktail napkins and poured a portion out for myself before sitting opposite him on the Ghery Wiggle chair. Sipping my wine, I waited for him to speak.

"So, I'm here because, as I said earlier, I want to be able to move forward with my life and I think it would be to your benefit, too."

"Well, that depends on what you're offering me, now doesn't it?" I said calmly.

"Why don't you tell me what you want and we can go from there."

I laughed. "You seem to be the one who's pretty clear on what they want and don't want, so I think it makes the most sense for you to go first."

"Fine," he said, clenching his jaw. He took another big swallow of wine and made a move to pour himself more, but I was closer to the bottle and picked it up first.

"Here, you're my guest. I'll do the pouring," I insisted, pouring him a very large quantity, figuring the more he drank on an empty stomach—and I knew his was empty because he never snacked at work and always came home starving for dinner—the more likely I was to get him to give me everything I wanted, and then some.

"Thank you," he said, taking another gulp. "Marcy, let me just start out by reminding you that I never wanted to hurt you. I couldn't help falling in love with Ainsley."

"We don't need to rehash this," I said.

He took another sip of wine before placing his glass carefully on the coffee table. Then he cleared his throat, straightened his posture, and adopted his "big pitch" tone. He used it at the office when he needed to convince his superiors of something, like longing natural gas because he was sure prices were going up, or at home with me when he had wanted to go to a restaurant that I didn't particularly like.

"Ainsley and I are getting married," he said slowly. "We're getting married very soon and we're going to need a place to live. I know that you were never as in love with this apartment or neighborhood as I was, and I know that the eco-friendly décor isn't your cup of tea, so I thought you would rather start over in a new place and Ainsley and I would move in here."

"I know the value of this apartment is seven million dollars."

"I'm prepared to offer you four million," he said.

I laughed. "John, that may be slightly more than half of what the apartment is worth, but we have other assets. Our bank account, stock and private equity investments, and retirement accounts. I'm also entitled to alimony, health insurance, and life insurance, and we still have to factor in your future earning potential. Don't think I didn't see that article about you in *Trader Monthly*. From my calculations you stand to pull down a sizable bonus this year. To the tune of—"

"So you've done your homework," he said, stopping me and picking his wine back up. "That's why I asked you what it is that you want. All I want is for us to make a clean split, no alimony, and, of course, the apartment." He took another gulp of wine, draining his glass.

I poured him another glass and splashed a little more wine into mine to give John the impression that I was keeping up with him. Really I'd barely had more than a couple of small sips because I was determined to keep my wits about me while hopefully he lost his.

"I don't get it. Why do you want this place when you're now in a position to buy a much bigger apartment?"

He shrugged his shoulders. "I like it here."

I considered his answer for a minute. It still didn't make sense to me why a guy as status conscious as John would want to stay here when—given the fact that he stood to make an estimated twenty to forty million dollars that year—he could afford a much bigger place in a much better building. It was possible that he was being truthful, that he really did love it here, and he had certainly been right when he pointed out that our apartment hadn't been my first choice (I prefer prewar buildings with old bones and working fireplaces to luxury, modern high rises with amenities like twenty-four-hour concierge services.)

"Okay, John, I'm willing to negotiate with you. I'm assuming you also want all the furnishings? You want those, too?"

"All except the couch," he said. "Ainsley never cared for it."

"What do you mean she *never* cared for it?"

"She doesn't like it, Marcy. That's it," he said, his nostrils flaring.

He was covering up something, I just knew it.

"You said *never*. Tell me John, how many times has she been to this apartment? And don't even think about lying to me. Because if you do, I'll know. You know I'll know. And then you'll never get your hands on this apartment or any of this furniture. You've been awfully presumptuous to think that I'd give up my home so easily. Who's to say I haven't fallen in love with all of our eco-fabulous tables and chairs and rugs and curtains and sheets and plates. I bought them, remember? I found everything, everything in this place. How dare you presume that I am not fond of it at all? So you better tell me the truth."

He took another sip of wine. "You don't want to know the truth."

"Oh believe me, I do. And start from the beginning. Did it start when you first met Ainsley at her Christmas party? Or at that dinner party at Jill's house? Or here, when she and Peter came over for dinner?"

He gave me a pained expression.

"You owe me this. At the very least, don't you think I deserve to know the truth?"

He nodded and parted his lips, hesitating a moment before finally and at long last satisfying my curiosity. "It started at the *House & Home* dinner at Jill's house. Not at the dinner itself but on the way home. She said she was heading uptown and wondered if I would give her a lift. We'd had a lot to drink at dinner and you know, in the car, one thing led to another."

It was hard for me to listen to the details of the affair and despite my best efforts I felt my eyes filling with tears.

"C'mon, Marce, why are you making me tell you this?" John asked.

"Just continue," I said, using my cocktail napkin to wipe away a tear.

"So we kissed that night, and I figured that was that. I felt really guilty about it and chalked it up to the wine, but the next day she texted me to tell me she had the worst hangover ever and I told her I was planning on heading over to the Parker Meridien to have a quick burger at the Burger Joint. She said that a burger sounded like just what she needed and that she would try and meet me there. I didn't think she'd come, but she did, and then, you know, we decided to get a room upstairs."

The day after Jill's party was the same day of my appointment at Dr. Delgado's office and the same day that John had given me the earrings from Bulgari. If I had been clearheaded, I would have realized then and there that something was amiss, but my mind had been clouded by my desire to have a baby and the thought that John had spent the day sleeping with another woman had never even occurred to me.

"So, let me get this straight? Instead of meeting me at the obstetrician's you decided to go screw Ainsley? And everything you swore to me that day about being caught in a meeting was a lie? And those earrings, you bought them for me because you felt guilty for cheating on me?"

He drained the rest of his wine and this time I didn't bother to stop him when he went to refill it.

"Again, I thought it was a one-time deal. I was attracted to her and I thought that if we had sex, I'd get it out of my system. I was more surprised than anyone when I realized that I was falling in love with her and that we had a one-in-a-million connection. You've got to believe me, Marcy. I never would have left you for her unless I was convinced that she and I had something really special."

"And how could you possibly come to the conclusion that you had something, as you say, special, with Ainsley based on one afternoon in bed together?"

"It wasn't one afternoon."

"So this became a regular thing between you two. Burgers and sex at the Parker Meridien? Was that your tryst spot?"

His nostrils flared again.

"Tell me."

"We made love here, too."

"In the apartment? On our bed?" I shrieked.

"Not in our bedroom," he said, slurring a little. I noticed that the bottle of wine was nearly gone. John was tipsy.

"Then where?"

He patted his left hand on the couch.

My couch, my favorite piece of furniture in the whole effing apartment and the one piece that Ainsley said she had never much cared for: That's where he fucked her.

It took everything, every ounce of self-discipline that I had in my body to keep myself from throwing the rest of my glass of wine in his face. I clenched my teeth and hands and forced myself to take a deep breath.

"You're right John. I don't think I need to hear anything else. Let's talk settlement. The sooner you and your gold-digging whore are out of my life, the better. I want fifteen million dollars post-tax. You can have the apartment and all the furnishings, *including* the couch. You've ruined it for me, just like you've ruined New York and ruined men and ruined everything."

"So does that mean you're moving back to Chicago?"

I didn't answer his question, partly because I didn't know the answer and partly because he didn't have any right to ask me about my future. "Fifteen million, John. Put it in writing."

"I need paper," he said. He waited one second before adding, "And I need you out of here by the end of next week."

"Happily," I retorted. After searching John's office, I found a legal pad and brought it to him in the living room, standing over him as he scribbled out an agreement. After he signed the document, I told him that he could leave.

He walked toward the door and I followed him, processing my shock that he had agreed so quickly to such a large sum. To be honest I couldn't even imagine what I would do with so much money. I'd have to buy an apartment, but then what? I could invest it and live off the interest for the rest of my life.

"Fifteen million dollars is a lot of money," I said, more to myself than to John.

He looked at me and smiled. "It's no big deal, I'll make more. And this way there are no hard feelings between us."

Oh yeah?

At the door John tried to give me a hug, but I stopped him with the heel of my left hand. He shook his head and frowned before delivering a few parting words that were more illuminating than anything else I had heard that evening:

"She really loves me," he said.

All I could think was: *What a fool.*

17

Baggage and All

Henry advised me to take John's offer.

Actually, what he said was, "That moron offered you fifteen million? He's given you everything, the idiot!"

"Except for the apartment," I reminded him. "And it's contents."

(Including one semen-soaked suede couch.)

"So?" he bellowed.

"I'm just saying," I grumbled.

Henry couldn't believe that John had rolled over and given us everything we wanted and then some, but he tempered our celebration by warning me that there was a big chance that John was being so generous because he was going to make even more money than either of us had anticipated by the end of that year.

"You might be put in a position to have to sit by and watch him and Ainsley enjoy the spoils of his success, having given up any claim on his future earnings," he said. But honestly, I didn't care if John made hundreds of millions of dollars. Fifteen million was more than I'd thought I'd get in the divorce and it was more than enough for me to live comfortably in any city I chose to, save maybe Dubai, but who wants to live in a city shaped like a palm tree, anyway? Also, if I invested my windfall wisely, which I certainly intended to, I'd have enough to put both of my sister's sons through college and maybe even leave them something to remember me by when I died (because at the moment it looked pretty darn unlikely that I'd have any children of my own).

Henry called a meeting with John's attorney, and the two of them began working on a settlement agreement, using John's scribbled notes on my legal pad as a template. Or make that *his* legal pad since starting Friday at 8:00 a.m. eastern standard time, the contents of John's office and every other room in the apartment, minus my personal effects, which included my clothes, jewelry, accessories, and toiletries, now belonged to my ex-husband.

Once we had both signed the document in front of a notary in our respective lawyers' offices, I was given exactly three days to pack up my belongings and leave the apartment. But I had really only needed one. It took me the full three days, however, to work up the nerve to call my mother and let her know that John and I were divorced. I'd phoned her earlier, after I'd gone to see Henry and he recommended (i.e., commanded) me to email or call all my close relatives and friends and tell them that John and I were in the midst of a divorce and that they should not talk to him or give him any personal information that would be harmful to me.

The result of my second call to my mother in Minnesota was to get an earful of I-told-you-sos and I-knew-this-was-comings. Apparently she had known long before John ever laid eyes on Ainsley that he would eventually have an affair and leave me for another woman. I asked her how she could have been so sure since it wasn't as though John was the kind of guy who checked out the waitress's backside as she walked away and my mother said that although John didn't have a "roving eye," it was also clear to her that I was not the love of his life.

"That doesn't make what he did all right!" I screeched. I couldn't believe that my own mother wasn't being more sympathetic to my anguish and humiliation.

My mother wasn't moved. "It's just that we could all see it. You two were friends and had similar interests, but there wasn't much chemistry."

Why was everyone so obsessed with chemistry? John and I had gotten along well and the sex was pretty darn good. It's not like we *never* had orgasms. We did, all the time. Just not simultaneously. (But show me a couple who does that. And Ainsley and John don't count because she has a personal trainer for her vagina.)

I wasn't about to tell my mother the explicit details of my sex life with John so I simply said, "Mother, you were not inside our bedroom and you cannot possibly understand our relationship."

"You got me there," she admitted, but I didn't like her tone. Her attitude enraged me.

"We loved each other," I bellowed. "Before everything started going wrong and I'd lost the baby, we made a wonderful team. We traveled well together, and enjoyed the same movies and books. We took good care of each other when we got sick—you remember that stomach flu I had the last winter we were in Chicago, don't you? John made me chicken broth and white rice with butter and stayed home from work one day to make sure I drank enough Gatorade."

"I hate to break it to you but that's companionship, not love. You two were always awfully considerate of each other, but, again, one day you or John were bound to meet someone who actually made each other weak in the knees."

So I hung up on her. I know, not nice, but it was either hanging up on her or spitting out a string of obscenities. And I figured the former was much less likely to earn me a strongly worded email from my father, which he would send only begrudgingly and only after being harassed by my mother for a solid day and a half. It would go something like this:

Dear daughter,

Please call your mother and apologize for yelling swear words at her. She is very upset.

Love,
Dad

If I hadn't hung up on my mom I would have been tempted to bring up the fact that until quite recently she and my father did not have anything close to what one would call "a good marriage." According to my mother, the expert on marital love, it was okay to fight with your husband constantly and threaten to divorce him at least ten times a month, as long as you had "chemistry" with him. If I hadn't hung up on her I would have had to remind my mother that she and my father's so-called chemistry brought the police to our front door on not one, but three Christmas Eves and two Easters. (Their fights were reliably more explosive on holidays.) All three times a pair of policemen armed with walkie-talkies and nightsticks came to our door and said that they had received reports of a "domestic disturbance" and needed to talk to my folks. They always left after giving my parents a warning to keep it down, and often my dad, his mouth drawn into a hard straight line, would kiss me goodbye "for a few hours" and take off in his ten-year-old Buick sedan. He would not return until he was quite sure we all had gone to bed.

Yeah, like that was a marriage I wanted to emulate. (Not.)

I'd take companionship over their chemistry every day.

I dialed my sister next, this time prepared to hear the same string of hurtful statements that had sprung forth from my mother's mouth. Annalise had always considered the fact that I'd married "up" and she, the beauty of the family, had gotten stuck living the life of a suburban housewife to be terribly unjust. She seemed to be terminally unhappy and expressed her dissatisfaction by lancing an endless stream of verbal arrows in my direction. I anticipated that she would take the dissolution of my marriage as proof positive that she was right all along; I should have never ended up with a man like John.

But she surprised me. On the phone she was encouraging and sympathetic and we ended up talking for hours. She admitted to being jealous of me all these years because I had more money, yes, but also because I could do what I wanted whenever I wanted since I wasn't saddled down with two kids like she was. "If you want to go out for a walk you can just walk out the front door, whereas I have to convince the kids that they also want to take a walk and then dress them appropriately and load the stroller with snacks and toys and diapers and wipes," she said, nearly exhausting herself with the effort of describing how difficult it was for her to run a few afternoon errands.

"And all along I thought you hated me because I was rich," I said.

"Yeah, well that didn't help," she laughed.

"What if I were to tell you that I was still rich?" I asked.

"I'd still love you. Now give me fifty bucks," she joked.

I laughed and we kept talking well into the night. It was two a.m. before either of us realized how late it was. "How about you and the kids come here, to visit me, during Christmas break? I'll find a nanny through one of my friends, so we can have a fun night out on the town, if the mood strikes."

At first Annalise balked and said that she wasn't sure if they could afford the three airplane tickets, but once I insisted on paying for the airfare—what good was a fifteen million dollar divorce settlement if you couldn't fly your sister and two nephews out

East for a visit?—she relented and agreed to look into flights and dates.

We were both about to hang up when she suddenly reminded me that I was going to be homeless in less than six hours. "But where will we stay?" she asked.

I hadn't given a second's thought to where I and my ten boxes of "personal effects" were going to be after I handed over my keys to John, but I didn't want Annalise to worry about me not having anywhere to go. New York had hundreds of hotels and last time I checked, they all accepted cash.

"Not to worry. I've got something temporary lined up and starting tomorrow I'm looking for a new apartment."

"So you're staying in New York?" she asked.

"Yep," I said. "This is home to me now."

The following morning, I checked in at the Morgans Hotel in Midtown, right across the street from the Morgan Library, for what eventually extended into a month-and-a-half-long stay. I spent my days meeting with wealth management consultants and insurance agents, and touring apartments with my real estate broker. When I wasn't busy trying to figure out my future, I drank coffee and ruminated over my failed marriage, unhappy childhood, and poor career choices. At night I turned to alcohol for comfort, bribing a porter to bring me up margaritas from Asia de Cuba, the hotel's lobby-level restaurant (the Morgans served wine, but try and order a cocktail and you're *merde* out of luck). The cocktails were tart and sweet and mind-numbingly potent—in other words, quite worth the extra expense.

One night, after downing three drinks in too-quick succession, I stumbled to the bathroom only to find my worst nightmare staring me right back in the face. I was skinnier, but there were wrinkles fanning out from the corner of my eyes and deep furrows running from my nostrils to the sides of my mouth. My hair was as flat and lifeless as my complexion. There was no doubt in my mind that the stress and alcohol had taken their toll. If I didn't want to look fifty by the time I turned thirty-six, I needed to get some help. I picked up the phone and dialed the only person I could rely on to come to my rescue, Gigi.

The following morning her driver picked me up and Maggie and Gemma showed up with the catering van to help me move my ten boxes of personal affects into the storage locker in the basement of Gigi and Jeremy's building. By nightfall I was ensconced in their spacious and luxurious guest suite, a tastefully appointed room that showcased Jeremy's collection of blue and white Chinese import antiques. There was a four-poster bed covered in a gold-embroidered ivory silk duvet and about fifteen down pillows. On the floor lay a trio of overlapping silk Oriental rugs in blue and ivory, and all around the room lay precious antique decorative items, including a pair of carved ivory lamps with peacock-feather shades and a trio of lidless porcelain congee jars that doubled as orchid planters. And that was just the bedroom.

The bathroom, which featured a deep, free-standing white marble tub and three enormous windows that turned opaque at the touch of a button, was equally luxurious. On the marble countertop a series of square-shaped crystal jars filled with jasmine and tuberose bath salts were lined up tallest to shortest, while the softest, fluffiest cotton bath sheets I'd ever had the pleasure of wrapping around my body hung from a pair of brushed steel racks that doubled as towel warmers. I opened a closet in search of a razor and found three shelves filled with every imaginable candle, soap, body cream, bath gel, shampoo, conditioner, styling product, face mask, and skin toner anyone could ever want or need, times ten.

By the time I emerged from my suite the following morning, I felt like another person. It had been months since I'd slept as well and about as long since I had taken a bath. Afterward, I sat in

Gigi's all-white kitchen and drank green tea out of an earthen-ware pot while Ken, the Cohen's house manager (don't call him a butler), chatted idly about the day's big story: Unemployment had jumped yet another percentage point according to the monthly jobless polls.

"Half of my friends are out of work," Ken sighed. "The first thing people cut is their domestic staff."

Dressed in khaki pants, polo shirt, and a fleece jacket bearing the emblems of Jeremy's two funds, Ken hardly looked like a butler. He was tall and thin, and had the placid demeanor of a yoga teacher. Gigi had told me that he was a specialist in Eastern medicine who Jeremy had found years ago on one of his business trips to Asia. He mixed Chinese herbs, feng shui-ed all their homes and the private jet, practiced chakra-balancing, cupping and acupuncture and led Jeremy through his Tai Chi routine every morning without fail.

After serving me tea and an artfully arranged fresh fruit plate, Ken asked me if there was anything he could get for me (Glass of Kombucha or Goji berry juice?) or do (Reiki session, reflexology?) but all I wanted was the morning paper. He left the kitchen for half a minute before returning with fresh copies of the *Wall Street Journal*, *New York Times* and the *New York Post*.

I opted for the *Times* and since it was Sunday, pored over a real estate supplement. After weeks of apartment shopping, I still hadn't made my mind up about where I wanted to live in the city, but I did know that I could afford to spend about five to six million dollars and that I didn't want to live in a luxury condo with floor-to-ceiling windows and impractical bathroom sinks. What sent my heart pitter pattering? Coffered ceilings and windows that didn't take a PhD in engineering to figure out how to open.

Gigi waltzed into the kitchen, already dressed for the day in a silk tunic dress and a pair of oversized tortoiseshell sunglasses perched atop her head. She sat down next to me and asked me if I'd found anything of interest.

"There are a few apartments that I've circled, but my broker is taking me today to show me some new places that aren't even officially on the market. She says the best values never even make it into the paper. But I like looking anyway." I slid the section across the table and showed her the ones that I'd marked.

"Looks like you're only looking at prewars in prestige buildings."

"Shailagh, Henry's sister, keeps trying to steer me toward condominiums, but they never feel as authentic and sturdy as the old buildings."

"You're using your divorce attorney's sister as your broker? That's convenient," she snorted.

I understood her reaction; I'd had it, too, when Henry slipped me Shailagh's card at our last meeting (right after he handed me a bill for two hundred and fifty thousand dollars for services rendered), but then he mentioned that Shailagh had survived her own nasty divorce from a trader with a secret penchant for high-priced escorts, and I decided that there wouldn't be any harm in meeting with her.

"I know it sounds all too cozy, but Shalaigh's an ex-hedge fund wife, too, and that practically makes her family in my eyes. Besides, you're the one who introduced me to Henry in the first place," I reminded her.

Clearly dubious of my ability to choose a broker let alone go apartment hunting on my own, Gigi decided to come along and meet Shailagh "just to make sure I was in good hands."

"When is she coming to pick you up?" Gigi asked.

I checked my watch. "She said she would be here in half an hour."

Then Gigi remarked that I better go get changed. I was wearing an old black cashmere sweater and pair of jeans that she deemed too "down market" for the task at hand.

We went to my bedroom, where I changed into a pair of wide-legged navy pants, nautical-print blouse, chain belt and heels and listened to Gigi try and talk me out of gunning for a co-op rather than a condo.

"These white glove buildings are so snooty, I don't see why you would want to live in one," she said, plopping herself down on the canopy bed, which had been magically made up for me while I was munching on my seasonal fruit plate in the kitchen. "They don't like hedge fund money, and they like ex-wife hedge fund money even less."

"Gigi, the economy is in the tank. These people have no choice but to accept my money, even if it's brand-spanking-new and covered with sequins. Don't you think they'd rather let me, than yet another Russian oligarch's daughter, inside their pearly gates? I'm a nice girl from the Midwest, and between you and Jill, I'll have sparkling letters of recommendation."

"I just don't want you to get your hopes up."

"My hopes are totally in line."

"You leave me no choice but to tell you the truth."

What now?

"A few weeks ago, I got a call from Ainsley," Gigi said. "I didn't know why she was calling me because it's not like we've ever been close."

"Not to mention the fact that you and I *are* friends," I added.

"Right. But I just let her keep talking and was cordial. You know that old saying, you catch more flies with honey? She asked me how everything was going with A Moveable Feast and mentioned that she had a couple big personal events coming up, which I took to mean her bridal shower and wedding, you know?"

"How dare she think she could hire you, my best friend in New York, to cater her wedding to John?" I nearly spit, I was so enraged by her audacity. Wasn't it enough that she had stolen my husband? Now she wanted to co-opt my friends?

"She offered me a hundred thousand dollar contract, which I have to tell you, A Moveable Feast could really use right now."

"Really?"

"Business hasn't been that good," she began to say, but then we were cut off by my phone ringing. It was Shalaigh, telling me that she was downstairs waiting curbside in a black Mercedes.

While riding the elevator downstairs, Gigi explained that the depressed economy, which had caused a lot of her clients to cut their budgets, compounded by rising food costs, crunched her profit margins down to almost nothing. And her clients who hadn't already sliced their budgets in half were switching to rival catering firms, in part because of the poor reviews of her last cookbook. Gigi said she was losing accounts left and right and had so few parties booked for the holiday season that she was worried she might have to lay off some of her staff.

Ainsley hadn't been coy about knowing how badly A Moveable Feast needed her business, but Gigi wasn't about to swap my friendship for the chance to cater what was being billed around town as the event of the season, aka my ex-husband's wedding.

"And how did she respond, when you told her thanks but no thanks?"

"She said that I'd better be careful who I associated myself with."

"Meaning me?"

"She told me that you had something of a checkered past and that you'd gone to great lengths to hide it."

I racked my brain for what Ainsley could be alluding to and came up with nothing. "That's crazy."

Gigi sucked in a breath of air and continued. "She suggested that you had been promiscuous at BlooMu and had an affair with your much-married managing director. According to Ainsley you unsuccessfully tried to blackmail this guy into giving you a promotion, so the bank shelved you away in private banking."

"That's a lie!" I screeched, which wasn't the smartest move since Gigi and I were at that moment cruising through her fancy, vaulted-ceilinged lobby (boy, did my voice carry) on the way out to Shailagh's car. I held my tongue until we reached the sidewalk and then, with my heart pounding hard against my breastbone, I swore to Gigi that nothing that Ainsley had told her was true aside from the fact that the bank had passed me over for a promotion a couple of times.

Gigi looked at me and grasped my shoulders. "Sugar, I know she's full of shit. I just wanted to tell you because I have a feeling she's been selling this story all over town and it might be a problem if you try to buy into any buildings that have her friends on their boards."

A car pulled up beside us and Shailagh jumped out and gave me a double air kiss. She had Henry's same wavy red hair and pale skin and was dressed in regulation hedge fund wife attire: sleeveless silk blouse, pastel tweed jacket, trouser jeans, and designer heels.

"Uh-oh, I sense something's the matter," she said, noticing my watery eyes and Gigi's concerned expression. "If you're not feeling up to this today Marcy we can blow off apartment hunting and go have brunch. I can send away the car and we can walk to Michael's around the corner."

"No, you've already set aside your time," I said, climbing into the backseat of the car. "Let's stick to the plan." Gigi and Shailagh followed me in and as we settled into our seats, I told Shailagh about Ainsley's smear campaign against me.

"Oh dear," Shailagh said.

Then she sat back in her seat and thought for a bit before inquiring politely about the veracity of Ainsley's accusations. I promised her that I hadn't slept with one person at Bloomington Mutual and wouldn't dream of blackmailing anyone, let alone my wonderful boss (whom I was never even the slightest bit attracted to).

"The whole thing is ludicrous," I said.

"Maybe so but the slightest whiff of scandal can scare off these co-op boards. Most of them are looking for a reason to turn down your application and Ainsley's served one to them on a silver platter. If I were to hazard a guess I'd say that she's trying to run you straight out of town."

"What should I do?" I asked, throwing my hands up in the air. "Bid my adieus?"

"No!" Gigi said. "But maybe it wouldn't hurt to look at some condominiums? What do you think Shailagh?"

"Sure, why not?" Shailagh said, patting my leg. "There are lots and lots of beautiful condos on the market. I can think of five meeting your qualifications just in this instant. But let's not get ahead of ourselves or make any rash decisions. Let's take it one day at a time. Okay?"

I nodded in agreement.

Gigi leaned over Shailagh to squeeze my hand. "Try not to worry too much about Ainsley," she said.

As the car pulled up to our first stop Shailagh put her arm around my shoulder. "I know what it's like to get divorced in this town and I know it isn't easy, especially when your ex is parading his kewpie girlfriend around town. But you'll survive. If I did, anybody can," she said.

18

Spread to Worst

Four hours and two bottles of champagne later, I felt more confused and blindsided than ever. All the apartments Shailagh had showed me that day were lovely, with lots of good light and charm. There was one four-bedroom apartment on Carnegie Hill that seemed perfect: It had a marble entrance gallery, spacious living room with a working white marble fireplace, and a kitchen with skyline views. But then Gigi pointed out that the master bedroom was too small, the ceilings were too low, and the kitchen would need a gut renovation, and I realized that the main reason I liked the place so much was because the walls were painted various shades of pink and robin's egg blue.

That was the third apartment Shailagh had brought us to and although we had two more stops before we were done, she could tell I was starting to feel overwhelmed. Gigi suggested we call it a day and head to the Carlyle Hotel for a drink, and after clicking our heels across the polished black marble-floored lobby to the Bemelmans Bar, we piled into a brown leather booth. I admired the gilt ceiling and murals covering every inch of wall space, while Shailagh ordered a bottle of champagne. As we toasted to new beginnings, we were interrupted by none other than Irina Khash-ovopova.

"Hello, ladies," Irina said, gazing down at us. I had forgotten how tall and busty she was, and the bright red platform heels and leopard-print dress she was wearing only served to highlight her Amazonian proportions.

"Are we celebrating something?" she asked, not waiting for an answer before sliding into the leather booth next to me. She motioned for the waitress to bring her another glass.

Gigi responded first. "Yes we are, in fact. Marcy, here, just settled her divorce."

"Congratulations," she said, her icy blue eyes narrowing as she studied my face. "We've met before, no?"

I nodded and took a sip of my drink. I wasn't going to remind her of the circumstances of our last two run-ins, how she had sneered at me in Ainsley's foyer and snarled cuss words at me at the bar in the Sky Hotel in Aspen. But this time I didn't feel so much intimidated by her as I felt annoyed. Who did she think she was to just plop herself down at our table uninvited? The woman had no manners—I didn't care if she was best pals with Denise Rich and Bill Clinton—and I wasn't about to cut her any slack given how rude she had been to me the last time we exchanged words.

"So, tell me, Irina," I began. "What is it that you do? We never got around to talking about that last time."

"My father very successful businessman," she said, her upper lip curling objectionably at me.

I gave her a look that conveyed exactly what I was thinking—*Russian oligarch's daughter, my ass!*—while the waitress filled her glass.

Gigi kicked me under the table and mouthed "don't antagonize her," but I had discovered that I was rather enjoying sparring with Irina. Doormat Marcy would have never taken on the mysterious and quite possibly dangerous woman seated next to me (Irina looked to be the type who had friends who broke legs for a living) but not Marcy 2.0.

"I'm not afraid," I mouthed back at Gigi.

After the waitress left, Irina took a sip of her bubbly and turned her attention back to me. "I heard you walk away with twenty-five million," she said.

"I don't think that's any business of yours," I responded coolly.

I swear she growled at me.

Shailagh cleared her throat, trying her best to diffuse the mounting tension. "I just love the scene in this place. Do you come here often, Irina? I'm always meaning to come here more regularly."

Irina smiled, baring a set of wide white teeth, clearly veneers, and dark purple gums. "Yes, I do," she said. "In fact just this past week I was here for the most unbelievable, spectacular baby shower. You could not see the ceiling there were so many balloons—light blue ones because she's having a boy. The papa is so happy. Flowers everywhere, delicious food from hot new caterer: I never tasted food so good," she said, eying Gigi challengingly. Irina brushed a few strands of pitch black hair behind her shoulder and turned once again to face me. Never breaking eye contact, she continued quite slowly, as if to maximize the pleasure of saying the words, "Jill really outdid herself for Ainsley."

It took me a few seconds to digest what she had said.

Ainsley was pregnant.

With John's baby.

And Jill threw her a baby shower.

I didn't know who to kill first—Jill, Ainsley, or myself.

The table fell silent as everyone waited for my reaction.

"I'd heard it was a wonderful event," I said evenly. "I was sad to have missed it."

She gave me a dubious look (the same kind of look I'd given

her not more than a minute earlier) and downed the rest of her glass of champagne before filling it again. Then she fished out a copy of the *New York Post* from her silver python-skin purse and dropped it in front of me on the table. "Lucky for you, a reporter was there," she said before standing up and rejoining her friend at the bar, a gorgeous young girl with wide-set eyes, long brown hair, and legs so long and lithe they made Heidi Klum's look chunky.

"Wow, you handled that well," Shailagh said, refilling the rest of our glasses until the bottle was empty. Then she turned it over, base side up in the ice bucket and signaled to the waitress to bring us another bottle.

"Did either of you know that Ainsley was pregnant?" I asked.

Gigi nodded. "I'd heard rumors, but I didn't know for sure and I didn't want to bother you with hearsay. She didn't mention it when we spoke, but that must have been what she was referring to when she said she had some personal events coming up. I assumed it was her wedding and wedding shower. Jill didn't invite me to the baby shower, if that's what you're wondering."

I opened the paper with trepidation. "Where do you think it is?" I said.

"Try Page Six or *Page Six Magazine*," Shailagh responded.

I didn't find anything on Page Six, but inside that day's glossy magazine supplement I did. Turning to page fifteen, I was assaulted by a three-page spread on the baby shower, with several pictures of Ainsley dressed in an empire waist, sleeveless wool knit dress, and surrounded by friends and presents. I counted about fifty other women in the room, including Jill, Dahlia, Caroline, and Irina and about double the number of gift boxes. The magazine had also run a picture, a society photographer-taken snapshot of John and Ainsley at a benefit this past summer in the Hamptons along with the baby shower pictures. In it John was tan and beaming, dressed in one of his white dress shirts and khakis, his hands spread wide on her bulging belly. That was this summer, which meant—I quickly calculated—she had gotten pregnant in the spring.

When John and I were still married.

I scanned the text, through nausea-inducing quotes from Ainsley about how she had met John ("At a party. We had an instant connection."), how happy she was ("My life with John is a fairy tale."), and how excited she and John were about the baby ("Even though it was an accident, we are so ecstatic. We've both wanted one for so long."). There was, however, no mention of me by name or of the fact that John had been married before Ainsley. There was a section on her divorce from Peter and a quote from Ainsley saying that she still loved Peter, but that they had met when they were too young and simply grown apart over the years.

If by growing apart she meant that Peter's bank account went in one direction (down) while her social aspirations went in another (up), then, yeah, they grew apart.

The story also mentioned that the baby, a boy, was due in two months, in late November, which meant that Ainsley was seven months along and had conceived in April, not long after she and John had begun their affair and John had made those tremendous trades at work. I didn't buy that her pregnancy was an accident. I was sure that Ainsley had lied to John about being on the pill, and getting John to go without a condom probably wasn't that hard to do. (He hated condoms because he claimed they reduced his sensitivity.) Suddenly I remembered that when I walked in on them together in Miami he hadn't been wearing one.

"I wonder if this is why he left me, because she was pregnant," I said. "What if he hadn't planned on divorcing me at all but only did because she was going to have his baby?"

"It's possible," Shailagh said gently. "But the only way you're going to ever find out is if you ask John directly. And that's assuming that he'll give you a straight answer. Though if I have any advice to give, it's that you don't even go there. Even if he did leave you because she was pregnant, would that necessarily make you feel any better about what's happened?"

"Yes it would," I yelped, sputtering champagne across the table. "John has this do-the-right-thing instinct that kicks in whenever he has a moral dilemma."

"Oh yeah? And where was that instinct when he was fucking Ainsley?" Shailagh asked.

"He's not perfect, okay? But at least now I'd know that he didn't leave me because he loved her more, but because she was pregnant."

Shailagh admonished me firmly. "Look, Marcy, you don't have to listen to what I'm saying to you, but I'm telling you, the only way to get past your divorce is to just not go there. No second-guessing yourself. What happened isn't your fault and if it hadn't been Ainsley it could have just as easily been some other hussy. John's an idiot and he'll get his one day. But in the meantime count yourself lucky for having figured that out before you'd wasted your entire life with him. You're still young, attractive, and full of life. You'll find someone else if that's what you want. Or maybe you'll find a new career for yourself and earn your self-esteem back one dollar at a time like I did. But that's never going to happen if you're walking around with your head up your ass, obsessing about what your life would look like if your stupid-ass husband had insisted on wearing a condom with his mistress." Shailagh took a breath and raised her eyebrows at me. "Got it?"

I gave her my best look of defiance. "I'm entitled to a few weeks of wallowing in self-pity."

Shailagh responded to that by forcibly wrestling the magazine right out of my hands and tearing out the article on Ainsley's shower. "Tomorrow we'll look at some more apartments," she said as she slowly, calmly ripped the pages into a dozen small pieces. "And all this," she said, throwing the pieces into the air like confetti, "will feel like a thing of the very distant past."

By the time Shailagh dropped us off at Gigi's apartment, we were tipsy and starving. Jeremy was in Miami visiting Lauren, who had once again gotten herself into trouble. Lauren had apparently been caught with a large quantity of Adderall, a methamphetamine commonly prescribed for attention deficit disorder but often abused by women for weight loss. Gigi thought that Lauren might be dabbling in even harder drugs, like heroin, but Jeremy refused to believe it. In any case, he was going to be gone for the next few nights, which meant that we would have full run of the apartment and twenty-four-hour access to Ken's unparalleled care.

As we stumbled into her apartment, Gigi hollered out to him, "Hey Ken! Order us some of those chile rellenos, huitlecoche tamales, and black beans and rice from that gourmet Mexican restaurant I like?"

While Ken placed the dinner orders over the phone, I mixed us up a couple of margaritas in the kitchen. Gigi walked in just as I was pouring the mixture into a pair of glasses I'd found, and quickly dispatched Ken to Blockbuster to rent us some movies. When I started suggesting some films I'd been hoping to see on video, she stopped me short, assuring me that Ken had such uncanny movie-picking abilities, she'd learned to trust his taste better than her own.

We took our drinks into the screening room, a dark annex outfitted with a small movie screen and six large leather chairs, each with their own wooden console and cashmere blanket. "You know, sometimes I think that I put up with all of Jeremy's crap just so I can keep Ken in my life," Gigi said as she threw herself into a seat and brought her knees up into her chest. "The guy can find other jobs. There will always be another job. But there's only one John. Now I know that I had it all backward. There are many Johns out there. I see them on the street walking by, all these men. All these men that I could have fallen in love with, that could have fallen in love with me. There's no such thing as The One. That's a myth, created to oppress women, to dupe us into exchanging our ambitions for the promise of true love, like it's some precious, rare thing. And it's not. If I could go back in time I would sit my stupid, naïve former self's butt down and tell her that there will be many Johns in my life, as many as I wanted, but that career opportunities are rare and you have to grab them and fight for them and hold on to them for dear life. You cannot depend on a man to keep you safe in this world." I stopped talking, took a deep breath, and held the table to steady myself.

The waiter brought out our orders and I forced myself to eat my salad even though I was the farthest thing from hungry. As I speared the tuna piece by piece, barely tasting each bite, Gigi and Jill exchanged stories about divorced women they both knew. My favorite was about a woman who had had to live with her husband, a derivatives trader, for two years while their divorce was pending. He hadn't wanted to give up the apartment and she refused to be bought out by him even if he could have raised the capital to pay for her half. The husband slept on the couch and she in the bedroom—for twenty-four months.

"And the most amazing thing is that *he* was the one who asked for the divorce," Gigi added.

"She had a child with him, right?" asked Jill.

"Yes, and he was so mean to her afterward, when she was struggling to lose the baby weight. He told her that she was so fat that he couldn't even get a hard on when he touched her."

Jill shook her head in disgust. "We're talking about a woman who was a size eight maximum."

"How did she survive living with him for that long, while they makes the only green tea I can bear to drink and massages my feet at least twice a week."

"I thought you didn't like that," I snorted, reminding her of her stint with a foot fetishist.

"Oh hush, there's nothing the least bit sexual about reflexology," she said.

As if on cue, Ken entered the room with our movies and the takeout we'd ordered on two laquered wood trays.

"Hey, if I had a Ken, I'd stay too," I whispered once he had left the room.

Gigi pressed the pause button. "Ken or no Ken, I can't leave. I'm stuck, and there's nothing I can do about it."

"What do you mean? You have plenty of options," I said.

"If I leave Jeremy I'll get nothing. A little child support but not much else, and since my business could close any day, my books aren't moving and my endorsement deals have all been pulled, there's no way I can take care of my parents if I were to leave him."

"But I thought you said he wasn't giving you any money for them, anyway."

"He's finally agreed to help. He made the down payment on the new house in the assisted-living facility."

"Well that's generous," I said, spooning a mound of rice and beans into my mouth.

"It would be if we weren't calling it a loan and I wasn't being charged interest," she said.

19

Take This Portfolio And Stuff It

The following morning I woke up to the sound of Ken rapping on my bedroom door. After opening it groggily, I was presented with a cup of Chinese herb tea, and the morning's activity schedule, which included a round of Tai Chi, followed by fresh fruit and microgreens frappe for breakfast and an Ayurvedic massage. After some haggling, Ken and I compromised on some green tea, a plate of buckwheat pancakes, and a ten-minute head, neck, and shoulder massage: this was followed by a hot bath, and by midday I was showered, dressed, and ready for business. I had a meeting with my private banker at Countrybank—today was the day he was going to present me with his asset allocation recommendations—and then I was meeting Shailagh to look at a few more apartments.

I was more determined than ever to find my own place; it was the only way I was going to be able to turn over a new leaf and really think about what I wanted to do with the rest of my life. Even after months of soul searching, I still had no clue what my next career move should be. All I knew how to do, besides balancing a tray of champagne flutes on my hand, was manage wealthy peoples' investment portfolios—and wasn't this the job I was paying my financial advisor to do?

As I hailed a cab outside of Gigi's apartment, it occurred to me that I could ask my banker, Thorne Van Buren (no relation to the president), if Countrybank was hiring. I had enjoyed working in wealth management when I was at Bloomington Mutual; my position was fun and rewarding and I'd regretted giving it up almost as soon as I tendered my resignation.

The job of a private banker was a lot like a quarterback in that we threw "balls" to the different departments. For example, if I thought a client should consider buying a piece of art in order to diversify their investments, I'd set him or her up for a lunch with one of our art advisors. Likewise, if a client wanted to ensure their grandchildren would be able to afford college, I'd set them up on call with one of our trust and estates officers. A lot of my clients wanted to explore alternative investments in private equity and hedge funds, and I had built my own sub-specialty in that area over the years. I loved helping people feel more secure about their finances (and thus future), but I also loved uncovering interesting investment opportunities.

So far my private banker, Thorne, hadn't impressed me. He spoke with a locked jaw, wore rimless glasses, and (I suspected) dyed the hair around his temples gray so he would look older. He dressed in monogrammed French-cuffed shirts, bespoke suits (with the first button on the sleeve undone so there was no mistaking it for off the rack), and wore the same shoes John did. On the wall of his office were diplomas from Deerfield, a prep school in Massachusetts, and Harvard, and on his desk there was a sepia-toned, studio-quality picture of himself and his skinny blonde wife. Thorne seemed to be capable enough, but I didn't feel like I was a priority to him. I only had fifteen million in my account, which for a guy used to dealing with clients worth upward of a hundred million, was small potatoes. He also seemed better suited to dealing with male clients, or at least ill suited to dealing with me, a woman who knew her LIFO (last in, first out) from her FIFO (first in, first out) and how to calculate the right WACC (weighted average cost of capital) for her DCF (discounted cash flow) analysis in less time than it took his secretary to pour a glass of Pellegrino.

Thorne's assistant met me in the lobby and took me up to the top floor of the building, where Countrybank kept its executive conference rooms. The room I was in had had sweeping views over midtown and two Warhol silk screens of dollar signs on the interior walls. I took a seat at the circular black glass conference table and spent five minutes pushing down my cuticles with my thumbnail before Thorne managed to make an entrance.

And when he did, he was talking on his iPhone, an inexcusable offense as far as I was concerned.

"No, there's no way I'm signing up for one more charity," Thorne was hissing into his phone. "Listen to me, Marissa. We can't. And as long as you're going to spend the next week moping about your missed photo ops, I'll tell you now that I've canceled the trip to Cap d'Antibes."

"Do you want me to come back later?" I asked loudly, scooping my crocodile handbag from off the floor.

Thorne jumped, surprised to see me seated in the conference room already, and told his wife he had to go. Walking toward me, he offered his hand.

"You're looking well, Marcy," he said, his lockjaw voice even more grating than I had remembered. Today he was dressed in pinstripes, a pink dress shirt, and a purple tie shot through with chartreuse stripes.

"You too, Thorne," I said.

"What do you think of the Warhol room?" he asked, gesturing toward the silk screens. He watched my face, waiting for me to express my amazement and appreciation for the art on the walls. He'd forgotten that I had worked in a bank and knew that all major financial institutions housed expensive art in their executive rooms.

"Well, that depends on what you've worked up for me," I responded, sitting back down in my seat.

"Oh great stuff, great stuff." Unbuttoning his suit jacket, he took a seat before sliding a slim pitch book across the table to me. "Take a look."

Eager to begin thumbing through his recommendations, I opened it and studied the first page, which showed a pie chart illustrating the allocation of my assets right now. It was all one color, red, and marked "cash." The subsequent pages offered three different investment scenarios: most conservative, midrange, and aggressive.

The more I read, the more upset I became. Thorne's recommendations were incredibly safe. In every chart, even the so-called aggressive one, I was too heavily weighted in municipal bonds and mutual funds. Where was the emerging market debt or private equity? And he wanted me to invest in a fund of funds (a hedge fund that invests in other hedge funds), which meant that I would be paying fees on top of fees. Thanks, but no thanks. Although I was all for protecting my assets, especially in a time of extreme economic volatility like the current one, every good portfolio includes a few higher risk investment plays. Thorne's proposal had provided for none.

I closed the book, laid my pen on top of it, and gazed at my banker across the table.

"I know what you're thinking. Where's the Manolo Blahnik shoe allocation?" he said, tipping his head back and chortling.

"No, Thorne, what I actually was thinking was, why on earth is this so plain vanilla? I was hoping I'd see something more exotic today."

He laughed again and adjusted his glasses on the bridge of his nose. "Now, Marcy, this is a very balanced portfolio."

"How can you say that when your most aggressive scenario is still fifty percent bonds!" I squawked.

He swiveled around to retrieve a porcelain plate loaded with pastel-colored macaroons and placed it on the table between us. If Thorne thought a dish of cookies was going to keep me from serving his favorite appendage to him on a stick, he was very wrong.

"It's a geriatric allocation and you know it," I said stridently. "I'd give this to a seventy-year-old retiree."

"Actually, Marcy, that's not a bad comparison. Think about it. You're pretty much retired, right? You're not going to work again, are you?"

"What gave you the impression that I was never going to work again?" I sputtered. I hated that he leaped to that conclusion. He never would have said that to me if I were a man.

"All right, let me rephrase that," he said carefully. "It's not like you're expecting to receive another windfall, are you? Or is there a husband number two in the wings?"

I'd worked with enough chauvinists at Bloomington Mutual to know that getting offended by their remarks served no purpose. The only thing pricks like Thorne respected was balls, and I was about to show him mine.

"Funny one," I said, chuckling gamely, adopting his same condescending tone. "Now, Thorne, if you're done with the stand-up act, do you think we can get back to talking about my money? There's too much in my fixed-income bucket."

He opened the pitch book and turned to the equities section. Pointing at one of the pie charts, he said, "Did you see the biotech section?"

"Yeah, but you've got a principal protected note on it," I parried.

"That's because with a PPN you're not in danger of losing anything you put in while at the same time you're getting exposure to a very sexy sector."

"First of all, I know how PPNs work," I said calmly. "And second, I don't think I'm at the age that I need to be wearing training wheels. If we're going to take a position let's take a position."

He offered me a few different options, none of which I found exciting or particularly intelligent. As a last ditch attempt to appease me, he threw me a low-volatility long-short fund that happened to be seeded by Zenith Capital, as in my ex-husband John's employer. I nixed that idea straightaway. Then I stood up and told Thorne that I would take his recommendations under consideration but was overall less than satisfied with them.

"These are good, solid scenarios considering your life circumstances. You may not be thrilled with your options now, but in the long run you'll be happy you played it safe," he said.

I collected my handbag and pitch book and stood up from the table. "The last person who said that to me was my husband, and look where that got me."

"From my perspective, it looks like it got you fifteen million dollars richer." He grinned.

And that's when I made up my mind that I would rather lose every single penny of my money, rather than let Thorne Van Buren get his pasty little hands on it.

Since Countrybank's offices were so close to the apartment building where Shailagh and I were planning to rendezvous after my meeting with Thorne, I decided to walk there instead of hailing a taxi. As I made my way east, down a block teeming with bankers out on their lunch breaks, the autumn wind whipped the hair off my face and my coat jacket open. I felt more alive, more unfettered, confident, and awake than I had in a very long time.

Thorne Van Buren was an asshole. John was an asshole. And I was better off without them both.

I arrived at the building shortly before Shailagh pulled up in her hired Mercedes. She was wearing a dark pink St. John suit and pearls and her shoulder-length wavy red hair had been blown straight. "I know I'm late," she said. "I had a closing this morning and you wouldn't believe how slow the other broker was. I mean, the buyers are getting the apartment for a steal, and they had the nerve to complain about the state of the guest bathroom? Anyway, I'm sorry for keeping you waiting."

I fanned off her apologies and told her I'd spent the extra time in the lobby watching the building's residents stream in and out. From what I observed, there were a lot of young mothers in jeans and pea coats, nannies pushing their charges in strollers, and older men and women with handbags and newspapers tucked under their arms—basically the same as you'd find in any luxury building in New York, with one key difference: These people stopped to talk to each other. They knew each other's names, their children's names, even their dog's names. They were courteous to the doorman and to each other. I even overheard one woman promising to bring the other a slice of her son's birthday cake.

"I have a good feeling about this one," I told Shailagh in the elevator on the way up to the apartment.

"Good, because even though this one is a co-op, you actually have a decent chance of getting in. The board has a reputation for being slightly more progressive. They prefer people with the right background, *Social Register*-y-types, but they won't hold your age or marital status against you. Some buildings won't let unmarried women into their building at all. The wives of the residents go to great lengths to make sure that any single, attractive woman under sixty-five gets rejected. It's happened to my female clients many times. Once I even advised a lovely interior designer to ugly-herself up for her interview, but she hadn't told me that her picture had appeared in *House & Home* a month earlier. She never stood a chance of getting into that building."

Shailagh dug a folder out of her Birkin and handed it to me. "This one has two master bedrooms and a huge walk-in closet that can be converted back into a third bedroom. There's a private security system, a laundry room, and you'll have access to the building's roof deck and courtyard. Oh, and the ceilings are ten feet high," she said as she opened the door.

I stepped into the foyer—inlaid marble floor, walls papered in salmon-colored suede, a sky mural on the ceiling. Shailagh pointed me to the right, down a hall, at the end of which we found the living room with dark hardwood floors, paneled walls, a ceiling medallion, and a marble fireplace with a matching overmantle.

"It's all Italian," Shailagh said, in reference to the marble fireplace.

I murmured my appreciation while I ducked into the kitchen, where I found a lot of wood paneling, a checkerboard floor, and an oddly shaped center island. The space would need updating, but ripping out the island and updating the cabinets and flooring wouldn't be too difficult or costly. Off the kitchen there was a dining room, small but big enough for my purposes, while on the other side of the apartment, the master bedrooms overlooked the East River. One held a large built-in bookcase and three large windows, and the other, slightly larger, featured a decorative cornice and carved frieze running along the top of the walls.

"I like that everything feels so solid," I said to Shailagh as I swung open the door to the walk-in closet.

It was indeed the size of a small bedroom. Specially sized cases and cabinets for shoes and clothes and racks for clothes lined all four walls. It reminded me a lot of Jill's closet, infact.

"This has to go," I said. "God help me if I ever have enough stuff to fill this room."

"This space could make for a great office," Shailagh said.

A home office, now that was an idea. I'd been secretly envious of John's office in our old apartment. He let me use the computer, of course, but the desk was stuffed with his papers and the computer configured to meet his needs and interests. Plus John's office was a masculine room, full of dark wood and leather. My dream office would be painted in pale mint green, with an off-white desk and a wall hung with a half dozen floral prints encased in ivory wood frames.

I turned to Shailagh. "This is my home," I said. "This is where I want to start over."

"The ask is five-point-nine, maintenance is five thousand three hundred a month and they require fifty percent down."

"Can we offer less? My plan was to spend closer to five," I said. I wanted this apartment so badly, but I also wanted to stick to my budget and I knew that in a down economy and buyer's market, major discounts were not out of the ordinary.

"We can certainly offer less, but there's no guarantee they'll take it. However I happen to know that the couple who lived here is divorcing and they need the cash to settle their debts. The husband worked on Wall Street, trading mortgage-backed securities. Spent a bundle keeping his wife in the manner to which she had become accustomed only to have her walk out on him as soon as he lost his job. And then, because she hadn't emasculated the poor slob enough, she moved in with his best friend from college as soon as they separated."

I looked around the closet and considered all the shelves for shoes and handbags. There were velvet-lined drawers for sunglasses, belts, and scarves, a built-in safe for jewelry and a cold-storage armoire for furs.

We walked through the apartment again, stopping in the living room. "Do you think five-point-nine is a fair ask? Is this apartment worth that?" I asked Shailagh.

She was tapping something out on her BlackBerry. "This apartment is worth what is sells for," she said, giving me a wry smile.

I ran my hand along the fireplace mantle. I loved the apartment, no question about it. Returning to the foyer, I admired the painted ceiling one last time before calling to Shailagh in the next room, "Offer five-point-five, and we'll go from there."

I took a cab to ABC Carpet and Home in Chelsea, and before we parted ways, Shailagh made me promise that I wouldn't buy anything until my offer had been accepted and we'd gotten past the board. "I just want to start getting ideas," I assured her, reminding her that one of the advantages of having let John keep everything was that it meant that I had an excuse to buy everything new. I needed glasses and plates, a bed and sheets, a dining room table and chairs, a couch and desk.

For the following three hours I giddily wandered through the store noting the manufacturers' names and prices of pieces and things I liked, until I was tired and hungry and my feet were killing me. Outside I passed one of those sidewalk newsagents and scooped up every interior design magazine I spotted before finding a little French café and settling into a table. I ordered a cup of European hot chocolate and a wedge of raspberry tarte.

The waitress brought my pastry and hot chocolate as I was flipping through the brand-new issue of *House & Home*, which featured an article on kitchen redesign on the cover. Taking a bite of the tart's buttery crust, creamy custard and fresh raspberries, I closed my eyes to savor all the flavors and textures.

My mistake was opening them.

On the page before me I saw for the second time in as many days Ainsley and John's smiling faces. This time they were sitting on my old couch (which had been reupholstered in silk hemp), with John's hand wrapped lovingly around Ainsley's pregnant belly. I had spent half a year of my life outfitting that apartment with environmentally friendly furniture and knickknacks to John's exacting specifications and now Ainsley was passing it off as her own. Disgusted, I flipped back to the first page and read the title of the article, "Two Find Bliss Going Green," and the author, Jill Tischman.

WTF!

I threw fifteen dollars down on the table and stormed out of the café. Jill knew for a fact that I'd decorated that apartment all on my own so how could she in good conscience report all those lies? And there was still the matter of the baby shower. Something fishy was going on, I just knew it. And it was time I found out exactly what that was.

At the Times Square headquarters of Oilliamson-Gerard Publications, a Paris-based publishing conglomerate that put out ten monthly magazines including *House & Home,* I told the downstairs security guard that Jill was expecting me. The guard had to call up because I wasn't on the list of expected visitors, but eventually a pretty young woman appeared in the lobby and escorted me upstairs and into the *House & Home* reception area.

"Jill wasn't expecting you," said the woman. Her breath stank of coffee and cigarettes and I wondered if the boys that dated her fed her breath mints before they kissed. "She's in a conference call."

"I know. I'm happy to wait," I responded.

She raised her dark eyebrows to say "suit yourself" and swished a handful of long glossy mahogany hair behind her back.

For the third time in one day, I found myself waiting. My stomach growled and I thought longingly of my raspberry tart and the plate of macaroons that had gone untouched in Countrybank's Warhol room. Finally, Jill's halitosis-inflicted assistant appeared and escorted me into Jill's tiny office, which was decorated in the same Maximalist fashion as her home—patterns on top of patterns, bright colors and bold bibelots. Jill sat behind a pink lacquer desk that was too large for the small space. A chunky gold statement necklace hung around her neck, and she was dressed in a floral-printed frock I had seen in the window at Barneys. On the floor a chartreuse crocodile purse lay on its side, spilling out a handful of cosmetics.

"Marcy, I'm so glad you came," she said preemptively as soon as her assistant closed the door behind her. "I've picked up the phone to call you so many times. But I—"

"What? You thought it would be easier for me to learn about Ainsley's pregnancy in the *New York Post*? Or in this month's *House & Home*?" I said, throwing the magazine down on her desk.

"When you hear what I have to say, you'll understand."

"I'm waiting."

"Ainsley has been blackmailing me," she said so quietly I had to move closer toward her to hear her. "She somehow found out about me and Blake."

So Jill had lied to me and Gigi about the extent of her involvement with Blake. "You slept with him, didn't you? You two were having an affair!"

She held her index finger against her mouth and mouthed the word *please*. Then she continued speaking, her voice low and controlled, "Ainsley threatened to go public with my indescretions if I didn't put her in *House & Home* with John. It was a logistical nightmare. Theirs were the last pages we shipped."

"So that's why John needed me out of the apartment so quickly," I said.

"Ainsley told me that if I dared to tell you, she would find out."

"So then why are you telling me now?"

"Because you deserve to know the truth and because I can't live with myself anymore knowing the pain I've caused you."

"But throw her a baby shower?"

"I swear all I did for her shower was show up; she handled everything else on her own. I didn't even handle the invitations or guest list," Jill said.

"I just don't know how you could expect me to ever trust you again," I said.

"Just think about it from my perspective. Try putting yourself in my shoes."

I looked down at her feet. She was wearing a pair of six-inch studded chartreuse suede platform booties. Something about them—the trendy color, the height of the heel, or the six-figure price tag I was sure that came with them—made me angry.

"I couldn't if I tried," I said, crossing my arms over my chest.

"Believe me, Marcy, I had no choice! You have to understand that. I would have lost *everything* if people found out about me and Blake. Glenn would have left me and taken the kids, and Oilliamson-Gerard probably would have fired me. The new creative director wants me out. He's assembled a new team and they're all just waiting for me to mess up so they have a reason to push me out. Blake is nineteen years old. I'm on the board of the New Yorkers for Children. Do you know what a scandal that would have been?"

"Oh, I don't know, maybe on par with having your husband stolen away from you by his mistress, whom he impregnated while he was still married to you, then having one of your best friends throw the baby shower?" I said.

Jill put her hands on her hips. "What if you could have prevented going through all of that? Wouldn't you have done anything in your power to save your marriage? Even if it meant hurting a friend?"

I looked at her standing there, so righteous, so perfectly put together. To an outsider, her life looked perfect: she had a handsome, successful husband, glamorous job, active social life, showplace apartment, and attractive children. But it was all façade.

Her husband was verbally abusive and she was barely hanging on to her job; she was a philanderer and shopaholic, and her children were neglected and desperately in need of their mother's attention.

"You and I are clearly very different people," I said. "I wouldn't dream of sacrificing one of my closest friend's happiness and trust just to save my own ass."

Then I turned on my heel and waltzed straight out of her office.

20

Money Ain't the Only Thing Green

In the short span of time I had been in the Oilliamson-Gerard building, the sun had set and a Northern wind had descended on the city, dropping the temperature outdoors by a good five degrees, if not more. Fumbling with my bag of magazines and handbag, I managed to thread one of my arms through the sleeve of my coat before I lost my grip on the bags and dropped them both. Squatting down to pick them up, I heard a familiar voice.

"Need a hand?"

It was Mr. Navy Suit, aka Warren Robbins, the charming widower from Jill's dinner party, the one who had refused to be sucked into Ainsley's vortex of pseudocharm. When I looked up he smiled at me with his adorable, lopsided grin, causing me to get flustered and lose my balance. Pitching forward, I nearly knocked Warren over on his backside.

"Whoa there, Marcy," he said, catching my shoulders in his hands. He held me like that until it was clear that I had regained my balance. "It's Marcy, right?" he asked as we both stood up.

"Yes," I said, surprised that he remembered. "You have a good memory. I can never remember anyone's name."

"I don't either, usually," he chuckled. "Yours stuck, though. Are you sure you're okay?"

"Oh nothing a big plate of cheese and an even bigger glass of wine couldn't fix," I said, buttoning my coat closed against the freezing wind.

"Ah, so that's your poison, *le fromage*?" he said, adopting a thick French accent. He tweaked his imaginary moustache and winked.

I laughed, snorting a little. "*Et le vin*," I added, winking back.

"How about we go get some then? I know a great place and just the other day I was telling myself that my cholesterol was getting dangerously low."

I looked at my watch.

"Or do you have to be somewhere?" he asked.

"No, not really." Gigi had a dinner party to cater that night so it was just going to be me, Ken, and a big bowl of Soba noodles. "I was just checking to make sure it wasn't too early to have a drink."

"Never too early, if you ask me," he said, hailing us a cab.

Warren directed the taxi to Artisanal, a restaurant in lower Midtown that specialized in cheese. Since it was still early, we were able to snag one of the little tables near the fromagier, and the smell of all those delicious wheels and wedges sent me straight to heaven.

"I've been dying to come here," I said, rubbing my hands together excitedly.

"How can it be that a cheese lover like yourself has never come here?"

"My ex-husband said it would be like taking an alcoholic to Ireland."

"Ouch."

"Yeah, John didn't want to encourage my addiction. But the

funny thing is that ever since we split up, I've barely touched the stuff." I didn't think it was necessary to mention that my abstinence had more to do with the fact that I couldn't afford my favorite creamy rounds of Brie, tangy pyramids of sheep's milk, wedges of crumbly, salty blue, or snowy globes of mozzarella than with any concerted effort to cut back.

The waiter arrived tableside and Warren ordered us a couple glasses of Riesling and an order of gougères—gourmet, lighter-than-air mini-cheese puffs. Then we left our table and walked over to the cheese display, where the maitre de fromage let us taste a half-dozen cheeses before we settled on a buttery French Comte (pronounced kom-tay), a bold Swiss Alpage (mountain pasture) cheese, a semi-soft washed rind cheese from Vermont, and a zesty Spanish goat's milk cheese, based on our wine order and taste preferences.

When we returned to the table, our wine and the bowl of gougères had already arrived. I dug in greedily and popped one of the pale orange puffs in my mouth. It was hot and buttery and made me want to devour the entire order in three seconds flat, but I restrained myself and pushed the bowl back over to Warren's side of the table.

"You were married when I met you at Jill's. That was how many months ago?" he inquired.

"About eight months," I said, taking a sip of my wine. "You do know that John left me for Ainsley, and she's having his baby."

"I try not to listen to gossip, so, no, I hadn't heard. But your ex-husband, if I may say so, is an idiot. I find that in situations such as these, one man's loss is sure to be another man's gain."

I didn't know what to say to that, so I popped another cheese puff in my mouth.

Warren's iPhone started ringing in his pocket and he took it out to turn off the sound. "If you need to get that, I understand,"

I said just as our cheese arrived along with a basket of baguette slices.

"And neglect all these delicious cheeses?" Warren laughed eye-balling the plate. "I think not." He cut a wedge of the Comte, placed it on a piece of bread and handed it to me. "Now tell me, Marcy, what did you do before you became a hedge fund wife?"

For the next two hours, Warren and I drank wine, ate cheese, and talked. I told him about my career at Bloomington Mutual, my childhood in Minnesota, and revealed my devastation at dis-covering John's infidelity. He regaled me with stories from his youth—he'd grown up in Michigan, the youngest of four—and had gone to Stanford on a swimming scholarship. At Stanford he majored in math and computer science, and did well enough to earn a spot in a graduate program at MIT, where he was recruited by GHBC, a blue-chip investment bank, to help develop their automated trading system. After 9/11 Warren formed Iceberg Capital, a "black box" hedge fund that invested money mostly by computer, using supersecret algorithms he and his partner had written.

That same year Warren married Meghan, a lawyer he'd met through friends. They had a son named Oliver a few years later. From a beat-up brown leather wallet, Warren produced a picture of a dark-haired little boy in a pair of navy and red swimming trunks, a pair of bright orange floaters holding his arms aloft. Oliver was smiling broadly—he had Warren's same grin—and beautiful big brown eyes that must have been inherited from his mother.

"I heard that your wife passed away," I said, handing Warren back the photograph. "You and Oliver must miss her so much."

Gazing down at the picture of his son, he said, "I do, but at least in Oliver I'll always have a piece of Meghan with me. I just wish we'd had a chance to have more children. That was her one regret, too. If I've learned anything about life through her death, it's that you never know what the future holds. The only thing that truly matters, that we have any control over, is the here and now. Meghan and I did so much planning. We were going to have another child, renovate our house, travel through the Far East and South America as soon as our kids were old enough to appreciate it."

Tears began welling in his eyes, which of course made me start to tear up, too. "Warren, I'm so sorry. To have found the love of your life and lose her must be devastating. Sometimes I think I'm lucky that John left the way he did because at least now I get to hate him, and hating someone is easier than missing them."

We sat in silence for a while until Warren motioned toward the plate. There was one piece of Comte left.

"Last bite, going once, going twice," I warned.

He made a motion toward his mouth and I leaned over the table to slide the cheese into his mouth. As he began to chew, he touched my bottom lip with his thumb.

I leaned back in my chair, my cheeks burning and heart racing. *Oh boy.*

"Sorry," he smiled. "It was sweet how you opened your mouth. Meghan used to do that whenever she was feeding Oliver."

"So what next?" I asked.

Warren waved the waiter over and handed him his credit card. "How about a visit to the green fairy?" he suggested.

Twenty minutes later, Warren and I were in the East Village in front of an unmarked building that resembled an old-time train car. Pushing open the wooden door he ushered me inside the tiny, dimly lit bar, which was full of people and decorated with dark wood-paneled walls, a marble-topped bar, crystal chandeliers, and suede banquettes with black-granite tables. The bar, named Death & Co., called to mind a 1920s speakeasy and, as I was about to learn from Warren, was inspired by a pre-Prohibition era advertisement that grimly illustrated the effects of alcohol on a man's health. Warren said that he had been taken there by a friend a year ago and it had become one of his favorite haunts.

We took the two remaining seats in the house, a pair of stools at the end of the bar. "Hey, Billy," Warren said to the bartender. "Meet Marcy, Marcy, Billy, the finest mixologist in all of New York."

"Aw shucks, Warren, you're makin' me blush," Billy said, smirking.

"Don't mind him. Billy's not used to seeing me with a girl. I usually come here to console myself after enduring yet another bad date."

"So you've never brought a girl here besides me?"

He shook his head. "You're the first I've wanted to."

When Billy returned, Warren ordered two "green fairies," and less than a minute later there were two etched glasses, each one-quarter full of absinthe, set before us on the bar. Billy balanced a pair of slotted silver spoons on top of each glass and set a cube of sugar on top of each spoon. Next Billy opened a bottle of champagne and poured it over the cubes, dissolving them into the green liquor.

After clinking my glass against Warren's I took a sip of the milky, fizzy cocktail, sloshing the anise-flavored drink in my mouth. "Like it?" he asked.

"It tastes like licorice. And I love licorice," I responded, taking another sip. "How about you? Do you like it?"

"If it's good enough for Oscar Wilde and Ernest Hemingway, it's good enough for me," Warren said.

"Oh, I loved *The Sun Also Rises*. In high school I wrote a paper about the novel's indictment of postwar society, the deterioration of values and fixation on wealth accumulation," I said, pausing. "But what I remember the most from that book was the female character, Lady Ashley."

"Brett."

"Yes, Brett. She was the kind of woman who could inspire men to ruin their lives and betray their friends. And on top of all that sexual power, she had the means to remain financially independent. She was totally liberated."

"Thanks to her two divorces," Warren interjected. "And I disagree that she was liberated at all. She needed a man to make her feel beautiful and powerful, so ultimately she was dependent on men for her emotional security."

"Hemingway was a misogynist. He couldn't handle women who were both powerful and beautiful."

"That's not true. In fact, he was quite drawn to them. He just didn't like the destructive, narcissistic man-eating ones."

"Oh really? Give me an example of a strong and beautiful woman—a real heroine—in a Hemingway novel."

"That's easy. Maria in *For Whom the Bell Tolls*. After witnessing so much brutality and death in war, Robert Jordan didn't care about life, until he met her. She restored him."

"But he died and she lived. Ultimately he was the hero, not her."

We had finished our drinks, so Warren ordered another round. This time Billy mixed us a cocktail made of absinthe, chambord, and rum, and we toasted to great literature. Warren confided in me that he had always dreamed of retiring one day and attempting to write the great American novel, and especially after Meghan's death he had become nearly consumed with the desire to run off to someplace quiet to write. If it weren't for Oliver's psychiatrist advising him against it he would have moved full-time to his ranch in Montana long ago.

"I've met more women than I care to remember in the past

year, and not one of them was able to carry on a conversation about a book, or make a literary allusion. You're different, Marcy," he said, grasping my hand in his. "You make me want to stick around."

It had been a long time since a man showed any interest in me, and the sensation of Warren's warm, enveloping hand on mine sent chills up and down my spine. I turned my palm upward to meet his and we sat like that in companionable silence, enjoying the effects of the alcohol and the feeling of each other's skin for a while. And then he kissed me. His lips were soft and smooth and left no doubt as to where our evening was headed. I let Warren pay for the bill, and then I let him take me to bed.

The following morning I woke up in Warren's bed and created a plan of action.

Priority number one?

Finding my underwear.

Number two?

Restoring my dignity.

Number three?

Getting the hell out of Warren Robbins's apartment.

Hopping out of bed, I cringed as I remembered my failed attempt at performing a pole dance with one of the four posters on Warren's bed. Stroking my bruised backside, I had a newfound respect for exotic dancers—their job was harder than it looked. As I hobbled around the room, I gathered my clothes and considered my chances of getting a second date (if I could count last night as our first, which I wasn't entirely sure I could), and came to the conclusion that I'd made a grave error by not only sleeping with Warren, but making a big heaping, failed-stripper fool of myself at the same time. Allowing myself one more minute— possibly my last opportunity ever—to admire Warren's masculine, perfectly symmetrical face and skilled hands (*oh, the things they could do)*, I forced myself to quickly dress and wash my face in the slate-tiled en-suite bathroom. If I could get out of his apartment without waking him, then at least I'd leave him wanting more. And then maybe he'd call.

I was still missing my underwear, purse, and my bag with all the décor magazines and Thorne Van *Sexist*'s pitch book. Not seeing them anywhere in the bedroom, I decided to search for them in the living room, where Warren and I had warmed up (*if you know what I mean*) on the rug in front of the fireplace before moving to his bedroom.

In the living room I found a big L-shaped couch, upholstered in dark gray suede and piled high with velvet pillows and cashmere throws. An ancient Buddha head and a pair of large hurricane lanterns encasing two thick ivory candles crowded the top of a square ebonized-wood coffee table, and a pair of leather triangle stools flanked the front of a gray stone fireplace. There was a silver-plated egg-shaped chest of drawers and a large wenge wood bookshelf stacked with books. After last night's conversation about Hemingway, I couldn't help being drawn to the shelves, and searched past the Marcel Proust and Shakespeare to find what I was looking for: Warren's well-worn paperback copy of *For Whom the Bell Tolls*. Thumbing through it, I found comments scribbled in the margins and highlighted passages. If I had had my purse, I would have been tempted to slip it inside and keep it as a souvenir of the previous night and proof that I had actually shared a night of naked bliss with *the* Warren Robbins.

Before bumping into Warren on the street, the last time I'd seen him was in the society pages of the *New York Times*. There was a photograph of him at the annual Robin Hood Foundation benefit. He was seated next to the Czech model and tsunami-survivor Petra Nemcova. I'd seen the snapshot during my lonely mid-divorce period, and had called Gigi to rant about Petra, but

Gigi refused to be sympathetic and told me that Petra was a nice person and I was acting like a jealous bitch.

Maybe she was right.

But it no longer mattered since Warren obviously preferred a woman of substance, a woman more like myself, to perfect facial features, long legs, and great tits.

And how did I know that?

He'd spent last night with me, not her!

Ha!

Little old me, Miss Never Been Kissed, Miss Never Went to Prom, spent the night with Warren Robbins and not only had sex with him, but *hot* sex that was just dirty enough—that is, if you didn't count my unfortunate accident with the bed post.

"Isn't it a little early for such heavy reading?" Warren said, interrupting my trip down memory lane. I wheeled around on my heels to find him standing in front of the fireplace in his plaid cotton boxers, scratching the dark stubble on his chin. His mostly bare swimmer's body—broad chest, strong shoulders, and trim torso—had my heart racing once again.

"I was looking for my purse," I said defensively.

"In the bookshelf?"

"I got distracted." I wedged the book back on the shelf.

"Have you found it? Your purse?"

I shook my head.

"Did you have it when we came in last night?"

"I can't remember." I felt idiotic standing there, talking about my stupid purse. But I couldn't leave without some money for a cab ride home, not to mention my personal identification, credit cards, and telephone.

"And it's not in the bedroom?"

I blushed at the word. I still couldn't believe some of the things we had done the night before. The absinthe had robbed me of all my inhibitions and good sense. Pole dancing? Performing a strip tease to *Purple Rain*? The reverse cowgirl?

Warren disappeared back into the bedroom and came back with my purse and cotton underpants.

"Thank you," I said, trying to hide my mounting embarrassment. Stepping out of my heels, I began to snake the underwear up my legs. *Oh why, oh why, couldn't I have worn my lacy pair of panties yesterday?*

"Marcy, I wouldn't—" he began to say but I cut him off. I didn't want him to give me the last-night-didn't-mean-anything or the equally horrid I'm-not-ready-to-be-tied-down speech . . . at least not yet.

Can't we just pretend that you really do prefer me to the Petra Nemcovas of the world?

"Let me just say that I'm not the kind of woman who—" I said.

"Takes her panties off in taxis?"

"Um, no. I don't usually do that," I mumbled, pulling my underwear up as modestly as I could in a nonstretch pencil skirt.

"And I take it, then, that you're also not the kind of woman who then proceeds to throw her panties in the gutter in front of not one, but two doormen, proclaiming the aforementioned undergarment, and I quote, 'useless given what I have in store for you Mr. Sexy Pants'?"

"I did not do that."

"Oh yes you did," he said, laughing.

"That means that . . ."—I shrieked, pulling off my panties (with zero regard to decorum this time)—". . . these have been on a New York City sidewalk."

"Not sidewalk. Gutter," he said, covering his mouth with his hand. He tried hard not to laugh, which only served to make his abs look even more defined.

Something a little farther south caught my eye.

Warren noticed me looking. "Come over here," he said, suddenly serious.

I swallowed hard. I wanted him, but I also wanted to leave him wanting more. I looked over to a picture of Oliver and his mother on the fireplace mantle. "What about your son?" I asked.

"Oliver," he said, scratching his scruff again. "I hadn't thought of him. You're the first person I've ever brought home."

"Oh come on. You can't be telling me that you haven't had sex with another woman since Meghan."

"What, you don't believe me?"

"But a man has needs," I said.

"Meet my needs meeter," he laughed, holding his right hand up in the air and wiggling his fingers at me.

"I don't believe you," I said, crossing my arms across my chest.

Grabbing my arm with his hand, he pulled me into his bare chest; the smell of his skin awakened my desire almost immediately. He kissed me again, this time for a long time before I pulled away.

"But Oliver?"

"He's in Greenwich. Spent the night with my parents in my house out there," he said, pushing my skirt up around my waist.

Then he picked me up and walked me over to the bookcase, where we did things that would have made even Lady Ashley blush.

21

Where's the Antacid?

When I got back to Gigi's apartment, I learned that two of Wall Street's largest and most venerated investment banks were no more. One had filed for bankruptcy and the other had been bought out by another bank that hadn't been so heavily exposed to the meltdown in the mortgage industry. But there was trouble rumbling in other sectors of the economy, and even while the government was making historic moves to ease the mounting liquidity crisis and come to the aid of major corporations in need of assistance, a full-on recession seemed inevitable.

The feeling of panic had already spread from Wall Street to the penthouses of Park Avenue. Gigi told me that all over town nannies and housekeepers were being fired, and she had already heard from five friends trying to find new jobs for staff members they had been forced to let go. A Moveable Feast was in big trouble, too: Three catering events that were in contract were terminated and another five events canceled just that morning. As a result, Gigi had no choice but to lay off one-third of her employees.

In light of the economic freefall, I felt silly talking about how my night with Warren had gone, but Gigi insisted that I tell her every last detail, if only to get her mind off of everything else that was waiting for her back in her office. From her perch at the foot of my bed, she listened quietly as I recounted everything from my chance meeting with Warren on the street in front of the Oilliamson-Gerard building to that morning's steamy activities (without offering too much detail), and when I was all done, she let out a long, withering sigh and embarked on a ten-minute-long lecture about "putting out" on the first date.

In an attempt to redirect the conversation to anything other than "the perception of wantonness," I told Gigi about my meeting with Thorne and then falling in love with that apartment on Beekman Place, when it occurred to me that I hadn't heard from Shailagh about the sellers' response to my offer, and rooted around in my purse for my BlackBerry only to find it missing.

I left my coffee on the Chinese box bedside table and followed Gigi into her office, where she looked up the phone number for Death & Co., while I checked my messages on a landline. Shailagh had indeed phoned that morning asking me to call her back as soon as I'd heard her message, and I didn't waste any time in returning her call right away. Once I had her on the line, she told me that the sellers of the apartment had accepted my offer, and the next step was for me to fill out a purchase application and assets-and-liabilities statement that would be reviewed by the board. At some point they would bring me in for an interview and make their final decision but this might not happen for several weeks, depending on how many other applicants they were reviewing. (There were apparently several apartments in the building up for sale.) She said she would be messengering the paperwork, plus her board interview tips over to me that afternoon.

After I called Death & Co. and left a message, I picked up the phone to dial Warren to tell him that I had lost my phone, but Gigi said that doing so would be the kiss of death.

"Negatory," she said, snatching the phone out of my hands. "Men like Warren can have any woman they want, so you have to be the one woman they can't," she said.

I reminded her that he had already had me and then some, but Gigi explained that all was not lost. If I had succeeded in giving him a taste of something he was going to want again (which I think I did, *thankyouverymuch*), I hadn't destroyed my chances of seducing him but had, perhaps, enhanced them.

"However you cannot call him because then he'll know he can have you whenever he wants. And sugar, no matter how delectable a morsel you may be, if he can get a free sample any time he wants, he's never gonna wanna buy the whole darn cookie."

"And here I was thinking that it was the milk you didn't want to give away for free," I quipped.

Gigi slipped her phone back into its charger. "Do Not Call Him."

"I don't see why I should follow your rules."

"You can try it your way, but speaking from experience, men like Warren place the women they are dating in one of two categories: easy hussy or precious jewel. And from which one of those two groups do you think they end up choosing their wife?"

"The precious jewel," I replied glumly.

When I finally managed to convince Gigi that I would rather eat a bloody tampon than call Warren and profess my eternal love and devotion, she left me to start packing for Miami. Feeling suddenly exhausted, I decided to catch up on all the sleep I had missed the night before, and by the time I woke up it was five in the afternoon and the sun had already started dipping toward the Manhattan skyline.

My stomach was growling, so I went to the kitchen in search of something to eat. Ken, who had gone to Florida with Gigi, had left me a bowl of soba noodles with tofu, scallions, and ginger and as I was heating it up, the doorman buzzed from downstairs to announce the arrival of a courier who ended up having the papers for my board application. I took them back into my room once I had finished my soup, and began to read through them.

The questions were far more personal than I anticipated. The board wanted to know my age, marital status (and marital history), occupation, and whether I had children, regular houseguests, or pets. After answering all the personal inquiries, I sailed through the section on my finances, until I got to the space for employment status and occupation. I was stumped.

The phone rang and I picked it up. "Cohen's residence," I said, mimicking Ken's smooth intonation the best I could.

"How are you holding up?" said the voice.

It was Warren.

"How did you find me?" I asked.

"It wasn't that hard. The Cohens are listed in the Hedge Fund Family Pages."

"Really?"

"No."

"So that was a joke," I said, walking to the bed and pulling my legs into my chest. My cheeks felt hot and my heart was thudding in my ears and I couldn't help but wonder if Warren felt equally flushed and flustered by the sound of my voice.

He told me he was driving back to the city from Greenwich and was going to take Oliver out to dinner but wanted to know if I could meet him for a drink afterwards. I knew I should say no, for the sake of my liver and because I knew Gigi would kill me if she found out I went out with him again, especially since drinks was not dinner, and Warren wasn't even offering to pick me up. Still I couldn't help myself and said yes. So what if Warren wasn't going to fall in love with me because I was too "easy"; maybe all I wanted was a fling, too. For crying out loud I had just gotten through a gut-wrenching soul-pulverizing divorce. Didn't I deserve to have a little no-strings-attached fun?

At ten o'clock that evening I met Warren at yet another hole-in-the-wall bar on St. Marks Place near First Avenue. The bar, called PDT, or Please Don't Tell, was located behind a dingy hot dog stand. You actually had to walk *through* the hot dog place to get to the bar, which was every bit as intimate and cool as Death & Co. It had a wooden ceiling, brick walls, a mirrored-back bar, and mounted deer heads.

It was also packed with people trying to forget the uncertainty of their own financial futures and the continued chaos on Wall Street. The Dow was down another four hundred points that day and the government had moved in to bail out an overleveraged insurance giant as well as the country's largest mortgage lender. Very few sectors of the economy would be spared by the liquidity crisis: Real estate prices were dropping precipitously, most new construction projects had been halted or scrapped indefinitely, the luxury goods market was tanking, restaurants were closing, as were Broadway shows, and two airlines were rumored to be on the brink of bankruptcy.

Even before the meltdown of the financial industry sent markets roiling, hedge funds were having the worst year in nearly two decades, with losses ranging from six to twenty-five percent. The recent turn of events only served to worsen the outlook for most funds because the investment banks, which were scrambling to fend off short sellers, were calling in their loans, making it next to impossible for the portfolio managers to continue trading, and many funds were forced into liquidating all their assets to make their margin calls. Needless to say, investors were trying to pull out capital left and right, and several funds had announced that they were shutting down operations completely.

Amid the atmosphere of massive panic, everyone had turned

to alcohol, including us. That night Warren and I ended up inebriated and once again in bed together. I left his apartment near the crack of dawn; this time little Oliver *was* at the apartment and had a six a.m. Cheerios date with daddy at the breakfast table.

The following afternoon, I finally received a call back from the manager at Death & Co. who told me that they had found my things at closing and had called directory assistance to find out my number. A woman answered, claimed to be me, and came by later that day to retrieve my things. Some wires were crossed, the manager said, and they'd thought I'd left my message *before* I, or rather the woman who had pretended to be me, was contacted. No one had put two and two together and figured out that the woman who had collected my belongings and I were two different people until I called the bar again to ask if either of the items had been found. The manager apologized profusely and asked me if I planned to contact the police, but I said no, I knew exactly who had my things (Ainsley) and would deal with it on my own.

"You've only seen the tip of the iceberg with this one," I said.

"That's all I usually get to see, and thank God for that," he replied before hanging up and wishing me a good day.

I called Verizon and had them make sure that there hadn't been any long distance phone calls or overage charges on my cell phone service since I lost it and then arranged to come into one of their stores to buy a new BlackBerry. Getting my pitch book back would be much more difficult, and I decided not to even bother. Ainsley would deny taking my things and John would defend her and probably think that I was crazy for making such an accusation—which, come to think of it, was probably exactly what Ainsley wanted to happen.

A few hours later, when I had returned from buying my replacement BlackBerry, Warren called again and arranged for us to meet at another clandestine bar, this one named Angel's Share

after the part of the alcohol that evaporates while the liquor's being aged in a cask. It was hard for me to locate Angel's Share—it
being situated behind a waiter's door on a second-floor Japanese
restaurant and all—and by the time I finally found it, I had
started having second thoughts about what I was doing there.
Maybe Gigi was right. It was no fun being treated like a good-time
girl. I wanted to be taken out to dinner and if dinner really was
impossible, then at the very least I wanted to be picked up.

Entering the dimly lit lounge, I saw Warren sitting at the bar
talking to the bartender and decided to play a little game. If he
noticed me coming in and sitting down a few seats away from
him then he really did like me, and if he didn't then he didn't. I
walked normally and chose a stool a few down from his, where I
was sure he could see me. I sat there for a full two minutes listening to the bartender talk about his previous life as an auto engi-
neer (GM had laid him off a few months earlier) before I made up
my mind to sneak out of the restaurant to call Gigi. She'd know
how I could restore myself to precious-jewel status with Warren.
It probably involved leaving him in the bar and texting him a
cryptic excuse and apology for not showing up, but I was finally
ready to admit that I had fallen hard for him and was willing to
do whatever was necessary to make him fall in love with me.

I slipped off of my barstool and made it about five paces toward the door before I felt a tap on my shoulder. I didn't dare look
around.

"Marcy," Warren said. "Were you trying to sneak out of here?"

"No," I snorted.

"Can you turn around?"

I did.

He gave me a puzzled look as he leaned in for a quick kiss on
the mouth. Then he took my hand and led me to the back of the
lounge, to a small square space decorated with purple leather arm
chairs and marble-topped tables. We sat down at one of the tables

marked reserved and ordered our first cocktail. As I sipped my drink, Warren told me about his day and the endless dinner with a couple of his old buddies from GHBC from which he had just come.

"We talked about the markets, what else? One of the poor guys just lost his shirt, lost a hundred mil in three months. He kept thinking he could make up his losses, but the market kept tanking. And then the bank called in his loans, and bam, he's out of business. His wife just had another baby, their fourth, and now they have to sell their apartment and he's looking to unload his Aston Martin."

"Oh no, not the Aston Martin! Anything but that," I said dourly.

"What's with you tonight?" Warren asked.

I shook my head. According to Gigi, whining was the second worst thing you could do on a date (or whatever this was). The first was acting slutty, and I already had covered that territory. Finishing my drink, I asked Warren if he could order us another round.

"Not before you tell me what's going on with you. You don't seem like yourself."

I took a deep breath knowing that what I was about to say would very likely drive Warren far, far away from me. But I had to lay my cards on the table, even it was against The Rules.

"I see a pattern emerging," I finally said. "And it troubles me. We've gone out for three nights in a row, and every night we've gone to some dimly lit, secret bar that no one's ever heard of. I think it's curious that you don't want to go someplace where we might actually run into someone we know."

"I like my privacy, Marcy. I don't want people to know what I'm up to."

"Or who you're with?"

"Isn't it easier for us to get to know each other without an audience," he said, grabbing my hand across the table. "It's not that I'm not proud to be with you. Is that what you're thinking?"

"You sound just like my ex-husband," I said.

Warren sat back in his chair and sighed. He looked weary and unprepared. And although I hadn't expected him to go down on one knee and ask me to marry him, neither did I anticipate seeing the look that was on his face, the look that said *not this again*. As difficult as it was to do, I made up my mind then and there to let Warren Robbins go.

It had become incredibly evident to me that I was making the same exact mistake with Warren that I had made with John. I was letting him sleep with me in secret, just like John had for all those months before we became a legitimate couple, and in doing so, had ceded all my power, not to mention self-respect.

"I'm not going to repeat the mistakes of my past. I'm not interested in having a secret relationship." I looked at Warren, waiting for him to insist that he wasn't ashamed of me and that he wanted everyone in the world know he was dating me, but he didn't.

I reached into my purse for my wallet.

He put his hand on my arm. "Don't. And don't go. I shouldn't have asked you to come out tonight. We should be taking this slower. And with everything that's happening in the markets, my head isn't where it needs to be able to really enjoy your company."

I took a step toward the door. I'd had enough of men who claimed they couldn't pay attention to me because they were too stressed out from work. Granted, the financial markets were imploding, and thousands had lost their jobs and hefty portions of their life savings, but I wanted to be with someone who could discuss those things *with* me, not use them as an excuse not to talk to me at all.

"Let me at least put you in a taxi," Warren said, but I could sense a degree of relief in his voice.

"That's okay, I respect your privacy," I snapped. "And I'm sure you have work matters to attend to."

He held his hands up in mock surrender. "Okay then."

I pushed open the waiter's door and didn't look back.

I spent the following week trying not to think about Warren. Gigi was still in Miami with Jeremy, but she called frequently to give me pep talks. The upside was that she was proud of me for walking out on my paramour and told me that he would no doubt be showering me with flowers and jewels as soon as he thought a prudent amount of time had passed. Gigi also filled me in on the latest about Lauren, her step daughter. Despite her father's offer to make an anonymous donation to the tune of one million dollars, Lauren had been placed on a one-year mandatory leave from Rollins College. Jeremy, his ex-wife, and Gigi had organized an intervention and had put Lauren on a plane to Silver Hill in Connecticut for rehab.

Gigi said Jeremy had finally gotten Lauren to confess that the reason for her drug abuse—they expected heroin—was heartbreak. One of her old classmates from Pruitt, whom she had been dating long distance without anyone's knowledge, had cheated on her, and Lauren had found pictures of him with the older "woman" on his computer when she had last visited him in New York. She'd confronted him and he'd responded by kicking her out of his absent parent's Upper East Side pied-à-terre. Her revenge? Sleeping with his best friend, who happened to be a rampant drug user.

Lauren had started with Adderall and alcohol in high school and quickly moved on to cigarettes and cocaine as soon as she'd arrived at Rollins. It was only after she'd been dumped by her boyfriend that she'd turned to heroin. Her weight had dropped from 120 pounds to 98, and she was failing all but one of her classes that semester. To top it all off, she had amassed a $50,000 bill on her credit card, mainly charges from Miami-area restaurants and clothing shops, and had stolen at least $15,000 dollars in cash from her mother and father in the last six months. ·

Surprisingly, Gigi had discovered that Jeremy, in addition to finally paying attention to Lauren, was being increasingly attentive to Chloe, whom he had bathed for the first time ever. He had suddenly realized that he hadn't been a good father to Lauren and felt responsible for her recent drug abuse and promiscuity. He knew enough pop psychology to know that troubled young women often looked for love from boys to replace the affirmation they weren't getting at home from their fathers.

"It's like he's a brand-new person," Gigi whispered excitedly over the phone.

At least there was a silver lining for one of us.

22

Just When You Think It Can't Get Any Worse . . . It Does

Aside from preparing for my board interview, I didn't have much to do, and the lack of activity in my life made me feel morose and useless. I was bored, lonely, and depressed, and knew that it was time for me to get a real job, something that allowed me to use my mind and skill set, something in finance. My best prospect, considering the abysmal state of the markets, would be with Bloomington Mutual in their New York office. At least there, people knew me. I had built a reputation as a hard worker and innovative thinker, and also still had plenty of friends who would offer recommendations if I asked them to.

On a blustery Monday morning in mid-October, I made a call to an old colleague in Chicago, who then referred me to a female financial advisor in the bank's New York office. Her name was Justine Peterson, and she agreed to meet me for lunch at Lever House, a hot lunch spot on Park Avenue near BlooMu's East Coast headquarters.

I arrived first, dressed in my pearls and power suit, and took in the scene. The restaurant was longer than it was wide, resembling the interior of a space ship, and was stacked with Wall Street heavyweights, real estate scions, and publishing wunderkinds. The lunch reservation was under Justine's name and I was originally taken to a table at the back, near the kitchen door. But then, shortly after I had been seated by the hostess, the maitre d' arrived, red-faced and apologetic, and moved me to a table closer to the action.

I was just getting resettled and enjoying a glass of sauvignon blanc (on the house) when Justine arrived, wearing a suit jacket that fit too tightly across her chest and a skirt that had been hemmed two inches too short. She had great legs and a face like a porcelain doll, and would have been extremely attractive if it weren't for the excessive eye makeup and the twenty or so extra pounds she was carrying, mostly on her hips.

She held out her hand and gave me a firm handshake. "So nice to meet you, Marcy," she said, brandishing an earnest smile.

We made our menu selections—jamón ibérico and arctic char for Justine, grilled shrimp and risotto for me—and spent five minutes playing the name game—we actually knew very few people in common—before I asked Justine how long she had been working at BlooMu. It turned out that she had only been there less than a year, and had previously been working at, of all places, Zenith Capital. She'd known John, she said, but hadn't worked with him intimately since her job was in Zenith's marketing division—she organized events, advertising, and other outreach programs to help the fund find new investors.

Of course I had to ask whether John had a reputation around the office, and if so, what it was. Justine smiled and said that he was considered "ambitious" and a "great hire."

"But?" I asked. "There's always a but. We're divorced so you can be frank."

"John struck me as a typical hedge funder: Thinks he's God, kisses Fred's ass whenever he can. He's an operator. But if you're wondering if he had a reputation for hanging out at strip clubs or tomcatting around, the answer is no."

Her answer made sense, and because I didn't want to spend another minute of my lunch with Justine talking about John, I quickly changed the subject. "So why did you leave Zenith?"

Our server arrived with our starters and Justine waited until he had left before answering me. "Between us, I was let go. There were some other girls in my department who had been there longer than I had, and they were out to get me. I received stellar reviews from the partners, not three months before my termination. They told me, point blank, what an incredible job they thought I was doing. And then, wham, I get into an argument with one of the other women, Serena, over what party at Art Basel Miami the fund should sponsor that year, and the next thing I know my boss is asking me to clean out my desk. He said it simply wasn't working out."

Justine's story sounded sketchy, but I gave her the benefit of the doubt. After all, I'd been screwed over at BlooMu by a woman. "Why is it that women turn against each other like that? We should be supporting each other, not masterminding each other's firings," I said.

"Serena was jealous of me from the get-go. Everyday she'd comment on my clothes. 'Oh, is that something new?' or 'Justine, don't you think that skirt's too short?' And she always wanted to know who I was dating. She was so competitive about men; even if she was married, she still wanted their attention. But it wasn't until I began outperforming her at the work that she really started gunning for me."

"But if you were doing a better job than her, why didn't they fire her instead of you?" I asked. "Doesn't Zenith pride itself on being a meritocracy?"

Justine snorted. "Meritocracy my ass," she said. "Serena had been there longer and . . . her husband is a Zenith investor."

"Oh," I said.

"I should have been more careful not to get on Serena's bad side, but, you know, I was just doing my job. I thought about suing them for sexual harassment since one of the managers had kissed me at the Christmas party and we'd had a secret thing going for a while, but Zenith's lawyers said that if I didn't sign the termination agreement right then and there, I'd lose my severance pay and they wouldn't write me a letter of recommendation. Maybe I made a mistake signing the document, but at the time I felt like I had no other choice."

Although I was interested in her story, the lunch hour was quickly slipping away and I hadn't even yet launched into the purpose of my invitation—namely, to ask about my shot at getting a job with Bloomu. "I made a grave mistake leaving the bank," I said. "And I'd like to come back. Do you know if any positions might be opening up in the near term?"

"Are you kidding? There's a hiring freeze, and even if there wasn't, no one is leaving. In fact, most of us are deathly afraid of getting kicked out. And it's pretty much like that at every bank in town. I wish I had better news, but I know I wouldn't be doing you any favors by sugar-coating the situation."

I dabbed at the corners of my mouth with my heavy cotton napkin. "No, I appreciate your honesty. Even if it is disappointing to hear," I conceded. We both took sips of wine. I sighed, and then laughed. "Ah well, back to square one."

"Can I ask you something?" she asked.

"Of course."

"Why do you want to work? If I didn't have to, I wouldn't be squeezing into my suits every day just to sit behind a conference table and tell someone who's actually done something valuable with their life what to do with their money. I'm slaving away my best years for what? I thought banking would be a good place to find a husband, you know? But it hasn't worked out that way. None of the guys want to date me because I'm too smart, but I can't afford to dumb myself down at the office. I think the fact that I graduated magna cum laude from Yale is actually an impediment. Jesus, I just want to find a husband, you know?" she said, almost blubbering now.

Justine then told me that she had dated a guy who had worked at another fund for three years until she finally got fed up and delivered an ultimatum—either you propose or it's over—during dinner at a fancy restaurant. His response was to push away his plate and deliver these crushing, final words: "I do not negotiate with terrorists."

"That's it? That's all he said?" I asked.

"Yep." She frowned. "He didn't love me at all. I should never have stayed with the asshole for so long. I suck at relationships, knowing how to pick the right man to pursue, et cetera. How do you do it, Marcy?" she asked.

"How do I do what?" I responded, perplexed.

"Land a husband," Justine said. She undid the first button on her jacket, snaked her arms out of the sleeves and looked at me with teary brown eyes.

"Well, it wasn't something I did on purpose. It's not like I have a method. But I have a friend who sort of does," I said, thinking of Gigi's rules. "Maybe I could put you in touch with her," I proposed.

She seemed exasperated by my answer and took another bite of her food. When she had finished chewing, she leaned forward over the table and whispered, "Did she set you up with Warren Robbins?"

"What? No!" I exclaimed too loudly, garnering the attention of a table of men, all four dressed in dark suits and chartreuse ties.

"You *are* dating him, aren't you?"

"Well, yes, I was, sort of, but, no," I stuttered. How did she even know about Warren and me?

"So the *Wall Street Journal* was wrong?" she asked.

Oh shit.

Managing to conceal my surprise, I told Justine I wasn't comfortable talking about my private life. Then after sensing that she wasn't going to get a short course in seducing billionaires from me, she changed tactics and tried to land me as a private bank client for Bloomington Mutual. At first I didn't know which of her efforts I should be more offended by, but, then, staring at her across the table as she made a pitch as heavy-handed as her cosmetic application, I began to pity her. It wasn't easy being a single woman in New York, especially if you weren't a knockout and hadn't yet learned, as I had, that marriage was perhaps the worst exit strategy of all.

I ate enough of my entrée not to appear rude and then asked the waiter for our check, apologizing for my early departure. Justine insisted on paying for our meal, saying that we both might as well enjoy a meal on BlooMu, and I didn't contest her. As we waited for her corporate credit card to be returned to the table, I decided to tell her what I thought she needed to hear, even if I knew it would most likely fall on deaf ears.

"Justine, if my friend, the one who does have a method for landing wealthy men, were here, she would tell you to lose ten pounds, invest in a better mascara and a tutorial from a makeup artist, and start playing hard to get. But I'm not my friend, and thank God for that because she, if I may use your word, landed her very rich husband and guess what? She isn't all that happy. So I'll give you the advice I have, based on *my* life experiences."

Justine sat up in her chair and her attentiveness reminded me of a small dog waiting to be thrown a table scrap. In other words, she reminded me of me, when I was "hooking up" with John and desperate to know the secret to making him mine forever. "The easiest thing in the world is marrying money. It is far harder but far better to make your own," I said.

She snorted with incredulity.

"Think about it. What's going to happen if you get your wish and marry someone rich, and maybe, if you're lucky, a little handsome, too? I'll tell you what. You'll be in a doomed marriage. You'll stay together and be miserable because your husband calls all the shots and you're pissed about that, or you'll be like me and be too stupid and insecure to be pissed but you'll still be miserable because you'll always feel like you're not good enough for him. Or, also like me, he'll leave you for someone else. Is that the fairy tale ending you're after Justine?"

"No," she scoffed. "Of course not."

"But imagine if you didn't look at getting married as your ticket to early retirement. Imagine if you were just looking for partnership and love and kept your job when you got married. Imagine if you had a full life beyond just your relationship with your husband. Wouldn't he respect you more? Wouldn't it be a more equitable union?"

"Easy for you to say. You've got money and you obviously don't have any trouble attracting the right sort of man," she said.

What the . . . ?

"You make it sound like all I have to do is choose to make millions of dollars. But you and I both know it's not that easy. The system is still set up against us; it's still harder for us to get promoted. Men dismiss us, and all women do is fight with each other, backbiting and gossiping and undermining," she paused momentarily before continuing, her voice increasingly impassioned. "When I was in college I majored in women's issues. I studied the great feminists; I was committed to honoring their legacy by taking advantage of the opportunities out there for women in the workplace. But, you know what? I've been out of school for ten years, and I can tell you, the glass ceiling is still pretty much fucking intact."

"But progress is slow and uneven. Sometimes you have to go back one step to go forward two," I argued. "Don't lose heart."

She threw her napkin on top of her plate. "It's too late, I already have. I'm done worrying about whether my boss knows I see a shrink, or if my secretary is listening in on my private phone calls and keeping tabs how long I spend at lunch. I'm exhausted. I want out."

"I hear you, I've been there. But marrying the first guy you can get to commit to you isn't the answer."

"Why not?" Justine said petulantly.

"Because no amount of money is worth compromising yourself. How much money do you think your love is worth?" I asked.

It was meant to be a rhetorical question, but she wanted to give me an answer. "I don't know," she shrugged. "Five million would make me happy."

"Trust me, that's not enough." I laughed.

"Then tell me what is."

"That's my point! It's never enough. That's just how it works."

"And now you're going to tell me that you'd be interested in Warren Robbins even if he wasn't loaded."

Clearly Justine wasn't going to be coming around to my way of thinking that afternoon, and I needed to get to the bottom of exactly what had appeared in the papers about Warren and me. I thanked Justine for lunch and got the hell out of Lever House.

Once back at Gigi's apartment I logged on to the Internet and Googled my name and Warren's and sure enough, there were several links. The first was from the *New York Post*'s Page Six. Holding my breath, I clicked on the link to find a brief, but scathing item about me, titled *Ex Hedge Fund Wife Digging for New Gold*.

> Marcy Emerson, ex-wife of up-and-coming hedgefunder John Emerson, who is engaged to pregnant socialite Ainsley Partridge, is looking to catch an even bigger fish. Sources say that the ex-Mrs. Emerson, a serial dater and social climber back in her native Chicago, was seen canoodling at the East Village speakeasy Death & Co. with widowered hedgehog Warren Robbins, founder of quant fund Iceberg Capital and whose estimated 500 million dollar fortune makes her rumored 15 million divorce from Emerson seem like a pittance.

I hit the back button to the Google search page and saw another link to an article in the *Wall Street Journal* and clicked on that. This piece, a profile of Warren dated that morning, must have been the article Justine had referred to over lunch. I scrolled downward until I found my name.

> "Mr. Robbins is known to friends as a mild mannered, immensely private man. Two years ago he lost his beloved wife and mother of his toddler-aged son to breast cancer. Recently Mr. Robbins, whose fund has emerged relatively unscathed by the recent market turmoil, has been squiring Marcy Emerson, ex-wife of Zenith Capital trader John Emerson. However neither Mrs. Emerson nor Mr. Robbins would confirm the relationship."

My first instinct was to call Warren. He had to know that I hadn't intentionally landed him in the gossip columns or broadcast our dating history to the *Wall Street Journal*.

So I called him and left a long message.

But he never called back.

Of course he didn't.

As much as I wanted to wallow once again in my misfortune,

I had a board interview to go to later that week. Because my name had been in the papers (and not in a flattering way), Shailagh and I figured that my chances of getting approved by the board had sunk from not likely to don't even bother. But I had to go anyway. I'd laid down a hefty deposit, thirty percent of the negotiated purchase price, when my offer was accepted, and the only way I'd get it back is if the board rejected my application. Before we hung up, Shailagh asked me what I was planning on wearing. When I told her that I hadn't given it much thought and ran through the very short list of options hanging in my closet she cheerfully suggested that I go shopping for something new. "Nothing builds confidence like a new outfit," she said.

"I just don't see what the point is. I have no chance of getting approved."

"I never figured you for the type to give up easy. C'mon, Marcy, you've come this far. So what if you don't get the apartment, the point is maintaining your dignity even in the face of rejection."

I couldn't quibble with that, so I promised Shailagh I'd go exercise my new American Express card. I decided to go to Bergdorf Goodman because it was the closest store to Gigi's apartment and I already knew the saleswoman in the Ralph Lauren department. She instinctually understood my aesthetic and knew which outfits would showcase my best assets (a small waist) and hide my worst (lumpy thighs). Within ten minutes she had me in a dressing room with a black and white wool crepe dress, tweed pants and chiffon blouse, and purple cashmere sheath dress with ruched sleeves and a sensible hemline.

I had just finished buttoning up the chiffon blouse and was about to pull up the pair of tweed pants when I heard an unmistakable peal of laughter coming from the Ralph Lauren department.

It was Ainsley.

"My breasts are gigantic," she was giggling. "Not that my fiancé is complaining, but nothing fits."

"But you couldn't be more than a four. How did you lose the weight so quickly?" my saleswoman asked. She led Ainsley into the dressing room next to mine and I could hear her hanging up several hangars.

"It's true what they say about nursing. I wasn't going to do it but then I heard that that was how Jessica Alba lost all her baby weight and I had to give it a try. I'm still about ten pounds away from my goal," Ainsley confided.

"May I suggest you try this little black one first? It's perfect for a honeymoon in Paris."

John was taking Ainsley to Paris for their honeymoon? It was where I wanted to go, but he wanted to go to Hawaii, so guess where we went?

The saleswoman gasped. "Oh. My. God. That is the most beautiful ring I've ever seen. I know it's rude to ask but—"

"The center stone is five-and-a-half carats and the side stones are two carats each," Ainsley said. "The ring was my push present."

"Was the labor hard?"

I expected Ainsley to say that she'd had one of those prescheduled C-sections but instead she surprised me by describing John as the perfect "birthing partner." He'd apparently gone to every Lamaze class with her and helped her through each one of her contractions. She'd not only given birth vaginally, but without the assistance of any pain medication. She said that she respected other women's need for medication but she herself wanted to bring a child into the world in as "organic and natural" a way as possible.

When the saleswoman started cooing over a baby picture, I decided that I couldn't stand one more second. Wriggling out of the pants I put my own clothes back on, gathered up my purse and the blouse I planned on buying, and flung open the door to my dressing room.

"Hello, Ainsley," I said. "Fancy seeing you here today."

"Shopping for something new to wear out with Warren Robbins, or has he already glommed on to the fact that you've got your two shovels out?" she tittered.

The saleswoman, sensing the tension between us, murmured something about going to help another customer and zipped out of the dressing room as fast as she could.

I couldn't believe it. After everything Ainsley had done to me, all the humiliation and pain I had endured because of her, now she had the temerity to stand there and accuse me of being only interested in Warren's money? No way. I took two steps toward Ainsley and said in a low but aggressive voice, "You and I both know who the real gold digger in this room is."

"You may like to think that I stole John away from you—like I had to go out of my way to seduce him—but, honey, John was the one who pursued me. He begged me to sleep with him. I can't help it if you weren't enough for him."

"It's no surprise no one but John was stupid enough to lay a hand on you. Don't think that everyone doesn't know that you got knocked up so he had no choice but to marry you?"

I watched her eyes dart nervously from side to side. "You're just jealous because I got the baby you always wanted. I bet you can't stand it," she spat.

"Not at all. In fact, I should probably *thank you* for taking John off my hands. Now I'm free to date whomever I please. But you already know about me and Warren. What was it that the paper said? His fortune makes John's look like a pittance?"

She bristled and fingered her ring nervously. "He won't be interested in you for long. Warren Robbins dates supermodels and social figures, women like—"

"Like you? Not from what I saw at Jill's dinner party. I saw your ridiculous attempt to get him to notice you. Didn't work, did it?"

"We'll see how this ends for you, shall we? And in the meantime I'll be getting married to John—at the Pierre under a blanket of Ecuadorian roses, with two hundred of our closest friends cheering us on—and living the cozy little family life that you always dreamed about. Won't I?" she said.

She put her arm out to shut the door of her dressing room, but I held it firm. "This isn't over, Ainsley, and it won't be until everyone in this town knows what a weak, manipulative hussy you are. Most people don't have to steal other people's husbands to find love, or blackmail their friends into throwing them baby showers. You're pathetic. I hope that ring keeps you warm at night."

"You're forgetting that I also have John."

"We'll see how that all ends for you, shall we?" I said, mocking her tone. "May you get everything that's coming to you," I added before I turned on my heel, grabbed my purse and walked out of the dressing room with my head held high.

The morning of my interview I had my hair blown out professionally and dressed conservatively in the chiffon blouse I'd bought at Bergdorf's and a pair of slacks I already had in my closet. I arrived as instructed, ten minutes early for the interview, and took the extra time to review all the notes and tips Shailagh had given me.

I had been coached not to ask questions—this was the time for the board to interview me, not vice versa—and to be prepared to discuss every aspect of my financial package. I was not to discuss renovations unless asked. And if I was asked about my plans for renovation, I was supposed to downplay them. If the board asked me personal questions I was to handle them without sharing more than necessary or, on the flip side, getting defensive. I didn't have anything to hide in my past, and if I refused to respond to certain questions, they might think the opposite was true. Shailagh advised me to try to enjoy the interview, and to think of the people across the table as my new neighbors rather than the building's gatekeepers.

"Be relaxed, be confident," she said over the phone, but as I walked into the meeting, all I could hear was Justine's disillusioned voice saying: "That's easy for you to say."

I walked into the room, a nondescript office on the building's first floor, just off the lobby, to find five people sitting along one side of a conference table. I sat in the middle, across from a balding man in his sixties whom I surmised to be the board president. On one side of him sat a man in his midforties, dressed in a blue oxford cloth shirt and khakis, and a white-haired woman in opera-length pearls and a cashmere twinset. One the other side another older gentleman and an attractive middle-aged woman with short dark hair and piercing blue eyes were seated. I couldn't place her, but she looked incredibly familiar. My first thought was that she was a former actress or maybe a model, and I wondered briefly if I had perhaps served her at one of the many parties I'd covered for Gigi.

The board president got the ball rolling by asking me why I had chosen the apartment building and what I liked about the apartment. I told him that since moving to New York I'd wanted to live in Beekman and in an apartment that had plenty of Old World charm and grace. "I'm not overstating it by saying that I've found my dream apartment," I said, which seemed to please the older woman and gentleman.

I was then asked how many apartments I looked at and for how long I had been looking, and then the woman with the white hair and pearls interrogated me on the building's House Rules. I was able to demonstrate that I was willing to abide by the rules, so she moved on to my personal habits: Did I smoke? No. Have a pet? No. Play a musical instrument? No. Entertain frequently? No. Have a boyfriend? No.

The woman raised an eyebrow, questioning my last response. "Oh really?"

I sat there quietly in my chair, hoping that my silence would convey my unwillingness to talk about my relationship status. Let them think what they wanted about me, whether or not I was dating a multimultimillionaire shouldn't have any bearing on my approval. There was a long pause in conversation that must have lasted half a minute but felt more like half an hour, before the man across from me took over once again and redirected the questioning back to my finances by asking me if I felt comfortable carrying the mortgage and maintenance fees. Then he asked me about my employment status. "It says here that you are unemployed," he stated, peering down at the pages in front of him.

"I'm in the process of transitioning back into the workforce. I'm trained as a private banker."

"But not employed as one," pressed the younger guy.

And before I knew what I was doing, I opened my mouth and replied, "I'm self-employed, actually."

I noticed the entire table sit up a little taller in their seats, especially the middle-aged woman, who seemed to view me with fresh eyes.

"Is that so?" she said, speaking for the first time, and I instantly recognized her gravelly voice. She was one of my first private clients at Bloomington Mutual and her name was Emma Wrightsman. She'd come to us shortly after her husband, a man who had made billions buying and selling recycled steel, had died, quite suddenly, from a massive stroke. I set her up with our trust and estates specialists and helped manage the bequeathal of several important artworks to the Art Institute of Chicago, the J. Paul Getty Museum in Los Angeles, and the Museum of Modern

Art in New York. And after we'd made sure her assets were protected and children's future secured, we went out to lunch. She was the first person I'd ever known who ordered a cheese course before dessert. It was at her side that I had my first taste of Époisses de Bourgogne.

"Tell us more," she said.

"I'm in the process of starting a boutique financial advisory, calling upon my years of expertise as both an investment banker and private asset manager for Bloomington Mutual."

They all digested my response for a while before the older man questioned whether I would be working from home. I knew that the safe answer was no, but I also didn't want to lie. "Yes, in the beginning. And then once we're up and running, I'll rent space in an office building," I said.

I fielded a few more softball questions and then the board president stood up to shake my hand and tell me that I could expect to hear back in a week, but there was a chance it could take longer.

Leaving the room, I felt pretty confident I'd won them over.

And if I hadn't, I knew my former client would.

Because I knew just what to send her: A basket of the best cheeses I could lay my hands on.

23

Down to Business

The board approved my application.

Shailagh called it a miracle.

And who was I to disabuse her belief in divine intervention? (Although I was pretty sure my approval was more a testament of how bad the economy was than proof of God's existence.)

I moved in to the apartment in January. As a housewarming present, Gigi, who had flown back from Miami with Jeremey to take Lauren to rehab, came over with a basket of food from Dean and Deluca and an enormous round of imported Parmigiano Romano. Shailagh sent a case of Perrier-Jouët and arrived with a set of eight crystal champagne flutes. We sat in my near-empty living room eating chunks of cheese and drinking champagne, and although it overwhelmed me to think of all the work that was ahead of me—the kitchen renovation, closet to office conversion, and all the furniture shopping—I felt more settled than I had in as long as I could remember. I finally had my own nest that I could decorate to my own taste, with comfortable, classic furniture that reflected who I was rather than who my husband wanted people to think we were. My life was finally taking shape in a way that I felt I truly owned, literally. I had my own home and soon, my own business.

Getting my professional life back on track wasn't going to be easy. The first step was passing a battery of tests given by the National Association of Securities Dealers (NASD), the hardest of which was the Series Seven, a test that all brokers, traders, and investment advisors have to take in order to deal legally in stocks and equities. I'd taken it once before, but because I had been inactive for two years and hadn't kept up with my annual course requirements I had to earn my license all over again and sit for the grueling six-hour, 260-question-long test in front of a computer. But that wasn't even the worst part—having to take prep classes in a Sylvain Learning Center downtown was because it made me realize how far I'd let myself fall behind.

But I gutted through it. And the more I studied the more my vision took shape. I'd start by investing my own money, finding interesting opportunities that would pay off in both the long and short term, and then I'd help other people do the same. In private banking, just as in any industry, the key to success was being able to corner the market in something, no matter how specialized. My niche would be independently wealthy women. I'd target widows and divorcées, heiresses, and self-made millionaires. At my firm, they wouldn't be teased about their love of high heels or given a pitch book better suited to an eighty-year-old retiree. I hadn't figured out what I was going to name my company yet, but I had a clear mission statement and more energy and focus than I've ever had in my life.

· I took my Series Seven in December, receiving a score of eighty, ten points above passing. One of the traders in my class happened to see my score on the computer screen and told me that I was lucky I didn't work on the floor because I'd get hazed to no end for overstudying. A perfect score on the Stock Exchange floor was a seventy and not one point higher. I laughed. That was Wall

Street, for these guys everything was a question of utility. Life was one long series of opportunity cost calculations. Even women and marriage were considered in terms of depreciating and appreciating value. (To hear these guys talk, a woman's value depreciates as she ages, while a man's increases. Since apparently the only thing women have to offer is their beauty and all men have is money, a marriage makes sense when a woman's beauty is equal to a man's wealth, but if either slips, then new calculations must be made.)

After passing my Series Seven, I signed up for a supervisory license and the Sixty Six, another NASD-administered test for investment advisors. These were both easier than the Series Seven, so I was finally able to dedicate some time shopping for a clearinghouse or "prime brokerage" for my trades. I might be making the investment calls but I needed a big bank to actually process my calls and act as my custodian by holding my assets. I thought about using Countrybank, but that would mean that Thorne would find out what I was up to, and I wasn't ready for that yet, so I chose GHBC. If it was good enough for Warren, it was good enough for me. Plus, it had the added benefit of being solvent, which was more than you could say for some investment banks those days.

My sister Annalise arrived with her sons Jack and Trevor in March, when Jack's school was on Spring Break. We spent the week shopping for furniture (me) and clothes (her) and taking my nephews out to the Children's Museum on the West Side, seeing Disney musicals on Broadway, and for lunch at kid-friendly places like Serendipity, where the boys polished off enormous ice cream sundaes and Annalise and I shared a frozen hot chocolate drink that made me forget all about fitting into my pencil skirts.

It was the first long, uninterrupted stretch of time Annalise and I had been able to spend together since she fell unexpectedly pregnant six years earlier and I was worried that we wouldn't know what to say to each other, or would fall back into our old pattern of zinging each other with passive-aggressive comments. To my relief, we didn't. She didn't point out my dimpled thighs and I didn't lament her wasted brain power. She held her tongue when I dressed in an unflattering (but comfortable!) pair of jeans for one of our excursions to the Doyle auction house, where I scored a nineteenth-century flame mahogany credenza, and I didn't chide her for her infatuation with all manner of reality television.

But our relationship had improved in a more profound way as well. Namely, we were no longer jealous of each other. And once I was able to see past my envy for Annalise's long legs and children, I noticed that she had, in fact, matured from the selfish, self-centered narcissist I had grown up with; motherhood had transformed her into a patient, loving, and empathetic person. Yes, her life was difficult, and her marriage, like most, was imperfect, but she felt fulfilled. I had been off the mark for a very long time about her. She hadn't been viewing her life through the prism of mine. *I* had. And I knew it was because I had been so wrapped up in the material aspects of my life (because, really, that was the only good thing in my marriage on which to focus) that it hadn't even occurred to me that Annalise could actually be happy having as little as she did.

I woke early each day so I could fix breakfast for Jack and Trevor and let Annalise get some rest. Dressed in their car- and truck-themed pajamas, their eyes squinting and hair matted, the boys were especially adorable in the morning. I made them breakfast, nothing fancy, and watched them swing their legs as they ate their toasted bagels or chocolate chip pancakes, excited to be in their long-lost aunt's Big City apartment. I relished the time with them, and Annalise was incredibly grateful to be able to lie in past six a.m. Her husband occasionally took over morning duties but she said it usually ended with the kitchen and living room in such a state of disarray that it wasn't worth the extra hour of sleep.

"It's easier if I just get up and make them breakfast," she said, her beautiful face awash with resignation. Seeing her in this new light, not as the popular, pretty cheerleader, but as a suburban mother who could barely manage to carve out a sliver of her day to remove her chipped nail polish or tweeze her eyebrows, reminded me of how sometimes in life, the worst things that happen to you—an unplanned pregnancy, a nasty divorce—can turn out to be the best things for your long-term well-being.

For her last day in New York, I surprised Annalise by hiring a couple of babysitters, friends of Gigi's nanny, so we could spend the afternoon indulging in spa treatments (European facials, hot stone massages, and paraffin wax pedicures) and the evening enjoying a delicious meal at Aureole, one of my favorite restaurants in the city.

Once we had settled into our square table at the restaurant, we ordered a couple glasses of champagne, which we sipped while studying the menu. A waitress came and took our orders and after she left I watched as Annalise took in the calm, but heady atmosphere and ran her hand over the pristine white table cloth. "It's easy to get used to all this, I bet," she said.

I nodded and took a sip of my champagne. "Money is like a drug. The more you have the more you want. In the beginning being able to go for expensive meals in restaurants or on a trip to a luxury resort is thrilling, but the more you do and spend, the more you have to do and spend to get the same rush you felt before." I thought of Jill and her spending problems, of Jeremy and his inferiority complex, and John and his misplaced adoration of Ainsley and everything she represented to him.

"I love you, sis, and I love New York," Annalise said, "but I sure am happy to be going home to my little split-level ranch in Minnesota."

Our appetizer, a plate of duck prosciutto, arrived along with two fresh glasses of champagne sent to us by another diner. I asked the waitress who we might thank for the drinks.

"He asked me not to say," she replied with a small smile.

"You have a secret admirer," Annalise giggled.

"How do you know the guy isn't after you?" I asked. My sister may have looked older than me, but she was still the more attractive one.

"He said they were for the lady in green," the waitress said.

I looked down at my top to double check that I was, indeed, wearing my green silk wrap dress that evening.

Annalise laughed. "See, I told you." Then, she leaned forward over the table and whispered, "Do you think it's Warren?"

I told the waitress to thank whoever was responsible for sending over the drinks, and informed my sister that Gigi had seen Warren at an auction at Christie's with his arm around a pretty art advisor from a well-known New York family. He'd clearly moved on; me, not so much.

We ate the rest of our meal, savoring our food and reminiscing over our grade school traumas (mine) and romances (hers) and returned home to find the boys fast asleep in the guest bedroom. I'd installed a pair of single beds with headboards upholstered in a navy and white French ticking fabric, and filled the remainder of the chamber with a pair of coordinating slipper chairs and framed old black and white photographs of city bridges and buildings. The walls had been painted cornflower blue and on the floor I'd laid a geometric navy and white rug.

With Gigi, Shailagh, and Annalise's help, I'd managed to decorate a good portion of the apartment with a mix of new and antique furniture. I had a few standout Art Deco pieces, but nothing overly fussy or precious. The general aesthetic I was after was clean lined and crisp, with a touch of Old-World glamour, like the enormous gilt chandelier in the dining room or a pair of shell-encrusted orchid planters on the coffee table in the living room. And after living for so long confined to drab olives, ivories, and beiges (John's preferred color palette), I couldn't help but bathe the walls in exuberant hues. My dining room was painted in fresh, cleansing cerulean blue, the living room in warm, glowing salmon, and my bathrooms in lush violet, amaranth, and Kelly green tones. However it was my office, which featured a Queen Anne sofa reupholstered in quilted yellow wool and walls papered in marigold suede, where I chose to spend the majority of my time. There was something about the saturated, sunny colors that made me feel cheery and optimistic, like I was finally on the right path—at least in terms of my professional life.

My personal life was another matter entirely. After Annalise and the boys left, the apartment felt even emptier than it had before. I missed the children's shrieks and laughter, and telling someone if I was leaving or coming home. I had so few friends in New York, just Gigi, Shailagh, Maggie, Davina, and a couple of the girls I'd met at my Series Seven prep class (we bonded over our mutual hatred of panty hose, Spanx notwithstanding), and ended up spending most of my nights at home, eating dinner in front of my computer or the television to distract me from my loneliness. There were times when I had to clench my hands to keep them from dialing Warren or, surprisingly, John.

It turned out that I wasn't the only one feeling nostalgic about the past. In late March, right after I passed my last two exams, John showed up unexpected and uninvited at my building. I was so surprised that when the doorman buzzed him up I asked "John who?" and almost dropped my plate—a French-Women-Don't-Get-Fat-approved amount—of cheese and crackers, when he responded "Emerson."

I probably should have refused to see him, but I was curious. I wanted to know how life with Ainsley was treating him and what he wanted from me. I wondered if his mother hated her, or if fatherhood had changed him. I set my cheese back on the kitchen counter and dashed into my bedroom to change out of my leggings and raggedy T-shirt and into jeans and a cashmere turtleneck. I had time enough to do a quick breath check and swipe on some under eye concealer, blush, and eye liner before my doorbell rang.

As soon as I opened the door, I knew John was drunk. His eyes were glazed over and he was swaying slightly in his shoes. *This was going to be interesting.* "May I come in?" he asked.

I stepped aside and opened my hand. "Sure," I said, shrugging. "May I take your coat?"

He handed it over and as I led him to the living room, he looked around with palpable awe, trying to take in as much of the apartment as he could, like a small boy being led through a candy factory.

John stumbled into one of my wingback chairs. Once seated, he chortled quietly to himself and slapped his knees.

"Something funny?" I asked, crossing my arms over my chest.

"You've done a great job on this place," he said. "Love the colors. Who would have thought to mix mauve and turquoise?"

It was actually amaranth and Columbia blue, but I wasn't about to correct him. He could learn his color wheel from Ainsley now.

I seated myself across from him on the claw-footed sofa and raised my eyebrows quizzically. "What are you doing here John? I'm sure Ainsley's wondering where you are."

He wiped a tiny amount of spittle from the side of his mouth. "I have a baby now," he said.

"So I gather. I heard it was a boy?"

"Yes, Hudson. We call him Hud for short. He resembles his mother, thank goodness."

It was a canned statement, given in a perfunctory, practiced manner, and I feared it was indicative of John's disinterest in the child. Could that be what was wrong, that he didn't feel a connection to Hudson?

I thought about telling John about Jeremy Cohen and how he was finally coming around to Chloe, but then decided against it since I didn't know if I could trust John not to tell Ainsley, who would then repeat the information to everyone. "It's normal for a father not to immediately bond with his baby. I've heard it can sometimes take years," I finally said.

He pushed forth his lips and tapped them with his index finger. "Naw, Hud and I spend lots of time together. You'd be proud of me. I change diapers and give the little guy his bath at night. But Ainsley's at a fancy spa in Texas with Hud this week. They have a special program for mommies and infants. She went to lose the last of her baby weight. She looks great to me, but you know women."

I checked my watch. I was getting impatient and didn't want to give John the impression that it was all right for him to come see me whenever he pleased. "Well, it's getting pretty late," I said, standing up.

"Wait, I have something to tell you. I'm sure you're wondering what I'm doing here," he said, slurring again.

"The thought did cross my mind, yes," I said, sitting back down across from him on the couch. I pulled my legs up and crossed them, and hugged a suede pillow to my chest.

"I feel really bad about cheating on you. And the guilt is killing me. I acted like a total shit head and I know God is punishing me for it."

"Oh, John, is everything okay? You're not sick, are you?"

"Jesus, no, Marcy. I'm fine."

"And your family? They're all okay?"

He grumbled impatiently. "What I'm trying to tell you is that I'm sorry I left you. Ainsley's a pain in my ass. All she does is whine and shop and come up with new ways for me to spend ungodly sums of money. And sex? Ha! I haven't gotten any in weeks. If I'd wanted to never get laid I would have—"

"What? Stayed with me?" I said, throwing the pillow aside.

"Marcy I know I fucked up," he said, his eyes catching mine. Suddenly he stood up, or tried to, and pitched forward over the coffee table. He instinctively held out his hands, one of which caught the edge of my shell-encrusted orchid planter, sending it skittering across the table and to the floor, where it cracked open.

Crying out in pain, John grasped his injured hand, which was split along the palm and bleeding. I grasped his shoulder and marched him into the kitchen, where I directed him to the sink to wash his cut while I went to look for the first-aid kit I'd bought in preparation for my nephews' visit.

When I returned to the kitchen John was leaning against the sink, his hand wrapped in a dishtowel. I wiped the cut down with an alcohol-soaked towelette and used a couple pieces of gauze and an Ace bandage to bandage the cut.

"Thanks," he said, opening and closing his hand.

"Maybe you should go to a hospital to get it looked at," I suggested.

"Would you come with me?" he asked.

I cocked my head to one side and shook it. "John, I'm not your wife anymore. I don't know why you came here tonight, but let me make it clear that we can't be friends."

"Why not? We had some good times together and I did you right by giving you all that money. The least you can do for me is take me to the hospital."

"John, you had sex with another woman on our couch. You impregnated her when we were still married. I don't owe you anything. You're lucky I even let you come up here."

"Marcy, you have to believe me when I tell you that she tricked me. That day that we slept together for the first time? *She* sug-

gested we meet at the Burger Joint. Not me. And then she arrived
wearing this supershort skirt and no panties. She told me she was
wet; she took my hand and made me feel her. What man would
be able to resist that?"

"You. My husband. You were supposed to."

"It was just meant to be an affair. But then she got pregnant.
She swore to me she was on the pill. Then she said it was an
accident—another one of her lies. I heard her talking to her
mother last week. She didn't know I was home, but I was, and I
heard her say that she wished she'd never gotten knocked up with
my baby. That she should have waited until she found someone
richer and more powerful than I am. She doesn't love me, Marcy.
I don't think she ever did. And now we have this kid and he's
great, but how's he gonna turn out if he has a mother like Ainsley?
What values is she going to teach him? I don't want him to end up
like all the entitled little pricks running around the city."

He leaned forward and cradled his head in his hands, and all
I could think was *poor John*. I knew this day would come but now
that it had I wished it hadn't. I opened my mouth to tell him that
I was so sorry, but he cut me off.

"I don't want to hear you say I told you so."

"I wasn't going to say that."

He looked at his hand and grimaced. He was starting to sober
up, and the pain of his injury was no longer dulled by his inebria-
tion. I offered him a glass of water and a Tylenol, which he gladly
accepted. As he swallowed the pill he peered at me over the rim
of the glass.

"Is it true that you were dating Warren Robbins?" he asked.

I bristled. "I'm not sure if that's any of your business."

He smirked. "He's a total weirdo, you know."

"Oh yeah?" I said, annoyed.

"Yeah, it's good that you're not seen with him anymore. People
were saying that you're only after him for his money."

Because your wife told them that.

"Really, John, who cares?" I said.

"I do! You're my ex-wife. I don't want people bad mouthing you."

The defensiveness tone in his voice was touching, and I wondered if, against my previous conviction to the contrary, we could be friends again. But then John reminded me exactly why I was better off having nothing to do with him.

"It reflects poorly on me," he whined.

I shook my head and laughed at my own albeit momentary stupidity. John had always been a selfish, spoiled boy and he always would be. Why did I think, even for a moment, that it would be possible for him to change? Maybe he'd seen his folly for cheating on me with Ainsley and then marrying her, but he was still entirely obsessed with how others perceived him. He'd always think of the women in his life as a barometer of his own worth. The enormous rock on Ainsley's finger was not a testament of his love for her, but rather a very clear fuck-you message to his circle of friends. He was destined to go through life collecting the cars and houses and maybe jets and boats he thought he should, but he would never be able to actually receive pleasure from any of these possessions. And he certainly would never be able to truly love a woman.

I thought of a book that I had once read about a woman who married a man who came from a wealthy family, and how she had later in life wished that she'd looked for a man whose wealth was self made because at least then she wouldn't have to kowtow to her in-laws. But I was not sure that one situation would be preferable to the other. Self-made men can be, as John is, incredibly vainglorious and at the same time rattled with insecurities that compel them to spend their lives continually proving their worth. Being tangled up in an elder's purse strings is no picnic, but neither is being trapped in someone else's psychological drama.

"You need to go," I said.

"Marcy," he pleaded.

The overhead lighting cast round, droopy shadows over his eye hollows, rendering his countenance effete, wasted. When we were married I'd only ever seen the perfect proportions of his face. His straight nose and high forehead were the attributes of an honest and reliable man, I'd assumed. But I was wrong to have tried to read his youthful features; only mature ones give any indication of the person beneath. I'd judged John too soon, but now, standing before me I could see him clearly. He was priggish and pretentious, and entirely unaware of his selfishness. And he would only grow harder and more rancorous as he aged, no matter what life had in store for him. If I were to have hazarded a guess then and there, however, I would have speculated that he was not destined for great things.

I turned away from him and started walking toward the door.

"Please," he said, grabbing my arm with his good hand.

"Please what? Your life is with Ainsley now. You made your choice and now you have to live with it." I wrenched free of his grasp, walked out of the kitchen into the entry hallway and opened the front door.

Sulking, he walked out of my apartment toward the elevator.

I shut my door quietly, before he could turn around and waste any more of my time.

24

Reckoning at Bergdorf's

In the spring I passed my last two exams and could finally execute my business plan. I'd spent an enormous chunk of my settlement on the apartment, but I still had plenty of cash to play with, and wasted no time in putting it to work for me. I made a few short-term plays, and turned over a tiny profit, but nothing remarkable. Until one day in the middle of June, I was flipping through a copy of the *Economist* and read an article about how sugar cane was better than corn because it could be transformed into fuel in one step rather than two and the entire cane was put to use whereas only the stalk of the corn could be utilized. The corn farmers' interest group in Washington was lobbying hard against importation of sugar cane fuel, but the article pointed out that Congress could keep it out for only so long. The skyrocketing price of corn was making everything from beef to bread more expensive—more farmers were converting to corn since it was a more profitable crop than, say, wheat—and consumer rights groups were starting to protest against the rising cost of food. Food cost inflation was a hot button issue with most constituencies, especially given the rising unemployment and crime rates, and congressional representatives were near-desperate to prove to their loyal voters that they were doing what they could to relieve the pricing pressure.

I decided to short ethanol.

And I made a killing.

Remembering all of John's conversations about offshore drilling, I also invested heavily in the companies that manufacture equipment for offshore deep-water drilling. I took strong positions on Petrobras, Brazil's big oil company that had discovered an estimated eight billion barrels of crude in a field near Rio de Janeiro, and followed T. Boone Pickens, the legendary oilman and hedge funder, on wind turbines. By the end of that summer, I had doubled my money several times over, and used my profits to open up my own financial advisory firm, called Demeter & Co., after the Greek goddess of grain and fertility. We even came up with a tagline that we put on our letterhead: Make Bad Choices with Men, Not Money.

The *Wall Street Journal* wrote a page-one piece about Demeter & Co., praising our savvy investment strategy and out-of-the-box marketing efforts. Since we were one of the only outfits growing in a down economy, the story took off like wildfire, and my business exploded almost overnight. All of a sudden women from all over the world, not just the United States, were calling my firm. Many were divorcées like me, but plenty had inherited wealth or were businesswomen. I even picked up some male clients, to my surprise.

I had so much work that I had to rent office space on Park Avenue to house the six private bankers, including Justine, I'd poached from Bloomington Mutual and a few of the other big banks. I brought on trust and estates specialists, art experts, and equity analysts to pad out our knowledge depth. We made tons of money for our clients and did so well, in fact, that all of Wall Street started clamoring for our business. Every day a new bank would call and try to sell me on their brokerage and custodial services, promising me I'd be happier with them than GHBC. Often they attempted to sweeten the pot with offers for tickets to the U.S. Open and the Super Bowl.

As I said, these guys were clueless.

And the most delusional of all was Thorne Van Buren, the dimwit financial advisor at Countrybank whose pitch book was so awful it inspired me to start my own firm. He called me on the phone to cross-sell Countrybank's brokerage arm on a sunny morning in late August. It was the last Friday before Labor Day and the city was already half empty, so I was surprised that he was in his office instead of on a beach in the Hamptons, or boating in Bar Harbour or some equally exclusive summer local. I supposed it was a measure of how bad the financial industry was doing—could it be that Countrybank's private banking arm was hemorrhaging clients?—that he was.

Still, I had a million better things to do than sit on the phone politely declining Thorne's invitation that we meet for lunch at the Harvard Club, which he, of course, did not fail to remind me was his alma mater. So I simply told Thorne that I was too busy to meet this month, and when he persisted in trying to nail me down on a date I patched him through to my assistant and told her to get rid of him for me.

Later that day I was about to start eating a ham and cheese panini at my desk when I stumbled across an article in the *Financial Times*. It's headline was "Cohen Capital to Close Down," and was no longer than a few paragaprahs:

> Two hedge funds managed by Jeremy Cohen are to cease operations and return money to investors. The firms manage about $6 billion in assets. In a letter to investors on Tuesday, Mr. Cohen said he is retiring from managing

capital after 30 years in the investment business. "My intention to spend more time with my family is at odds with the responsibilities of a hedge fund manager who must be immersed in the markets around the clock in order to look after clients' interests properly," Mr. Cohen said in the letter.

When I looked up Gigi was standing in my office. She was wearing her sunglasses and a colorful retro tent dress. "You're coming to lunch with me," she announced before I could ask her anything about the article on Jeremy's funds. If it was true that Jeremy was really shutting them down because he wanted to spend time with Gigi and Chloe, then this was a great thing, something worth celebrating. But if Jeremy was simply using his family in an attempt to make a graceful exit from a burning building, well, then, I could only forecast more problems for my friend's marriage.

"C'mon you heifer, get up," Gigi said.

"Who are you calling a heifer, you cow?" I protested.

"Not one word. Get up."

I wanted to have lunch with her, but I had three stacks of papers to read through and some phone calls to return. "I can't—"

"Zip it. I made reservations at BG."

That was tempting. BG, the café in Bergdorf Goodman, was located on the seventh floor of the department store, the same floor where they sold all their gorgeous home goods and tableware. I'd been dying to go back there for ages, but hadn't been able to carve out the time. There always seemed to be some work waiting for me back at the office.

Justine Peterson appeared in my doorway. Since leaving Bloomington Mutual to come work for me she'd completely transformed her life. She took up yoga and tennis, which had been her childhood passion, and rented a house in the Hamptons with a few other girlfriends. Her once pasty, pinched face looked relaxed and tan, and her suit jacket no longer struggled to close over her chest.

"Go to lunch, Marcy," Justine seconded. "I checked your schedule and it's pretty much clear for the rest of the afternoon." I knew why she wanted me to leave; she'd met a nice bankruptcy attorney (his practice, like that of Henry's, was firing on all cylinders, thanks to the recession.) Justine was probably hoping to make it out in time for dinner with her new beau.

"All right," I sighed, turning off my computer. "Let's go."

Downstairs Gigi hailed a taxi.

"What, no car, no driver?" I asked.

"Nope. Hope you weren't my friend just because I had a driver and a jet, because we don't have either of those anymore," she said, opening the door to the cab.

Stuck in traffic on the way to Bergdorf's, she showed me recent pictures of Chloe and Jeremy on her iPhone and I asked her about Jeremy's funds closing down. Taking off her sunglasses, Gigi told me that although it was true that Jeremy had a lot of investors pull out during the past year and had seen his personal net worth fall by several million dollars, that wasn't the real reason he decided to get out of the game, family was. "He didn't want to lose another wife and see another one of his daughters turn into a drug user," she said.

I patted her knee. "That's great, but it must be hard for him to have to scale down so much."

"Actually, this whole thing has been good for us. It's given Jeremy a new perspective on life. And the fact is that we're doing just fine. It's not like we're starving and can't pay our bills on time."

I told Gigi that I was impressed with how she and Jeremy were taking the decline of their personal fortunes in stride, and leaned in to give her a hug. She felt meatier than I remembered and when I pulled back she could see on my face that I'd noticed the difference.

"Before you go accusing me of getting fat, I'll have you know that I'm pregnant," she said, patting her rounded tummy beneath her dress.

I shrieked, embracing her again. "How far along are you?

"Four months. And we already know that it's going to be a little boy. Jeremy and I want you to be the godmother, if you'll do it?"

"But I'd be honored! Of course!" I shrieked again.

At the restaurant Gigi and I were seated at a pair of high-backed pale blue chairs overlooking the small park in front of the Plaza Hotel. We both admired the décor, and how the dark wood floors contrasted with the cool blues and greens of the seating and silvery chinoiserie wallpaper. I ordered a ton of food, plus wine (for me), and as I sipped my chardonnay Gigi caught me up on all the gossip I'd been missing since I had started my business and basically checked out of the social scene.

Ainsley and John were still together, but just barely. Rumors swirled around town that she intended to leave him. After cleaning up last year—my fifteen million dollar settlement barely made a dent in his income—John's streak of good luck had come to an abrupt halt when he decided to long ethanol. He'd made a few other bad calls on oil derivatives as well, and since, like most funds, Zenith didn't tolerate losses of over twenty percent, he was under an incredible amount of pressure to bring his portfolio back into the acceptable range, or they'd have to let him go.

There was more bad news: Jill and Glenn were headed for divorce, and it was likely to be a brutal public battle over their estate and children. The *New York Post* had printed an item about Glenn having fooled around with a woman who worked at his hedge fund, and a few weeks later broke the even more scandalous story of Jill's affair with Blake, the nineteen-year-old son of an eccentric publishing heiress. I couldn't believe that Jill had been so stupid as to allow Blake to videotape them *in flagrante delicto*—and in his dorm room at Columbia, no less, but apparently there really was a sex tape floating around out there in the ether. Jill had been put on probation at work, and Glenn was suing for full custody of their two children. Given the circumstances, he had a decent shot at getting it.

Gigi tucked into her truffle-coated lobster napoleon and I took a bite of my steak au poivre, and as we both chewed I began to digest all of the information that had been unloaded upon me: Ainsley's rumored infidelity, John's perilous position at Zenith, and Jill's affair coming to light after all she had done to keep it secret. None of it surprised me, but I was surprised to feel as saddened as I did by it all.

I looked out the window and down at the crowd of tourists milling about the fountain in their sneakers and jeans and a few boys on skateboards doing their best to stay out of everyone's way. The Plaza's front door opened and closed for a trickle of European residents. I'd learned from Shailagh that residential real estate values had plummeted over the summer and the only two buildings that hadn't been drastically effected by the downturn were the Plaza and another newly built building on Central Park South, and that was because they were mostly inhabited by wealthy Europeans who wouldn't dream of selling when the dollar-to-euro exchange rate was so disadvantageous. There seemed to be no sign of an end to the U.S. recession—believe me, I spent my days looking for bright spots I could turn into investment opportunities—and I feared that the correction would drag on for many more quarters.

There, in the luxuriously appointed café in the city's most lavish shopping emporium, one was supposed to feel quite high above the fray; and, indeed, the room was swarming with hedge fund wives, who were holding on to that conviction with all their might. Magdalena Zimmer was eating with Dahlia Kemp at one table; and several of the other women I had met while I was still with John were quietly savoring their lunches and purchasing power, which was, although diminished, still a far cry from diminutive. Out of the corner of my eye, I saw Ainsley enter through the café's double doors and take a table on the opposite side of the room. Following behind her was Lauren, Gigi's stepdaughter.

Gigi read the shock on my face, and turned to see the pair settling into their table.

"What the hell?" she nearly shouted, and jumped to her feet. She grabbed my arm and pulled me across the room with her.

"Aren't you supposed to be in Connecticut this week?" Gigi asked Lauren as we sidled up to their table.

I was well aware that by Connecticut she did not mean Jeremy's sprawling nineteen-room manor in Greenwich but Silver Hill, i.e., rehab.

I'd seen some recent pictures of Lauren, but they hadn't prepared me for the vision before my eyes. Her eyes were sunken in and glazed over and her skin was so translucent I could see blue veins traveling the length of her forearms into her boney hands. She was wearing a short dress that exposed almost the entirety of her painfully thin thighs.

"I had some things to do in the city this week," Lauren responded.

"I am calling your mother, I hope you know," Gigi said.

This did not seem to faze Lauren, who in lieu of a response, or perhaps as one, adjusted the Chanel sunglasses perched on her head and yawned.

"So, Marcy," Ainsley said, "I was at a dinner recently and heard that Warren Robbins is dating this lovely young girl, Anna something or other, who works at Gagosian. And he takes her out. In public and to parties, if you can believe it? Not just to bars where you can't see two feet in front of your face," she cackled. "Guess this proves, definitively, what calibur of woman he wants."

I chuckled gamely and leaned over on their table so my face

was no more than six inches away from Ainsley's. "No, darling, the only thing definitive is that you're still a miserable shrew," I said.

"Lauren, you never told me that you and Ainsley were friends," Gigi said.

"Huh?" Lauren said. Her pupils were dilated, a sure sign that she was on some sort of drug.

"Ainsley, how do you know her?"

"Oh, we met at a Rollins alumni party here in New York. She's been like the big sister I never had." "She helped me get through my heartbreak, and she says she's going to get me an internship at *Vogue*."

Now I understood perfectly: It had been Blake who had broken Lauren's heart. And when Lauren, who had tattled on Jill's affair to Ainsley, had found out about the adulterous affair, she'd confided in Ainsley in hopes that she would scare Jill away from Blake.

But Jill hadn't known about Lauren, Blake's spurned teenage lover, and had wrongly assumed that she could continue her affair with impunity if she satisfied Ainsley's demands. I wondered if Blake and Lauren had continued sleeping together in secret, despite her relationship with his drug-dealing friend, and if they met only when Blake was lonely and Jill couldn't see him. That would explain why Lauren had been whipping through all that money: She was buying plane tickets with cash rather than credit cards so her parents wouldn't find out she was making long-distance booty calls. Lauren had put all of her self-esteem in the hands of a stupid, cocky young boy who couldn't care less that she was destroying and debasing herself for him.

"I'm going to the ladies room," Lauren said, standing up from the table and heading out the door of the café.

"Blake's the one who broke her heart," I whispered in Gigi's ear, and she instantly understood, like I had, what exactly had transpired.

"I'm going after her," Gigi said before running out of the restaurant in search of Lauren.

Ainsley made a move to get up but I pushed her back down in her chair. "I think your lunch with Gigi's step-daughter is over, and if I ever find out that you have tried to get in touch with her again, I will make sure everyone knows you blackmailed Jill," I said. "No one will ever speak to you again. And you can kiss all your precious little society page photo ops goodbye."

Ainsley opened her mouth in protest, but before she could, I picked up the glass of champagne the waiter had just delivered to the table and dumped the whole thing on her head. "I've been meaning to do that for a very long time," I said, clicking away on my heels.

After quickly paying our bill, I left the restaurant and was outside standing on the sidewalk hoping to catch a cab home when I noticed Dahlia exiting Bergdorf's loaded down with several shopping bags. Behind me I heard a car skidding to a stop, and turned to see five men dressed in black, with ski masks pulled down over their faces, jump out of a black SUV. Before I could figure out what was happening, they had grabbed Dahlia, pushed a gun in her face, and shoved her into the back of their car, which peeled off with a loud screech.

I fumbled in my purse for my cell phone and dialed 911 with shaky hands. "I just witnessed a kidnapping on the corner of Fifty-eighth and Fifth," I said. "Dahlia Kemp has been kidnapped."

25

Baby Shower 2.0

Four years later . . .

I was messing with the pink balloons tied to the backs of all the chairs when Gigi came into the dining room and instructed me to stop fussing with the decorations. I'd already fiddled with the pink dahlia flower arrangements on the tables, rebuilt a pyramid of strawberry macaroons, and sprinkled more flat-leaf parsley on a tray of filet mignon-wrapped asparagus. Gigi was starting to get annoyed.

"Why are you more keyed-up than I am?" she asked, her voice half amused and half perturbed. "It's just a baby shower, you know."

"I know, but I just want everything to be perfect," I laughed, surprised by my own jangled nerves.

I mean, it's not like I hadn't ever had a party thrown in my honor before.

There was my wedding, a great big 300-person affair in Montana, with the summer air giving flight to the skirt of my wedding dress and a hundred Japanese lanterns lighting up the Big Country sky. I'd been nervous then, too, as I walked down the petal-strewn aisle toward my beaming fiancé, the love of my life: Warren.

Yes, Warren Robbins and I were married. He'd proposed a year after we bumped into each other at GHBC. We were both there for meetings with our brokers. I was coming in and he was going out, but he held me by the bank of elevators long enough to tell me that he thought of me often. I gave him my number, and he called later that same day to ask me out for dinner. Over steak frites and a bottle of red wine, we both discovered that the old chemistry between us was right where we left it, but this time I didn't jump straight into bed with him. We dated for two months before I spent the night with him again, and he didn't ask me to leave before his son woke up. A year later he proposed on bended knee, with a six-carat diamond of unbeatable quality.

We didn't waste any time after we were married to start our family. I was lucky this time around—no miscarriage, although I did have to go on bed rest for the entirety of the last trimester, which meant that I had to leave the day-to-day operations of Demeter & Co. to Justine, who had already become my right hand and was very much up for the job.

Besides opening offices in Chicago and San Francisco, my big focus at Demeter and Co. had been building and maintaining a woman-friendly work environment. We instituted several companywide policies to make it easier for the moms on our staff to balance motherhood and work, which has given us some of the best employee retention rates on Wall Street. We also offer several internships for high school students from middle-to-low income families, and have sent a handful of our most promising interns, including Gemma, through college via the scholarship program partially endowed by my upstairs neighbor and fellow turophile, Emma Wrightsman.

It probably would have made a lot of sense for me to move in with Warren and Oliver in their apartment downtown because it was *much* bigger than mine and already perfectly decorated, but I'd fallen in such deep love with my home, and Warren wasn't opposed to starting over in some place new. Plus, my building was closer to Oliver's nursery school, and by moving to my place, I was able to walk him to school in the morning instead of taking a car. Now that I'm pregnant again, I'm probably going to have to call Shailagh and tell her that I'm in the market for someplace bigger.

Gigi and I heard a loud clang coming from Chloe's bedroom and rushed—well, I waddled—to make sure no one had gotten seriously injured. Our children played together well on most days, but sometimes Charlie, Gigi's three-year-old, forgot that my Ernest was only two and hadn't yet mastered the art of sharing.

Teaching our children the value of sharing is something Warren and I do a lot of these days. In fact, I spend most of my time working at the philanthropic fund we set up in the name of Oliver's mother. Most of our donations are directed to breast cancer research centers and subsidizing mammograms in low-income neighborhoods, but we also give to educational outreach programs in the United States and school building initiatives in Latin America and Africa. More than anything Warren and I want to make sure our children understand that wealth isn't the key to happiness, and collecting material things won't give you long-lasting satisfaction.

"He bit me," yelled Gigi's son, holding his index finger out for his mother to inspect.

Gigi planted her hands on her hips. "Well, sugar, what was your little finger doing in Ernie's mouth in the first place?"

Charlie burst out crying while Ernie stood rooted in his spot. He gazed downward, chin glued to his chest.

"Say you're sorry for biting him," I instructed, pushing my son's little body over to where his friend lay prostrate and wailing on the floor.

Ernie mumbled his apologies and looked at me with bewildered little eyes. "Mommy, he's still crying." He shrugged.

I asked him what he thought would make Charlie feel better and he fished out of the pocket of his corduroy pants a small toy car, a die cast Ferrari that Warren had bought for him that winter at the International Auto Show. "Here," he said, holding out the little red car. "I'll let you play with my favorite one."

Gigi gave me a thumbs-up sign over the kids' heads as Chloe rushed in, whining about Lauren's refusal to let her have one of the cupcakes in the kitchen.

"They're for the guests," Gigi explained. "And if there are any left over, you can have one. But I mean *one*."

Lauren, after finally completing a full twenty-eight-day program at Silver Hill, had stopped using drugs and entered an outpatient program for eating disorders. She'd also started working for Gigi's catering company while studying fashion design at Parsons. Blake had been fired as A Moveable Feast's bartender when Gigi had learned that he was not only sleeping with Jill *and* her stepdaughter, but several other older women around town, most of them hedge fund wives. Some were even paying for his company.

Gigi had called Blake's mother to inform her of the destruction her son had wreaked and suggest that she send him to see a psychotherapist. Blake's mother, a publishing heiress who spends most days in seclusion drinking gin and reading mystery novels, responded with her own tirade, accusing Lauren of being a deranged young girl who belonged in an insane asylum, forget the therapist's couch. The conversation quickly ratcheted up from there. With blood pumping furiously in her ears, Gigi came to a dramatic, passionate defense of Lauren, whom she insisted was an intelligent, sensitive, and trusting young woman, worthy of far better things than a guileless lothario like Blake. Lauren overheard her step-mother's defense and decided, at that exact moment, to get some help. She'd been 100 percent clean ever since leaving rehab.

Lauren's transformation convinced Jeremy to stay retired even though after six months away from the investment business he found himself itching to get back in and worrying almost obsessively about "mental atrophy." Gigi's response was to introduce Jeremy to her parents' favorite game: Bridge. Now the two of them spent much of their free time traveling to tournaments in exotic places like Monaco, Sydney, and Hong Kong, and playing in local leagues in New York and Miami. When Jeremy wasn't playing cards, he could usually be found in his office, studying Eastern medicine or in Central Park practicing yoga and Tai Chi (weather permitting).

Gigi, meanwhile, had followed up *Wow Their Socks Off* with another entertaining guide two years later. *Magical Feasts* was more attuned to the cost-conscious reader and ended up being an enormous hit. Soon after its publication, she was approached by the Style Network to host a one-hour special that received such high ratings that they signed her on for an entire season of shows. *Magical Feasts with Gigi Ambrose,* which featured Gigi sourcing antique linens from neighborhood flea markets and making sophisticated table decorations with inexpensive flowers and backyard finds—think gold spray-painted rocks—regularly drew hundreds of thousands of viewers and became one of the network's premier productions.

Since this was my second baby shower, I wanted to do something a little different than the usual luncheon followed by opening presents. Gigi came up with the concept of throwing a co-ed party (since we can all agree that we spend enough time away from our husbands) with lots of fun games. I was most looking forward to the men-only doll-diapering contest. The prize, in addition to bragging rights in perpetuity, was dinner for two at Per Se—which was no longer an easy reservation to secure, given that all of Wall Street was once again flush with cash.

Even John, last I heard, had found a new job with a hedge

fund. He'd been let go by Zenith, and Ainsley had left him for another trader, just as I had warned John she would. After she left, he became depressed and developed an addiction to painkillers (in addition to the Ambien he still took every night) and eventually ended up in rehab. When he emerged, six months later, he sued Ainsley for joint custody of Hudson and won. Every once in a while Warren and I would run into John and Hudson in one of the playgrounds in Central Park. I was glad my ex was putting the pieces of his life together, and hopeful that he wouldn't fall prey to another woman like Ainsley.

As for the economy, when it was all over and done with, the recession lasted a little more than five years. Hundreds of hedge funds had closed, and thousands of bankers lost their jobs. The real estate market went into free-for-all on a national scale, as did the market for various luxury goods—designer clothes and accessories, jewelry, cars, and personal gadgets. It was a tough, sobering five-year stretch, but the overall effect of the recession, from a long-term, historical perspective, was a good one. Americans started saving more and spending less, and the national average household debt began to decline for the first time in dozens of years.

Dahlia's kidnapping had made national news, and even though she was held against her will for less than forty-eight hours before the feds tracked her down in a warehouse in Queens (her dim-witted captors, a group of unemployed construction workers, had ordered Chinese food with her black American Express card), she was forever changed by the event. Dahlia believed that her kidnapping was a form of karmic retribution for snubbing so many people, and made a desperate plea to God that if she survived the ordeal, she would do everything she could to atone for her past behavior. She shook every hand she could, hugged her friends, and spent most of her time volunteering in soup kitchens and tutoring underprivileged children.

I felt my daughter kicking in my belly, and placed my hand on my stomach. She, I imagined, knew something was up, that today was a special day for us both. One day I would tell her everything about my life, how I studied as much as I could in high school and college and had made the most of the opportunities I was given after graduating from Northwestern, and how I was distracted, temporarily, from my goals, but eventually, with a little hard work and determination, was able to get myself back on the right path. I would teach her the value of resilience, and to never, ever look to a man for your emotional or financial security. I hoped to impress upon her that nothing in my life had come easily and that I had made a fool of myself more times than I cared to remember, but that I wouldn't change anything about the circumstances of life. Everything I'd gone through had made me into the person I was today. And I liked her, Spanx-necessitating thighs and all.

The doorbell rang, announcing the first of the thirty-some guests who had rsvp'd for my shower, and we all hustled into the living room to commence the festivities. There were pink balloons covering the ceiling and cheese trays on every available surface that wasn't already covered with cookies and tightly wrapped bouquets of pink roses. Some light music, a pop song I wouldn't remember later, piped in over the surround-sound speakers as Justine and Shailagh, followed by Dahlia and Caroline, Magdalena and a dozen other women and their husbands, floated through the front door bearing presents and warm wishes. In the mix I noticed a new face, and assumed that it was the wife of one of Warren's employees at Iceberg Capital.

I walked over to her and held out my hand. "My name's Marcy, and you must be Genevieve," I said.

She shook my hand tentatively and fussed with a wayward lock of her hair. "You know, when I first opened the invitation to your baby shower, I thought I received it by mistake," she said.

A+

AUTHOR
INSIGHTS,
EXTRAS, &
MORE...

FROM

**TATIANA
BONCOMPAGNI**

AND

AVON A

Q & A with Tatiana Boncompagni, Author of HEDGE FUND WIVES

Q: What inspired you to write *Hedge Fund Wives*?

When I started thinking about *Hedge Fund Wives*, the title I had in mind was *When the Parties Ended*, and my idea was to depict life in New York after a stock market crash or other cataclysmic economic event that plunged the city into a recession. I had just finished writing my first novel, *Gilding Lily*, which is about a group of New York socialites who are driven by their desire for fame and status, and I wondered what would happen to the social swirl here in the New York if there was a sharp economic downturn, because most of the fund-raisers and parties are paid for or underwritten by luxury goods retailers and investment banks. My assumption was that if these businesses went belly up, so would the good times.

Then I had a conversation with my editor, Lucia Macro, and mentioned that my characters would include a bunch of hedge fund wives, and Lucia pointed out that *Hedge Fund Wives* would actually be a great title and focus for the book. It was quickly settled: I would write my next novel about women whose lives revolved not around status (like in *Gilding Lily*) but money and the consumption of material goods.

Q: Why did you decide to set your story against the backdrop of a recessionary U.S. economy?

Historically, economies go through cycles of growth and retraction, and it was clear to me and plenty of other smart people (this was in the summer of 2007) that at some point the economy would take a nosedive or undergo a "correction" of some sort.

Times of great economic volatility are rich with drama, and I was excited about exploring how a market downturn would affect the personal lives of a handful of characters. This seemed infinitely more interesting than simply cataloging the excess and privilege of a certain group of women.

Once I settled on writing about hedge fund wives and setting my story in a period of tremendous uncertainty, the story started taking shape. The first thing I found myself wondering was what would happen if, for example, one woman's husband lost everything while another woman's husband made a fortune. How would a really unscrupulous woman handle that redistribution of capital? From that point I built the characters of Marcy and Ainsley and their husbands, John and Peter.

Next I created Jill, a binge shopper with a neglectful and verbally abusive husband, and Gigi, a woman whose husband refused to help her with her personal problems despite a vast reserve of cash. The economic downturn would change the dynamics of both of these women's marriages, one for the better and one for the worse.

Q: There's a lot of discussion of real estate, as well as art and interior décor in the book. Are hedge fund wives really that obsessed with material possessions?

Yes and no. Some of my HFW friends are businesswomen working as hard or harder than their husbands, some are loving mothers, and some basically do nothing all day other than work out at the gym with a personal trainer, get their hair blown out, and make dinner reservations. Oh, and they shop like crazy. If you've ever wondered who shells out a few thousand dollars for a pair of shoes, well, now you know.

It's true, however, that most of the hedge fund wives I know are fortunate enough to be able to spend a larger portion of their life shopping the hallowed halls of Bergdorf Goodman and flipping through Christie's latest auction catalog for their next antique or art acquisition, but there's nothing inherently bad in exercising your spending power, is there?

I personally don't think there is anything wrong with shelling out vast sums for beautiful things (provided you can afford them), but what is wrong, or, rather, pathetic, is when a woman shops to fill a void in her life. No amount of money or possessions can make up for the lack of love, self-esteem, friendship, and personal accomplishment in a woman's life.

Here's my bottom line on the topic: The vast majority of us look at women who can drop thousands of dollars a day on clothes, accessories, and other nice things, and wish we could be in their (overpriced) shoes, if only for a day. But the truth is that just because these women are richer than us doesn't mean that they don't have problems or that they lead lives that are happier or more fulfilling than we do.

Q: The marriages seem pretty unbalanced. Do you think a woman can be married to a wealthy man and expect to have an equal amount of power in the relationship?

The short answer is that it depends on the dynamics of the relationship. I know a woman who is married to a very rich man, but she calls almost all of the shots at home because she has a strong personality and a job where she makes an impressive amount of money (though not as much as her husband). That said, I know far *more* examples of women married to absurdly rich men who have near total control of the relationship.

That's why I'm a big believer that all married women should keep working and networking even if they don't "have" to, because not only will their husbands respect them more for it, but they will respect themselves more for it, too. (And if you have children, you'll be teaching them about the value of hard work and the importance of being financially independent.) Also, if worse comes to worst, as it does for Marcy, you have a job or career to fall back on.

One of the main themes of *Hedge Fund Wives* is how foolish it is to depend on a man for your emotional and financial security. Most of my characters learn this lesson the hard way, and I hope that my female readers feel inspired to keep working or go back to work after reading this book.

Q: One of your characters, Warren Robbins, is a hedge fund manager obsessed with Hemingway, and there are a lot of Hemingway references in the book. Why did you include them?

By making reference to Hemingway's novels and memoir, *A Moveable Feast*, I hoped to underscore the idea that we are another "Lost Generation" in the sense that we exist in a society with unclear morals and ethics.

Hemingway and his cohorts, Gertrude Stein, F. Scott Fitzgerald, and others, wrote after World War I, when, culturally speaking, there was a great sense of disillusionment. I think we are a society that also suffers from a great sense of disillusionment with our country and government.

As a character, Warren Robbins reads Hemingway because it provides him with a prism through which he can understand his both great and horrible fortune (he is wealthy, but bereaved by the loss of his beloved wife). His love of Hemingway also demonstrates that he is, unlike other male characters in the book, a man guided by his value system, rather than by greed, with interests that reach beyond the limits of his own affluence.

Q: What's with all the chartreuse?

One of the tricks a lot of writers employ is called repetition of physical motif. The basic idea is that by mentioning a certain object, color, or even a certain song (as Jay McInerney does in *The Good Life* to fantastic effect), the book somehow holds together.

But beyond wanting to use the color of chartreuse to tie the scenes together, I think the fact that most of the hedge fund wives own chartreuse clothing or have decorated their home with the color reflects how trend-driven they are and we are as a culture. This is the color the women are told they need or should covet by various tastemakers (interior designers, magazine editors, etc.), and therefore it is the shade that quite literally colors their lives.

And for those of you who don't know exactly what color chartreuse is, it is either yellowish green or greenish yellow. (It is also the color most visible to the human eye.) It is showy, vibrant, and, not coincidentally, the color of money . . . on acid.

Q: Were there any Hedge Fund Wife anecdotes that didn't make it into the book?

A few, but one of the funnier ones was about a woman who insists on wearing a clean pair of pajamas every night. Not so unusual except that they must be the exact same brand and style of pajamas and they must be washed in a particular kind of laundry detergent. This means that when she travels, she brings a set of pajamas for each night she is away. I heard that she once brought twenty-five pairs of freshly laundered pajamas on a trip (all folded into their own plastic bags for the purpose of maintaining their freshness).

Top Ten Hedge Fund Wife Must-Haves

1. Eff-you diamond engagement ring. This can have many variations, but the ring of choice includes not one, but three flawless, colorless diamonds amounting to no less than eight carats.
2. Van Cleef & Arpels Alhambra necklaces. Heap them on, ladies!
3. Extensive collection of exotic skin handbags and shoes, designer clothes and furs, plus a climate-controlled, thousand-square-foot closet to house it all.
4. Multimillion-dollar art collection. For shame if Christie's doesn't already have a dossier on you.
5. Refrigerator stocked with face and body creams based on your own DNA, bottles of vintage champagne, and ½ lb. tins of Beluga caviar.
6. Pilates instructor, personal stylist, lawyer, dermatologist, nutritionist, hair stylist, makeup artist, interior designer, masseuse, architect, acupuncturist, astrologer, psychiatrist, bodyguard, and vagina trainer, all on speed dial.
7. Full-time, live-in domestic staff, including household manager, housekeepers, driver, nannies (one per child), and personal chef.
8. Table at the annual Robin Hood Foundation benefit; co-chairmanship of at least one A-list fundraising event.
9. Private jet or regular invitation to ride on someone else's, ditto for super yacht vacation to St. Barth, Cap d'Antibes, Monaco, or Portofino.
10. Chalet in Aspen, Beach house in the Hamptons, Palapa-roofed winter getaway on Mustique. Bonus: Pied-à-terre in Paris, plus a front-row seat at the Chanel Haute Couture show.

TATIANA BONCOMPAGNI is a freelance journalist based in New York City. Her writing has appeared in the *New York Times*, *Wall Street Journal*, *Financial Times* and *Vogue*. She is married with two children. This is her second novel.

Tatiana Boncompagni